Leave Her to Heaven

By Ben Ames Williams

HOUGHTON MIFFLIN COMPANY · BOSTON

1 9 4 4

THIS BOOK HAS NOT BEEN CONDENSED. ITS BULK
IS LESS BECAUSE GOVERNMENT REGULATIONS
PROHIBIT USE OF HEAVIER PAPER.

The characters in this book are
fictitious; any resemblance to
real persons is wholly accidental
and unintentional.

LEICK and the boatman adjusted a bridle on the canoe so that it would tow without yawing, and they loaded the dunnage into the motorboat, and then Leick came to where Harland was waiting. Harland had been standing apart, looking down the lake, his eyes fixed upon that distant notch between the mountains which was the threshold of the River. Above the wharf, where the road ended at a garage made of sheet metal with stalls for half a dozen transient cars, three men sat on the concrete base of the gasoline pump, watching him and the others. While he waited he had heard the low murmur of their voices, needing not to hear their words to be sure what they were saying and to wince at that knowledge.

Leick said mildly: 'We're ready any time you are.' Harland came to the wharfside and stepped into the motorboat and sat down in the stern while Leick cast off the mooring lines. The engine caught at the first spin and they moved away. Wes Barrell, at the wheel, looked back and lifted his hand in farewell to the three men by the gas pump, and to Harland his gesture seemed to promise that he would have a tale to tell when he returned. Leick too looked back; but then he went forward and stood with the boatman, engaging him in conversation. Thus Harland was left alone.

He turned his head for a brief survey of the garage, the neat little hotel, the half-dozen houses and the store. This would be his last sight of the world of men — except for an occasional glimpse of individual men — for a long time. 'Forever, I suppose,' he thought, not bitterly but with a calm acceptance, as he set his back toward the scene they had left and turned his eyes ahead.

— II —

This hamlet at the head of the lake — it bore the lovely name of Hazelgrove — seemed to Harland today an ugly huddle of houses, an ugly huddle of humanity. Probably there were people here who if you met them singly were pleasant, simple, friendly folk; but in a group, here as elsewhere, they became a mob, sinking to the level of the lowest of them, degenerating into a gabbling, yelping pack, a hunting pack ready to pursue and tear and rend.

He and Leick had arrived on the early train, and Leick when they alighted went forward to the baggage car to see to the unloading of their gear. Jem Verity, the station master — Harland remembered him from another morning four years before — followed to talk with Leick there, and Harland as the train pulled out was left alone by the station. Three men whom he shrinkingly supposed had come to have a look at him stood in a loose group a little along the platform, and he was uneasy under their speculative contemplation. When Leick and Jem Verity returned toward him, Jem stopped to speak to these men a low-voiced word, and they drifted away while Leick came on to where Harland stood.

'He'll take us to town and then come back and truck our gear down to the wharf, and the boat's all ready,' Leick said. 'We'll go get your license and your forest permit.'

Jem joined them and drove them into the village. The game warden's house was next door to the store, and his wife answered their knock. Her eyes were fine and merry, and two small children, a boy and a girl, pressing beside her, were ready to make friends with these strangers; but when the young woman saw Harland, she said quickly to the children: 'There now, run along! Don't bother the gentlemen!' They vanished, and she told

Leick, as though she knew their errand: 'Come in. Ed's in the woodshed. I'll call him.'

The warden was a broad-shouldered young man with a fine brow. He heard Harland's name without any outward sign that it was familiar, though Harland had expected — and dreaded — a look of startled recognition. When, their business done, Leick said they must find the forest supervisor, the young man volunteered to show the way. As they passed the second house, a boy nine or ten years old came running out to hail them.

'Hi, Ed!' he called. 'Where you going?'

'I'm busy, Jimmy,' the warden told him. 'You stay home.' The boy lagged and reluctantly turned back; and the warden apologetically explained: 'The kids always trail along with me if I'll let 'em. They like to have me tell 'em about deer and bear and fish, and birds and things.'

Harland judged children would like Ed; but he understood that today the news of his own presence in the village must already have been spread abroad, and mothers would keep their children indoors till he and Leick were on their way.

The forest supervisor had a small farm along the shore; and an old woman, presumably his mother, watched their approach through a curtained window. As they reached the front gate, the supervisor, a blocky young man with an expressionless countenance, came out to them. 'This here's what you want, I guess,' he said, in a hurried, embarrassed tone; and Leick took the permit and glanced at it, and Harland felt a wry amusement at this proof that his coming was expected. 'Starting right away?' the supervisor asked. Leick nodded, and the man said: 'Ed and me'll see you off.'

Harland almost nodded, in submissive understanding. They meant to make sure that he left the little community unharmed. As they all walked back toward the wharf, Harland at some sound looked behind them and saw the supervisor's mother following along the dusty road. She turned into the first house of the village, and he guessed she would watch from that vantage their further movements, while she told an avid audience there all she had seen and heard and thought of him.

Except for her and his companions, no one was visible till at the wharf they found Jem and the boatman. Wes Barrell would set them down the lake to the outlet, and when he returned, his wife would have a thousand questions. Harland had encountered her avid curiosity four years ago; and on the wharf now, seeing Wes ostentatiously ignore him while they prepared to depart, he imagined Barrell's homecoming and his wife's persistent interrogations so completely that he was almost sorry for the man.

While the gear was being loaded and the canoe made ready for towing, Harland, although the three men by the gas pump were the only ones in sight, felt many eyes upon him. There were, he supposed, fifty or sixty people who lived either in the village or near-by, their lives devoted to defending their fields and garden patches against the encroachments of the wilderness. They traded work among themselves, and now and then Jem Verity hired them for one of his enterprises, or placed them as guides for sportsmen bound down the River; for Jem dominated this small community. Wes Barrell and the boat were alike Jem's property. Probably not even the warden and the forest supervisor could hope to hold their places without his good will.

Harland felt the eyes and the thoughts of all these people fastened upon him, felt himself naked before them. They knew his most secret hopes and sorrows. They knew when he had bedded his wife, and when he left her bed, and why; they knew his bliss and his agony; they knew his dreams, and they had witnessed, though from a distance, the catastrophe which had so nearly destroyed him. All about him during the hour since he and Leick alighted from the train he had seemed to hear their whisper: 'Murderer! Murderer! Murderer!'

So, gladly, after that one farewell glance when the boat pulled away from the wharf, he turned his back upon the scene, turned his back upon these men and women and upon the world. There was nothing so ugly as an ugly town — unless it were the people in it. He was hungry to bid the place good-bye.

– III –

Harland turned his back upon the world, and almost at once there began to be a subtle change in the bearing of the man himself. As long as, standing on the wharf, he had felt many eyes upon him, he had been a little stooped, as though half-crouching under an expected blow, with his head thrust slightly forward, his shoulders bowed. His hat, pulled low over his eyes, seemed a part of a vain effort at concealment. But now, when Leick went to join the boatman and they stood together with the wheel between them, their backs to Harland, he felt himself for the first time in weary months blessedly alone.

To be lonely is one thing, to be alone is another. There is no loneliness so acute as that of a man upon a pillory, facing ten thousand eyes; but to be alone is to be free, free from eyes and tongues that watch and question and condemn. Feeling himself now thus alone, his shoulders began insensibly to straighten. His head lifted, and after a few minutes he removed his hat, baring his pallid countenance to the strong sun. Their course was northeasterly, and it was still well short of noon, so the sun was in his eyes; and the glare and shine on the water made Harland blink and squint and finally shut his eyes altogether, for they were not yet used to the fine and splendid light of day. Yet the very hurt of the glare pleased him, and he embraced it, leaving his hat on his knee, opening his eyes again, drinking the beauty of the scene. His glance swung a slow circle clear around, but always he avoided looking backward, and always his eyes lingered hungrily on that deeper notch, still miles ahead of them, through which the River escaped from this high basin where like a gem the lake was set, to begin its rushing journey to the sea. He sat erect and eager now, and the wind and the sun made their play with him; and when a gust of spray flung up by the boat's blunt and plunging bows whipped back to wet his cheek, something like a laugh leaped in his eyes. How long was it since he had laughed before? He dared not remember.

Leick looked astern to make sure that the towed canoe was

riding easily; and his eye rested on Harland with a faint surprise, and Harland felt this and hurriedly replaced his hat again. But then, and this was a brave and valorous thing he did, he took it off once more.

Leick came back to him. 'Fine day,' he remarked.

'Yes, fine.'

'It's been an awful dry spell, and hot; but it's some cooler to-day. The sun feels good.'

'It does to me.'

'Be'n so dry they tell me it's hard going to the second dam,' Leick reported. 'Not bad beyond there, though.'

'I won't be able to help you much. I'm pretty soft.'

'We'll get along. You'll toughen up quick.' Leick spoke in an easy reassurance, and Harland's courage quickened like a young fire when fuel is laid freshly on. He stood up and took off his coat and necktie and opened his shirt at the throat and rolled his sleeves. Leick said warningly: 'Don't get too much of a burn too quick.'

'I'll take it easy.' After a moment, Harland asked uncontrollably: 'Leick, is she really all right?'

He had asked that question a dozen, twenty, fifty times in this scant score of hours since the heavy doors shut on his heels and Leick met him with car and train tickets and luggage and gear all prepared and every plan in order. He had asked the question over and over; but Leick answered it again, as he had answered it each time before.

'Yes, she's good. She couldn't be better.'

Harland after a moment, with an awkward gesture, touched the other's arm. 'I appreciate you, you know,' he said. 'The way you've stood by.'

'Sho!' Leick spoke casually. 'Why wouldn't I?' And he said gravely: 'It's time you started to forget all that. It's done.'

'I can't help remembering.'

The other smiled, wise and gentle. 'Remembering can be a hard thing on a man,' he suggested. 'I wear life like an old pair of shoes that's easy on my feet. I might figure ahead some, what we'll have for tomorrow breakfast, say, or what job of work there might be to do today, and how best to do it. But I've already done the best I could with yesterday, so I never could see the sense of fretting about that.'

Harland, about to speak, saw Wes Barrell watching them; and his face changed, and Leick saw this change and looked at Wes. Wes was wishing he could hear what they said, and the wish was in his eyes; so Leick went to him, took him in conversation. Harland, thus protected, was left again alone.

He resumed his slow survey of all that lay within his vision here, looking right and left and far ahead; but he did not look back. He would never look back again. He must never look back through these six years. Since that one outbreak, like madness, which had prolonged his sentence for half a dozen unnecessary months, he had sought to drill his mind to forget these years, had tried to teach himself the hard lesson of forgetting, had forced himself to look ahead — and by so doing had won back to sanity again. To remember now was to risk the loss of all that he had won.

– IV –

The lake was sometimes wide, with deep bays on either side; it was sometimes narrow and confined, when the forest-clad mountains came plunging down to the water's edge. Once Leick caught Harland's eye and pointed toward the shore where a deer fed among lily pads a quarter-mile away. As they advanced, the horizon slowly changed its character. Mountains which, seen from one angle, were smoothly rounded off revealed from another point of view precipitous slopes; or steep bluffs and cliffs were lost to sight as gentler contours were revealed. Except for an occasional naked cheek of rock, where even in this dry season a trickle of water reflected the sun in a flash of brilliance, the forest was everywhere unbroken. There were no clearings here, no farms along the lake, no camps or cottages. The civilization from which men came was far away;

and those who ventured here were lumbermen with permits to take out a few thousand feet of spruce and pine, or fishermen bound for the River, intent upon the great salmon there, scornful of the lesser fish with which the lake abounded. Watching the changing profile of the mountains and the passing shore, Harland realized that they had long since rounded the point of land which shut out the village whence they had come; but even then he did not look back, fearing his calculations might be wrong, fearing he might catch one more glimpse of the world he wished to leave behind.

An hour before noon, they reached the dam at the foot of the lake, the gateway to the River. The sluice was open, but no water flowed through it, and there was only a little leakage through the timbers of the dam, trickling among the boulders in the narrow stream bed below. The dam-tender's cabin was deserted, the dam-site solitary. Leick and the boatman put the gear ashore. There was a crate of oranges, and a small packing box was full of staple supplies; sugar, coffee, flour. Two wooden pails held cooking dishes and the little provision they would require today and tomorrow. Bedrolls and a canvas fly, Leick's small pack and Harland's old, familiar duffel bag, the axe and the paddles and the pole made up the lot. To unload this little was no long business. Harland left them at it, walking over to look at the dam and the thin stream below; and Leick swung the canoe up on the landing. A moment later the engine started, and Wes Barrell went his homeward way; but he stood sidewise to look back at them, giving only scant attention to his course, as the motorboat drew up the lake again.

Leick above the landing began to build a little fire. When he was ready, he called and Harland joined him.

'Where's the dam-tender?' Harland asked, remembering the wheezing old man who had been here when they passed this way before.

'He died,' Leick said. 'Died all alone here last fall. There was an early freeze that caught him so's he couldn't get up the lake. They didn't find him till the ice was thick enough to travel. He'd been dead a week anyway, by then.'

They ate toasted corn bread and bacon and drank hot sweet tea. 'Where was everybody in the village this morning?' Harland inquired, remembering the solitude which had been drawn like a wall around them there; but Leick did not know. Harland watched the departing boat half fearfully, dreading to see it turn and retrace its course toward them; but before they were done with eating it was far away, and presently it passed behind a jut of the shore and disappeared. He filled his lungs with a deep inhalation.

'He's gone,' he said, in a great relief.

Leick nodded cheerfully. 'Yup. I'll clean up, and we'll be on our way.'

– v –

The first stage of their journey was tedious, for the stream that would so soon become a broad river, marching through its deep valleys to the sea, was here no more than a shallow rill. They surveyed the prospect together, and Leick said:

'No use to try to float the canoe right here. We'll carry to the mouth of the brook.' He added: 'You take it easy till you get your strength back. I can handle it all right alone.'

'I'll see how it goes,' Harland decided; and when Leick had swung the canoe, paddles and pole lashed to the thwarts, across his shoulders and set out along the half-mile carry, Harland burdened himself with Leick's small pack and his own duffel bag and picked up the wooden bucket which held the cooking dishes and took the carry trail.

The way at first ascended at a steep zigzag, climbing for a few rods to top the rocky point which was, on this side, the anchor of the dam. Before he was halfway up this short climb, Harland was gasping for breath. He set his teeth and pushed on to the top, but by the time he reached it his heart was pounding in his throat, his lungs ached, and he was sweating hard. He stopped to rest, mopping his forehead, feeling a strong distaste for himself. This was not the clean, honest sweat of a body lean and hard, but

the oily exudation from soft layers of pale yellow fat which over-
laid all that was left, after months of sedentary life, of what
had been his muscles. Once he had been proud of his fit condition, with skiing in the winter, and in the summer at Back of the
Moon long afternoons of strong tramping through the forests
when his morning's work was done. But now he was a soft,
pulpy, white thing like one of those grubs which live out their
lives in dark, humid soil; like one of those fat, eyeless, flabby fish
which dwell in subterranean waters and never feel the sun. Even
his hands were trembling with fatigue from this short climb.

'I'm like a man who has been sick,' he thought, looking at these
shaking hands; and for a moment a profound and hopeless depression overwhelmed him. He sat down, his shoulders sagging. Was
it worth while to go on, to try to fight down the past, to submit to
all the pangs the future held? Were it not wiser and easier and
even braver to make somehow, here, now, a quick and peaceful
end? The world, if he lived, would always be ready with its side
glances and its whisperings, wherever and whenever he should
face the eyes and the tongues of men again. Here in the solitude
was peace. Could he not stay here, let his body come here to its
last corruption and set his tormented spirit free? Death would be
so easy and so sweet.

He sat in half-surrendering self-scorn until he heard at some
distance in the stillness of the forest the sound of Leick returning;
and he was ashamed that Leick should find him here, and yet
ashamed too to pretend a strength he did not possess. So he sat
where he was till Leick came up the path to face him; and when
the other paused he said honestly:

'I got this far, Leick, but I played out.'

Leick nodded, assenting calmly. 'Take your time,' he advised. 'I'll need a couple more trips myself.' He went on down
to the landing by the dam, wisely leaving Harland to fight his
battle out alone.

Harland rose and resumed his burdens and proceeded. When
Leick, bowed under the bulk of fly and bedrolls, overtook him,
he moved aside to let the other pass and followed on. His de-

pression had somehow vanished. Perhaps the deep and labored
breathing provoked by that first short ascent had purged his
lungs, had burned out some of the sooty dregs with which they
were encrusted. He was sweating freely now, like a squeezed
sponge, and he savored the salt taste on his lips and found it good.
Leick went on and disappeared, and Harland stopped once to
rest — he merely paused this time, without sitting down — and
then proceeded. When he met Leick returning, the guide grinned
approvingly.

'Keep straight ahead,' he said with a backward nod to show the
way. 'You'll see the canoe. I'll fetch the rest of it this time.'

When, a few rods farther, Harland came down to the waterside, it was where a considerable tributary brook flowed into the
main stream; and the River even in this half-mile had drawn rein-
forcements from little spring brooks, so that it bore now enough
water to free the canoe. Yet Harland knew that there would
still be shallow reaches where he might need to wade, perhaps to
help Leick drag or carry the loaded canoe across these obstacles
into deeper water. There were boots in his duffel, but he chose instead a pair of shoe pacs, and he changed his clothes too, stowing
coat and trousers away in a careless roll, thinking with a grim
satisfaction that whether his trousers were creased would not
matter soon again. He put on stag pants and a flannel shirt
which Leick had brought for him from Back of the Moon; and in
the well-worn garments — a little too big for him now, for he had
lost weight in these months while his muscles turned to fat — he
felt strong and alive again. He caught himself starting to sing,
and checked suddenly, long habit of silence clamping his lips; but
then he remembered that he could sing now if he chose, and he
flung back his head and like a dog that bays the moon, he shouted
at the serene and cloud-swept sky:

> 'Oh a capital ship for an ocean trip
> Was the Walloping Window Blind . . .'

He wondered why he sang that particular song. The words had
not entered his mind for — how long? Then he remembered the

last time he heard the song, and the past pressed down on him again, silencing him, bowing his shoulders under a load that seemed unbearable.

When Leick returned, Harland was lying on the gravel bar beside the water, his duffel bag for a pillow, his arm across his eyes against the bright sky and the sun. Leick said in approval of his change of costume: 'Well, you look more natural!' But Harland did not speak nor stir till by the sounds he knew the canoe was loaded. Then he rose, and Leick without a word put the duffel bag in place in the canoe, and set the craft afloat, and steadied it while Harland stepped in.

To float free upon the mirror surface of the infant River was a release; but it was not yet all easy going, for sometimes there were sunny rips where the clear bright water sparkled and chuckled over gravel, and the canoe might scrape or even ground. At such times Leick, stepping out into the water and coming to the bow to drag the canoe a few feet, always freed it quickly. At frequent intervals lesser streams added their waters to the larger. The travellers came to a region where beaver had been active centuries ago, their dams backing up the water and catching silt and gravel in the spring floods till they had created wide marshy intervales, which, now that the dams were gone and the water was drained away, were pleasant meadows where the tall grass grew head high to a man. Sometimes the stream clung close to the foot of the mountains on one side, and arching trees on that bank made a shady canopy, and the water, barely deep enough to carry the canoe, glided easily over a bed of fine gravel; while on the other side the intervale might lead the eye pleasantly away, sometimes a scant hundred yards, sometimes half a mile or more, to wooded higher land beyond. Once they saw bobbing white flags ahead where two or three deer, playing some game or other, bounded sportively to and fro in the reedy undergrowth which clad a low gravelled island in the stream itself. They came close to these deer unseen, till the creatures, at last alarmed, turned to blow at them challengingly, and finally took flight, their tails visible for a while as they made their way in effortless bounds through the shallows and off toward the cover of the woods.

'A pile of deer up here,' Leick said. 'They ain't bothered much, only poachers come in most every winter and take out a few sled loads.'

Twice more they had short carries to pass dams built by the lumbermen, and once the stream threaded a cedar bog where blowdowns blocked their way; and sometimes they lifted the canoe over these obstacles, and sometimes Leick, wading knee deep, used his axe to clear the channel.

Thus the pleasant afternoon droned on, and an hour before sunset they came to a gravelled point where men had camped before, and landed there.

'Well,' said Leick contentedly. 'We're past the worst of it. Mostly all straight going now.' He took from where it was coiled around his hat a six-foot leader with a Parmachene Belle at the tip, a Silver Doctor for a dropper. 'Get us what you figure we can use tonight,' he directed. 'I'll be settling things.'

A few rods above the point, a little brook made in, and Harland turned that way, supplementing the leader with a bit of twine and a birch shoot. The trout were young and bold and hungry. He brought back half a dozen, not too large for the pan, and cleaned them; and then he took his ease while Leick with the skill of long experience spread their beds, stretched the fly for security against a chance shower, set his fire and so presently had supper ready. Afterward, he washed the dishes, saying little, letting Harland drink the healing silence of the wilderness. Before dusk turned to dark they were ready for the night, a smudge drifting smoke across their beds to keep insects away; and a little after full dark they rolled in their blankets side by side.

The night was long, and it was all one silence through which at intervals some soft sound came. Once, lying awake, savoring the fragrant darkness rich with the scent of the pine spills which carpeted the ground, Harland heard a train whistle far away in the direction from which they had come. More than once he heard the movement of some wild thing near them; the interrogative

thump of a rabbit, the heavier tread of a deer drawn by the salt
smell of their bacon frying, the querulous whining bark of a fox
not far away; and once they heard the busy teeth of a porcupine,
and Leick rose to drive the creature off, and then all was still
again. These sounds and these silences alike entered into Harland, became an enriching part of him. He had known silences
enough, in the months just gone; but those were the dead silences
of a tomb inhabited by living men. This night was all alive and
free. He slept at last, and for the first time in long, he slept
dreamlessly.

– VI –

At gray dawn Leick rolled out of his blankets; and, still half-
asleep, Harland heard the stroke of the axe and smelled the first
smoke. He rose to go to the stream side, and strip his pale body
and bathe, hurrying afterward into his clothes to protect himself
against the swarming mosquitoes, coming back to find immunity
in the drifting light smoke of the fire. While they ate, Leick
baked corn bread for their nooning, and before the sun lifted
above the wooded mountains to the eastward, the canoe was
loaded, and they embarked.

Harland, measuring the distance in his mind, decided they had
still some thirty miles to go; and he took a paddle to make greater
haste, but the unaccustomed exertion soon tired him and his ribs
began to ache and he put the paddle down again. Leick said
understandingly: 'Don't wear yourself out. I'll hump her
along. We'll be there by mid-afternoon, with the current to
help.'

'Even that little paddling tired me.'

'You'll harden up quick. Set back and enjoy yourself.'

So Harland submitted, filling his eyes with the passing scene.
For the first two hours they rode in beauty. The River gathered
to itself many little brooks and trickles; it threaded a region of
rugged hills that were not quite mountains, rising steeply seven
or eight hundred feet above the water. The hills were clad in

good second growth of spruce and pine; and along the waterside there were hardwoods, birch and beech and oak and an occasional elm.

But at the end of those two hours they came into the burnt land. The River was the same, the hills the same, the sky the same; but instead of forest, there were charred and lifeless stumps, scattered thinly across the steep slopes, standing erect like the chimneys of ruined homes. Most of the burned trees had fallen, to be covered by the quick springing undergrowth; but the gaunt black fingers of those which continued to stand still pointed as though in stubborn accusation at the heedless sky. In some places, even the humus which once covered the rocky slopes had been consumed by the fire, and the ashes had blown or washed away, so that no vegetation yet found a foothold there; and the naked rocks and ledges lay like bleached bare bones. In other places, the new growth, poplar and birch and brier and miscellaneous underbrush, was waist or shoulder high; and once or twice, on the slopes this thicket covered, they saw browsing deer which watched their passing, standing at a distance unalarmed.

Once Harland asked a low-voiced question. 'Was this all that same fire?'

Leick said: 'Yup! It burned a strip twenty-five miles wide and half as long again, right through here.'

'It hasn't grown up much, even in four years.'

'Takes time for the new growth to get a start,' Leick agreed. 'But it'll come along fast now.'

Four years? His own words stayed in Harland's mind. Was it in fact four years since, sitting in the shallows of the river with only his face out of water, he had seen these hills all a sea of leaping, hungry flames? It seemed a lifetime and a bitter one, interminably long; yet the new growth began to conceal the wound the earth had suffered, and ten years from now, or fifteen, these hills would all be healed again, clad once more in the seemly garment of the forest. For even in these burnt lands there was the potentiality of beauty. The ashes left by that conflagration were not dead after all; but caught in crevices and hollows of the rocky slopes they waited to receive and to nurture the seeds of life once more.

Harland thought his own life had been in some ways like this progress down the River, beginning with hard toil, coming then to a land of smiling intervales with a strong stream to bear him into lovely shaded reaches of even keener beauty. Afterward, just as they had come this morning, so he had come to desolation; yet, just as this ravaged waste one day would smile again, when the forest flowed back across the land to hide its scars, so too the future held its promises for him.

The sun lay scorching in the valley where the River ran. Harland watched the passing water, and sometimes as they drifted quietly through the great pools, he saw the swirl of grilse and salmon moving away from the canoe. The big fish were a translucent green. It was as though they were a part of the water in which they dwelt; and only their shadows, following them along the bottom, testified that they had solid substance. He stood up now and then, balancing himself against the paddle surge of the canoe which was like a pulse beating under his feet, the better to see these fishes and these shadows on the clean bottom of the stream.

They found no shade for their nooning, but a little grassy level beside a brook mouth served well enough, and a burned stump furnished splinters for a small fire to boil the kettle. Harland ate little. 'How much farther?' he asked, when they were done. The landmarks, which he had not seen since the fire, were strange and confusing now with the forest stripped away.

'Not far,' Leick told him, and Harland sat staring at the River flowing free, and Leick saw his fierce impatience and made haste to clear away and they pushed on. Two miles below, they saw on the high bank a cabin, built of new logs since the fire, and the warden who lived there came to watch them pass, and Leick lifted his paddle in greeting and had a sign of recognition. 'He'll telephone ahead,' he said. 'Let her know we're coming.'

Harland did not speak. The broad Sedgwick contributed its waters, and the River thereafter was twice what it had been before. Though it might narrow to pierce some deep defile between crowding hills, or where gravel bars flanking the main current had built out for half its width, it was always a strong and steady stream, the constricted waters flowing faster so that the canoe on their breast darted ahead as though suddenly it were alive, to slow and move sedately on the easier flood below.

The River ran through burnt land still, through a waste of blasted rocks and blackened stumps; yet always there was the thin green carpet of new life that would give birth to forest by and by. Harland, watching as each new prospect opened out before them, began to tremble with anticipation — and with a sort of terror too, as though he could not yet believe this scarred ugliness would ever end. He searched the hilltops far ahead for some hint of living forest standing there, but as each new vista opened, the prospect was the same; ravished slopes and a naked skyline with the pillars of the dead trees black against the blue. When he saw at last that for which he had looked so long, his eyes stung with sudden shaking happiness.

They had rounded a bold point rising steeply from the water where the River made an S-curve, undercutting the banks against which its full force was flung. For half a mile beyond the turn the stream ran straight and free; and at the end of that half-mile, Harland saw — for the first time since they had entered the desert of the burnt land — the dark green of spruce and hemlock and cedar and pine, their foliage mingled in varying hues; and he saw the brighter foliage of hardwoods too. These trees were not packed together in a forest mass, but were scattered pleasantly across a level sweep beside the river; and it seemed at first glance that there were hundreds of them, receding into the distance in a contenting perspective.

He watched and could not speak, and Leick said behind him: 'Purty, ain't it? It was some job, too. Every one of them trees we had to fetch from down-river. You can't transplant forest trees so they'll live in the open; have to get 'em where they've growed out in the field like. We moved seventy, but there's some will die.'

Harland nodded, unable to speak, feeling his throat choked as though with tears, and Leick said in the tone of one remembering proudly and happily a labor that was loved: 'Yes sir, it was a job! Every one of 'em, we had to dig a trench around it that first summer and fill it up with fresh loam so's the roots would branch out and ball up. Then come winter and the freeze, we horsed 'em out of there and fetched 'em up here on sleds on the ice. We'd already dug the holes for 'em up here, and levelled the ground and got grass started and all. There was around thirty of us working steady, just on the trees and the land, only when the snow was too deep for any use. And a crew putting up the house besides.' Then he added quietly: 'You can see the house now.'

They had been following till a moment before the main current which ran close under the north bank of the River; but it veered, angling out into mid-stream, and as they went with it the house indeed came into view. It was built, not of logs as the forest custom was, but of sawed boards and timbers. It was a low, sprawling house with wide verandas and a huge foursquare chimney; and shrubs already bound it to earth, and there was young grass all around.

And as Harland looked with hungry eyes, a woman left the house to come toward the landing that was still a quarter-mile ahead of them.

She was in white. That much Harland could see, and he could see the rhythm of her walk. By that alone he would have known her anywhere; for there was always about her manner of walking something unmistakable — and indescribable. It was not enough to say that she held herself erect, her head high, her back flat, her slim legs moving easily; there was in the way she moved something gracious and serene. She seemed never to make haste, yet Harland knew by experience that it needed his best gait to match that easy, lovely way she had. He tried, since this was his almost forgotten trade, to put her walk into words; and he thought that as she came toward the landing — which they too now approached — it was as though she were about to drop him a curtsy. Without actually doing so, she nevertheless seemed to hold her skirts caught between her fingertips and lightly outspread like a fan. Her garments borrowed grace from her.

A path came down at an angle to the landing, and by it she reached the narrow log float even as the canoe rubbed lightly and was still. Harland stepped out upon the logs to meet her, and could not see her clearly because his eyes were full; but he saw the white of her gown, and then her hands touched his. She spoke in that voice he had always been able to hear so clearly, even during the shadowed months that now were done.

'Welcome home, Dick,' she said, and then, seeing the muddled dregs of agony in his eyes, she whispered: 'Oh my dear!'

So he was in her arms.

T HESE SIX YEARS which Harland wished to forget had begun on a day in July, and upon a train westbound from Chicago. Harland's destination was Glen Robie's New Mexican ranch. They had met the summer before, on the little steamer *Fleurus*, which took salmon fishermen from Quebec to Anticosti Island. Robie and his son Lin were bound for the Jupiter River; Harland and Danny, his much younger brother, for the Becscie. Danny was twelve, and Lin Robie was a year older, and aboard the *Fleurus* the two youngsters quickly made friends and brought Robie and Harland together.

Robie, in his middle forties, was an oil man; one of those generous and friendly individuals whom the great Southwest produces. He had begun as a wildcatter; and a combination of driving energy, luck, and good judgment in choosing his advisers enabled him to bring in the first wells in one of the big Texas fields, and to build on that foundation a complete producing and distributing organization. His life was a success story of the sort not uncommon in the oil country. He had sold out his interests, four or five years before he and Harland met, for a sum so vast that it converted the transaction into a real-life fairy tale; and one of his first acts thereafter was to buy some two hundred thousand acres of New Mexican mountain and desert land. He specialized in Dutch Belt cattle and in the breeding of polo ponies; but also, since the mountain brooks were alive with trout, he had a fishing lodge a day's ride from his ranch house. A common interest in angling drew him and Harland together.

Harland had caught salmon in Newfoundland and on the Restigouche, and Robie was eager for the advice and instruction which
the other was able to give. Robie in turn described the angling in
the waters he knew; and he insisted that Harland and Danny
plan to come out next summer and sample the sport there.

Harland said they would like to come, but he assumed that
would end the matter. Summer friendships and summer flirta-
tions were pleasant while they lasted and rich in promises, but
they were apt to fade with the first parting; and easy invitations
were easily forgotten by the giver.

He and Danny had a good week on the Becscie. The rest of
the summer they spent at Back of the Moon. When Harland
was a boy his father put him every summer in charge of a woodsman named Leick Thorne, and he and Leick went adventuring,
sometimes for days at a time, into the forest lands near the Harland summer home. On one of these expeditions, ascending a
turbulent brook through young second growth, they came to a
lake like a half moon bent around the foot of a rugged hill. The
hidden beauty of the spot delighted Harland, and when later he
and Leick brought his father to see the place, the older man in a
characteristic enthusiasm bought the land. Leick and Harland
spent the next summer there, building a log cabin near the outlet, putting in a dam to maintain the lake at a good level and a
boathouse in which to store a skiff and a canoe. Harland, since
his father's death, had come to call the place Back of the Moon,
because no one except himself and Danny and Leick nowadays
ever saw it.

He and Danny stayed there, after their return from Anticosti,
till September. The two brothers were alone in the world, Harland some seventeen years the older. Their father had died just
before Harland went to college. Mr. Harland's income — he
was a lawyer — had been substantial, but he left only a house on
Chestnut Street in Boston, and an annuity barely sufficient to
support Mrs. Harland and Danny and to pay Harland's bills at
Harvard. Mrs. Harland, who had always been querulous, after
her husband's death became under the pinch of semi-poverty

increasingly fretful; and Harland's four years in Cambridge were, as a result of her complaints at the necessity of financing his education, shadowed by a resentful sense of guilt. He felt himself on the defensive; and as soon as he was graduated, he found employment on the *Boston Transcript*.

As a sophomore, Harland had fallen passionately in love with a girl named Enid Sothern; but since he could not hope to be married until he should become self-supporting, he and she could only plan, and could not seize, the future. Nevertheless they spent every possible hour together, and, for a while, in an equal intoxication; but a young and leaping fire must have fresh fuel or die down. The ardent caresses which never reached a climax lost their savor, and the week before Harland's graduation, Enid told him with a pretty ruefulness that she would marry another man. Harland, when the first shock to his vanity had passed, assured himself that he felt a deep and genuine relief. Nevertheless, like a betrayed husband, he dreaded facing either the smiles of his friends or their loyal sympathy; so he spent many solitary evenings at home. He had won distinction in English at Harvard, and writing was his natural bent; and to occupy his empty hours he began to write a novel. He put three years of painstaking labor into the book, and as is apt to be the case with first novels, this one was autobiographical, himself the hero. He called it *First Love*, but his heroine — Enid almost undisguised — was so little endearing that the rupture between them gave the book an unconventional happy ending.

The first publisher to whom he showed the manuscript accepted it. Harland had a youthful gift for irony, and a dangerous facility at pillorying human follies and frailties. Since the critics, reviewing too many pedestrian volumes, are always eager to welcome a first novel which shows promise, his book won an enthusiastic though limited audience.

Its mild success permitted Harland to resign from the *Transcript* and begin another. Before this was finished, his mother died. He and she had never been congenial; but her sudden death made him forget her faults and remember her virtues, and it left in him an unaccustomed sense of loneliness. One result was that although Danny was at the time only ten years old, Harland turned to him hungrily. Danny had always, in a shy, boyish fashion, worshipped his big brother, and he welcomed this offered comradeship. Thereafter, except when Danny was at school and Harland at his desk, they were as often as possible together.

Harland's second novel was an improvement on the first; he finished his third in June, before he and Danny went to Anticosti. Published in October, the book quickly sold into six figures; and at once hundreds of women who had enjoyed the novel were eager to see him 'in the flesh' at luncheons and dinners and club meetings. Upon the assumption that anyone who can put words on paper can also speak amusingly, he was besought to lecture not only in Boston but elsewhere; and these flattering seductions consumed that winter so much of his time that he saw less than usual of Danny. When in April the boy contracted infantile paralysis, Harland blamed himself, thinking that but for some omission on his part, Danny would not have been thus stricken.

Danny's illness seemed at first likely to be fatal; and though he survived, his legs were left almost useless. As soon as he could safely travel, Harland took him to Georgia for treatment. Thus they were at Warm Springs when Glen Robie's letter reminded them of that invitation to New Mexico.

Harland had at first no thought of going, but Danny said at once that he must do so. 'My gosh,' he cried. 'That's the only thing that will make up to me for not going myself! You can come back and tell me all about it, and it will be almost as much fun as if I were along.' And with that wisdom which is sometimes given to the young and afflicted, seeking an argument which Harland would accept, he urged: 'Besides, Dick, we're getting a little stale on each other! We're all talked out. You'll come back with so many things to tell me that we'll never run out of talk again.'

Harland yielded not too reluctantly. The thought of fine sunned days in the saddle and of streams alive with trout evoked in him a hungry longing. He wrote Robie his acceptance, explaining why Danny could not come. He went by way of Boston to pick up a pet rod and some other needed gear, and when he departed, Danny gave him a cheerful farewell.

'Keep a diary, Dick,' the youngster insisted. 'Put everything in it, and I'll ask a lot of questions too. Lin said there are wild turkeys on the ranch. Shoot one for me, and catch a lot of trout, and tell me all about everything when you come back. Good-bye! Good-bye! Good-bye!' The clear, happy boyish tones rang in Harland's memory as he drove away.

– II –

Harland's train left Chicago late in the evening. After breakfast next morning, with a book under his arm, he sought the observation car; but he sat down at the desk at the forward end of the car to write a long letter to Danny. His scrawl was rendered at times almost illegible by the motion of the train; and he made a joke of this illegibility, converting an occasional erratic pen stroke into a little sketch — an absurd face, an animal of no recognizable species, a flower — smiling as he imagined Danny's hilarious enjoyment.

He finished the letter and took a chair facing a young woman who was reading — it was this fact which determined his choice of a seat — his own recent novel. Probably half a million people had read the book, or would; but to see some stranger engrossed in one of his novels was an experience of which he never tired, and particularly when as in this case the reader was almost extravagantly beautiful. This girl was small, and her hair was dark, was perhaps black; but it was not straight as black hair is apt to be. It was not straight, but neither was it curly. Rather it seemed to have a playful tendency to curl, as though if permitted it would do so. Her skin was smooth and of an olive hue, with the flush of warm blood just below the surface; and her lips, though they seemed innocent of lipstick, were vivid. Watching them, he thought of a wine jelly which has dried a little and is lightly crusted over. Her lips looked — he chose the word advisedly, since the choice of words was his delight — delicious, as though if you bit them it would be like biting into a sweetmeat, one of those candies which are filled with a pleasant warming liquid. The tips of her ears, below the soft line of her hair — which was long enough to be knotted at the nape of her neck — were almost as pink as her lips. He had the feeling — permitting his thoughts to range as they chose — that it would be delightful to nibble at them! Her throat was a little paler than her cheek, and her body would be paler still, like a sweetly shaped figurine of old ivory, with round small breasts, and slim waist and gently swelling hips and slender thighs. While he watched her, exotic words drifted across the mirror of his mind as summer clouds drift across the sky; words that bore the flavor of the mysterious East. He remembered the tales in the *Arabian Nights*, heroines with alabaster brows, and almond eyes, and lips — was it lips? — like pomegranates. He was not at all sure what pomegranates were, and probably that simile was wrong, but its sound pleased him. He thought of myrrh and frankincense and potpourri — or was it patchouli? — and of nameless mysterious fragrances; of sloes, and of clusters of purple grapes, each richly full of blood-red juices which spilled when you crushed them between your teeth.

The train checked with a jolt that brought him back to — Kansas, to sweeping miles of level wheat lands reaching to the horizon; and he reminded himself with a faint amusement that this was no way to think of a nice girl! Nevertheless most men probably had such thoughts when they looked at a pretty woman. If this were not so, there would presently be an end to the human race!

However, if this girl chanced to raise her eyes and met his glance and read it, she would be made uncomfortable; so Harland turned his attention to the pages of his neglected book. It was Conrad's *Victory*, long familiar. Conrad's heroine was one of those quietly beautiful but almost bovine women who provoke in man the paternal instinct; but this girl across the aisle, though she sat perfectly still, was certainly not bovine. Even in her passivity there dwelt something like a flame, as though the very tips of her fingers, if you touched them, must be warm.

He looked at her again to confirm this impression and saw that she had fallen asleep! The book lay unheeded in her lap, her relaxed hands barely holding it there. Her head was tipped to one side against the back of her chair, and she was sleeping like a child.

Harland smiled, amused to find himself astonishingly provoked. So she was bovine, after all! Certainly no one in whom dwelt — he remembered his own phrase — something like a flame would go to sleep over his book! His Book! If his thoughts had affronted her, surely she had now by going to sleep insulted him!

When the unheeded book slipped off her knees to the floor, thus rousing her, he leaned forward to pick it up — observing as he did so that her ankles were exquisite. She accepted the book, nodding, speaking a quiet word. 'Thank you.' For a moment when she spoke he met her eyes, and he saw them, though still warm with sleep, widen in a quick surprise; and when he opened *Victory* again, he felt her watching him.

Well, he had watched her! Let her watch him if she chose. He remembered his own thoughts of her and wondered whether there were any similarity between her thoughts of him now and his thoughts of her then. Like most men, he sometimes derived a secret satisfaction from seeing himself reflected in store windows; and he amused himself, while he pretended to read, by putting her imagined comments into flattering words. Perhaps — his photograph had been printed along with many of the reviews of *Time Without Wings* — perhaps she recognized him, was mustering courage to speak to him. She might even ask him to autograph his book for her! Strangers had before now taken this flattering liberty.

But at length under her steady and continued scrutiny he became uneasy, changing his position, lighting a cigarette and smoking it furiously and stubbing it out again; and he began to be a little angry too. At last he lifted his eyes from *Victory* and met her glance squarely and held it, intending frankly to stare her down.

Her eyes did not falter. They explored his searchingly and deeply, with a sort of longing in them, till he could no longer support this visual encounter.

'Well, I'll be damned!' he said, under his breath, flushed with wrath; and he rose to return to his compartment, feeling himself driven from the field. Yet he paused for a moment, looking down at her still.

She seemed to rouse then with a sort of start. 'Oh, I'm sorry!' Her voice was low and husky. 'I was staring at you, wasn't I?' She extended her hand in an appealing gesture, and he saw a solitaire diamond on her third finger. 'Forgive me! You see — you look exactly like my father!'

And at the word her eyes, incredibly, filled with shining tears.

He cleared his throat, awkward and uncertain. 'It's all right,' he blurted, and turned hastily away. He hurried back to his own car in a sort of flight, something shaking him, his pulse racing.

He felt as though he had never been alive before.

– III –

Harland, since the day Enid told him of her engagement to another, had felt no particular interest in any girl; but he was now unable easily to forget the young woman who had gone to sleep while she was reading his book. The fact that because he looked like her father she had burst into tears suggested that she was recently bereaved and her appearance indicated that she was of the nervous and emotional type. Her translucent skin through which deeper flesh tones showed, her large eyes and lofty brow and her low, vibrant voice persistently suggested the mysterious East, the indolent seductions of hot desert days and starlit nights.

He smiled at his own fancies and set himself to forget her, staying all afternoon in his compartment, reading or idly watching the passing scene. The world hereabouts seemed to be made of vast plane surfaces which met at angles almost imperceptible. The horizon was sometimes fifteen or twenty miles away, sometimes close at hand; yet these near horizons were hardly above the level of the eye, and a straw stack or a group of farm buildings miles beyond might lift above them like the top-hamper of a passing ship at sea. Once he saw a shower approaching from the northwest, the emptying clouds casting across the wheat a shadow as blue as the ocean. Rain lashed the windows of the train and then was gone, leaving the rich lands teeming in the sun; and Harland knew these wide fruitful levels could feed a hungry world.

But the girl continually intruded in his thoughts, and he wondered idly why it was that an ocean voyage, or a long train journey, so often awoke romantic imaginings. Perhaps it was the feeling of irresponsibility which arose from the certainty that you would never see your fellow travellers again.

In the morning he had time to breakfast before they reached the junction point where he alighted. On the platform, while he was feeing the porter, young Lin Robie came running toward him with a shout of welcome. The boy wore dungarees and a silk shirt, high-heeled boots and a wide hat; and he was lean and brown and strong, and — remembering Danny who would never run again — Harland felt a shaking twist of pain. Then Lin was grasping his hand and saying many things all at once. 'Gosh, we're sorry Danny couldn't come, Mr. Harland; but I'm glad you did! How is he? Is he going to be all right?'

'Some day, perhaps,' Harland said. 'But it will be a long fight.'

'He wrote to me,' Lin explained. Harland had not known this. 'He told me to give you a good time. There's a washout on the branch line between here and the ranch, so Dad and I came down with the car and the truck to meet you. He's looking for the others. Did you meet them on the train? There, he's found them! Come along. Charlie will look after your things.' Harland saw in the background a young man with a broad, friendly face under his wide hat, and fine shoulders in a checked shirt, and the narrow hips of those who spend their days in the saddle; and Lin introduced him. 'This is Charlie Yates, the ranch boss. This is Mr. Harland, Charlie.'

Harland shook Charlie's hand, finding the other's grip, as was so often the case with outdoors men, as gentle as a woman's. Conscious of their strength, they were careful to hold it in restraint. Then Lin cried eagerly: 'Now come on!' Harland followed him, and a moment later he saw Glen Robie, in business clothes but wearing the wide hat of the region, standing with three women. One of them was old, white hair drawn smoothly back to a knot on her nape, with deep-set dark eyes; one was young and wore a pleasant friendliness; and the third was the girl whom Harland had decided to forget!

Robie when they approached turned to grasp Harland's hand in warm welcome. 'And now meet Mrs. Berent, and Miss Ellen, and Miss Ruth!' he said. So her name was Ellen! Harland saw her meaningly clutch her mother's arm, saw them exchange glances. 'I've told them about you,' Robie said. 'I thought you might get acquainted on the train.'

'Ellen had her eye on him,' the older woman declared. 'She insisted he looked like Professor Berent, but I told her that was nonsense! It is, too! He's only a boy!'

'I don't see it, myself,' Robie assented, looking at Harland appraisingly, so that Harland felt like a child whose resemblance to its father or its mother is under discussion.

When they set out, Mrs. Berent sat in the front seat of the big touring car with Robie. Harland found himself between Ellen and Ruth in the tonneau, while Lin perched on a drop seat, turning around to face them. After three or four blocks they emerged from the town into the open desert. Robie drove fast, and he talked over his shoulder as he drove, and Harland, saying, 'Yes,' and 'Yes, I see,' as Robie called his attention to this and that, wished the other would keep his eyes upon the road. Mrs. Berent finally said irascibly: 'For Heaven's sake, man, look where you're going!' Robie laughed and mended his ways; and after a moment Ellen, turning to Harland, asked curiously:

'Are you really the Richard Harland who wrote *Time Without Wings?*'

'I suppose I am,' he admitted, wishing that he did not always feel, when such a question was asked, an inane desire to simper.

She laughed softly. 'And I went to sleep reading it, before your very eyes! No wonder you scowled at me! But I sat up half the night to finish it afterward, honestly.'

Harland could find nothing to say. The rapid motion of the car, causing them all to lean one way and then the other as they rounded occasional curves, pressed her against him, pressed him against her. Lin chattered steadily, and Harland answered him; but the sisters sat now in an equal silence. Harland forgot Ruth, but he did not for a moment cease to be conscious of Ellen, close on his other side.

– IV –

Robie's home, planned by an artist who worked under no financial restrictions, was perfection, completely suited to its surroundings, never emptily luxurious yet never unnecessarily lavish. When they arrived, Mrs. Robie, surprisingly young and with an appealing beauty, welcomed them; and Harland saw the firm devotion between her and her husband, and their mutual pride. She was not quite as tall as her daughter Tess, whom Harland judged to be about eighteen — although Mrs. Robie might have been no more than thirty — and who met them with an unspoiled friendliness.

Harland's room — to which Lin escorted him — was at the end of the wing just above the pool which, tiled in blue, seemed to catch and reflect the pure beauty of the cloudless sky; and beyond, Harland could look out across the desert where every changing light produced a shifting panorama of colors to enchant the eye with swimming beauty. After an easy lunch, he went with Robie and Lin to see the stables, immaculate as a laboratory, which housed the polo ponies, and the wide pastures where fine cattle grazed; and they drove a few miles up the canyon to Robie's hunting lodge, so Harland did not meet the other guests again till they all came together for cocktails under the pergola beside the pool. During dinner, Robie explained for Harland's benefit — since the others of course already knew this — that Professor Berent had been his chief adviser during the years when he himself was active in the development of new oil fields.

'And after I sold out and bought the ranch here,' he said, 'he — and Ellen — came out, last year and the year before, to collect specimens, birds. That was his hobby. He had a collector's license, used to skin them and then send the skins — and sometimes he made the mounts too — to museums. Ellen helped him.' He said to Mrs. Berent: 'I'm sorry you could never come with them.'

'Ellen wouldn't let me!' she retorted, with that harsh asperity which seemed to be habitual to her, and she went on: 'Long before that, she had claimed her father as her private property, monopolized him so completely that I was surprised she didn't sleep with him!'

Ellen said quietly: 'Father needed someone to help him with the birds, Mr. Harland; and neither Mother nor Ruth cared to do the things he wanted done.'

'I should think not!' Mrs. Berent exclaimed, with an indignant jerk of her head. 'Snipping away at a dead partridge's eyelids is not my idea of a way to spend an afternoon! I'd rather do needlepoint!'

Ellen, as though the older woman had not spoken, added: 'And Mother was afraid of the arsenic, and Ruth was apt to be careless with it, and that sometimes worried Father.' Harland, who like most authors knew a little about a great many things, remembered that powdered arsenic was used to preserve raw skins.

'I was afraid of it, I admit!' Mrs. Berent said crisply. 'I don't like poison!' There was frank malice in her tones as she added: 'But Ellen seemed to enjoy handling it. She treated it as casually as so much face powder. I'm not at all sure she didn't sometimes dab it on her nose!'

Everyone — even Ellen — laughed. After dinner, they had

coffee beside the pool, sitting in quiet talk under stars that seemed to stoop close to peer at them, till Robie said presently: 'We'll start early in the morning, breakfast at seven. It's a long day's ride, so some of you may want to turn in.'

Mrs. Berent asked in quick protest: 'Ride? Horses?'

'There's no road to the fishing camp,' Robie admitted. 'The trail's rough even for a horse.'

Ellen said in quiet triumph: 'I told you, Mother, there was no need for you to come. You can never ride so far. You'll have to stay here. You might quite as well have stayed in Bar Harbor.'

'I came this far and I'm going the rest of the way,' Mrs. Berent retorted. 'So you might as well make up your mind to it! You did your level best to shut me out of your father's life; but I intend to see the last of him in spite of you! Horses or no horses! I'm going through with it, even if they have to tie me on top of one of the creatures.'

Robie laughed reassuringly. 'You'll have no trouble, no more than if you sat all day in a rocking chair,' he assured her. Harland smiled, suspecting that Robie had overstated the case for mountain riding.

When the others departed, Robie and Harland stayed to drink a highball together; and Harland, making his tone casual, led his host to speak of these other guests. Robie recalled the years when he and Professor Berent were together in Texas; but it was not of Ellen's father Harland wished to hear, and at last he asked directly: 'How old is Ellen?'

Robie looked at him, momentarily hesitant. 'She's twenty-two,' he said briefly. 'Ruth's twenty. She's a fine girl.' It was as though he compared them, and to Ellen's disadvantage, and Harland wondered what it was he did not say; but then Robie returned to Professor Berent. 'After the wells came in, I didn't see him for years,' he said. 'Then I sold out.' He chuckled in an agreeable fashion. 'You know, Harland, I like money. It makes it possible to do so many of the things we all want to do. I gave Professor Berent a million dollars — it was his knowledge and his advice on which I'd cashed in — and we were such good friends that he took it.'

Harland hid his astonishment, smiling. 'Most of us, at an offer like that, would be torn between pride and avarice; but you'd better not try it on me. I'm not proud!'

Robie laughed. 'Find me a new oil field and I'll do it,' he retorted, and he went on: 'Then when I built this place, I asked him out for a visit; and Ellen came with him.'

He hesitated again, said: 'You asked about Ellen.' Harland had only asked her age, but there were many questions in him. 'She's a strange girl. They spent two months here; took a couple of the boys and some pack horses and kept on the move. Before they left I came to see behind Ellen's beauty, see the iron in her. She has an absolutely immovable will. It seemed to me her father was a mass of small bruises, beaten numb by his constant exposure to the impact of that will of hers. She never let the men do him any personal service at all. They saddled the horses, made camp, did the routine things; but she spread his bedroll, prepared his meals, almost fed him by hand. Of course, she was crazy about him; but he couldn't call his soul his own.'

'I suspected her of a — father fixation, something of the sort.'

Robie nodded. 'I've heard of men and women in medieval times being "pressed to death," whatever that means. It was as though he were being pressed to death by the weight of her devotion.'

Harland smiled. 'Looks bad for the man she marries.'

'I notice she's wearing an engagement ring.'

'I saw that. I suppose after her father's death her life was empty and she snatched at a straw — or at a straw man. How long has he been dead?'

'Died this spring.'

'Mrs. Berent said something tonight I didn't understand, something about seeing the last of her husband?'

'Why, they've brought his ashes out here,' Robie explained. 'There's a place up in the mountains, a high pasture with a low rim of forest all around it, nine or ten thousand feet above sea level. Professor Berent used to say it seemed to be pressed against the sky; and you have that feeling when you're up there, that the sky is within arm's reach overhead. He loved the spot, and he hoped his ashes might be scattered there. I think he knew he wouldn't live long. That's why they're here. I judge Ellen would have preferred to come alone, but for once her mother apparently insisted.'

Harland was silent, hushed in thought. They sat in darkness save for the fair light of the stars; and he remembered that for ten thousand years men had told tales under the quiet stars, sometimes beside a flickering little fire, huddling to its warmth for a while before they sought the solitudes of sleep. It was in darkness, surrounded by the mysteries of night, that the story-teller first found his imagination stimulated into speech, and there he first found his audience too. Robie's cigarette glowed under a last drag, and he stubbed it out; and Harland said: 'Well, if we're starting early . . .'

– v –

The fishing camp lay at the junction of two canyons, and the spot was walled in by steep wooded slopes rising four or five hundred feet above the level greensward where the cabins were placed. The riders reached there in late afternoon, the horses picking their surefooted way down the last sharp slant of rocky trail; and already in the bottom of the canyon shadows lay, so that it was as though they went down into a clear pool of faintly tinted water. The brooks sang in the high silence; and when they paused to alight, Mrs. Berent groaned and declared she would never let herself be set upon a horse again. 'I feel as though I'd been paddled with a hammer,' she cried, and demanded to be lifted from her horse, gasping with angry pain at every touch.

Harland and Robie next morning fished downstream two or three miles to where the main brook plunged into a narrower canyon, with cascades a dozen feet high and deep pools alive with trout. Robie said this lower gorge extended six or eight miles till the brook came to desert lands and lost itself. 'It's hard walking,' he admitted. 'But there's good fishing all the way. Sometimes when we're going out to the ranch I fish down through, have a horse meet me at the lower end.'

'I'd like to try that.'

'Better wait till we leave,' Robie advised. 'It's too long a tramp down and back in one day.' So this adventure was postponed.

Harland at first, though he was intensely aware of her, saw little of Ellen. She took a horse every morning and rode away alone, reappearing just in time to change for dinner. But on the fourth day, ranch business would engage Robie; and when Harland heard this, preferring not to fish alone, he asked:

'What about a wild turkey?' On the twenty-mile ride in from the ranch, they had seen three flocks of hens and chicks. 'Danny told me to be sure and shoot one for him.'

'Go ahead,' Robie assented. 'They're out of season, but we can spare one. Take a gun and ride around till you see a flock and then put your horse right at them. They hate to take wing, and they never try it unless they can get a level or a downhill run for a takeoff. If you can drive them uphill you can often get right among them. It's tricky shooting, but you'll have some fun out of it.'

Ellen — they were at breakfast — spoke from across the table. 'I can help you get a fine gobbler, Mr. Harland, if you wish. I watched six of them, feeding on grasshoppers, yesterday; and they're sure to be back today.'

Robie said at once: 'That's the idea! Ellen knows every turkey on the ranch by its first name, Harland. You go along with her.'

Harland, afraid his voice would betray the sudden quickening of his pulses, hesitated; and Ellen said: 'We needn't start till after lunch. They only feed there in the afternoon.'

'Why, fine,' Harland agreed, and he explained: 'You see Danny, my brother, has had infantile, and he made me promise to bring back a full report of everything the ranch had to offer.' To conceal his eagerness he turned to Robie. 'He spoke of wild horses, too; said Lin told him there were some here.'

Lin cried quickly: 'You bet there are! You come along with me tomorrow — I'm going with Dad today — and maybe we'll see them.'

Harland, to hide his excited anticipation, turned to his cabin and spent the forenoon writing a long letter to Danny. He began by describing the pretty girl who sat opposite him in the observation car and who read his book and went to sleep over it. He knew how amusing Danny would find that episode, and he made much of it; but when he came to speak of his arrival here, some impulse led him to avoid saying that that same girl was in the party, and that they were to hunt turkeys together this afternoon. He stayed in his cabin till Mrs. Robie called that lunch was ready. When they had eaten and their horses were at the door, Harland would have forgotten the need for a gun, but Ellen reminded him, and they went to the rack and she bade him take a pump gun and a handful of shells. He put the gun in the saddle boot, and they mounted and set out.

Ellen led the way, turning up the north canyon, taking almost at once a side trail that climbed steeply through the pines. Riding behind her, he watched the light sway of her shoulders and her pliant waist. When now and then on a level reach they trotted briefly, she did not rise but held her seat after the western fashion. Harland, more used to an English saddle with shortened stirrups, found it hard to relax; and he tried to imitate her yielding grace. They went in silence, pausing briefly now and then where on the lofty trails a break in the forest allowed them to look down some far canyon to the desert like the sea beyond.

They crossed two ridges and descended into a valley like a park, through which a trickling brook meandered; and since the canyon floor was wide and smoothly turfed they rode now side by side, and flower masses, fringed gentians by the thousands and many other blossoms, were a carpet everywhere. Harland silently chose words to paint the beauty of the scene, but Ellen showed no desire to talk and he did not speak till after half a mile she turned aside.

'We'll leave the horses here,' she told him, and led the way into the forest that cloaked the canyon walls, and they tethered the beasts where from the open they could not be seen, and went back afoot. 'We must lie and wait for them,' she explained. 'They feed down this canyon almost every afternoon.'

'There's not much cover,' he commented. There was in fact, except for slight irregularities of the ground, none at all. The grass was cropped short, and the flowers were only inches tall, and no underbrush grew in the open anywhere.

'We'll just lie still,' she said. 'As long as we don't move, they won't notice us.'

She led the way to a single tree of some dwarf variety which Harland could not name, and which grew near the brookside and about equally distant from the forest on either hand. Its lowest branches were five or six feet above the ground, but at its base there was a slight saucer-shaped depression. Ellen lay at length, face down, in such a position that she could, even without raising her head, look up the canyon; and Harland hesitated, uncertain where to post himself, till she said: 'Here, beside me. We'll be able to see them coming for almost half a mile.' She added: 'I was here yesterday and they passed close by me, never noticing.'

Harland took the place she indicated, so near her that he could have touched her if he chose, could without moving have laid his arm across her shoulders. Since the lone tree gave scant shade, the baking sun was strong upon them, warming them through and through; the little saucer-shaped depression was as full of warm sweet-scented air as a cup is full of cream. For a while she did not speak, and this long silence seemed to enter into Harland like a fragrance in his nostrils; and he caught the scent of the sunned grass on which he lay. When his neck began to ache from long staring up the empty canyon, he looked down among the grass roots, watching the busy insect life there. A small green bug climbed one grass blade, crossed to another, and descended to the ground again. A grasshopper landed a yard from their faces and stared at them with tremendous eyes and then with a wooden clatter of wings leaped away. An ant threaded a circuitous path through the grass till it reached Harland's sleeve. It climbed on his wrist and then went along his arm to his elbow and down out of sight; but her elbow was so near his that almost at once the ant reappeared on hers. She was lying with her chin on her crossed hands, looking up the canyon; and Harland followed the ant's progress up her arm and across her shoulder. Her shirt was open at the neck, and it embarked upon the smooth sea of her throat before she felt it and quickly brushed it off.

'I was watching it,' Harland said lazily. 'Wondering how far it would dare go. It went along my arm and across to yours.'

'Father and I used to lie like this and watch the little things in the grass world,' she assented. 'When we were waiting for birds, sometimes we lay for hours side by side; but it never seemed long to me.'

'You and he had fine times together.' She nodded, and he asked: 'Collecting specimens, birds and things?'

'Not only that.' Her murmuring tones could not have been heard a dozen feet away. 'From the time I was able to walk, we were both happiest when we were together, and out of doors. Sometimes in the winter we took skis and carried packs and slept in the snow; and sometimes we went fishing, for salmon, in Newfoundland, and in New Brunswick, and around the Gaspé.' Harland found it hard to believe that their paths, so often parallel, had never crossed. 'Once we went to Georgia, went into the Okefenokee swamp, and found an ivory-billed woodpecker; and we talked there with a man who had seen passenger pigeons within five years — or thought he had. Father was never convinced of that. And — especially since he gave up teaching — we went to many places.'

'You haven't fished here, since we came.'

'No. When he and I were here we caught trout to eat; but catching salmon has taken the sport out of fishing for trout, for me.'

'I've done some salmon fishing on the Codroy, and the Restigouche, and at Anticosti. Danny and I. We met Glen Robie and Lin at Anticosti.'

She turned her head, resting her cheek on her folded arms, looking at him steadily. 'I told you once that you were like my father,' she reminded him. 'I mean you are like him when he was younger, when I was still a child. He too was fair, and lean, and gentle.' Harland felt his color heighten, and she asked: 'How old are you?'

'Thirty.'

'I thought at first you were older. You look years younger since we reached here. I think you were tired when we came. You were tired on the train.'

He did not answer this, but after a moment, feeling close to her, wishing to draw closer, he said: 'Robie told me about your father. He told me — why you have come here now.'

She turned her head, looking once more up the canyon. 'We mustn't move,' she explained. 'Their eyes are keen.' He thought her words were a rebuff, as though she meant to ignore what he had said; but then she told him frankly: 'Mother isn't used to riding, but I hope she can sit a horse tomorrow. Then we'll take his ashes up to the high basin he loved.'

He did not speak. The sun lay on them strongly, but the air that drifted down the canyon was dry, so the heat was no discomfort. Silence drew them closer, and as if she felt this and sought the release of conversation, presently she asked: 'Is your father alive?'

'No, my father and mother are both dead. There's just Danny and me.' Without looking toward her he felt her head turn, felt her watching him again. 'We've always been close, Danny and I,' he said. 'Although he's much younger than I, only thirteen now. Since he had infantile, I've spent all my time with him, till this trip.' He added: 'I even put my work aside.'

She asked curiously: 'Your work and Danny — are they all your life?'

He smiled, understanding what she did not say. 'I suppose you mean — why have I not married?'

'Why have you not married?' she assented.

'Well, I've been busy, working hard.' Then he added: 'I noticed your ring.'

She looked at her hand where the diamond caught the sun.

'His name is Quinton.' Her voice was empty of all expression.
'He's a lawyer, lives in Maine.'

'Russell Quinton?' Harland was surprised.

'Yes. Do you know him?'

'I met him once,' he told her. Quinton was almost fat, almost
bald, almost middle-aged; and Harland wondered what common
ground these two could have found. 'We were both fishing the
Upsalquitch. He came downstream, stopped to eat lunch, then
went on.' Quinton had been in ill-humor that day, and Harland
had not liked the man, had not liked what Leick afterward told
him about Quinton.

'He was a friend of my father's,' she said, 'and father liked
him, and Mr. Quinton wished we might be engaged. But I will
never marry him.'

Harland felt his heart quicken, as a horse quickens at the faint
warning touch of the spur. Conscious of her eyes upon him, he
paid for a moment no attention to the movement far up the canyon. Something, probably some of Robie's cattle, had drifted out
of the shadows of the trees into the sunned open there, but he
hardly saw them. Her quiet words had carried an astonishing
impact. She wore Quinton's ring — but she would never marry
him! A turbulence possessed Harland, but then he realized that
those cattle up the canyon were very dark, almost black; and as
his eyes and his mind focussed upon them, he said in a low whisper: 'I see turkeys!'

She did not move, still watching him. 'How far away?' she
asked.

'Quarter of a mile at least. They're so big I thought they were
cattle.'

From the corner of his eye he saw her head turn, very slowly,
till she too could look that way. 'Big gobblers,' she said then.
'Six of them.' One of the tremendous birds made a running leap,
its wings half opening; and she murmured: 'Catching grasshoppers. They'll work down this way. Be very still. Completely
still.'

Harland obeyed her, and they lay motionless, watching the

slowly approaching birds. Now and then she whispered some word almost soundlessly; and he answered, hardly moving his lips, feeling his pulse pound, at once completely conscious of her beside him and yet trembling with the keen tension of this waiting. The turkeys seemed gigantic. Lying prone, looking up the canyon toward them as they approached, Harland's vision was to some degree distorted, so that the birds appeared to be larger than they were, and very near; but when at last he slid his gun a little forward, she whispered warningly:

'No, wait! Let them come as close as they will.' And she added: 'I'll tell you when to shoot.' And a little later she said: 'Watch the one that's second from the right, now. Take him when you shoot. He's magnificent! Can you see his beard? Keep your eye on him.'

Harland muttered an assent. His hand was tight on his gun and he felt it slipping with sweat and released his grip to wipe his palm dry on his trouser leg. The turkeys, moving straight toward where they lay, came within fifty or sixty yards; but then Harland thought the birds saw them. Certainly he and Ellen were by that time in plain sight, and certainly the actions of the turkeys were subtly modified. They changed course, and instead of coming on they drifted nearer the border of the woods and, keeping the same distance away, described a third of a circle around the two watchers. Harland wished to shoot, but he waited till Ellen whispered:

'Careful! Now!'

He swung the gun's muzzle slowly toward the birds, and at that cautious movement they stood for an instant in motionless attention. In that instant Harland fired.

The turkey he had chosen fell; the others fled like speeding shadows. As he leaped erect, the stricken turkey also scrambled to its feet; and Harland, running toward it, fired again, knocked it down again. Before he reached it, it was up once more, and once more Harland shot it down. It was still struggling when he caught its neck, smothered the great beating wings, gave it a quick quietus.

And he thought then suddenly that his chest was about to explode! The violent exertion through these few seconds at this high altitude had called on his heart and lungs for an extraordinary effort. When Ellen, coming more slowly, reached him, he was lying flat on his back, breathless and helpless, his hand clasping the softly feathered neck of the dead bird.

She knelt beside him, quickly understanding. 'Just rest!' she said. 'I should have warned you. You're not acclimated to the thin air. We're up nine or ten thousand feet here, you know.' Then she cried, looking at the turkey: 'Oh, what a pity! One of your bullets cut his beard. He'd have made a splendid specimen!'

Harland, grimly amused at his own distress, thought he himself was in a fair way to become a splendid specimen! He tried to sit up, but she bade him lie still. 'Wait,' she insisted. 'You'll be all right presently.'

He did not protest. He was content to stay passive till his laboring heart slowed to a normal beat again; content even then to sit with her while they admired the big gobbler on the ground between them. Its wingspread was wider than his gun's length would span, and she guessed the bird would weigh twenty-five pounds. 'It's bigger than the best my father killed,' she said. 'I'm sorry the beard's spoiled. I might have saved the skin and mounted it in the group he made last winter, out of turkeys he killed here.'

'Do you still do that sort of thing?'

'I haven't, but I could. I've kept his workrooms as they were, in Boston and at Bar Harbor, with everything ready, just as he left them.'

'Do you mean to — go on with his work?'

Her eyes met his. 'I don't know what I mean to do,' she said quietly. Then with a quick movement she rose. 'Stay here. I'll bring the horses.'

'I'll go.'

'You shouldn't move around much for a while.' Her solicitude at once flattered and compelled him, and he felt a momentary rebellion at her assured domination; but she was already moving away. When she returned, herself mounted and with his horse on lead, under her direction he loosed the yellow slicker bound behind his saddle and wrapped the turkey in it and secured it on the horse's back. Then they turned homeward, jubilant together, talking much and laughing easily. There was a like intoxication in them both, and every thought was amusing, every word provoked a shout of mirth. On the crest of the last ridge they paused to watch the level sun dip below the heights northwestward, and when it was gone, like bathers venturing into the sea at night, they descended into the cool dusk which filled the canyon; and Ellen began to sing a doleful song:

> 'Are we almost there? Are we almost there?
> Cried the dying maid, as they drew near her home.
> Are them the slip-per-y el-lums that r'ar
> Their proud green forms 'neath Heaven's blue dome?'

He laughed in amused appreciation. 'Where'd you get that?'

'Charlie Yates taught it to me when father and I were here two years ago.'

'It's a classic!' He began to sing it with her, and when he erred she corrected him.

'Not "slippery elms"!' she protested. '"Slip-per-y el-lums"! Soulful and woeful! Try it again.'

So they began afresh, and their singing voices went before them as they neared the lodge, and their shouts of triumph summoned the others out to see their prize.

– VI –

Harland before he slept that night planned eagerly to spend next day with Ellen; but at breakfast Lin reminded him that they were to go looking for wild horses and he could think of no ready pretext to escape. Tess decided to join them, and shortly after breakfast, lunch in their saddlebags, the others on the veranda to watch their departure, they set out.

From the first it was clear that Lin felt himself to be — and was — in charge of the expedition. Harland found it hard to re-

member that Lin was no older than Danny; the boy seemed so
completely at home in these surroundings, so sure of himself, so
mature in all his ways. Tess, in dungarees and checked shirt and
big hat, wearing leather chaps to guard her knees against the buck
brush through which sometimes they rode, seemed as much a boy
as Lin; and they vied with each other like puppies, spurring their
horses into sudden headlong races not only on the level but up or
down the steep trails, shouting and laughing, the victor deriding
the vanquished while after each sprint they waited for Harland
to come up with them.

They were charming, but he wished it were Ellen with whom he
rode through these sun-filled canyons and these park-like open-
ings carpeted with flowers. He might have forgotten their quest,
but Lin did not. Whenever they were about to emerge from some
forest cover he paused to scan the scene ahead; and thrice he
showed Harland tracks of the quarry upon which they sought to
spy. At noon, as efficiently as any guide, he boiled the kettle beside a tumbling little stream, and Harland smiled at the
youngster's gravity, and thought how Danny would have enjoyed this day, and they ate their lunch and then rode on.

It was mid-afternoon before fortune gave them at last the
glimpse they sought. Emerging from an aspen thicket into one
of the lovely parks which lay everywhere, Harland saw Lin pause
to look ahead, and the boy called a low, quick word, and Harland
and Tess brought their horses up beside his, and then they all
spurred into the open.

Two hundred yards away, gleaming like bronze statues in the
sun, nine horses stood with crests flung high, watching them. As
Harland's eye found them, they turned in thundering flight. The
stallion herded his mares away, and Lin shouted and gave chase,
and Tess and Harland, at full gallop, followed; but in a dozen
bounds the wild creatures reached the rimrock and plunged over
it and were gone. Only the stallion paused for one last defiant
backward glance before he followed his harem over the brink.
When the riders came to the spot, it seemed impossible that anything larger than a fox could have descended the broken decliv-

ity; but the horses were gone, already out of sight in the wooded deeps.

'Did they go down there?' Harland cried, doubting his own eyes; and Lin laughed.

'Sure. They're a mile away by now. They're like mountain goats, and just about as wild.' He was tremendously proud of this success, and Harland to please him asked many wondering questions, till presently they moved on, now homeward bound.

Half an hour after they saw the horses, they emerged upon a tree-clad rim from which they looked out across a high grassy basin perhaps a mile wide. Lin checked his horse in the fringe of trees; and Harland, pausing beside him, saw three mounted figures sitting quietly in the center of the basin. He recognized at once Robie's big, light-colored hat, and the two people with him were clearly feminine; but far away across the basin another rider went at a swinging gallop, describing a circle around these three; and even at a distance Harland was sure this was Ellen.

Tess said in quick dismay: 'Oh, I didn't know they were coming up here today. Get back, Lin.' Lin reined his horse among the trees again. 'They won't want us butting in,' Tess explained, and Harland too retreated; and for long minutes they stayed there watching, while Ellen rode at a headlong run the circuit of the basin.

When she passed below where they hid, Harland saw that she held something in the curve of her left arm, pressed against her breast as a mother holds a child; and her right arm swung in the motion of a sower, regularly as a pendulum; and he understood what it was she thus broadcast upon the rocky sward, and he thought of a priestess at her rites, and he thought of old pagan festivals, and he thought there was a pounding and barbaric rhythm in the thudding of her horse's hooves, and he thought of the ride of the Valkyries. For there was a singing in the way she rode, erect and sure, her head high and proud; and he heard that singing in his blood while he watched her bring her father's ashes to the spot the dead man she loved had chosen, to this high meadow pressed against the sky.

The three watchers stayed hidden, and they saw her turn at last, still at full gallop, and plunge into the forest at the border of the basin, diagonally across from them. So she disappeared; and Harland heard a choked sound beside him and turned and saw that Tess had tears in her eyes; but she smiled at him.

'That was — sort of wonderful, wasn't it,' she said frankly. 'Professor Berent was a fine old man.'

Harland nodded, and Lin said in a low voice: 'That's the trail to camp, the way she went.' Even the boy had felt the solemn beauty of this scene. He turned his horse back among the trees. 'Come on,' he called softly. 'We'll go home another way so they won't know we were here.'

They went headlong, plunging down rocky draws, racing at full gallop through the forests; and the horses, instantly responsive to the neck pressure of the reins or even to the inclination of the rider's body, wove through the trees in a graceful measure like a dance. They reached camp before the others. Walking to the lodge from the corral where they left their horses, Tess said warningly: 'We mustn't let them know we were watching, Lin.'

'What do you think?' he demanded, scornfully indignant at the suggestion.

She touched his arm in affectionate reassurance. 'I know you won't,' she assented. 'But I'm glad we saw them, all the same.' Lin nodded soberly, and she said to Harland: 'It was — sweet, wasn't it, Mr. Harland.'

'I'm glad we were there, yes,' he agreed.

While Harland was in his shower, Robie and Mrs. Berent and Ruth returned, and Harland heard Mrs. Berent bitter in complaint at the torment the ride had imposed upon her; but he did not hear Ellen's voice, and when they all gathered at the dinner table she had not come home. Mrs. Robie was concerned.

'Are you sure she's all right, Glen?' she asked doubtfully.

'Don't worry,' he told her. 'She probably wanted to be alone a while. I've known her to ride all night, on a moonlit night; and she knows these trails as well as I do.'

Mrs. Berent tossed her head. 'She probably imagines her

father is up there with her right now,' she exclaimed. 'I don't know where she gets her notions. Certainly not from me!'

'I like to be out at night myself,' Robie admitted. 'There's a lot of good company in the stars. Did she have a blanket, anything to keep warm?'

Ruth said quietly: 'She packed a heavy sweater in her slicker roll. She'll be all right, I'm sure.'

Mrs. Berent snorted. 'She's a fool — and so am I, to go gallivanting over mountains on a horse at my age. Ruth, I've one of my coryzas coming on!' Harland reflected that she treated Ruth more like a paid companion than a daughter.

'I'll fix you up, Mother,' the girl promised, a twinkle in her eyes.

When dinner was done, Mrs. Berent had begun to sneeze; and she and Ruth said good night at once. Harland, his emotions deeply stirred by that scene he and the children had witnessed, was alert for Ellen's return, wishing he might be with her in this hour of her lonely grief, and he waited a while on the veranda, listening for the hoofbeats of her horse. Mrs. Robie presently joined him, and he confessed that he and the children had chanced upon the scene on the heights that afternoon. 'It was a moving thing to watch,' he said.

'Tess told me,' she assented. 'And Glen saw you, but the others didn't know you were there.'

His own hunger to see her made him resent Ellen's long delay, and he said: 'Ellen ought to come back. She must know it will worry you. You've enough of a job, keeping us comfortable here, without riding herd on us too.'

'Oh, I enjoy this,' she assured him. 'I mean, making things nice here for Glen and our friends. But Ellen really is difficult, sometimes. It's not so much selfishness as a sort of — is egoism the word? When she wants to do a thing, she doesn't take into account the wants of others at all. It isn't that she overrides them. She simply goes her own way — and they can only submit.' There was no resentment in her tones, merely a half-amused appraisal. 'I've never seen anyone so wholly sure of herself,' she confessed.

Harland nodded, feeling himself aggrieved. 'I know. When we went after turkeys, she told me exactly what to do. It never occurred to me to argue with her.'

'Of course not.' She added after a moment: 'Her father couldn't call his soul his own. I used to feel like — slapping her, sometimes. I loved that old man. I'm glad he wanted to come back here.'

Someone stirred in the shadows, coming quietly toward them, and Harland till she spoke hoped this might be Ellen; but it was Ruth.

'I saw your cigarettes,' she said. 'Don't feel you must wait for Ellen, Mrs. Robie. She's all right.'

'We weren't sleepy,' the older woman assured her, and Harland asked:

'Where do you think she is?'

'I think she'll stay up there till dawn,' Ruth told them. Her voice was warm and heartening in the night. 'She probably hid to let us pass, and then went back there after we were surely gone.' She added in faint amusement: 'Ellen dramatizes things, you know.'

Lightning flickered far away, sending a faint wave of radiance across the cloudless sky; but it was so distant they heard no thunder rumble. 'There's rain north of us,' Mrs. Robie doubtfully remarked.

As she spoke, Robie joined them. 'Ellen knows her way home, if she wants to come,' he reminded her.

Ruth added: 'Yes. Don't worry, please.' She bade them good night and turned away, and Harland noticed how pleasantly she moved. He was surprised to find that in the darkness she wore a beauty of which in the light of day he had never been conscious.

After a moment Mrs. Robie likewise said good night, and the lightning flashed again, and Harland said: 'That must be an old roncher of a thunderstorm.'

'We get some terrors,' Robie agreed. 'Real cloudbursts. I've seen the brook rise three feet in an hour, even here where it has room to spread all over the canyon.' He turned away. 'Good night, old man.'

Harland at last abandoned his vigil, telling himself he was a fool to be concerned; but he wondered whether he would hear Ellen's horse if she returned during the night. He woke before sunrise and at once thought of her and dressed and went out. No one was stirring in the bunkhouse; but one of the men must already have gone to find and bring in the horses for the day's use, and Harland walked up to the corral — a lonely milch cow, secured to one of the posts, was its sole occupant — and stayed there till he heard the clatter of hooves up the canyon. The horses came at a gallop, with tossing heads and flanks wet from the night's fall of dew. Penned in the corral they circled excitedly, the cow shrinking and making herself small as they milled past her; and then Charlie Yates, who had brought them in, stopped to roll a cigarette and to exchange a word with Harland.

'She hasn't come home yet,' he said looking up the canyon trail; and after a moment he added: 'She's a hot one, always doing the damnedest things. You'd think she'd know Mrs. Robie would be upset.'

Harland surprisingly resented this echo of his own criticism. 'Can I have a horse?' he asked stiffly. 'I think I'll ride to meet her.'

'Sure thing,' Charlie agreed. 'I'll go along if you say so.'

'No need,' Harland told him. 'She's all right.'

'Sure,' Charlie drawled. 'She knows all the answers.' Harland realized that even Charlie must be uneasy, to speak thus of a guest.

When his horse was ready, Harland set out, at first at a foot pace to conceal his own eagerness; but once out of the other's sight, he lifted his horse to a trot and then to a lope. The sun struck the ridges high above him; but here in the canyon the air lay damp and cool, and he rode in shadows while in the sky the level rays swept away some shredded skeins of golden cloud. When in due time he passed the bars and left the main trail and began to climb, he ascended into sunlight that came pouring over the heights behind him in a shining flood; and on the crest of the ridge he met Ellen face to face.

The sun was in her eyes and the sun was all upon her, so that she seemed for an instant to wear a sort of incandescence. Harland imagined the stains of tears upon her cheeks, and the ravages of solitary grief in her countenance. Phrases formed themselves in his writer's mind and he thought of a white-hot ingot coming from the fire, of molten gold in a bone-white crucible. Sorrow, the night long, had brayed her in a mortar, and her soul was swept and burnished.

'All right?' he asked, hoarse and husky.

She nodded, smiling radiantly. 'Come,' she said, and touched his hand, inviting him to share with her some pleasant prospect. 'I'm ready now to return to the world again.'

They rode back to the lodge, and till they left their horses — Charlie was there to take the reins — she did not speak, nor did he; but then she said gravely: 'Thank you, Mr. Harland.'

So they parted and Harland was alive with a mysterious excitement. He heard her mother's querulous greeting, heard the sound of a sneeze, as Ellen went into the cabin where they lodged.

– VII –

Harland after breakfast waited for Ellen to reappear, and he stayed at the lodge all day, refusing Robie's suggestion that they try the brooks; but she remained invisible till dinner time. Even then he had no chance to claim her, for when they rose from the table, she joined Tess and Lin at one end of the wide veranda, and they chattered together like children, flying into gales of laughter at their own words or at nothing. Harland, sitting with Glen and Mrs. Robie twenty feet away, wished he might join them, but would not without an invitation. The moon was waxing, and the canyon was paved with magic shadows that were broken by silver light patterns, and presently the two young people and Ellen strolled away down the trail together, and their voices came back softly through the night, blurred by the steady chuckle of the brook. After a time, at some distance, he heard them singing the nonsense songs of which children — young or old — never tire.

He was so abstracted that Robie noticed it and suggested they join the singers; but Harland, feeling that Robie had read his mind, reddened in the darkness; and he said he was sleepy and would go to bed, and did so.

At breakfast Robie proposed a day of fishing, and Harland agreed and hoped Ellen might go with them; but when Robie invited her to do so, she declined. 'Lin says he and Charlie Yates and one of the cowboys want to try to locate a trail out of the box canyon up in the horse parks,' she explained. 'I'm going with them.'

So to Harland the fishing was dull and profitless. Back at the lodge they found she had not returned, and they sat on the veranda for a while, and the sun sank lower in the west, till at last Glen said:

'Look yonder!'

Ellen and Lin had appeared on the crest of the ridge above camp, and now they brought their horses plunging down the steep descent, refusing the trail, starting a small avalanche of tumbling loose stones, the horses as often as not sliding on their rumps, plunging through the pines and aspens which clad the slope, the riders with shrill cries urging them on. When they reached the level, Lin was one jump ahead; but as they raced toward the lodge, splashing through the brook, his hand lay too heavy on the reins, so that he twitched his horse off stride. Ellen passed him and came first to the goal triumphantly.

Lin had lost his hat, and from a deep scratch on Ellen's cheek fresh blood trickled, bright crimson against her warm dark skin. They were panting and laughing, and Lin explained to his father, while he gasped for breath:

'We raced the last mile, Dad; took a straight line, up and down, over everything. I'd have beat her, too, but I swung too far south on the first pitch. I thought she was headed wrong.'

Glen laughed. 'Ellen always knows exactly where she is, and where she's going,' he said drily.

'She'll never beat me again,' Lin declared, and Ellen laughed and told him she could beat him whenever he chose. She was in dungarees, hot and soiled from her long day in the saddle, that scratch on her cheek a red flame, her face as smudged and sweat-stained as the boy's; but she appeared for dinner in something light and soft and completely feminine, and the contrast beween her delicate and pulsing beauty now and the disordered hoyden she had been an hour before seemed to Harland so intoxicating that he became suddenly wary. When Robie next morning proposed an inspection trip to the upper pastures, he accepted, determined to put her out of his mind.

He and Robie rode all day, scouring every covert, starting the scattered bunches of cattle and inspecting them. Robie and Charlie decided it was time to brand and earmark the young stock, and settled on Tuesday for this task. When they returned to the lodge they found Ellen and Lin together on the veranda, and Robie asked: 'What have you two been up to?'

'Not a thing,' Ellen smilingly assured him. 'We didn't feel like doing anything strenuous, so we've just been sitting here talking all day.'

Harland wondered whether he could spend a long day alone with any fourteen-year-old boy — unless of course it were Danny. Clearly Ellen liked boys, and understood them too. The youngster's eyes were shining as he watched her now.

That evening the moon was brighter, and the sky a cloudless bowl of paling stars. Lin went early to bed, and Ellen after a little rose and stood by the veranda rail. 'I've sat still too long,' she said. 'Mr. Harland, will you walk with me?'

Mrs. Berent — this was her first appearance at dinner for days — made a derisive sound. 'Quoth the spider to the fly!' she said sharply; and everyone laughed in dutiful fashion, and Harland as he joined Ellen felt hot and angry; but when he was alone with her his anger passed. They followed the brook trail half a mile down the canyon to the lower bridge — the moon was bright enough to show them every pebble in the way — and they went at first in silence, till Harland said at last, remembering Danny:

'You and Lin get along.'

'I enjoy being with him,' she agreed.

'I like him, too, but I can't imagine sitting and talking to him all day.'

Her tone was lightly quizzical. 'You're ever so dignified, aren't you? I think you're one of those men who wear a sort of mental beard. You try to seem more reserved and mature than you really are. Except the day you shot the turkey, I've never seen you really let go and throw back your head and laugh!'

'"'T' see ourselves as ithers see us,"' he quoted, amused. 'I suppose I don't laugh much. Laughter is the luxury of the indolent, isn't it? Busy people don't have time to laugh.'

'You're on vacation here, not busy at all!'

'An author never has a vacation. He's a walking sponge, sopping up impressions till he's saturated, then going to his desk and squeezing them out on paper.'

'I'd forgotten you're an author,' she confessed. 'Probably that's why you like to make phrases. Of course I know you must have worked hard, to be so successful so young.' She laughed at him in a teasing way. 'I suppose you think you must live up to your position, pretend a — gravity you do not always feel. And then of course you're terribly shy!'

Harland chuckled. 'I wonder why men always feel a little flattered at being told they're shy.'

'They like to feel they're — heroes,' she suggested smilingly. 'Keeping a stiff upper lip against heavy odds.' They came to the bridge and stopped, leaning on the handrail, looking down into the clear water; and she cried: 'Look! You can see the trout, even in the moonlight.'

The night air was damp and cool and fragrant. 'And you can smell flowers,' he agreed. 'All your senses seem so much keener here.'

'I know,' she murmured. Her shoulder almost touched his, and he caught a dizzying hint of some faint scent she wore. She looked up at him and an overhanging bough between her and the moon laid a dark shadow across her nose and mouth and chin; and he thought again, as on that first day he saw her, of those mysterious beauties of the harem, who wear a veil which hides all but their eyes as the shadow hid all but her eyes now; and he smiled and spoke of this, said the shadow on her face was like one of those veils.

'Yashmaks? Is that what they call them?' he suggested. 'Or it's like one of the handkerchiefs train robbers used to wear as masks, when this country out here was young.'

'I suppose we all wear masks,' she assented, and turned, and he moved at her side; and as they walked slowly back toward the lodge she asked questions about Danny; asked where he was, and how long he had been ill, and how he progressed; and Harland answered her, and to speak of Danny woke tenderness in him, and it was in his tones, so that she said at last:

'You love him almost too much, don't you?' Her words faintly disturbed him, seemed to be in some way he could not define a threat to Danny. She said: 'I wish I knew him. I get along well with boys his age — and Lin's.'

That sense of danger to Danny, groundless though it was, made his tone dry. 'I'm sure you do,' he assented. She looked at him in surprise and let her hand rest lightly on his arm, as though in reassurance; but he did not speak again and they came back to the lodge.

– VIII –

On the day set for the branding, they all except Ruth and Mrs. Berent went to watch the proceedings. Cowboys rode into the mass of milling cattle, dropped their ropes over the necks of the calves they selected, and dragged the bucking victims toward where little fires were burning and the irons were hot. Sometimes a cow followed her offspring, excited by its bawling, making alarmed or threatening movements till she was driven away. Lin helped to throw the calves, but he was not big enough to handle them easily, and his ambition sometimes outran his powers. When he tackled a lusty antagonist there might follow a protracted struggle, the calf bucking and bawling, Lin's feet as often in the air as on the ground, till he was spattered with blood and smeared

with dirt and grime — and completely happy. Harland, laughing
with the others at the boy's activities, had an itching impulse to
dismount and try his hand; but he could picture too clearly the
ridiculous figure he would cut if he proved inept. He thought no
one guessed his wish, but when they all rode homeward, descending from sunlit heights into the cool and shadowed canyons
again, Ellen brought her horse beside his and said with a twinkling amusement in her tones:

'You were just aching to try to throw a calf, weren't you? I
could see it in your eyes.'

He grinned. 'Yes, I wanted to; but I had sense enough not to
try.'

'I did it, last year,' she assured him. 'It's a knack, that's all.
Not hard. If there hadn't been an audience, you'd have chanced
it.'

'Another week here and I'd feel young enough to tackle the
job, even with an audience.'

'Another week, yes,' she echoed in a lower tone. 'But we've
only another day.' He looked at her in sharpened attention, but
then the trail narrowed so that she moved ahead, and they went
single file and spoke no more. Yet at dinner that evening —
Harland found himself between Ellen and Tess — she referred
again to their approaching departure.

'It doesn't seem possible that we've been here almost two
weeks,' she said. 'And yet it seems too as though we'd always
been here!'

'It's been very pleasant,' he agreed.

She nodded and, her eyes downcast, she said softly: 'I'll never
forget these days.'

As she spoke she moved her hand in such a way that the movement caught his eye, and he looked at her hand on the table
here beside him and felt a shock of surprise. For the ring —
Quinton's ring, whom she would never marry — was not now on
her finger! He stared at her hand so long that she looked at him
inquiringly.

'What is it?' she asked.

'Have you lost your ring?'

She shook her head, her eyes holding his. 'No. I took it off, forever, an hour ago.'

The moment was simple, yet there was an electric message in it. Meeting her glance, he read that message plain; and his eyes were the first to fall. He looked at the fork beside his plate and absently turned it over and turned it back again. She began to talk to Lin, across the table, and he tried to put his thoughts in order. He felt himself entangled, held in light yet tenacious bonds; and a stubborn anger that was half alarm took hold of him. When they rose from the table he excused himself. There was a letter he must write, he said; and he sought the sanctuary of his own quarters, admitting not even to himself that this was flight.

He tried to write to Danny, tried to read; but he could not, so he went to bed, yet not at once to sleep, for the message in her eyes a while ago had been clear beyond any doubting. Since his books began to succeed he had been more than once the target of flattering feminine glances, but never before had his own interest been in the slightest degree aroused. Ellen, he knew now, would marry him if he chose; but he had been sure for years that he would never marry anyone, and he was sure tonight that he would never marry Ellen. 'We'd always be either on the peaks, sublimely happy, or in the bleak valleys of anger and despair,' he told himself; and he knew he would prefer to dwell in a pleasant intervale, one of those lovely spots which so often he had seen along a northern river, where the grassy meadows were dotted with tall graceful elms, and quiet deer came feeding, and a little brook sang near-by, and there were friendly hills all about, and perhaps a few mountains, not too closely seen, visible far away.

Yes, it was peace a man wanted. He reflected with an amused smile that Ruth was much more the sort of woman an author ought to marry: self-effacing, strong, serene, with a sense of humor which occasionally revealed itself in her pleasant eyes. But of course there was no question of his marrying Ruth!

For that matter, there was no question of his marrying anyone!

Ellen would marry him if he chose — but he did not so choose! If in the future he ever regretted this decision — he chuckled with resolute amusement at the thought — he could always write a book about her. He began to imagine such a book, to imagine the emotions and the actions of which such a woman might be capable, and the deeds to which she might provoke a man; and just as Ellen had once fallen asleep while reading a book he had written, so he now fell asleep while he shaped in his mind a novel in which she should play the leading role. Thus he had his revenge.

– IX –

Harland's decision, it seemed to him next day, had set him free. They all sat together at breakfast and for a while on the veranda afterward, with no plans for this last day here. Without avoiding Ellen, he nevertheless was able to ignore her, and not once that day were they alone together. He remembered his plan to go out to the ranch tomorrow by way of the canyon below the lodge, fishing on the way; and after dinner that evening he spoke to Robie about it. Robie readily promised to send a horse to meet him at the foot of the canyon.

'You'll want to pack a lunch,' he advised. 'It's only about ten miles, and the first two or three miles you've already fished; but it's slow going from there on. You'll be all day at it.'

Harland, with a malicious satisfaction in thus escaping Ellen, decided to tell no one his plan, to leave early the next morning before the others were about. Robie agreed to this.

'Start as early as you like,' he assented. 'Cook will put you up a lunch. I'll have Charlie go down to the head of the gorge with you, to bring back your horse.'

So in the morning before the others appeared, Harland was on his way. Robie had said he would sometimes need to wade; but boots were heavy walking, so he had chosen sneakers with stout soles. He carried no fish basket, but wore a sleeveless fishing vest with many pockets. His lunch was stowed in one of them, and in another a roll of cheesecloth in which he would pack any particularly handsome trout which he decided to save.

When Charlie said good-bye to him and he was alone, Harland felt a deep relief. The beauty of the mountains and the deep canyons, the long days in the open, the nights when the stars stooped low and the moon turned the shadowed world into a silvered glory, all had combined till now to create a stage setting hard to resist. Another week here and he might have lost his wits; but now, though he would see Ellen again tonight and tomorrow at the ranch, the spell she might have cast over him was broken. In frank gratefulness he knew he was secure.

He began to fish. Whenever he cast a fly, the greedy trout rushed to seize it; but they were mere hungry youngsters, and so numerous that after an hour the sport began to pall. Then in a pearl-gray swirl where bubbles from a little cascade made the water opaque, he saw a great trout rise to suck in some tiny insect floating in the boil. That was a fish worth keeping, and he decided to try for it. Dropping his fly where the big one had risen, he caught at once a little native, and another and another. Not till he had taken — and thrown back — seven of these small fry did he hook a respectable fish. This one may have been a foot long, and he caught and released four more of a pound or a little over. When the fish he had seen did rise at last, Harland saw its broad side and its wide tail as it turned. He lifted the tip and the trout was on.

He held it, giving it no play. It drowned quickly, and Harland, standing at the water's edge, stooped down, and after two false tries hooked his thumb into its gills and lifted it clear. With the rod in one hand, the fish in the other, he turned and climbed out on the ledge above where he had been standing; and he cracked the trout's neck and disgorged the hook and drew out his strip of cheesecloth to pack the great fish tenderly away. It would run, he judged, a fair three pounds; and he was admiring its fast fading colors, his ears filled with the roar of the water here beside him to the exclusion of all other sounds, when a shadow fell across the ledge on which he stood, and he looked up and saw Ellen, ten feet above him, between him and the sun.

After his first instant of surprise, he knew the shock of terror which a wild thing in a trap might feel.

3

ELLEN'S possessive devotion to her father began when she was still a baby. They spent their summers at Bar Harbor, and as soon as she could walk, he took her down to the beach to watch him dig clams under the rocks at low tide, and he hauled aside great scarves of seaweed to show her the little crabs scuttling for cover, and when neap tides exposed a whole new world to view he helped her hunt for starfish and sea urchins.

This was before she was four years old, but already she thought him all her own; and one of her baby tricks pleased him and amused everyone else except her mother. If Mrs. Berent spoke of him as 'Daddy,' Ellen would cry indignantly: 'He's not your Daddy. He's mine!' This delighted him, and he was apt to snatch her in his arms and hug her hard.

When Ellen was four, Ruth came to live with them. She was Professor Berent's niece, his brother's daughter; and after her mother died, Professor and Mrs. Berent gave her a home and on her father's death two years later they legally adopted the little girl. Ellen, till Ruth's coming, had ruled the household, and from the first she resented her father's interest in this intruder. When Ruth was old enough to follow them down to the beach, Ellen fiercely rebelled, crying: 'I don't want her! You're my Daddy! You're not hers! I don't want her!' He at first laughed in affectionate amusement at her jealous protests; but Ellen, if he insisted on bringing Ruth along, took every means to make her miserable, toppling her into puddles, tweaking her pigtails, bringing her sometimes to the point of tears. Eventually

Ellen's persistence outwore them all, so that Ruth stayed at home with Mrs. Berent while Ellen and her father resumed their long summer days together.

By that time she was old enough to go out with him in the dory to pull the half-dozen lobster pots which he kept set off their landing; and he taught her to swim in the icy water, and to sail the little dinghy. He was already dabbling with the collecting which would become his hobby. He began with shore birds, and the islands off the rocky Maine coast were his fruitful hunting grounds. Sometimes he and Ellen went off in the dory or in the sailing dinghy for two or three days at a time, taking a tent and bedding and supplies; and Ellen tended camp while he tramped the shores or sought the island ponds to find his specimens. As she grew older he took her with him to Newfoundland or to the Provinces to fish for salmon, or into the woods to try for a deer in the fall. Their hours together were for her one long content.

These delights were interrupted when he began to spend most of each summer in Texas with Glen Robie; but when she was twenty and Robie invited Professor Berent to come to the ranch, she went west with him. The raw beauty and the bold colors of deserts blazing in the sun, snow-tipped mountains bright against the cloudless sky, parks and canyons carpeted with countless wild flowers and slopes clad in luxuriant forest green, intoxicated them both. They stayed, that first summer, two months at the ranch, and ten weeks the next.

The second year, as though he knew he might never come again, Professor Berent twice or thrice postponed their departure, revisiting over and over beloved scenes. The day before they were at last to depart, they rode far together, and in late afternoon they came to a spot which had always held for each of them a particular charm. This was an upland pasture shaped like a saucer and surrounded by a low wooded rim which shut off any view of loftier peaks either near or far away. Their horses moved at a foot pace out across the basin, and the sky was fair and blue.

'It's like riding across the front lawn of Heaven,' Ellen said in a hushed voice.

'It's beautiful, certainly,' he agreed.

'When I die,' she declared, 'You must bring my ashes and scatter them here. Will you, Father?'

'Why should you think of dying? You'll outlive me, you know.' He smiled, but there was no mirth in his smile. Able to interpret certain signs and symptoms, he had of late often contemplated his own death.

'Then we'll exchange promises,' she urged with a sweet gravity. 'If you die first, I'll bring your ashes here; and if I die first, you'll bring mine.'

For a moment he did not speak, and when he did, it was half-laughingly. 'After I'm dead, Mother can decide what becomes of what's left of me!' he said, and lifted his reins. 'Come along. We'll have to move if we want to make the lodge before dark.'

Ellen's engagement to Russ Quinton resulted, in oblique ways, from this moment in the high pasture with her father. That fall, as they had sometimes done before, they went into the Maine woods to try for deer, lodging in Quinton's cabin on a remote and lovely pond; and for the last few days of their stay, Quinton himself came unannounced to join them there.

He was at that time about thirty-five years old, a lawyer, a graduate of the University of Maine and of Harvard Law School, with political ambitions which, since any opposition was apt to provoke him to a venomous and uncontrolled anger that made him many enemies, were as yet unrealized. He and Professor Berent had met seven or eight years before, casually, as fishermen do, on the Mersey River in Nova Scotia. A mutual interest in trying to bring back eastern Maine rivers as salmon streams gave them a point of contact out of which grew a casual friendship, which Quinton, from the day he first saw Ellen, assiduously cultivated. He showered upon Professor Berent many favors — the gift of an occasional salmon or a basket of trout, a haunch of venison, a brace of ducks, the use of his hunting cabin — which it was impossible graciously to refuse, and which Professor Berent repaid by making Quinton welcome in his home.

Ellen was at the time in her early teens. Quinton taught her to call him 'Uncle Russ' and to let him kiss her when they met and when they parted. She accepted him at first as her father's friend, but as she approached maturity she realized that to be with her produced in him a flattering excitement, and with the precocity which resulted from her constant companionship with her father, she suspected that he was in love with her. When this fall he came to join them at his cabin she soon decided that he was trying to muster courage to ask her to marry him, and in a lively curiosity she helped the moment to arrive.

The event was disappointing. He said it would surprise her and perhaps frighten her to hear what he wished to say, but she was neither surprised nor frightened; and she bade him go on. He did so, haltingly; and when he was done, willing to prolong the game, she told him she would never marry anyone as long as her father was alive.

'He needs me, and he comes first,' she said.

Quinton resentfully protested that her father would not want her to take such an attitude; but she told him: 'It's not what he wants. It's what I want.' He persisted, and at last, roused by her coquetry, he caught her in his arms and kissed her. She enjoyed the sense of power it gave her to feel his shaken passion, and when after a moment he released her, stammering apologies, she said sweetly:

'I'm not angry, Russ. I know men like to do things like that to girls; but I love my father too much to marry any other man as long as he needs me!'

In a sudden anger — she knew his high temper, had seen him storm at the guides — he demanded: 'Do you mean you want me to just stand around waiting till he dies?' Then, at her reproachful silence: 'I'm sorry, Ellen. I'm sorry I said that.'

'I know you are,' she assented, and smiled forgiveness. 'When you get mad, you blurt out things like a little boy!'

'You drive me half-crazy,' he told her hoarsely.

Deliberately, she said: 'Maybe that's why I like you. I do like you, you know, as well as any man I know.'

But then she saw the quick leap of delight in him, and, a

little dismayed by the emotion she had roused, she turned quickly indoors to join her father. Quinton had to follow her.

This was the last evening of their stay, and they sat long around the stove in the cabin and Quinton asked questions about New Mexico, and Ellen and Professor Berent answered him, each supplementing the other. It was Ellen who spoke of that high mountain meadow so near the sky, describing the beauty of the spot. 'Father and I both loved it,' she told Quinton. 'We agreed that we want our ashes to be scattered there when we die.' She was so accustomed to assuming that her own wishes were decisive that she did not remember Professor Berent had failed to join her in this compact; but her father did not contradict her. Changing the subject — perhaps it was distasteful to him — he said casually:

'It's up in a region they call the horse parks, Russ, because some wild horses range there.' And he told Quinton how the old Spaniards brought the first horses to the Southwest, three or four hundred years ago, and thus stocked the whole vast region.

So he turned the talk into other channels; but Ellen, months later, at a time of need, would remember that conversation and use it for her own ends.

The following spring, her father died quietly in his sleep. Ellen had so long thought of him as her possession that not even his death shook her feeling of ownership. When Mrs. Berent, after the first gush of grief, began to plan that he should be buried in conventional fashion at Mount Auburn, Ellen with a jealous instinct to make every decision that concerned him, cried:

'Oh, no, Mother!'

Mrs. Berent exclaimed in surprise: 'For Heaven's sake, why not, I'd like to know?'

Ellen unhesitatingly found an answer. 'Because that wasn't what he wanted! He wanted to be cremated, wanted me to take his ashes to New Mexico!'

'New Mexico?' Mrs. Berent was astonished. 'Why, that's the most outlandish thing I ever heard of! He never mentioned it to me!'

'There were lots of things he didn't tell you,' Ellen said cruelly.

This was so true that Mrs. Berent made no effort to deny it. 'Now you want him stuffed away underground in Mount Auburn, because that's what all your friends do with their husbands when they die; but Father wasn't like them! He'd hate being shut up to stifle in a grave.'

Her mother urged, near tears: 'Why, Ellen, I simply can't believe it. He'd surely have told me . . .'

'You mean you think I'm lying?'

Mrs. Berent sniffed in sudden anger. 'I wouldn't put it past you! You never saw the day you wouldn't lie to have your own way.'

Ellen persisted; but Mrs. Berent was for once as stubborn as she, and Ellen tried to enlist Ruth's support. It was often possible to win the other girl by tender cajolery, but in this matter Ruth was firm. 'I think Mother's the one to decide, Ellen,' she suggested.

'But Ruth darling, I tell you Father said . . .'

Ruth smiled affectionately. 'Are you sure? You know, Ellen, you're always apt to believe things happened the way you wanted them to happen.'

Their incredulity, coupled with her own secret memory that they were right, infuriated Ellen. It was bad enough to be called a liar; it was worse when the accusation was true. But, suddenly recalling that night in Quinton's cabin, she was sure she could make him support her, and she telegraphed him: 'Father died yesterday. Please come to me.' She knew what hopes that message would arouse.

He came at once, and she met his train — this was the morning of the second day after Professor Berent died — and told her plight and demanded his corroboration. 'Mother thinks I'm lying!' she said. 'But you heard Father say that he wanted his ashes taken out there. She'll have to believe you!'

'Why, I remember you said something about it, but . . .'

'No, no, it was he who said it,' she insisted. 'Surely you haven't forgotten! It was the night you asked me to marry you.' She caught his hand. 'You can't have forgotten that night!' She was so distressed and beseeching that he could not deny her; so he told her he did remember, and — this was in the taxicab, on their way to her home — she clung to him, weeping with relief and triumph; and he cried, holding her close:

'Ellen, darling, darling, your father doesn't need you now. But I do, I do.'

'I know, Russ,' she agreed, heedless and unthinkingly. The future was unimportant, if she could bind him to her present cause. 'But first I must do this last thing for him.'

When he confirmed her testimony as to Professor Berent's wishes, Mrs. Berent surrendered; but before Quinton went back to Maine, he had Ellen's promise that she would marry him in the fall. His grateful kisses neither pleased nor offended her. He was her ally against her mother, and for the moment this was her only concern.

She expected to go to New Mexico alone to do her errand there; but this proposal Mrs. Berent flatly rejected, and with the invincible inflexibility to which weak people may by long persecution be provoked, she insisted that she too — and of course Ruth — would see her husband's ashes to their last resting place. Robie, in response to Ellen's letter, said business this year would keep him from the ranch till late June. He fixed a date for their coming, and hospitably suggested a fortnight's stay. This would cause them to miss part of the summer at Bar Harbor, and Mrs. Berent fretted at this disturbance of her routine; but when Ellen repeated that she could quite as well go alone, her mother retorted:

'Nonsense! I'm ready to do my duty! Of course, I've never been west of Philadelphia!' Her tone confessed the confirmed Bostonian's misgiving at venturing into the hinterland. 'But I'm prepared for some discomfort, and I'm sure Mr. Robie will make things as easy for us as he can.'

— II —

During the weeks of waiting, while spring came to Boston and tulips bloomed in the Public Garden, Ellen refused to re-enter

with Ruth and her mother their familiar ways, telling herself that
by resuming their weekly attendance at Symphony, by going
sometimes to the theatre or to the moving pictures, they proved
themselves heartless and callous. She spent her time sorting her
father's papers and possessions. He had converted to his own
use the topmost floor of their Boston home, putting a skylight in
the roof, building moth-proof cabinets around the walls to hold
his sets. She cleaned the scalpels and dissecting scissors and
needles, put the spools of thread in their rack and the rolls of cotton on the shelf, set the jars of arsenic and of plaster of Paris and
the tray of assorted glass eyes in order, labelled and put away
some unmounted skins. She devoted long hours to this self-
imposed task, and one day the glass jars of arsenic caught her
attention. She took up one of them and poured a little of the
white powder into her hand. For years the poison had been to
her just one of the materials which she and her father used in their
work together, but she remembered now that it was deadly stuff.
If she swallowed even a little of it she would die; and she imagined
Ruth and her mother finding her here lifeless, and she heard them
say sorrowfully: 'She loved her father so!' Her eyes misted
with wistful tears and she pitied herself profoundly — but she
poured the arsenic from her palm carefully back into the jar and
covered it again.

A week before their prospective departure, Quinton came to
Boston to see her. He arrived on Saturday, and suggested that
they spend Sunday together. 'I'll hire a car and we'll drive down
to the shore,' he said, and Ellen indifferently agreed.

At the appointed hour he called for her, slick and shining, perspiring with delight, and she felt a brief distaste; but she took her
place at his side. He drove to the tip end of Cape Ann. When
they left the car to walk down to the rocks he produced from the
rumble a magnificent picnic basket fitted with thermos bottles,
paper plates and cups, plated knives and forks and spoons, and
canisters for salt and pepper and sugar, with a compartment for
ice, and neat aluminum containers for sandwiches. He showed
her all these wonders with a pride which hid his misgivings.

'Oh Russ, you shouldn't!' she said reproachfully. 'It's so extravagant!'

'It's a start toward furnishing our house!'

'It's a whole dining room in itself,' she declared; but later, while they lunched on the rocks above the shore, she saw his almost miserly pride in this treasure. Maliciously curious to see what he would do, sweetening her coffee, she allowed the small sugar canister to escape from her fingers and roll off the ledge. It fell into a deep crevice among the rocks, and Quinton labored for an hour in a vain effort to recover it, moving heavy boulders, wetting his feet and staining his trousers with sea slime, while Ellen with her arm across her eyes lay baking in the sun. In spite of the fact that the kisses she had had to accept upon their arrival had rather irritated than pleased her, she resented his neglecting her while he sought so long to get back that absurd canister; and when she said they must go and he urged that they had had as yet hardly any time together, she said chidingly that he should have thought of that before.

'But I couldn't just let the sugar thing go without trying to reach it,' he protested, so disturbed by this wasteful loss that she smiled and forgave him. So they stayed a little longer and she gave him enough of herself to make his head swim with dreams and sent him back to Maine a happy man.

In due time thereafter, with her mother and Ruth, she started for New Mexico. Leaving Chicago, Mrs. Berent and Ruth shared a drawing room, and Ellen had the adjoining compartment. She retired early. Among the parting gifts from friends in Boston there had been a book called *Time Without Wings*, about which everyone — said Janet Mowbray, who had given it to them — was talking. On the first night out of Chicago, Ellen began to read this book, and in the morning when she went back to the observation car, it was under her arm.

But Ellen was never much addicted to reading, and she presently fell asleep in her chair. As her grasp upon the book relaxed, it slid off her knee and thumped her foot and woke her from a dream in which she had been happy with her father; and in that dream he was young again, with fair hair, and merry, unwearied eyes. When now she woke, her father — or someone, to her sleepy eyes, incredibly like him as he had been in her dream — picked up the book and handed it back to her. Seeing his face, her throat constricted. She thanked him automatically, but after he resumed his seat across the car she watched him with a breathless attention. Her thoughts — and her eyes — remained fixed upon him till at last his glance met hers. He stood up, coloring with anger, and she realized that she had embarrassed him. To her apology, he muttered something and walked away; and she hastened to her mother, an eagerness in her which she made no effort to disguise.

'Mother,' she demanded,. 'Did Father have any relatives, brothers or nephews or anything?'

'Of course! Ruth's father, and another brother in Philadelphia; but he died ten years ago. For Heaven's sake, why?'

'Did that other brother have any sons?'

Mrs. Berent said sharply: 'I should hope not. He was a bachelor! What's got into you?'

Ellen said in a hushed tone: 'There's a man on the train who looks exactly the way Father used to look, enough like him to be related anyway.'

'What of it? That's not surprising! Your father was a perfectly ordinary-looking man.'

Ellen's eyes flashed with anger, but Ruth smilingly played peacemaker. 'I always thought Father looked rather wonderful, Mother,' she protested. 'Ellen, point this man out to us if you get a chance, won't you?'

But Ellen, resenting her mother's attitude, said coldly: 'You probably wouldn't see any resemblance. Neither of you saw Father with my eyes.' She went into her own compartment and closed the door.

Yet her thoughts clung to this stranger. She hoped to see him again in the diner, but he did not appear for lunch nor for dinner, nor when she frankly tried to find him was he in the club or observation cars. After Ruth and her mother were abed, she walked the length of the train, but her search was fruitless. Knowing he must be shut away behind some closed door, she wished to knock at every one, imagining him secret and alone, wishing to share his solitude. When, surrendering, she returned at last to her compartment and to bed, she lay long awake, crushed under a weight of loneliness because he was lost to her forever.

But in the morning they left the train and Glen Robie was on the platform, and after the first greeting he asked Mrs. Berent: 'Did you see Mr. Harland?'

'Harland?' she echoed. 'Who's he?'

'Richard Harland,' he said. 'He's the man who wrote that new book, *Time Without Wings*. He's coming to the ... Oh, here he is now!'

Ellen, half-guessing the truth, turned to look where Robie pointed; and she saw Lin and a tall young man coming toward them and felt as though a firm hand had gripped her heart. Her senses clouded dizzily, and when presently she was seated beside Harland in the touring car, her shoulder against his, she pressed her hands to her cheeks, thinking they must feel hot to her palms! All the surface of her body everywhere was tingling deliciously and frighteningly too. She was glad that Robie talked as he drove, so that she need not speak for a while. Her voice, she feared, might betray her, and when at last she dared turn to Harland with some careful, laughing word, she saw Ruth, sitting on his other side, look at her in wonder at her tone.

- III -

The fortnight that followed, at the ranch and then at Robie's fishing lodge in the mountains, was for Ellen a time of breathless wonder, of longing almost insupportable, of suspense almost too keen to be borne. She was caught in a torrent of emotions so strange and new that she was at first bewildered and overwhelmed; a torrent so strong that she could not resist it.

At first, instinctively, she sought to avoid Harland and the others too; and she took a horse every morning, disappearing sometimes for the whole day, returning only at dinnertime. But though she went alone, yet in her thoughts Harland was beside her. There was one day when she rode to a lofty outlook and secured her horse and sat for long hours on a bold rim high above a hidden canyon, basking in the sun, her eyes ranging unseeingly; and in her fancy she welcomed him there to share her solitude, speaking aloud, carrying on with him long conversations that were tinglingly impersonal and polite, rich with unuttered meanings. She lay for a while, her arms tight across her breast, her big hat shading her face against the sun, her eyes closed; and at every near-by sound she seemed to hear his step, imagined him coming ardently to seek her here.

This complete and absorbed attention to everything a man did or said, this constant hope that Harland would turn to her, coupled with a breathless anticipation that was something like terror, was new in her life. Her devotion to her father had armored her against those hours of tremulous and unadmitted longings which almost any chance-met boy may provoke in a girl still in her teens, rendered intensely sensitive to masculine approaches by forces within herself which she has been taught she must not recognize. Once when Ellen was twelve there had been a senior at Tech who sometimes came home with her father to discuss a thesis upon which he was at work, and who for weeks seemed to her the most completely wonderful person she had ever seen, so that she dreamed of him both awake and asleep and gave him openly a youthful adoration which she was not yet old enough to conceal. But this keen awareness of Harland was at once less frank and more profound; for she had been incapable at that time of those reactions — a quickened pulse, a warm flush on cheeks and throat, a faintness, a soft readiness for surrender — which even the sound of Harland's voice could provoke in her now.

Hoping his thoughts might be drawn to her as hers were drawn to him, she wondered whether he knew from Robie their errand here; and she wished her habit of seeking the solitudes would provoke his curiosity, lead him to question her. She planned her answers, planned the very words in which she would tell him, wistfully, about her father; and she pictured the sympathy and the new understanding which would appear in his eyes as he listened. She played, without admitting it even to herself, the part of one silently enduring a hopeless grief; and she imagined him observing and conjecturing.

But he made no approach to her; and when at breakfast one morning she saw an opportunity to suggest that they go together to seek turkeys, she seized upon it, hiding her eager hopes beneath a casual tone. He assented, and it was a flurry of soft panic, a delicious fear of what these hours alone with him might bring, which led her to say that they need not go till afternoon. All morning alone she blamed herself for that weakness. They might, if she had been bold, have spent the long day together. Till the lunch hour she waited in dread lest he change his mind, cancel this plan.

Yet when the time came for them to start, she was — at least outwardly — perfectly composed. She led the way, sure that his eyes rested upon her as he followed close behind. She rode well, and knew it, and wished him to remark it. He did not speak, but she was as conscious of his watching her as though she saw his eyes.

All her senses seemed on that ride together to be sharpened. The sky and the mountains had never been so beautiful, the odor of the sun-warmed pine spills upon the ground never so keen, the occasional bird song in the thickets never so liquid and clear and true. Even to watch the sliding shoulder-muscles of her horse as he breasted a steep climb or picked his way down an abrupt descent contented and delighted her. She had an extraordinary awareness of the life currents within her, and of Harland close behind, and of the solitudes in which they rode; and alone with him she felt a breathless terror which was half longing too.

At the spot she chose they hid their horses in the wood and walked out to the middle of the park-like canyon floor; and she led him to a shallow grassy depression and bade him lie beside her. Then for a while they did not speak, and she lay with her chin on her hands, staring up the canyon, feeling her heart pound against the turf beneath her breast, not looking at him yet seeing every line of his profile and the bulk of his shoulders thrust upward by the position of his crossed arms, and feeling the length of him along her own, so near that a careless movement of her foot might have touched his.

He spoke at last, some laughing word about the ant she brushed from her throat, and she found herself talking of her father; and though their talk was commonplace she felt in every word she spoke and in every word of his a quality of suspense, of overwhelming forces held for the present in abeyance yet which might at any moment break all bounds. She turned her head at last to look at him, and met his eyes, and he said he knew her errand at the lodge; and this knowledge on his part seemed to her to draw them close together, so that in an instinctive defensive gesture she looked away again. He spoke of his brother Danny. She had, as have many whole and healthy people, an innate repugnance for any sickness or deformity, so that she shivered slightly when he referred to Danny's illness. Then she remembered that she knew so little about Harland, only his name and his work and that he had this brother who was crippled. It was even fearfully possible that he was married, and she found herself questioning him; and when he said he was not married she controlled her breathing so that he might not see her sudden relief. Then he spoke of her ring. She had for these days completely forgotten Quinton. She told Harland about him and added calmly:

'But I will never marry him.'

Until that moment she had not known this, but as soon as she remembered Quinton she knew it certainly and beyond doubting.

From that quiet word of hers, she thought as she spoke, much might have followed; but then Harland saw turkeys coming, and at her direction, when the time came, he shot one. It was only wounded, and he had to run to dispatch it, and the unaccustomed exercise at these high altitudes exhausted him, and she wished to take him in her arms and cherish him, and forced herself to look at the turkey instead, and to speak, as though this were important, of the fact that a shot had cut its beard. Yet even then, on pretext of fetching the horses, she hurried to leave him so that he might not guess the tenderness which his distress had provoked in her; and when she returned with the animals she was controlled again. He was triumphant and gay and laughing and full of eager conversation, and she entered into his mood and they rode merrily back to camp. She thought exultantly that night that she would never lose what this day she had gained.

Next morning before breakfast her mother announced — she had been lamed till now by the all-day ride from ranch to lodge — that she was ready to go to see her husband's ashes sown across the high meadows. Ellen had almost forgotten this duty; but she welcomed it now as one welcomes the turning of the last page of a book, when another, full of promise, waits to be opened. She agreed that this should be the day; but when Harland and Lin and Tess planned at breakfast to ride to the horse parks, Ellen wished she might go with them, thinking that Tess was beautiful and that Harland might find her so. She could not change plans already made, but she was wretched all morning, her thoughts following them jealously.

On the ride up to the heights that afternoon, Mrs. Berent groaned and complained; for the way was steep and she was ill at ease in the saddle. Professor Berent's ashes were in a sealed bronze casket which till now had been in Ellen's charge, and which now, wrapped in sweater and slicker, rode at her cantle. When they came to their goal, she left Robie and her mother and Ruth sitting their horses together in the center of the basin, and rode out toward its rim; and at an easy lope, she began a wide circle around them, carrying the casket in the curve of her arm, lifting the ashes a handful at a time, letting them sift through her fingers as she rode.

Then the pricking ears of her horse led her to look across to the trees that fringed the basin, and she saw the two children and Harland come there into view. Almost at once they drew back out of sight again; but to know that Harland was sharing this moment with her sharpened her emotional reaction, and — unconsciously dramatizing her own part — she put her horse to a faster gait, feeling Harland watching her; and she rode like a soldier on parade, eyes straight ahead, looking neither right nor left, sowing the ashes broadcast with a rhythmic sweep of her arm. When with the circle of the basin not half completed, she found the casket almost empty, she had a sense of anticlimax; but since no one could at a distance guess the deception, she continued that motion of a sower till, completing the circuit, coming back to the head of the trail, she saw the chance for an effective exit and plunged into the forest and was gone.

She rode halfway back to camp before a new thought occurred to her, and she took a side trail to avoid the others and circled back to the heights again. If she did not return to the lodge for dinner, Harland — after their hour together yesterday — would surely come to seek her. She found the basin deserted, and on the highest point along its rim she built of scattered rocks a cairn where she bestowed the empty casket upon which her father's name had been engraved. Staying there where she could overlook the open sweep below her, she waited for Harland to appear.

At sunset he had not come, nor at dark; but the waxing moon made night as light as day, and still she waited, at first surely, then half-angrily, then in deep self-pity, telling herself none cared, not even he, whether she returned. She decided stubbornly to wait here till he came. Sweater and slicker were scant protection against the chill, frosty night, and she built a small fire and huddled near it. Night had no terrors for her, and she began wistfully to enjoy the part she played, thinking of herself as a bereft daughter mourning here on the heights the whole night long. When her horse, tethered to an oak sapling, became restless, she unsaddled him and secured him in such a way that he had more freedom. The saddle blanket, unfolded, served as a ground sheet on which she sat and which when she grew chilly she drew over her shoulders. The horse was cold and uneasy, stamping and blowing; but she kept the blanket, let him endure the penetrating chill.

She stayed there stubbornly till dawn, at once hungry for Harland to come and furious because he did not. If he had from the

first revealed an eagerness as great as hers, she might before this
have been ready to forget him; but since he had not, and since any
denial of her wishes was always a spur to her determination, this
night alone fused her vague dreams into a hot resolution. The
fact that, returning, she met him on the trail seemed to promise
the victory she coveted; but to whet his appetite she devoted herself that evening to Lin and Tess, and next morning she rode
away with Lin and Charlie Yates and one of the cowboys who
had ranch business to do. Because she was an overflowing vessel
full of tenderness which must find some outlet, she was that day
extravagantly sweet to Lin; and after lunch they left the others
and rode home alone, and in a charming fashion she made laughing love to the youngster till his head was whirling, giving him all
the smiles, the winning glances, the affectionate words, the en-
trancing laughter she was ready to offer Harland.

That evening after dinner, since he still held aloof, she summoned Harland to walk down the brook with her in the moonlight; and when she came back to the cabin which she and Ruth
and her mother shared, Mrs. Berent demanded:

'Ellen, are you trying to start a flirtation with that young
man?'

Ellen answered quietly: 'No, Mother.' 'Flirtation' was not the
word for the passionate certainty which filled her.

Mrs. Berent tossed her head. 'You act mighty like it to me!'
she declared. 'Butter wouldn't melt in your mouth! But you're
engaged to another man, and I'm going to see to it that Mr. Harland knows it! You'll have your trouble for your pains!'

Ellen smiled icily. 'You ought at least to ask what his inten-
tions are before you warn him off,' she said, and went to her room.
But next day at the branding, remembering that their stay here
was almost done, something like panic seized her. She had so
little time! Recalling her mother's threat, that night before dinner she laid aside Quinton's ring, and when Harland noticed this
and spoke of it, she looked at him, meaning him to read her eyes,
meaning him to know she was his if he would have her. When his
eyes fell, she knew he had understood.

After dinner he excused himself and disappeared, and she was sure that when the others had retired he would come to her, and she stayed on the lodge veranda to wait for him. But he did not come, and she wished to go to him and could find no pretext to do so. The longing in her was almost unbearable, and she went to her room at last, her lips dry, her heart wrung, her breath coming shakenly.

Next morning before breakfast, making her decision irrevocable, she packed Quinton's ring and addressed it and put it in the mail pouch. She told herself Harland would surely turn to her that day, but he did not, and tomorrow they would ride out to the ranch, and the day after or the day after he would go his way and she must go hers! That night she lay long awake, considering — and discarding — a thousand devices by which she might draw Harland to her side, sure only that in the few hours which remained she must somehow win him to be hers forever.

When she came to breakfast on the last morning, Harland was not there. At her carefully casual question, Robie explained that he had made an early start, that he meant to fish down through the canyon below the lodge, following the brook to where a horse would meet him in the late afternoon and fetch him to the ranch.

Her hands, hidden under the table, clenched hard. 'I shall go after him,' she said, half to herself. Then, realizing that her tone and her words suggested open pursuit, and willing to dissemble, she added quickly: 'I've always wanted to make that trip. You can send a horse to meet me, too.'

Robie courteously assented; but when they rose from the table Mrs. Berent drew Ellen aside and said sharply: 'You're not going chasing after Mr. Harland! You're coming along with us! You're making a perfect fool of yourself over that young man!'

Ellen said recklessly: 'I love him. I'm going to marry him, Mother.'

'Marry him! Don't be absurd! You're engaged to Mr. Quinton.'

Ellen looked at her ringless hand. 'I'm not engaged to Russ, not now,' she said, and Mrs. Berent made a startled sound. 'I mailed his ring back to him yesterday.'

'You're making a mistake,' her mother urged. 'Mr. Quinton isn't the sort of man with whom you can play fast and loose! Heaven knows I can't imagine what you ever saw in him, but I'll tell you one thing. He won't submit easily to being jilted!'

Ellen remembered that Quinton was by repute a dangerous enemy, but she shook her head. 'I'll not be frightened into marrying him, Mother,' she insisted. 'If that's what you're trying to do.' And she repeated: 'I'm going to marry Mr. Harland.'

Mrs. Berent wrung her hands, defeated; she tried pleading. 'Ellen, don't do this. Ride out to the lodge with us, please. I want you to.'

Ellen looked at her in a sort of wonder, astonished that her mother should persist in this attempted interference with her plans. 'But I want to be with Mr. Harland,' she said, and giving the older woman no chance for a further word she turned away.

One of Robie's men rode with her down the canyon as far as horses could comfortably go, and she went on afoot. She had dressed this morning for the ride out to the ranch, discarding dungarees for a divided skirt and a light silk shirt of many colors like a Scotch plaid, and knotting a yellow handkerchief loosely around her throat; and since before she made her new plans the pack horses had already departed with her luggage, it had been impossible to change. So her movements were somewhat hampered, and her riding shoes were ill suited to this clambering over boulders, their soles slippery, forever threatening to betray her. Yet she proceeded in a heedless haste.

But when she saw Harland — he was intently fishing a little pool — she was content to watch him for a while, scanning every line of his body, delighting in the set of his head upon his shoulders, in the way his waist narrowed to slender hips. Only when at last he caught a great trout did she reveal herself. Her shadow lay across the rock where he stood and she moved so that her shadow moved and he looked up and saw her there.

– IV –

When Harland's startled eyes met hers, they were empty of welcome, and Ellen saw this and her breath caught; but — she would somehow make him glad of her company. She climbed down to stand beside him, and cried admiringly: 'Oh what a beauty!'

'Why did you come?' he asked in sharp challenge.

Something thudded in her throat and her cheeks burned and at his tone her heart contracted in a knot of pain; but she spoke lightly.

'I asked where you'd gone,' she explained, 'and Mr. Robie told me. I've never fished down through here, so I thought you wouldn't mind if I came along.' Her answer was matter-of-fact and reassuring; and she spoke quickly of the trout again, exclaiming at its size, exerting herself to make Harland glad she was here. She succeeded, felt his resentment abate. He wrapped the trout in cheesecloth and packed it away in the big game pocket of his vest, and they went on down the canyon.

Ellen was full of a singing triumph because he had accepted her companionship. It was enough, for the moment, that they should be together. For the first hours, she fished as earnestly as if it were for this she had come. They caught many trout smaller than his big one and threw them back, enjoying the sport together.

Toward one o'clock, he proposed that they eat lunch. She had neglected to bring sandwiches. He was sure he had enough for both of them, but when he opened his packet she said laughingly:

'Heavens, I'd eat all that and cry for more. I'm famished. We'll catch some little trout and cook them.'

While he started a fire, she landed four small fish and — proud to display her capacities — borrowed his knife to clean them, and spitted them on sharpened twigs, and salted them well and set the twigs upright beside the fire. When they were cooked through, she toasted them briefly above the coals till they were crisp and curling. She and Harland ate them like small ears of corn, holding them crosswise, plucking off the sweet pink flesh with their teeth.

They sat together on a warm ledge on the sunny side of the stream; and Ellen was merry, laughing easily, sure he was happy with her now. A strong exhilaration ran through her like the fumes of wine, and to feel him by her side gave her a keener pleasure than she had ever known. When they were done, he lighted her cigarette and his own, and seeing his strong hands cup the match so near her lips made her heart beat against her ribs. She filled her lungs with a long inhalation and expelled the smoke, her eyes meeting his as he flipped the burned match into the stream. Then she spoke quickly, at random, saying anything at all to end this moment's silence — for which she wished only one ending.

'I'm sorry for the poor little fish here,' she said, in mock sympathy. 'The falls are so many and so steep that they can't get upstream, and down below the brook just sinks into the desert and disappears. There's nowhere they can go. I expect it's a relief, really, when someone like us comes along and catches them!'

'They don't act relieved,' he reminded her, and they laughed together for no reason except that the day was fine, and they were young and well-content. He stirred a little, as though to rise and go on; and she felt time slipping through her fingers, dreading the end of this day they would spend together. She might devise some accident which would delay them, keep them overnight here in the canyon, and she thought, smiling inwardly at the notion: 'If that happened, Mother's sufficiently Victorian so she'd think I was compromised and that he'd have to marry me!'

At the same time she felt, rather than heard, a deeper rumble like thunder. The small segment of sky which they could see was clear and cloudless, and she thought rain might be near; and if they were caught by one of the drenching mountain downpours, it might raise the brook and make this canyon impassable. So she spoke quickly, to delay him here as long as possible, ingeniously dilating upon the hard fate of the trout imprisoned in these rushing waters, knowing only this constricted and unchanging world. 'They've such narrow horizons,' she said, and he argued, amused by her foolery:

'But aren't all our horizons limited? We're no better off than the trout! Not so well off, perhaps! Certainly they couldn't ask a lovelier spot in which to live.'

'All the same, I'm sure a lot of them are dissatisfied,' she gaily insisted. 'Probably the young gentlemen trout want to go off and see the world, and the young husbands, I'm sure they love to wander, and their wives complain. I can just hear them. "It's all right for you, John, traipsing away up and down brook Heaven knows where, while I have to stay at home drudging from daylight till dark."'

He chuckled and — as though he were the husband thus reproached — retorted: 'Nonsense, my dear! I've given you a charming home here. Deep, cool water, and rocks under which to hide, and a nice hatch of flies every day all summer. What more can any self-respecting trout-wife want?'

'Well, I want to travel, for one thing,' she declared, delighted to have won him to this foolery, hoping he would not heed the distant thunder sounds. 'I never thought when I got married that it meant just settling down with my nose rubbing the same gravel bar for the rest of my life!'

'All right, come along with me, then,' he proposed. 'If you think you'd like it.' He coughed importantly. 'As a matter of fact, it's just a business trip I'm taking today. Old Bill Cutthroat up in the falls pool has worked out a new way of trapping grasshoppers, and if it's as good as he says it is, I want to get in on the ground floor.'

Ellen put on an affectedly querulous tone, keeping up the play. 'How can I travel? With my figure, I'm just a public laughing-stock! Having fifty thousand children every fall is no fun, I can tell you. Try it yourself some time!'

'They're my children too,' he reminded her, and added with an exaggerated leer: 'And — I always thought having them was fun!' Then, with ponderous tenderness: 'Seriously, my dear, you know I'd spare you all that if I could!'

She found it hard to control her breathing. This idle make-believe with which they amused themselves carried overtones which rang like great bells deep within her; but she tossed her head, continuing the play. 'I'll remind you of that, next spring; but a lot of good it will do! You'll start talking about our duty to the race! I know you!'

Their eyes held for a moment and then they broke into laughter, and she thought this shared mirth drew them closer; and then the sunlight where they sat suddenly faded and was gone. Harland looked up.

'Hullo,' he said, surprised. 'There's a cloud! You know that's almost the first cloud I've seen since we came out here!'

She spoke in casual reassurance: 'Oh, there are always thundershowers somewhere in the mountains.' But he rose, and she saw that he too was conscious now of an ominous tingling in the air, a quickening in the breeze that drew down the canyon.

'We'd better move,' he suggested. 'We don't want to get caught in a cloudburst up here.'

She knew better than Harland how serious this might be; nevertheless perversely she delayed to clean up their picnic ground, prolonging in every possible fashion these pregnant hours. She gathered the paper in which his lunch had been wrapped, burning it in the embers of the little fire, wetting down the ashes till not even steam arose.

Below the great pool, the stream snaked its way through a narrow gorge, pinnacles rising straight up a hundred feet or more on one side or the other; and they had to pick a careful way, sometimes wading in the shallow border of the brook, sometimes stepping from one rock to another, sometimes clambering along the slopes above the stream. The sky was darker, and once there was a flicker of lightning, and Harland instinctively made haste; but Ellen would not be hurried. Looking up, she saw a churning, wind-torn mass of cloud which seemed to be descending, falling straight down upon them smotheringly. She paused to watch it, but Harland pushed on till he was well ahead, not knowing she had stopped, so that she had to scramble after him; and when they emerged from the narrow reach of the gorge, she was panting.

Within half an hour after the sun was first obscured, the rain caught them. It came down the canyon on their heels, slowly, so that they saw the solid wall of falling water two hundred yards away; and they could see, as the rain came nearer, individual drops as big as buck shot which struck the sunwarmed ledges and exploded, quickly turning to steam, till the rain wetted and cooled the stones. When the first downpour overtook them they found shelter under an overhang to wait for it to pass. The rain fell with a frightening violence, the drops pelting into the brook and turning the opposite wall of the canyon into a sluicing cascade of muddy water. The din was deafening, and they had to shout to be heard. Harland brought his lips close to her ear to say:

'I never thought rain could fall so hard.'

She nodded, leaning so that her cheek brushed his. 'Oh, yes, I've seen it like this often, up here. Remember there was a washout on the branch line of the railroad, the day we came. These mountain streams become rivers, rushing out across the desert plain.'

The brook at their feet had already begun to rise; and Ellen watched the water on a slanting stone which was sheltered as they were from the direct downpour. The flood crept up its sloping surface, visibly higher minute by minute. There was, she guessed, almost three miles of canyon which they must still traverse; but rain fell harder, and it was darker all the time, and she thought, half-frightened now, that the rain would not relent till night came down and caught them here. Yet — it would be bliss to huddle with him beside a little fire, finding warmth and shelter in his arms, whispering together the long night through; and her eyes softened at the thought. Harland looked at his watch uneasily, but she did not ask the hour. The rain fell as though it would persist forever, and she said:

'Isn't it curious that when it rains we always think it's never going to stop?'

'We ought to move on.'

'Oh, this will be over soon.'

The brook boiled past, yellow with mud brought down from the canyon walls, rising steadily, and after a little Harland grasped

her arm. 'Come along. It will be waist-deep here in half an hour.'
He drew her to her feet so forcibly that she was thrown against
him; and for a moment, as though he had snatched her into a
swift embrace, all the strength drained out of her so that she hung
heavy on his arm.

'All right?' he asked.

She hid her eyes from him. 'Perfectly,' she said.

They had to wade to their knees to pass the end of the overhang which sheltered them, and the current was strong against
their legs, and Harland gripped her hand to steady her. As they
took the first steps, the brook seemed to reach up for them. It
rose six inches in a single hungry surge, a solid wall of water like
a tidal bore plunging down the canyon as though somewhere
above them a dam had let go. It swirled about their knees before
they reached the end of the overhang and scrambled out on firm
ground.

Yet even here, water pouring down the slopes ran ankle-deep,
and they came into the full beat of the rain, and it was as though
they had stepped under a waterfall. The big hats they both wore
— Robie had outfitted Harland on his arrival, but Ellen's was an
old friend left over from former visits to the ranch — sustained
the first impact; but from shoulders down they were instantly wet
through, and almost at once the hatbrims surrendered to the
weight of water upon them and drooped about their ears. Ellen
thought they could not travel far in this. The buffeting of the
rain, hitting them a thousand blows each second, would speedily
beat all their strength away. As though he had the same thought,
Harland looked all about, and saw on the slope twenty feet above
them a boulder which hung at an angle, with a slanting face that
promised some protection; and — holding her hand, tugging her
after him — he turned that way. They had to climb on hands and
knees, through muddy water inches deep which made many little
torrents, and they slid helplessly backward now and then, fighting
to recover the lost ground, laughing and panting, wet and be-
grimed. The struggle to achieve even that short ascent was a hard
one; but at last they reached their goal and found some shelter
from the bruising beat of the rain.

Ellen's lungs were bursting with the effort, and for a while she could only gasp for breath. When she could speak, she told him smilingly: 'This is as bad as chasing turkeys!'

He nodded, and they sat with their backs against the boulder, pulling their feet up out of the downpour. The din about them was too great to permit easy speech. The rain was so heavy that they could only dimly see the brook below. They were wet through, and when the wind came it was cold. Ellen remembered that when Harland lighted their luncheon fire he had taken a match out of a waterproof box, and she was glad his matches were dry; for unless the rain relented, they would have to spend the night here, and though she half hoped this would happen, without a fire it would be a wretched business. Robie of course would guess their situation, but not even the sure-footed western horses could pick a way through this jumble of great boulders to come to the rescue.

She was content to sit in silence, waiting for the pounding of her heart to ease. If she had not overtaken him, Harland would be alone here in this downpour; and thinking of him drenched and cold and alone, she felt toward him a brooding, almost maternal tenderness, glad that she could be here with him, could share with him whatever was to come. She watched him as though he were a child whom she must comfort and defend. He was staring at the flood with frowning eyes, and she told him, her lips close to his ear:

'We're all right. This will pass.'

'We're so damned helpless!' he said rebelliously.

She pressed closer, huddling against the insinuating cold, wishing to make him feel her trust and her reliance. They could make no move till the violence of the rain should abate. It came in gusts, slatting and spattering against the rocky slopes as if it were thrown out of a gigantic bucket. Its violence was frightening, and even Ellen felt this; yet since they were together, nothing else mattered to her. If they were never to be parted, then she had no fear.

When at last the rain slackened, Harland stirred like a prisoner who sees open the way to an escape; and then, as suddenly as it had come, the shower moved on down the canyon. The clouds began at once to vanish, the sun fighting through; and steam from the quickly drying ledges curled thinly in the warming air.

'We've got to move,' he told her, and with no other word they started, Harland picking their path while she obediently followed. At first their chilled limbs were awkward and uncertain, but their own exertions warmed them. For a while they made good time.

But to advance was difficult. The canyon walls were high, and rimrock barred their escape to the heights above. Sometimes they slipped on muddy footing, sometimes on wet rocks; and where the way was steep, they clung like cats. Sometimes, as Harland chose what promised to be the easiest path, they were high above the water, sometimes, at its very brink. Once Ellen called to him, and he stopped to hear what she said — the roar of the brook was like fists pounding them — and she cried:

'We forgot the rods, left them back at the big pool!'

He nodded shortly. 'I've had enough fishing for today,' he shouted, grinning; and she laughed with him, loving him immeasurably.

The brook was so much risen that they could never cross it, and they had to stay on the south side of the canyon. Once they were near disaster. This was at a spot where at the foot of an abrupt declivity a slope of rubble and mud slanted down into the stream. They worked precariously across, and Harland found more secure footing on the further side and turned to give Ellen his hand; but when she reached out to take it, the loose stuff beneath her let go, and she slid in a small avalanche of shale and mud fairly into the water. She had a moment of sharp terror as she saw the torrent about to engulf her; but by good luck there was a shallow bar, and although she was rolled over and over, and bruised against the stones, the water was no more than waist-deep. Harland plunged in to catch her and help her to her feet and back to solid footing again, and she clung to him for an instant breathlessly, wishing he would never let her go.

'All right?' he challenged, harsh in his concern.

She nodded, wiping the water from her streaming face, pushing back wet strands of hair that lay plastered on her cheeks. 'I've lost my hat,' she said, smiling up at him.

'It's gone on downstream.'

'That was pretty close, wasn't it?'

'Yes. For God's sake, watch your step,' he warned her. 'Now come along!'

She followed him, and her teeth chattered, for the cold plunge had chilled her through and through; and the weight of her soaked and muddy garments wearied her, and their progress slowed; and always the stream, swollen now into a hungry river, roared past just below them, like a shark which follows a steamer, rolling up a wicked eye at the passengers along the rail. The footing was so hazardous that any error could precipitate them to destruction, and Ellen thought that if she fell again, because she was so weary, they might not be able to win free from the hungry flood. At increasingly frequent intervals they paused to rest, their tortured lungs laboring, their bodies trembling with fatigue. But the air was warmer, and presently the sky blew clear and the sun blazed on the upper slopes so that rocks and mud alike seemed to steam and smoke.

Also, the sun renewed their courage — and at the same time it warned them that the afternoon was well-sped. Harland looked at his watch, and this time she asked a question, and he said it was almost five o'clock, and added urgently: 'Can't you travel any faster?'

There was no reproach in her tones as she replied. 'I'm sorry. I'll try,' she said. But she lagged, and he drew a few paces ahead, till reaching easier footing, he paused to wait for her. 'I'm coming,' she assured him; but then she stepped on a stone which turned under her foot. She threw herself sidewise and fell, with a low cry, and he came quickly back to her.

'It's nothing,' she declared, but when she took a step she limped and winced, and he said:

'I'd better bandage that.'

'I'm afraid so,' she confessed, catching her breath with pain.

'I don't want to play out on you. But — what can you use?'

'My shirt?' he suggested. She nodded and sat down and loosed the laces of her shoe and stripped off her stocking, while he laid aside his fishing vest and removed his shirt and tore out the back of it as far up as the neck yoke, and ripped it into lengths. His body, bare to the waist, wet and shining when he took off his shirt, dried quickly in the sun, and the muscles in his arms slid smoothly under the smooth skin. When he knelt to apply the makeshift bandages, his water-logged hat hid his face from her, and because she wished to watch him she took it off his head, and he looked up at her, a question in his eyes.

'It's so heavy,' she said. 'Throw it away.' She tossed it aside.

'How do I do this?' he asked. She told him how to place the bandages, and when they were affixed, he wrung her stocking as dry as possible, and with some difficulty, over the bulk of the bandages, she drew on her shoe and laced it tightly.

He put on again the fragment of his shirt. It was whole in front and still had sleeves, but they laughed together at his appearance.

'It's like a hospital night shirt,' he suggested.

She stood up to try her foot, facing him steadily. 'That feels fine!' she declared, and saw his quick approval of her sturdy courage.

Thereafter he let her lead the way, and their progress slowed accordingly. Presently, as they worked along a rocky slope, she heard over the tumult of the brook a rumbling sound, and looked ahead with startled and then amazed eyes. The flood had under-cut one of the perpendicular canyon walls which towered two hundred feet or more above the stream bed. This wall was a mixture of hard clay and shale and soft stone strata; and when its foundations were gone, the face collapsed. Like the front of a glacier when it meets a river swollen with spring floods, it sheared off, leaned a little outward so that for an instant Ellen saw the sky through a widening crack high above them, and then crumbled like a falling chimney, collapsing on itself, thousands of tons of debris smashing down into the gorge so violently that the earth trembled under the impact; and the water geysered high as though a charge of dynamite had been set off in the depths, and a mighty blast of air struck them, throwing them off balance so that they fell sprawling and clung to each other, still watching with staring eyes.

Ellen, after the first moment of awed terror provoked by that majestic spectacle, saw that the fall had completely dammed the stream. They were penned here like flies in a stoppered bottle. The waters began at once to rise, the canyon to fill as rapidly as a goblet fills when it is held under a faucet. Harland shouted:

'We've got to climb out of here! Come on.'

He took her hand, and they clambered upward, the rising water close on their heels. Something like panic touched them both, and they made unnecessary haste, till, looking back and down, they saw that the water would soon top the great mound of earth which sealed the canyon, and their hands held fast as they paused to watch.

The first trickle found a way across the barrier, and that trickle widened; and as easily as a hot knife cuts through butter it cut down through the dam. They saw boulders as big as barrels swept away and submerged; and abruptly the flood, making its own channel, began to fall again.

It had broken through at a point on the opposite side from where they were; and the heap of mud and rubble left on this side would for a while serve as a bridge which they could cross. To do so meant passing close under the face of the cliff from which the fall had come, and from which even now small clots of mud and rocks occasionally descended; but if they waited till the loose stuff was all washed away, they might not be able to pass at all. They must cross while they could, and Harland told her so.

'We can't, possibly,' she protested, holding fast to him, her teeth clicking with real terror now.

'We've got to!'

'We'll mire like flies on flypaper,' she cried. 'Or another slide will bury us!'

He gripped her hands so hard she thought the bones must break. 'We're going,' he told her strongly, and smiled and drew her toward him. 'We'll make it,' he said in calm certainty. 'It's all right, Ellen. I'll get you out of this. Now come.'

So hand in hand they plunged down the slope and began that dangerous passage. There was a moment when they sank knee-deep in mud, and Ellen thought they were caught; and a clod of dirt falling from a hundred feet above them landed so near that spattering particles stung their faces. But they crawled free of the muck and passed the face of the cliff and from a safe vantage looked back to see the last of their precarious footing, devoured by the hungry stream, dissolve and swirl away.

He laughed aloud, in a high pride because he had beaten the enemy; and because he could laugh at such a moment her heart swelled. 'I thought we were going to die together there,' she said huskily.

'We're all right!' he assured her. 'We're going to make it. Ankle pretty bad?'

'It's better all the time.'

'If we ever come to anything like level ground, I can carry you.'

'Exercise will do it good,' she said, but that was so absurd that they laughed together, and they drew together, united by this which they endured. Behind them the sun dropped below the last ridge and was gone; yet its rays still touched the loftier slopes above them, and though dusk began to fill the canyon, the sky was clear and fine. Ellen saw too that the way was easier now, the footing more secure; and the heights that walled them were no longer so abrupt. It was as though the mountains were relenting, relaxing their grasp, permitting these two small living creatures to escape. Yet full dark was almost come before the gorge widened out, and the violence of the stream, loosed from the canyon's close constriction, began to ease. They followed its margin, and the farther shore was all an indistinguishable shadow, and they came into a little clump of aspens, and pushed through and found themselves among pines beyond.

Here at last Ellen sank wearily down. 'I can't go any farther for a while,' she said helplessly. 'Do you think they might find us if we just waited here?'

It was almost dark among the pines, but the roar of the racing water no longer deafened them. 'Of course,' he said. 'Be sure they will. Rest. I'll see if I can start a fire.'

She remembered that Robie's ranch lay to the northward, and they were on the south side of the brook, so rescue could not reach them till the flood ran off; but she did not tell him so. On his knees, groping in the darkness, he collected by the sense of touch a supply of dead wood for his fire. He found none that was dry, but the small twigs of the pines would burn, wet or dry. When his wood was ready, he broke off a handful of these twigs from the lower branches of standing trees, and at last tried his matches.

The first one started a little flame, but it died as soon as the match burned out. While she watched, he used half a dozen to dry the kindling before at last it burned of itself. In five minutes thereafter he had a roaring bonfire, the sparks flying twinkling upward through the boughs overhead; and he stood back and brushed his hands triumphantly.

'There!' he cried.

Ellen, sitting near-by, facing the blaze, her shoulders resting against the trunk of a huge pine, smiled approvingly, looking all around. The flames pushed the darkness back — so far but no farther. At a little distance blackness ringed them still; but the circle of firelight seemed to her almost palpable, as though it built a wall around them and a roof over their heads, built a habitation in which they could rest secure. She was conscious of the weight of the vast wilderness in the heart of which by the fire-magic he had carved out a shelter for them both; and she was happy in this sanctuary he had made.

Her eyes turned back to him, and he asked: 'All right now? How's the ankle?'

'Fine,' she declared. 'But I'm terribly cold.' Yet the heat from the fire filled this circle from which the darkness was excluded. She was cold because she was wet through, as he was.

'You'd better take off some of your clothes,' he suggested. 'We'll dry them; and you'll be warmer without them, even while they're drying.'

She obeyed him without question, rising to step out of her skirt and hand it to him, and she gave him that bright-hued shirt she wore, sadly draggled and muddy now. He hung the garments so that they felt the heat of the flames, and his manner was wholly impersonal and reassuring.

But what she did had for her a significance deeper than the simple, reasonable act itself. Under the circumstances, for her to remove her wet and sodden outer clothing was the sensible and the intelligent thing to do; but because he was to her what he was, it seemed to her a symbolic gesture, as though she laid aside all her defenses. This circle of firelight was their bridal bower, and by doing what she did she surrendered herself to him — and bound him to her by that triumphant surrender.

To Harland, clearly, the moment had no such connotation. 'Stand here by the fire till you're warm,' he advised, his tone completely matter-of-fact.

She obeyed, turning back and front to the blaze; but after a moment she said: 'It's scorching me!' She went to the tree and sat down again, a small white huddle, hugging her knees, watching him with her heart in her eyes. He brought more wood and the flames leaped higher; and he took off his fishing vest with the many pockets, feeling the weight of the trout which he had forgotten there, and he exclaimed with a quick satisfaction: 'Here's our supper anyway!' He laid the trout on the ground, and took off his ruined shirt and hung it to dry, and stood stripped to the waist, the firelight gleaming on his chest and flanks; and to her swimming senses it seemed they were alone in a world of their own, intimate and close as lovers, the fire on their hearthstone burning bright between them.

Then, across the fire, through the tongued tips of the flames, their eyes met and held, and she gave him her eyes unmasked and full of yearning. They looked at each other for a long moment, neither speaking nor moving; and then with her eyes she drew him so that he came around the fire to stand above her. She knew the hour she had dreamed was come. Her eyes still held his, insistent and compelling.

With a low wordless cry Harland dropped on his knee. He set his hands on her bare shoulders, gripping hard, so that she felt his fingers bruise the soft flesh. She still watched him, eyes wide and waiting; and he leaned down, and when he did so, her lips reached hungrily to his. He kissed her with a sort of violence, crushing her lips, lifting her close to him by his grip upon her shoulders; and she tasted his lips against her teeth between her soft lips faintly parted. She threw her cool arms around his neck, tightening them there half stranglingly, holding him hard.

He spoke against her lips, words without meaning, and her arms tugged harder; but then her head fell back, and looking up at him, the firelight sending flickering shadows across her face, she spoke, low and tense and fiercely triumphant now.

'I will never let you go,' she whispered.

If in her word and in her eyes he saw something implacable and unyielding, so that for a moment he felt a deep alarm, she did not know it; for in that instant from across the flood they heard a long halloo. Harland leaped to his feet to answer. The rescuers had come.

- v -

Ellen when she heard that distant halloo felt a jealous disappointment, wishing she and Harland might have had this hour alone; but Harland hurried at once to the water's edge to shout that they were safe, and she followed him. When she came to his side, the moon, almost at the full, had risen; and now that the skies were clear the night was bright. She saw someone swimming his horse across to them, and she pulled Harland's head down and kissed him and said laughingly:

'There! Now I must go make myself decent!'

She slipped away through the trees back to the fire, and Harland waited till Charlie Yates, bringing a vacuum bottle of coffee and a packet of sandwiches, reached the shore where he stood. When they came together to Ellen she was fully clad again.

Charlie said Robie and Lin were on the other bank, and that Robie had sent word back to the ranch that they were found; and since the water now fell as swiftly as it had risen, the others were presently able to cross with the led horses, and with dry clothes for both Ellen and Harland which Mrs. Robie's forethought had provided. They left Ellen by the fire to change again while Harland told Glen and the others the tale of their adventure; and a little after midnight they came home to the ranch.

When she heard Ellen was safe, Mrs. Berent, exhausted by her day in the saddle, had gone to bed; but Ruth and Mrs. Robie and Tess were waiting. Ellen, overflowing with triumphant happiness that embraced all the world, kissed each one of them; and she felt Ruth's glad astonishment — it was years since they had kissed each other — and said in ironic apology:

'I'm sorry, dear. It's just that I'm so happy!'

She saw Ruth's quick understanding, saw her look at Harland. Then Tess excitedly demanded to know all they had endured, and Ellen told the story of their arduous journey down the canyon, her eyes forever turning to Harland in proud possession. When she was done, Mrs. Robie said in a quiet concern:

'You must be tired after all that. I think we'd better all go right to bed.'

Ellen nodded. Harland was beside her. 'Good night,' she told him softly. 'I'll meet you at the pool at seven.' Mrs. Robie said they might sleep late if they chose, but Ellen protested: 'Mercy, no! I don't want to miss any of our last day here.' Her eyes met Harland's once more as she turned with Ruth toward the stairs.

Ruth said Mrs. Berent had bidden them wake her. When Ellen softly opened the door, her mother snapped on the bedside light. 'Come in, come in!' she exclaimed. 'Don't stand there whispering.' Then as she saw them: 'Well, I see you're not drowned! You were bound to go. I hope you're satisfied!'

'Oh, I am! I am!' Ellen cried, her eyes dancing, looking toward Ruth as though they shared a secret, and Mrs. Berent saw that glance.

'Eh?' she demanded. 'What are you grinning at? You look like the cat that swallowed the canary. You're practically licking your chops!' And then, in shrewd conjecture: 'I can guess what you've been up to! Well! I thought Mr. Harland had more sense!'

Ellen laughed and leaned down to kiss her. 'You don't fool me, darling,' she said affectionately. 'I know you're really as happy as I am — if only for my sake.' And she told them both, lifting her arms, whirling around in a sort of dance, carolling in delight: 'Yes, it's true! It's true! It's true! It's true, true, true; and we're going to be married right away, before we leave here, day after tomorrow . . .' She saw the travelling clock on the table by the bed. 'No, yesterday's gone! So we're going to be married tomorrow morning!'

Mrs. Berent, with a grim deliberation, sat up in bed to join battle. 'Now, Ellen Berent, you'll do nothing of the kind!' she said flatly.

Ellen was still soft with happiness. 'Hush, Mother! It's all settled,' she declared.

'Settled, my foot! It's not decent, Ellen. As good as engaged to one man and marrying another! What does Mr. Harland say to that?'

Ellen's eyes twinkled. 'Oh, he doesn't even know we're going to be married in the morning.' There was music in her tones and a singing in her veins. 'I haven't told him, but it's settled all the same!' she cried.

'It's not settled till I've had my say!' her mother insisted strongly. 'Wait till fall and I won't say a word; but I won't have this marry-me-quick business! It looks too much like a force-put!'

Ellen felt her cheeks flush with the anger which opposition always roused in her. '"What will people say?"' she suggested in a light, scornful tone. 'Is that what worries you, Mother? Haven't you any other standard?'

'It's better than having no standard at all except your own wants,' Mrs. Berent retorted. 'You've always done exactly as you chose, Ellen, but not this time!'

Ellen hesitated, wishing it were possible to avoid an outright defiance. 'Do we have to quarrel tonight, Mother? It's the first time I've ever been completely happy, like a brimming cup. Must you spoil it?' She looked at Ruth appealingly. The other girl sat on her bed, facing Mrs. Berent, and Ellen sought her support, sat down beside her and, as though unconsciously, caught her hand and held it. She knew Ruth's capacity for affection, played upon it now. 'Don't you want me to be happy, Mother? Richard and I are just being sensible. His brother has infantile, and has to stay in Georgia, and Richard must go straight back to him; and he needs me, and I need him. We want to be together! I must go with him, Mother. I want to be with him always!'

She saw that the older woman was shaken, but as though to fortify her position Mrs. Berent cried: 'Want! Want! Want! That's all you ever think of, Ellen; what you want! What others want never means anything to you!'

Ellen pressed Ruth's hand, wishing the other would speak without prompting, would take her side. 'But Mother darling, it's my life,' she urged. 'Mine and Richard's.'

Mrs. Berent pleaded: 'Well, you're my life, you and Ruth, Ellen.' And she said weakly: 'All I'm asking is that you wait a little, a few weeks, wait till fall.' Her eyes filled.

Ellen made an exasperated sound. 'Oh, for Heaven's sake, don't start sniffling, Mother.' She rose, her voice hardening. 'There's nothing to discuss, anyway. I'm of age. But even if there were anything to talk about, crying wouldn't help.' She still held Ruth's hand, and she turned to her now, bent and kissed her cheek and felt quick affection in Ruth respond to that caress, and thought in a derisive inner scorn that Ruth was like a dog which, no matter how many kicks it may have received, comes at a kind word, tail wagging, to its master's hand. She played on the other's hunger for her love. 'Make Mother see my point of view, Ruth,' she urged.

Ruth hesitated. 'Why Mother,' she said honestly, 'I do think that if I wanted to marry a man, and he wanted to marry me, and people objected, I'd think they were pretty unreasonable.'

'There, you see, Mother!' Ellen cried.

'I want you to be married decently, at home, and not in such a tearing hurry!'

'Lovers are always in a hurry,' Ellen declared, laughing again. 'Love's in a hurry, Mother, like a racing river.'

'I'll never consent to it,' Mrs. Berent insisted. 'Not this helter-skelter business!'

Ellen faced her with hot eyes, hating these weak and ineffectual protestations. Since her mother had to yield, why could she not surrender gracefully? 'You know you can't prevent my doing as I choose,' she said in icy tones.

'No, I never could.'

'Then why not be nice about it? Why make me unhappy when to do so can't accomplish anything?'

Mrs. Berent looked at her for a long moment; then she lay down and turned on her side, her back to them. 'Very well,' she said grimly. 'You've always had your own way. I can't expect you to change. I'll dance at your wedding, my dear.'

– VI –

Ellen had hoped to be alone with Harland at the pool next morning; but Robie and Tess and Lin appeared, and it was not till after breakfast that she was able to draw him away with her into the garden. When she told him her plan — that they should be married here at the ranch, so that she could go to Georgia with him — he was surprised and doubtful; but Ellen said surely:

'It's so sensible, my darling! Do you expect me to go back to Boston, to Bar Harbor, and let you go off to Georgia all alone? Don't be ridiculous! For one thing, I want to see Danny, right away. I want to get to know him. I'll sit with him, read to him, talk to him, keep him happy while you go back to your work again; and when you're through working every day, we can all be together. Won't that be fun? You need me, darling; and oh, I need you so. I want you so!' In his arms she whispered breathlessly, half-sobbing: 'I'll die if we're ever parted again!' She felt resistance in him still, and flooded him with tenderness that broke it down.

He made at last only one condition. She must telegraph Quinton, tell him the truth.

'But of course, dearest!' she assented. 'I was going to! I'll even let you read the telegram. Give me paper and pencil. I'll write it right now!' He confessed that he had neither pencil nor paper, and she laughed at him. 'A fine author you are! How do you ever expect to write anything?'

'I've plenty in my room.'

'Then we'll go get them.' She caught his hand and led him indoors and upstairs, hurrying, hurrying, hurrying, deliberately giving him no time to make objections; and when they were alone and the door was closed behind them, she kissed him in rapturous ardor, and felt triumphantly his full surrender. He gave her pen and paper, and she wrote a swift scrawl:

> Find we made mistake. Marrying Richard Harland tomorrow.
>
> > Ellen

She turned to Harland. 'There!' she said.

He read what she had written and chuckled; but then he said seriously: 'Good God, Ellen, you don't have to kick him in the teeth! After all, the man loves you! That ought to entitle him to some consideration.'

She challenged mischievously: 'Will you always be so considerate of my lovers?'

'Think how he'll feel when he gets this!'

'I don't seem to be able to think much about him,' she admitted, her eyes full of tenderness. 'You've crowded everything else out of me, Richard; everything but you.'

He took another sheet of paper, took the pen. 'I'll write it,' he decided, and sat down at the desk, and she perched on the arm of his chair, watching over his shoulder. He made one or two false starts, wrote at last:

> I am terribly sorry and unhappy, Russ. Please believe me, and please forgive me. I know now that I never loved you. I

think it was because I missed Father so, and you and he had been friends. I know your generosity, know you will release me. I'm not coming home, so we won't see each other for a long time. It is best this way, believe me, and good-bye.

Ellen

When he finished, it was her turn to laugh. 'Mercy, you're extravagant! It will cost a fortune to send that. Do you always have to write a book to say what you mean? Never mind, we can send it as a night letter.' She picked up the paper, read again what he had written. 'But Richard, this doesn't sound a bit like me! It's so literary!' She added, smiling at him, teasing him: 'And you don't mention yourself at all? Skeered, Mister?'

'Leave me out! That would just be rubbing it in. This gives him a chance to be generous, to release you.'

Her eyes narrowed thoughtfully. 'I don't think Russ is particularly generous,' she reflected, then laughed in tender assent. 'But I'll send this if you say so, darling. Night letter?'

'No,' he insisted, 'a telegram.' He added: 'I'd feel a lot better if we had an answer from him before — tomorrow.'

'He won't give us his blessing,' she warned him.

'Well, send it anyway.'

'Aye, aye, sir.' She kissed him, clinging to him, whispering ardently: 'My dear, dear man!'

When the message was gone, Harland insisted that they seek her mother. Ellen had misgivings about that interview, but Mrs. Berent's surrender of the night before had been complete.

'Take her and welcome, Mr. Harland,' the old woman said, when he had spoken. 'And I wish you joy of her! She'll eat you alive and gnaw your bones!'

Harland laughed, but Mrs. Berent did not. Ellen nibbled playfully at his cheek. 'See, I'm beginning to eat you up already,' she whispered. Then, catching his hand, she cried: 'Now let's go tell Mr. and Mrs. Robie. After all, if we're going to be married in their house, they have a right to know!'

She swept him away. When Robie heard what they planned, she saw his startled glance turn doubtfully toward Harland, but he gave them congratulations, and Mrs. Robie met this emergency as she met all others, with at least outward composure. There was some talk of details, and Ellen, exactly sure what she wanted, made every decision. Watching Harland, she felt uneasy reluctance in him; and she decided that he must have no chance to voice his misgivings. Robie said there was no minister in the little village near the ranch. The nearest was fifty miles away. 'But we can telephone him and he'll be glad to come,' he said.

'No, no,' Ellen insisted. 'That's not dignified. You and Richard drive over and talk to him. And you help Richard see about the license, Mr. Robie; and I must have a ring!' She thrust them toward the door. 'Go on, go on,' she urged laughingly. She kissed Harland good-bye. 'That's the last one till we're married, darling,' she warned him. 'You're not supposed to see the bride before the wedding, you know!'

So they drove away, and Ellen and Ruth and Tess and Mrs. Robie began to plan and to devise. Ellen wished to be married in the pergola by the pool, and Mrs. Robie said flowers must be found and arranged, and Ruth and Ellen discussed what Ellen should wear. They were busy all morning, and after lunch Ellen announced that she was exhausted and went to her room, excluding even Ruth. Harland and Robie had not yet returned, and she was still alone there when Quinton's telegram was telephoned from the station.

Tess took it over the phone and brought it to Ellen. Quinton had wired:

> Refuse to accept your decision. Coming at once. Love.
> Russ

Ellen read it with a flashing glance, and Tess said doubtfully: 'Maybe I shouldn't have taken it, but I didn't know what it was.' Then she asked in uncontrollable curiosity: 'Who is he, Ellen?'

Ellen caught in her tone the accent of doubt, and for a moment there was an inner hardening in her. 'A man old enough to be my father,' she explained. 'One of Father's friends, in fact.

He's always insisted he'd wait for me and marry me when I grew up, ever since I was a little girl. He even thinks we're engaged! He gave me a ring I used to wear sometimes.'

'I noticed it when you first came.'

'He's awful,' Ellen assured her. 'Fat, and bald, and hairs in his nose!' Tess laughed gleefully at this description; and Ellen remembered that Harland must not see the telegram, and she tore it across and across and tossed it aside. 'That for Mr. Quinton!' she exclaimed. Then, quickly enlisting the other as her ally: 'Tess, you must stay with me every minute from now on. There are people coming for dinner, aren't there?'

'Yes, Mother planned it a week ago. They're just friends from the ranches around here, but that means some of them are driving a hundred miles. Of course she could call it off.'

'No, she mustn't! That's all the better! But you be my chaperone, Tess. Don't leave Richard and me alone a minute.'

'Oh, the poor man!'

'I'll make it up to him,' Ellen declared. 'Maybe it's a foolish notion, but — brides have a right to have notions, don't you think? So you stick to me like a burr! Promise?'

Tess was delighted to be a party to this conspiracy; and she stayed with Ellen till time to dress for dinner. Harland, when he and Robie returned, came to the door and knocked; but Ellen called:

'You can't come in, darling. Tess and I are busy. Did you get everything?'

She felt his hesitation through the closed door. 'Yes, everything's all set,' he assented.

'Wonderful! Then I'll see you later. I love you.'

'I — wanted to talk to you.'

'We'll have all our lives to talk together. 'Bye.'

She heard him go away, and Tess whispered, her eyes dancing: 'He sounded so forlorn!'

'He's just scared,' Ellen laughingly assured her. 'But bridegrooms always are!'

At dinner — Ellen had arranged this with Mrs. Robie —

she and Harland were seated the length of the table apart; but Robie announced their plans, and invited everyone to stay for the wedding, and toasts were drunk to them, and Harland and then Ellen responded. But Ellen was thinking of Quinton, wondering how he would come, whether he would fly, how soon he would arrive; and she was desperate with haste. When they rose from the table, she drew Tess to her side; and almost at once she excused herself, turning away upstairs. Harland saw her move away and came after her; but Ellen — holding fast to Tess — told him smilingly:

'No, you mustn't, dearest! It isn't done!' She kissed him lightly. 'There! Au revoir, my darling.'

When her door was closed, she leaned against it, shivering, her teeth chattering; and Tess was half-frightened, coming close to her, holding both her hands. But after a moment Ellen was herself again. 'It's all right, Tess, perfectly all right,' she said breathlessly. 'I'm excited, of course; but that's all!' She caught the younger girl, kissed her. 'Thank you for everything. I'm all right now. Good night, my dear.'

So she sent Tess away, and for precaution's sake she locked her door, drawing back from it warily as though outside it there were a threat, a danger. In a panic haste she stripped off her garments, hurried into bed. Belowstairs she could hear the murmur of voices, and later there was music and she caught the hushed whispers of feet as they danced, and someone strolled out to the pool below her windows, and she heard laughter in the night. By and by someone knocked at her door, and she answered drowsily, and Ruth asked whether she could do anything, and Ellen murmured: 'No thanks, darling. I was asleep. Good night!'

But she did not sleep till the house was quiet; till the guests were gone.

They were married while the sun was still low in the eastern sky, under the pergola by the pool as Ellen had wished. Robie lent them one of his cars for the first stage of their departure. 'Leave it anywhere you like,' he said generously. 'Just send me a

wire where to find it. I'll have someone pick it up.' Rice pelted
them as they drove away, and Ellen looked back, waving as
long as there was anyone to see.

Then she sighed with a great relief, and slipped her hand
through Harland's arm. 'There!' she exclaimed. 'That wasn't
so bad, was it?'

He touched her hand affectionately, but after a moment he
said in a regretful tone: 'I'm sorry there was no word from Quinton.'

'I suppose,' she suggested, 'he was off fishing or something,
didn't get my wire.'

– VII –

Their room in the hotel at Taos faced the west, and Ellen
waked at first dawn and lay for a while, blissfully happy, serene
and fulfilled. As the light crept into the room she looked at
Harland, still asleep, sprawling like a child; and she was content
for a while to watch him, studying the shape of his head, the con-
tour of his shoulders, the way his fingers curled over his upturned
palm, loving all of him. But at length she sat up to look through
the windows across the desert to distant mountains far away.
The world lay in the cool shadow of dawn, still undefined and
featureless; but as she watched, a rosy light began to fill the sky
beyond those remote mountains, bringing them to life as a dark
silhouette against that brightness. Then sunlight touched their
peaks, tipping them with crimson. The sun was rising behind
Taos and behind Ellen as she watched, its rays, diffused through
earth mists, lancing across the sky above the village to lift those
ranges yonder into the day.

The sunlight flowed down the flanks of the distant mountains
till they were all in brightness, and their rocky slopes and shadowed gorges formed a pattern of changing color which seemed to
Ellen wondrously enchanting. Then the coming day began to
race toward her, as though this sunrise came from the west instead of from the east. The illumination revealed in turn each

successive fold of the rolling desert, and each fold was gray-brown in the dusk of dawn till at the sun's touch it showed pink and crimson with shadow patterns for relief, and then the bright hues became shimmering bronze. While the miracle continued, the desert was barred by bands of color changing constantly. Ellen had seen northern lights play across the autumnal skies, and except for their greater brilliance these colors changed and altered in the same way, manipulated by some Godlike hand, as though God himself experimented, laying His pigments across a palette, considering which to use to adorn the world for this newborn day.

There was in the spectacle something sublime and breath-taking, and Ellen's eyes filled; but then she smiled, and asked herself happily whether yesterday she would have been as deeply moved by this beauty as she was today. Since she first knew Harland she had been intensely aware of all the living world, her senses sharpened and responsive to every stimulus; but there had been in that awareness a restless questioning, an eager hunger. Now she was at once more awake than she had ever been in her life before and at the same time more at peace.

Watching the spectacle that progressed outside her window, she thought those far mountains which had first reached up to snare the sun and pull it down to warm the earth, as a sleeper's hand reaches for a coverlet when night takes on a sudden chill, must be scores of miles away; for the sunlight which raced toward her was not yet near at hand. She had no impulse to wake Harland, content to have this moment to herself; but when at last the desert was all bright, she lay down again, stretching luxuriously, her arms extended over her head, her legs at full reach, her toes pointed, deliciously conscious of every muscle and sinew and of every drop of blood in her body, feeling herself complete, perfected, attuned to life and to the world.

She turned on her side to look across at her husband, watching him with a proud triumphant smile; and she thought in a blissful peace: 'Mine, mine, mine! There's nothing in my world but you, Richard; and there's nothing in your world but me!'

Yet after a moment she remembered that this was not wholly

true. She remembered Danny; Danny who was ill, crippled, his legs shrunken and distorted; Danny who was a maimed and ugly thing. The thought of him thus deformed made her shudder as one shudders when a snake with a broken back writhes in the dust. Her eyes narrowed, and her brows drew together in a thin frown. She had cast out of her life her mother, and Ruth, and Quinton, so that all her life now was Richard's.

But would he ever cast out his love for Danny, so that he could be altogether hers?

She lay for a long time, fixed in thought, till she was cold as ice; and she shivered faintly, and with a sudden movement then she sat up and took her pillow in both hands and flung it at Harland's head. He roused with a startled grunt, and she leaped out of bed and pounced upon him, catching his ears in her hands, thumping his head on the pillow, laughing at him, crying over and over:

'Wake up! Wake up, sleepy head! Pay attention to me! Pay attention to me!'

4

F OR AS LONG as he could remember, Danny Harland
had been sure that his big brother was one of the lesser gods.
Even while he himself was still almost a baby, Dick had treated
him as an equal, sharing his enthusiasms and interesting himself
in the things which interested Danny. Dick was so wonderful that
Danny was a little shy with him. When they met after any separation he wished to throw himself into the other's arms and hug
him rapturously; but for fear Dick might not like that, he assumed a mature dignity, and they met with a firm handclasp,
greeting each other as man to man. He had always felt nearer to
Dick than to his mother; and after her death the two brothers
drew closer still, and sometimes when they were together, if Dick
were reading or otherwise absorbed, Danny might just watch him
with wide eyes, thinking happily how wonderful he was, humbly
praying that he himself might some day be as fine.

Before Danny's illness, they had been comrades, and Dick
never seemed to remember that he was so many years the older;
but afterward there was a deep, almost maternal tenderness in
Dick, and whenever he came to where Danny lay he bent down
to kiss him — although they had seldom kissed before — and
these caresses and this loving kindness made Danny so blissfully
content that he sometimes thought it was worth being sick, to
find out Dick loved him so. At the same time, because he knew
how Dick grieved and worried over him, he took pains to be jolly
and cheerful whenever they were together, making light of any
discomfort he suffered, meeting this catastrophe which had

struck him down with a high valor that was so complete it never seemed to be what it was. Once — his hearing was keener now than it had been — he heard his nurse say to Dick in the hall outside his door: 'He's so brave sometimes it's just heartbreaking, Mr. Harland.' And he heard Dick's reply: 'He's so brave he never lets you see he's being brave!' Danny was mighty proud when he heard that. It had not occurred to him that he was brave. He was simply making things as easy as possible for Dick. If thereafter his courage ever failed or weakened, he had only to remember that overheard conversation to be strong again.

When the acute stage of his illness had passed, and Dick told him that they would go south to a place called Warm Springs where he might be helped toward complete recovery, Danny dreaded leaving home; but Dick saw his fears and banished them. 'I'll be with you there just as much as I am here, Danny,' he promised, and grinned reassuringly. 'You and I are always going to stick together.'

'Is it a hospital?' Danny asked dubiously; but Dick said:

'No. The people there aren't sick. You're not sick yourself, now, you know. They're like you, all over being sick, busy getting well.'

So Danny was reconciled. The long trip by train tired him; but at the Foundation, set high enough in the hills to be cool even in summer, with loftier mountains visible in the distance, he was soon happily content. It was, he told Dick, almost like New England. He would be for a long time unable to move about without assistance, and he must endure a wearying routine of medication, minor corrective surgery and weeks of immobilization in plaster casts and splints before the underwater physical therapy which would follow; but Dick was with him, living in one of the small housekeeping cottages near-by, bringing him many bright surprises day by day.

He looked forward to Dick's appearances, and when they were together he watched the other so closely, attentive not only to Dick's words but to every shade of expression in his tones and every shadow in his eyes, that he saw how concern and sorrow wore upon his brother; and when, not long after their arrival at the Foundation, the question of Dick's going to New Mexico arose, Danny was completely and wholeheartedly delighted, refusing to think how lonely he himself would be while the other was gone. But after Dick's departure he was at first sick with longing for him, sobbing heartbrokenly through silent night hours when he could not sleep, lying with dry, blank eyes through the long empty days. Then little by little his spirits rose again, and he remembered that Dick would soon return, and that he himself must have progress to report; and this necessity of getting better as fast as he could for Dick's sake made him presently forget his loneliness.

He read Dick's New Mexico letters over and over, devouring every word. In the second letter he was puzzled by something he sensed but could not define; for it did not sound like Dick. The first, written on the train, full of squiggles and little comic sketches, had made him laugh till he cried, and that sounded like Dick all right; but the second was different, with no jokes in it, or at least none that were particularly funny; and Danny had, when he read it, a curious feeling that Dick was holding something back; that there was something on the tip of Dick's tongue — or the tip of his pen — which he was always about to write and never did. There was a quality Dick put into his books, of which Danny was perhaps the most ardent reader. Without ever actually saying so, Dick in his novels always made you feel that something tremendously important and interesting was just about to happen. Danny got the same feeling from Dick's letters now, and he found them a little frightening.

But as the time for Dick's return approached, Danny lost himself in excited anticipation, counting the days. He woke one morning full of happiness, and for a moment could not remember why he was so happy; and then as he came wide awake he recalled that today Dick would leave the ranch and start the return journey back to him. Day after day after tomorrow, three days from now, he would be here!

Danny was so merry all that day that the nurses teased him

about his love for Dick, declared he was as excited as a girl waiting for her sweetheart; but Danny laughed at their teasing, enjoying it, thinking from hour to hour: 'Now he's left the ranch!
Now he's on the train to the junction! Now he's on the train for
Chicago!' He lay awake that night, unable to sleep, counting to
himself every turn of the wheels which brought Dick nearer and
nearer; and he hummed to himself that song which the wheels
sang in Kipling's story, and which so exactly fitted the sound of a
racing train. It was like a lullaby. He hummed himself to sleep.

Next morning there was a letter from Dick, which had come by
air mail, and when the nurse put the envelope in his hands
Danny's heart quickened with an instant alarm; for the envelope
was a thick one, and Dick would not have written a long letter on
the eve of his departure from the ranch. The boy tore off the
end of the envelope and found half a dozen closely scribbled
sheets in Dick's small, regular hand; and he began eagerly to
read.

> Dear Danny —
> This is going to be in some ways a hard letter to write, and
> I wish it didn't have to be written, wish I could be there to
> tell you my fine news, instead of writing it.

Danny's breath caught at that. It had an alarming sound;
but the next sentence began to reassure him.

> For it is the best of news I have to tell you, Danny. I'm
> going to be married tomorrow morning, to — as the fellow
> said — 'the most wonderful girl in the world.' Only in this
> case it happens to be true. We'll be married in the morning
> and leave here at once, and have a few days together before
> we come back to you. It won't be long, not more than a week,
> I'm sure. I know you'll be disappointed just at first, because
> you'll be expecting me about the time you get this; but I know
> you'll forgive us. You know how honeymoons are. We
> haven't decided yet just where we'll go; but it will only be
> for a few days, that's sure.

Danny muttered weakly: 'Gosh!' The letter slipped from his
hand and he stared at nothing, and for a moment he had again

that terrible sense of aloneness which had oppressed him when Dick went away. If Dick were married, probably things would be mighty different between them from now on. But of course he wanted Dick to be in love and married and happy. He picked up the letter again.

> Well, now you want to know all about her. Her name's Ellen Berent, and she's lived all her life on Mount Vernon Street and at Bar Harbor in the summer. It seems impossible that she and I never met before; but there it is. I've already spoken of her in my letters, though I may not have told you her name. She was the girl on the train. Remember? And she went with me the day I shot the wild turkey. She's done a lot of hunting and fishing with her father, and she's about the loveliest thing you can imagine. She and Lin are fine friends, and I know you and she will be.

Danny looked up from the letter again, staring at the wall of his pleasant, sunny room, wondering how it would seem to have Dick loving someone else, wondering whether he himself would like her as Dick expected. Even if he didn't, of course, he would have to pretend to like her very much, because it would make Dick unhappy if he didn't. He licked his lips and swallowed hard and for a moment he was just a frightened, sick little boy; because of course he would never again have Dick all to himself. But then he set his jaw and grinned and nodded to assure himself that this was fine and that he was glad, mighty glad, because Dick now would be so happy.

He read on. There was more and more about Ellen. At the last, Dick described the trip down the canyon, and the hardships and the dangers he and Ellen endured together. 'For of course it really was dangerous,' he explained. 'Things might have gone badly wrong.'

And he concluded:

> Something happened to me on the way down the canyon. I had liked Ellen before that, and yet I had felt a certain antagonism toward her too, for no reason, except that I was a

confirmed old bachelor, and bachelors always shy off from
any sort of matrimonial pitfall.

But before we came to the end of our journey it seemed to
me that she and I were, in all the ways that mattered, already
married, and that she was the bravest and finest and altogether the most desirable woman in the world.

And I saw in her eyes that she felt the same way about me.
Maybe it's a conceited thing to say, Danny, but I think she's
quite as much in love with me as I am with her. For instance,
my idea would have been to wait till you could be at our wedding; but she doesn't want to wait. To wait would mean her
going back to Boston and my going back to you, and our not
seeing each other for weeks or months; but she's anxious to
come with me, and to know you, and I'm anxious for you to
know her. And neither of us wanted to wait.

We'll be married here tomorrow morning, and Glen Robie
is lending us a car, and we'll drive away somewhere for a day
or two and then start to come to you. Be ready with a big
welcome for us, Danny. I want you to be as happy as I am.
It will be three of us instead of only two, from now on, and
that will be just twice as fine. We both send love, and we'll
see you soon.

Dick

Danny read that letter slowly, devouring every word; and he
grinned at Dick's happiness, and he thought Dick sounded different already, younger, gay and merry and more like a boy than
a man. There were two or three passages which, to his sharpened
and sensitive mind, seemed a little as though Dick were trying to
reassure himself; but Danny decided that was just his imagination. Certainly Dick would not have married anyone unless he
wanted to very much indeed; so Ellen was bound to be all right.

He told the nurses and the doctors, joyfully, the news. 'Listen! Isn't this wonderful? Dick's married! To a girl out there!
They're coming right on here!' He even read them parts of
Dick's letter, telling who she was and what she was like, telling
the story of the adventure in the canyon. But he saw their exchange of glances, significant and troubled; and he knew what

they were thinking, because of course they knew how much Dick meant to him. So to make them see that he did not feel badly, he put on an excessive enthusiasm, insisting over and over on his delight.

But when he was left alone, his eyes shadowed with doubts. Would Dick love him as much as ever, come to see him as often, stay as long? Would she like him — or would she resent Dick's devotion to him? After all, you couldn't blame her for not wanting Dick tied down, forced to stay near a sick, crippled, bed-ridden boy who couldn't do anything; who could never do anything again except perhaps lurch around on crutches, and sit in a wheel chair, and, of course, swim. It was only his legs that were useless, and when he was a little stronger he would be able to swim with his arms, and they said he could even use his legs in swimming, too. But all the same, he would never be good for much; and Dick said she was pretty, and probably she liked good times, parties and dances and fishing trips and travelling. And naturally she wouldn't ever love him as Dick did.

Maybe Dick would leave him here among strangers — who were as nice as they could be, of course — and take her home to Boston, take her next summer to Back of the Moon, take her fishing at Anticosti, take her with him to all the places to which he and Danny had planned to go. That would be pretty terrible, but he mustn't let them know he minded. Just because he was crippled, that didn't mean he had any right to boss their two lives. He would send them away to have their good times together, just as he had sent Dick away this summer.

Only perhaps when he was stronger he could sometimes go with them and not be too much of a bother. He would be able to walk on crutches by then, and perhaps after college he could become a writer, like Dick. You didn't have to be able to walk, to write books.

During the next two or three days Danny convinced himself that he could avoid hindering their happiness. No one wanted an invalid hung around his neck all the time, and he certainly didn't want to be a burden to them. They would be happy, and so would he.

One evening a telegram announced they would arrive next day. As long as the hour of their coming had been uncertain, Danny had been able to think pretty clearly and to plan how gladly he would greet them, so that not even Dick should guess the terror he had felt; but now in the imminence of their arrival he was just plain scared again! If she were the sort of girl some men thought beautiful, all made up, with red fingernails and a red mouth, it would be pretty awful. During the daylight hours before they came, he lay still, trembling terribly, perspiring, cold with lonely terror of the unknown; and when at last he heard Dick's voice along the corridor, heard them coming nearer and nearer his door, he shut his eyes tight, dreadfully afraid that he was going to cry; and he did not open his eyes again till they were in the room.

Then he saw Dick, and instantly the fear all went out of him; for Dick looked so well, fit and lean and strong; and Dick's eyes were clear and bright, and his whole face was different, glowing with a transfiguring peace and content. Then Dick bent over him, saying huskily, 'Hi, Danny!' and leaning down to kiss him; and Danny flung his arms around Dick's neck and hugged him tight, and they were both laughing with tears in their eyes, Danny's small body straining up to Dick's; and oh, but Dick felt good in his arms!

Then Dick said: 'And here she is, Danny!' He still held Danny with one arm, sitting on the edge of Danny's bed, and with the other hand he caught hers and drew her near. 'This is Ellen, Danny.'

Danny looked at her, suddenly shy, conscious of the fact that he was in his nightgown, swept by the modest embarrassment of which only a boy of thirteen is capable. She was so wonderfully beautiful, just as Dick had said; but Danny was terribly afraid she would make a fuss over him, call him, 'You poor boy,' or kiss him or gush over him or something. But she didn't! She just held out her hand and said, 'Hi, Danny!' exactly as Dick had done, and he gripped her hand gratefully, and said: 'Good morning, Ellen.' And he smiled a little, and she smiled; and he knew at once that she was all right, and that he was going to love her just as much as Dick did.

- II -

That winter was for Danny so brimming with happiness that there was a singing in him all day long. Love and tender care surrounded him, and each day brought or seemed to bring some small measure of new strength to his wasted legs. He gained victories in the battle to recapture as much of life as he could ever hope to seize; and in addition he could watch and share in the enriching happiness which Dick and Ellen found together. Just to see them was like swallowing a great draft of delicious, warming wine. They seemed to shine. Their eyes were bright and clear, the whites faintly tinged with blue; their smooth cheeks were full and glowing; their heads were high and laughter sang in their tones and in their every word. They walked together through the world as though the world were theirs and all desired things in it; and Danny took Ellen into his heart to share Dick's place there, because she and Dick were so clearly one.

It was as Dick had promised it would be. There were three of them now, and life was twice as much fun as when there had been only two.

Dick was working again, absorbed once more in the novel which he had laid aside when Danny fell ill and to which since then he had not turned at all. To it he gave every morning; but Ellen came to Danny as early as the routine of his treatment would permit and stayed with him till Dick appeared. Then they were all a while together, till Dick took Ellen away to lunch. In the afternoons, as soon as Danny was well enough, and if the day were fine, they drove for hours; and they were sometimes grave and serious together, having long talk of people and of places, of passions and of power, of the thoughts in a man's head and of the serenity that underlay the scurry of the world. But on other days they were gay and jolly, talking nonsense and laughing all together, not because what they said was particularly funny, but because they were happy and this happiness could become a merry madness with no sense in it at all.

When Ellen and Danny were alone, she asked him many questions about Dick, as though she could never hear enough of him she loved; and Danny liked nothing better than to talk to her endlessly about this big brother of his, searching back through his life under her hungry questions for every smallest memory. More than once he said laughingly: 'Gosh, you just want to know all about him, don't you?' and she nodded, smiling, her eyes shining.

'M-hm,' she assented, through closed lips. 'Yes, I do. I'm jealous, you see! I'm terribly jealous of all the years when I didn't know Richard, and of all the people who did know him then, and of everything he did and said and thought from the very first, when he was a baby. So now tell me. . . .'

And she winnowed his memory with a wind of questions. Danny had heard his mother tell anecdotes of Dick's childhood, and he had to repeat them all to Ellen now. She wished to know what Dick had looked like when he was a baby and a little boy; and Danny had seen pictures of him and tried to describe them, and he promised to find these old photographs when they all went back to Boston together. She asked about their house in Boston, and about the cabin at Back of the Moon; and Danny told her how beautiful the lake was, and he told her about Leick who always took care of him and Dick there, and he told her about the trout brook that flowed into the lake, and about the great trout which the lake itself occasionally yielded, if you knew just where to drop your fly, above the spring hole where the water was icy cold. Her appetite for these details was insatiable.

'I bet you just ask so many questions because you know I love to talk about Dick,' he said one day, and she answered with a laughing intensity:

'No! I don't do it for you. I do it for myself! I want every bit of him, of his whole life! I want to have it all!'

But they did not always talk about Dick. She told him about herself, and about her father, and about all the things they had used to do together; and she might read to him for hours on end. Her low musical tones were sweet and pleasing to his ear, so that sometimes he forgot to listen to what she read, content to watch her, to watch the sun in her hair and glinting on her cheek, to watch her lips move as she shaped the words, and her breast stir with her easy breathing, and the way her hair lay across her brow. Sometimes she caught him at this, and laughingly protested that he was not listening; and he grinned redly and confessed: 'I forgot to! Just looking at you is more fun than any book.' He thought he could never have imagined anyone so completely beautiful and so altogether charming as she was.

These two began to have small secrets, plans designed for Dick's pleasure and delight, which they concerted between them and perfected till the time came to astonish him with some wonderful surprise. Thus when Danny began to practice on his crutches they did not tell Dick, till one day Danny, already up and dressed and ready when they heard Dick coming, went proudly on his crutches to meet Dick at the door; and Dick was so surprised that for a moment he could not speak, and his eyes filled, and he and Danny and Ellen all had a good laughing cry together! There were other such surprises, though there were none so big as that one. Danny's strength, in arms and body, was slowly returning, and he now swam regularly in the pool; and one day he and Ellen planned that next summer at Back of the Moon, if the doctors would let him go there, he would practice till he was strong and then some day he would swim clear across the lake! They decided not to tell Dick beforehand, but just do it and surprise him.

There was only one break in that happy winter. In February, Mrs. Berent and Ruth came south to spend some time at Sea Island; and Dick and Ellen decided to go down for a week end with them. Danny, when they asked his consent, felt a secret pang; but he stifled it. He must never let them see that he was unhappy when they went away. So he told them to go, to stay as long as they wished; and Dick asked doubtfully:

'Are you sure you mean it, youngster? I hate leaving you even for a day; and if you feel the same way about having us go, just say the word and we'll stay right here!'

– Danny hesitated, and he was tempted; but then he saw that Ellen wanted to go, so he laughed at Dick and said jocosely: 'Nuts to you! I can get along without you, all right! Don't think you're so darned important! Give them my love. I'll bet they're swell!' He was as convincing as possible, and he saw the relief in Ellen's eyes, though Dick's were thoughtful still.

They had expected to be three days gone, but Dick telephoned Monday morning to ask whether it was all right for them to stay on another day or two, and Danny said of course it was. Yet he reflected miserably, after Dick had hung up: 'Maybe he'll call up again and say they want to stay even longer. Maybe they'll stay away a week, or a month. Maybe they won't ever come back at all!'

But he told himself he was a darned fool to think such things; and sure enough, on Wednesday evening they returned, brown from the sun, and Danny thought they were the two most beautiful and wonderful people he had ever seen.

In March Ruth and Mrs. Berent, driving north on a leisurely schedule, stopped over for a week end at the hotel; and Danny found Mrs. Berent and her sharp tongue tremendously funny. He liked Ruth too.

'She's not as pretty as you are, of course,' he told Ellen after they were gone. 'But she certainly is swell! You can feel a sort of warmness in her, feel her liking you. Dick likes her a lot, doesn't he?'

'Yes, of course,' Ellen agreed. 'Ruth's sweet as she can be!' But he felt she was sorry he had liked Ruth, and he wondered why.

– III –

In the back of Danny's mind, as winter turned to spring and the early southern summer began to flow richly across the hills, lay a single question: Would he be well enough to go this summer with

Dick and Ellen to Back of the Moon? At first, he and Ellen had often talked about the camp there. Danny loved the place, and liked to tell her about it; but little by little, because he was thinking of it so constantly, and hoping so dreadfully that he could go with them, he put a seal on his lips and never spoke of it unless she or Dick led him to do so. He wanted to go to the lake more than he had ever wanted anything in the world. Everyone here was wonderful to him, and he was grateful to them, but it wasn't like being at home; and Back of the Moon, though they had never done more than spend there some of the summer months, was home to him much more truly than the house in Boston.

Yet no matter how much he wanted to go, if it were best for him to stay here he would stay and not complain and never let anyone know his longing. This was his determination and he held to it; and when Back of the Moon was mentioned he was careful not to allow his eagerness to appear.

Sometimes when they were all three together, Dick talked to Ellen about Back of the Moon, telling her its charms, describing the routine of their lives there; but as summer drew near, Dick and Ellen began to avoid the subject, and Danny knew this meant there was doubt whether he would be well enough to go. He felt that he was running a race against an opponent whom he could not see, so that he could never be sure whether he were ahead or behind, gaining or losing ground. The worst of it was that this was a race in which the harder you tried, the more poorly you ran. To get better, it was necessary to be calm and serene, and to do what he was told, neither more nor less; and this was hard when he felt all the time that he must hurry, hurry, hurry!

Then one day when he and she were alone together, Ellen brought up the subject which filled his thoughts so constantly. 'I want to talk to you about something, Danny dear,' she said tenderly. He knew what was in her mind even before she went on: 'It's about this summer.' He did not speak, and she took his hands in hers, leaning near him, and explained: 'You see, Richard is homesick for Back of the Moon. He's worked hard all winter here, but now he's beginning to bog down. The novel isn't going so well. He needs to go back there where he loves to be, to go at it fresh and renewed again.'

Danny nodded. 'Sure,' he agreed, and kept his voice as steady as he could. 'Dick always got more work done there than anywhere else!'

'But you see,' she confessed. 'He hates leaving you here, so far away; and Doctor Mason isn't sure the life there would be the best thing for you.'

Danny wetted his lips. 'I thought I was getting along pretty well.'

'You are, darling,' she assured him. 'But that's a rugged life up there — and a hard trip in. You'd have trouble getting up and down those steep paths on your crutches. Richard says he and Leick can carry you, but I've told Doctor Mason about the place, how far it is from the nearest town, and what it's like after you get there.' He wished she hadn't told Doctor Mason that. 'Richard doesn't realize how hard it will be for you,' she went on. 'And how hard it will be for him and Leick, taking care of you.'

'I guess it would be pretty bad, all right.' He spoke in careful tones.

'Of course,' she added, 'Richard hates to leave you, thinks you'd be unhappy here alone; but I know how brave you are, and I know how you love Richard, and I know you want him to do what's best for him and for his work.'

'Sure!'

She kissed him fondly. 'You're sweet, Danny! If it turns out that you'd better stay here, you'll make Richard go, just the same, won't you? And we'll all be together again in the fall, when we come back down here.'

There was a lump like a rock in his throat, and a stinging in his eyes; but he said steadily: 'Sure! I'm fine here. This is the place for me, all right, till I get so I'm not such a bother to people.'

She told him he was wonderful, brave and strong as a man; but he was glad she did not kiss him again, for if she had, he would certainly have cried. There was a wail of terror in his heart; and he told himself hopelessly that if Dick and Ellen, who were all his world, went away and left him here, he would surely die.

After that day, no matter how hard he tried, he could not be as jolly and as gay as he wanted to be for Dick. Then one day Doctor Mason came to him and talked with him for an hour, wisely and gently, probing with delicate questions. He was a man full of understanding, as much concerned with the minds of his patients as with their bodies. Danny, thinking of Ellen, leaned backward to be fair in admitting the hardships he might face at Back of the Moon, till the doctor said in tones curiously stern:

'You mustn't feel that Mrs. Harland doesn't want you with them there, Danny.'

'Oh, I don't,' Danny cried. 'I know she's just thinking what's best for me.'

The doctor smiled, and he led Danny to tell him about the cabin and the lake, and about the things he and Dick had used to do there; and as Danny talked his eyes began to shine again. Doctor Mason watched him and listened to him and made him talk on and on, and once he said:

'You and Dick have always had a lot of fun together, haven't you?'

'We sure have,' Danny agreed. 'We've hardly ever been separated since my mother died.'

The doctor nodded, his eyes almost grim. 'I don't think it would be good medicine to separate you now. No matter what anyone says!' Danny thought he seemed to be talking to himself. 'And as for Back of the Moon, you're better just from talking about it.' He asked with a quizzical smile: 'Suppose I made you stay in bed, take a good rest for a few days? Would you mind?'

'No, sir,' Danny told him. 'I'll do whatever you say.' His heart pounded with happy understanding.

That afternoon he heard Dick and Ellen arrive, heard their voices in the corridor; but then one of the nurses spoke to them in a low tone, and instead of coming straight to Danny they went away from him toward Doctor Mason's office. A little later Danny heard them coming, heard Dick walking fast and eagerly; and his throat filled with a deep excitement, and then they appeared in the door.

Ellen stayed there, watching these two; and Danny saw her over Dick's shoulder and he had never seen her look as she was looking now. There was something puzzlingly like anger in her eyes. But then he forgot her, for Dick said in a great voice:

'Well, Danny, old man, take care of yourself, this next week. Store up a lot of strength! Because a week from today we're starting for Back of the Moon!'

Danny's eyes filled. 'Oh golly, golly, golly!' he whispered in breathless happiness, grinning from ear to ear. Dick laughed aloud, and then Ellen came to Dick's side, her eyes now alight with fondness, and she said tenderly:

'Isn't that wonderful, Danny dear?'

5

DURING those months — almost a year — at Warm Springs, Harland was like a man intoxicated. Ellen fitted herself to his moods as a dog does to its master's wishes, eager to do with him whatever he wished to do, equally happy to be idle with him at his desire. He discovered new wonders in her every day. Her beauty was a continuing delight, yet even in their richest hours, with the impersonal mind of the novelist he sometimes thought their rôles were reversed; that she was the eager lover, he the consenting mistress; that her passionate abandonments were more profound than his. She might be lost in ardent raptures while he was almost calm, and to see her thus moved filled him with a proud tenderness.

She recognized this difference, said more than once, after a lavish yielding: 'I love you so much more than you love me, Richard. If you ever stopped loving me, I'd die. And I'd want to die!' This was true of her, yet he knew — with a faint sense of guilt — that it was not true of him. Most men, he suspected, were or might be self-sufficient; it was women who lived to the utmost only through surrender — which was at the same time possession.

His life after their marriage took on a new dimension, and — the creative instinct in him again awake — he turned to his work with a keen zest he had never known, and with a fecundity of invention so greatly increased that it was as though he had acquired a sixth sense. He perceived in the pattern of human life complexities he had not hitherto suspected, and he began to com-

prehend emotional depths which till now had seemed to him unreal, theatrical, factitious. His hours at his desk were filled with
a high excitement, his hours with her were wholly contenting.
Only rarely did any shadow cloud their days. Once she asked, as
though wishing to be reassured: 'Am I all right with Danny,
Richard?'

'Wonderful,' he assured her.

'Sometimes I just hate him,' she confessed, only half-jesting.
'He's had so much of you that I can never have.'

He laughed teasingly. 'Ellen the Desirous! Never satisfied.'
Then, suddenly husky: 'When I watch you with him, I'm always
imagining what you'll be like with our own sons.'

She asked, her eyes searching his: 'You want a son, don't you,
Richard?'

'Some day, of course. Don't you?'

'Some day, yes.' Then she caught him fiercely close. 'But not
soon, Richard!' she whispered. 'I want you all to myself for a
while. No one else! Just us two! Just you and me!'

He held her strongly. 'Just us two!' he assented. 'And, of
course, Danny.'

'Oh, of course!' She spoke without emphasis. There was often
this disturbing flatness in her voice when they discussed Danny.

'We're all he's got in the world, you know,' he reminded her in
steady warning. 'We've got to stand by!'

She laughed and kissed him. 'Don't worry, darling. I love him
as you do, my dear.'

– II –

A later incident made him remember the brief misgiving he had
felt that day. They had left Danny for the Sea Island week end
with her mother and Ruth, and he found Mrs. Berent's tongue as
sharp as ever. 'Well, Mr. Harland, you don't look as though
you'd suffered any yet,' she commented, when they arrived, and
Harland laughed and said:

'No. Being married to this daughter of yours has been pretty tough sometimes, but so far I've been able to stand it.' He dropped his arm affectionately around Ellen's waist, and she clasped his hand with hers, pressing his against her side.

'I haven't begun to bite any pieces out of him yet,' she assured her mother; and the older woman made a stubborn sound.

'Time enough!' she declared. 'You will!'

She told them at dinner that evening that Quinton had arrived at the ranch a few hours after their departure. 'He came breathing out threatenings and slaughter,' she declared. 'If you're wise, Ellen, you'll not cross his path again.'

Harland was troubled. 'Why didn't he answer your wire, I wonder?' he asked Ellen, and he saw her mother look at her sharply.

'He did, Richard,' Ellen said at once. 'Don't you remember? His answer came while you and Mr. Robie were off after the preacher.'

Harland started to speak, then held his tongue; yet he felt Mrs. Berent's sharp eyes upon him, and when he and Ellen were alone he said: 'See here, Ellen, you didn't tell me about any telegram from Quinton.'

She smiled. 'Poor darling! And I made you back me up when I fibbed to Mother, didn't I? Did your New England conscience hurt? Mother's always been a troublemaker, Richard. We'll have to teach her not to interfere.'

'What did Quinton go out there for?'

'To forbid the banns, I suppose! Russ is a hard loser. Forgive me? I couldn't have him bothering us. I'd made up my mind I wanted you, you see; so talk would have done no good.' Seeing his doubt, she came to kiss him, crying: 'I'd do worse than lie to keep you all mine and always mine, my dear! Don't ever blame me for loving you, will you?'

So she won him to quick forgetfulness, and the days were bright. With Ruth they rode the beaches and the island trails, Mrs. Berent preferring a sunny corner by the pool. The bridle paths ran through groves of ancient live oaks hung with sweeping scarves of warm gray moss which might after a night of rain show pale green. Yellow jasmine spangled the forest with gold, and there were flowers everywhere, and they spent hours exploring the hidden ways. Harland, now that he began to know Ruth better, no longer thought of her as plain, though of course she was not beautiful as Ellen was beautiful. She rode, he found to his surprise, as well as Ellen did; but while Ellen's horse, when they returned to the stable, was dark with sweat and flecked with foam, Ruth's was always cool and unwearied.

One night there was dancing at the dinner hour. When he took a turn with Ruth — she danced, he found, as well as she rode — she said: 'I want you to know, Dick, that Mother and I are ever so glad about you and Ellen.'

'I know,' he agreed, thinking she meant that he need not be disturbed by Mrs. Berent's habitual tone. 'Your mother's bark is worse than her bite.'

'She was doubtful at first,' Ruth confessed. 'But she's content now that she's seen you together.'

'I was doubtful myself at first,' he admitted, with a chuckle. 'I was a bachelor and liked it. But now I know I was only half-alive.'

'Ellen is sweet, really,' she assured him. 'I don't need to tell you that. But she's strong, and till she learned to love you, she never — yielded to anyone. She's nicer than ever now.'

'There never was anyone like her,' he agreed. 'You should see her with Danny.'

'She loves him because you do,' she assented.

The night Harland telephoned to Danny to say they would prolong their stay, Mrs. Berent asked many questions about the youngster, and Ellen told her the routine of their days.

'I'm with him all morning,' she explained, 'while Richard works. Danny's such a dear, lovable boy. Then Richard joins us for the afternoons, and sometimes we have lunch together, and sometimes if it's fine we take long drives, the three of us.'

Mrs. Berent asked shrewdly: 'Doesn't she ever let you and Danny have a minute alone, Mr. Harland?'

Harland realized, with a disturbed surprise, that he had not in fact been alone with Danny since he and Ellen were married. 'We like to be all together,' he told her, evading a direct reply; yet he wondered whether Danny did sometimes wish they might have an hour to themselves. Then he felt Ellen watching him and met her eyes and smiled. 'We wouldn't have it any other way,' he declared.

'You never will have it any other way,' Mrs. Berent assured him. 'Ellen will see to that. She'll never let you out of her sight again.' They laughed at her together, but Harland, though he smiled with them, brushed his hand across his face with the gesture of a man who, walking through the forest at dawn, feels laid across his cheeks the tiny, clinging strands which spiders during the night have spun.

– III –

Spring came drifting northward, flooding these southern lands with flowers, and on moonlit nights the mockingbirds were singing. Harland wrote to Leick to make all ready for them at Back of the Moon, and he told Ellen more and more about the spot so dear to him.

'But I'm worried about how you're going to like it,' he admitted. 'It's rather primitive, you know.'

'I'll love it. I'll always love any place that means so much to you.'

'You'll like Leick,' he promised, and he told her something about the years when he and Leick from spring to fall had been inseparable.

'I'll probably hate him,' she laughingly declared. 'He's known you so much longer than I. I shall make him tell me all about you.'

'Well, you'll have chance enough. Up there, I get up at daylight, work till noon; so you'll have Leick to yourself all morning. Leick and Danny.'

She spoke slowly. 'Have you talked to Doctor Mason about Danny's going, Richard? I'm not sure he wouldn't be better here, for a few months more.'

'Oh no! He loves it there as I do. He'll have all the swimming he wants, of course; and you can help him with his exercises.'

'What does Doctor Mason think?'

'I haven't asked him.' He laughed in forced confidence. 'If he doesn't agree, we'll take Danny anyway!'

She linked her arm in his. 'Don't be too disappointed, Richard, if it seems best to leave Danny here.'

He knew she might be right, and to hide his own fears he spoke curtly. 'There's no question of leaving him here. If he can't go — why neither can we, that's all.' Then, realizing that his tone had been abrupt: 'But I'm sure he'll be able to go, Ellen. Don't worry about it.'

'Oh, I won't,' she promised. 'If Danny is better off here, you and I will stay, of course. Don't consider me at all. Last summer here was really quite comfortable. I didn't mind it much.'

She was so patiently submissive that he exploded. 'Damn it, of course I'll consider you! But we have to consider Danny too!' Then when she did not speak he regretted his tone and said cheerfully: 'You'll find I'm a different man at Back of the Moon. The trammels of civilization — whatever they are — fall away. I go pagan up there.'

'Men are all pagans,' she assented, nodding. 'They love to get off by themselves and pretend to be savages. But I've some pagan in me, too, my dear.' She drew his head down, kissed him with a tender ferocity: 'I wish there were going to be just the two of us, this first summer there. I'd be as pagan as you choose!'

A few days later — he postponed this as long as he could, dreading what the answer might be — Harland asked Doctor Mason's opinion.

'Well, I'm not sure,' the other confessed. 'Mrs. Harland's told me about the place. It seems pretty rugged for a boy on crutches.'

Harland resented this advantage she had taken, forestalling what he might say to the physician. 'She's never been there,' he pointed out. 'So she doesn't know what it's like.'

'Tell me about it,' the doctor suggested.

Harland did so, explaining how easy it would be to make Danny comfortable. 'Talk to him yourself,' he urged. 'He knows better than either you or I what it will be like for him.'

Doctor Mason nodded. 'I will.' He smiled. 'Probably Mrs. Harland sees it from the feminine point of view.'

Harland said: 'Well, she's a woman!'

'She put it pretty strongly,' the other remarked, his eyes veiled, his tone conveying an unspoken criticism. He added a saving word. 'But I'm sure she's only thinking what's best for Danny.'

'Why, naturally!' Harland assented, coloring; and he spoke strongly. 'She's devoted to him!' He wondered as he spoke why he felt it necessary to defend Ellen.

'Of course,' Doctor Mason agreed. He rose, nodding in dismissal. 'Well, we don't need to decide the question yet. I'll talk to him.'

So in the end it was Danny himself who cast the deciding vote. When Harland heard the verdict, he was too jubilant to wonder whether Ellen was as pleased as he. He wrote to old Mrs. Huston, who had served his mother and father and who since Mrs. Harland's death was in fact mistress of the house on Chestnut Street, to expect them in mid-June; and when they arrived there she greeted Danny with tearful affection, putting him at once to bed, tending him devotedly. To Ellen she gave a welcome so restrained that Ellen laughingly told Harland she felt like an intruder.

'She couldn't disapprove of me any more obviously if I were a light-o'-love you'd picked up on the street somewhere,' she declared.

'She's jealous,' he explained. 'She's ruled the roost so long! But if you want to win her, just get sick. She loves taking care of people. You see how she is with Danny.'

'We might leave him here with her,' she suggested, her tone light enough to make it clear that she was joking; but she added: 'Even the trip north tired him. Maybe it would be wiser if we stayed here in Boston with him?'

'He wouldn't let us. He knows how much Back of the Moon means to me.'

'We might leave him in Bar Harbor,' she proposed. 'With Mother and Ruth. He likes Ruth, and she'd be happy taking care of him, and we could see him often.'

He said at a tangent, resenting her persistence: 'You're always so ready to turn things over to Ruth! As though she were a maid of all work, or something.'

She nodded indifferently. 'She's adopted, you know,' she explained. 'She was Father's brother's daughter, and he died. She's lived with us since she was a baby, and of course Mother's made a regular slave out of her. She could take care of Danny all right.'

He was astonished at this revelation, yet it seemed to make clear many things in Mrs. Berent's attitude toward Ruth, and in Ellen's, which had puzzled him. His suddenly awakened sympathy for Ruth sharpened his irritation. 'I see,' he commented. 'Well, we won't dump Danny on her hands, anyway! He's our job, Ellen.'

So she was silenced. On the way to Back of the Moon they stayed a night at Bar Harbor. After dinner, Ellen led Harland out of doors, and she showed him the wide gardens and the lawn sloping to the rocky shore, and the small study and workshop which Professor Berent had built many years ago on a knoll above the water. In the workroom, Harland watched her go to and fro, lifting things and putting them down again, seeming to find happiness in thus touching objects her father had touched. He saw a jar labelled 'Arsenic' and felt, as normal persons will, a cold shiver of distaste. 'Why don't you throw that away?' he suggested. 'Someone might get hold of it.'

'No one ever comes here but me — and sometimes Ruth, to dust things,' she assured him. 'It's perfectly harmless, as long as you don't swallow it.'

'I've always heard that even breathing the dust might kill you,' he remembered. 'Didn't people get arsenic poisoning from wallpapers or something?'

'Fairy tales!' she said smilingly, and they turned out of doors again. The fine moon had risen and the night was warm, and they lay on the turf above the sea and watched the moon across the water, and the slow surf surging against the rocks below made the ground on which they lay faintly tremble. Harland was conscious of a deep intangible disturbance in him, an emotional anticipation like that which one may feel before the curtain rises at the opera, when the orchestra sets the key for the tragedy to follow. The night was fine, the moon was bright, Ellen was lovely and tender here beside him; yet there was a vibration in the very earth itself, transmitted from the rocks on which the long swells beat, which seemed to warn him that this sweet and stable world was insecure.

They stayed long there above the sea, their low tones mingling. Once Harland suggested that they go to say good night to Danny, but Ellen would not.

'Just forget everyone else but me for once, won't you?' she pleaded, and she said in a low tone: 'There's never been a single day — except maybe just at the very first — not a single day, and hardly even a single hour since we were married when you've thought of no one in the world but me.'

'I don't have to think of you, dearest! You're a part of me. The biggest and best part of me.' He meant to reassure her, yet there was a profound intensity in her words which were inadequately met by his inanity.

'You don't understand how much I love you, Richard,' she said gravely. 'You'll never understand how jealously I love you. I hate sharing your thoughts with anyone else at all. Even with Danny!' The hot passion in her tones was like the first rumble of a distant storm.

'You've been wonderful to him,' he insisted, uneasily clinging to the commonplace.

'I know! Oh, I know!' She drew closer to him till she lay pressed against his side, and he dropped his arm across her waist, turning toward her, tugging her closer. 'It's ever so good of me, too!' she assured him lightly. 'Because I'm so jealous of him I'm ready to scratch his eyes out all the time!'

He laughed as she was laughing, and he said honestly: 'I know, Ellen. You're swell about it. I know it's tough for you, but —

he has no one but us. He's shut off from all his old friends. We've got to be his whole world for a while.'

She asked after a moment, in a small voice, her face buried in his shoulder: 'Will you send him away to school in the fall?'

'Yes, if he wants to go. He'll want to go on to college with the boys he's always known.'

'Boarding school?'

'He's always gone to day school. He'll probably live at home, at least till he goes to college.'

'I'll be good to him, Richard,' she promised, turning for his kiss. 'As good as I know how.' He held her close and gratefully, and the moon was silver on the sea.

- IV -

At breakfast Mrs. Berent was in an unaccountably malicious humor. She told them that Russ Quinton had called upon her a few days before to ask for news of Ellen. 'He was elected prosecuting attorney, last fall,' she said. 'He's very proud of himself!'

'I can't imagine Russ in politics,' Ellen declared. 'With his temper he makes so many enemies.'

'Probably he thinks he can work off his bad temper by sending people to jail,' Mrs. Berent suggested, and she added: 'He hasn't forgiven you, Ellen. He makes a joke of it; but if you're wise you'll never give him a chance to get even.'

'I'm not planning to murder anyone, Mother,' Ellen said evenly. 'If that's what you mean.'

Harland chuckled. 'This sounds like a meeting of hardened criminals, discussing their enemy, the law,' he protested, and turned the talk to other things.

After breakfast they set out for Back of the Moon. They took the familiar road through the forest to Cherryfield, and turned north then for ten or twelve miles — the way was rough and rutted, and Richard drove slowly, easing the car over every irregularity — and so came to Joe Severin's farm, where the wood road to the camp began and where Leick was waiting.

On the way, Harland at the wheel listened smilingly to Danny's eager and excited voice as the youngster pointed out to Ellen familiar sights and scenes; and again and again Danny appealed to him for confirmation of some statement he had made, crying: 'Remember, Dick?' or: 'Isn't that so, Dick?' or: 'We did, Dick, didn't we?'

Harland always agreed, till Ellen said gaily: 'You're in a conspiracy, you two; just a team of great big liars backing each other up! I don't know which of you is worse.' And she told Harland: 'You're as bad as he is, Richard. You act about two years old.'

'I warned you,' he reminded her. 'I'm a different man up here.'

'I don't want you to be a different man,' she assured him. 'You suit me very well as you are.'

They turned into Joe Severin's farmyard — Harland always parked his car in Joe's shed when he went in to camp — and Leick and Joe himself and Joe's two sons, brawny young men who had near-by farms and families of their own, were waiting to meet them. Joe was a little Frenchman with the longest legs and the shortest body that were ever mismatched to make a man. He was not much more than five feet tall, but his shoulders were tremendously wide and he had a merry mouth and twinkling eyes. His wife, beaming on them from the kitchen doorway, was as tall as her sons, with the flaxen hair and the clear complexion of her Scandinavian blood.

Harland looked first to Leick, for it was almost two years since they had met; but his first greeting was for Joe and the two tall sons, before — keeping the best for the last — he turned to Leick and their hands clasped in the silent pressure of long understanding. Danny, shouting with glee, not waiting for help, launched himself out of the car and took his crutches, and Joe turned to touch him — softly as a woman — on the shoulder and to say how he had grown in these two years, and Leick went to Danny too; and then Harland saw Ellen still in the car, holding herself aloof, watching his proud delight at this reunion with old friends, her brows faintly narrowed in a frown; and he called Joe and Leick to meet her, and chuckled inwardly at the quick appreciation of her beauty in Joe's eyes. With Ellen and Danny and Leick, the three people dearest in the world to him, now at last brought together, he was a happy man.

He left them by the car and went to give Mrs. Severin a hug and a smacking kiss, and she insisted that they stop long enough for a bite — a cup of coffee, oatmeal, a hot doughnut — while Joe and Leick hitched the horses to the buckboard. So Harland led Ellen proudly indoors, and Danny was nimble on his crutches, his cheeks bright, his eyes dancing with happiness. For a while they stayed in the immaculate and sunny kitchen, and Harland saw regretfully that with Ellen Mrs. Severin was not at ease; that Ellen too was restrained. He left them together, hoping Ellen would know how to win the other woman, returning presently with a secret excitement in his tone to call to Danny:

'Come along, m'lord! Your carriage waits!'

As Danny came out, Joe's sons brought from the barn a comfortable armchair on each side of which two iron rings had been bolted to hold spruce carrying poles; and Danny, when he saw it, shouted with delight. 'Oh, that's swell, Dick!' he cried. But his eyes filled even while he smiled, and Harland knew that this more than anything that had gone before had brought home to Danny his own helplessness.

'Try it for size,' he directed, and Danny took his seat and declared the chair was perfect, and Leick met Harland's eyes and wiped his mouth with his hand and Harland knew that Leick too understood Danny's sudden shocking realization of his disability; and he remembered how in the past Danny had taken the trail from here to Back of the Moon at a jog trot, tirelessly pacing off the miles, and he swallowed hard.

To cheer Danny and himself he hurried their departure. He would drive the buckboard — or walk and lead the horses, if the road became too rough. 'You can ride or walk as you prefer,' he told Ellen. She elected at first to ride with him, and they set out, the four men carrying Danny in the chair and making the pace.

Harland, once they were under way, forgot his sadness of the moment that was past; yet he felt restraint in Ellen still. 'Does it scare you?' he asked gently. 'It's fine when we get there.'

'I don't think I'd quite realized how hard it will be for Danny,' she said. 'There'll be so many things we'll do together which he can't do.'

'We'll just do things we can all do,' he assured her. 'I've sent up an outboard motor and one of those light speedboats for him to run around the lake in. I haven't told him yet. It's a surprise. And he can paddle a canoe, and we'll concentrate our good times around the lake shore, so he can share them.'

She looked at him briefly. 'I suppose we can order our lives to his,' she agreed, and added: 'It's as though we were all three — crippled, isn't it? Because he goes on crutches, so must we.'

He felt the bitterness in her tones and spoke in quiet warning: 'We'll have to be careful not to let him think he's cramping our style.'

'And of course,' she suggested hopefully, 'if we wanted to take a trip — go to New Brunswick after salmon, for instance — we could leave him with Leick and he'd be all right.'

He hesitated, said slowly: 'I'm afraid I'll never go fishing without Leick. He's a habit with me.'

'He and Danny both!' she commented in a dry tone.

'And now you,' he reminded her, refusing to hear the rancor in her voice. 'Three mighty happy habits, it seems to me.'

They left the buckboard, after five or six miles, at the spring where the wood road ended, and went on afoot. The trail followed the stream's cascading course upward toward the pond from which it flowed, and Harland pointed out places where Leick had widened or improved the path, to make it easier for the chair to pass.

'And he's done the same thing at camp,' he explained. 'Put in some zigzags, eased the steep pitches, so Danny can get from the cabin down to the boathouse on his crutches. Maybe not just at first, but when he's stronger.'

'I can help him, of course,' she agreed, in a flat submission; but he was too happy to heed. From the top of the first ridge he pointed out to her the roof of the cabin on the flank of the lofty hill ahead and still a fair mile away.

'You can just make out the break in the trees where the sunny ledges are,' he said, and told her where to look. 'And there's a high rocky shoulder on the northeast face of the hill, not far above the cabin, where you can see all over the pond, see for miles.'

They were well ahead of the others when they reached the foot of the pond and the boathouse beside the dam, built of logs and two stories high. 'I've a study upstairs there where I work,' Harland explained. 'But we won't stop to inspect that now.' The cabin was a hundred yards, and a hundred feet of altitude, above the water; a long, low structure to which — the freshly peeled spruce logs were evidence of this — a new wing had been added. The central living room ran from front to back, and the kitchen and storeroom were on the northeast side. Their bedroom and Danny's were side by side in the new wing, with a screened porch for sleeping in the open air when the weather made it more pleasant to do so.

Before the men arrived with Danny, Harland had time to show Ellen the little there was to see. 'I had Leick build this new wing,' he explained. 'Danny and I had just the one bedroom, of course.' He looked at her hopefully. 'Like it?'

'It's very nice,' she assented in a flat voice. The wall between their room and Danny's was a single thickness of smoothed boards. 'If Danny wakes in the night and needs us, we can hear the slightest sound.'

He understood what she did not say. 'It's pretty close quarters, of course,' he admitted apologetically. 'We won't have much privacy. But we'll be out of doors most of the time when the weather's fine.'

'Where does Leick sleep?' she asked, like one making polite conversation. 'Off the kitchen, where we can hear him too?'

He tried to laugh her out of this humor. 'Now, now!' He put his arm around her; but she freed herself, moving toward the door, and he said: 'No, he has a room down in the boathouse.'

'Here they come,' she remarked. He heard the voices of the men outside. 'I'll put Danny right to bed.'

Harland followed her out to meet the others, watching her with unhappy eyes. He had looked forward to their arrival here with the eagerness of a boy, anticipating Danny's delight, tasting beforehand the happiness of showing Ellen this spot which meant so much to him; but now her disappointment was so plain.

She and Leick helped Danny from his chair; and despite his insistence that he was not tired, they led him indoors. Harland stayed to thank Joe Severin and his sons for their help; and Joe must have read his troubled thoughts, for the little man said reassuringly: 'Let her get settled and used to it here and she'll like it fine.'

Harland was astonishingly grateful. Joe and his sons departed, and Leick presently came out and said, looking toward the cabin: 'Time she gets to work fixing things to suit her, she'll feel different.' Both Joe and Leick had read her well, but Harland had learned long ago not to be surprised at the understanding hearts of simple men.

– v –

During the first days, Harland saw how skillfully Leick woke in Ellen the homemaking instinct which lies dormant in every woman. That first afternoon, the woodsman went to her with a question. 'I didn't put up any pegs in your bedroom, ma'am, because I didn't know just where you'd want them. What would you think of here behind the door?'

So she consulted with him, and when that problem was solved he proposed another, till she began to have ideas of her own. Leick, who with an axe, a draw shave, a ship auger, and a few nails could work miracles, placed shelves and pegs where she wished them to be, built a rustic table and some chairs, delighted her with his capacities. Harland let Leick work his magic upon her, remembering how often the other had solved for him problems which seemed insoluble; and he never made any comment to Ellen, suspecting that to do so might make her recognize her own surrender and fight against it. But more than once he spoke of her to Leick.

'She's happy here now all right,' he said, at the end of the first week, triumphantly.

'She is so,' Leick assented. 'Making over the place to suit makes it seem like her own. That's the way you get to like a place, or a man; doing things for them. We'll want to keep her busy.'

'She's wonderful, isn't she?' Harland's pride needed sharing.

Leick's eyes twinkled. 'She thinks you're hung to the moon.'

Harland said soberly: 'I know it. I've got a full-time job, living up to what she thinks of me.'

'It would suit her a lot better if there was just the two of you here,' Leick reminded him. 'It ain't any picnic for a pretty woman, hid away up here with two men and a lame boy, and no outside good times at all.'

Harland acknowledged that this was true; but he had no long misgivings, for their days soon settled into a pleasant routine. They rose at dawn, waked usually by the sounds Leick made in the kitchen; and Harland and Ellen raced down to the boathouse for an early dip in the cove, where morning mists might be curling up from the shallow water which in the cool dawnings seemed so much warmer than the air. By the time they returned, Leick would have helped Danny dress; and they breakfasted together, sometimes indoors, sometimes on the screened veranda which caught the early sun. Harland spent the mornings at his desk in the study above the boathouse; and Danny conscientiously made his way down to the wharf, using the easy grades of the new path, and grew stronger all the time. Usually he and Ellen in the late forenoon swam in the shallow cove; and when he was upborne by the buoyant water, his disabilities were no longer so obvious. If the day were fine, he swam again in the afternoon, Ellen and Harland with him. Sometimes they took canoe or rowboat — Harland had here two canoes and a flat-bottomed skiff which Leick had built to bring firewood from along the shore, as well as the frail speedboat to which the powerful outboard could be attached — and went exploring the lake. At its farther end, as distant as possible from the boathouse, there was a sandy beach so smooth and level that a hundred yards from shore the water was still no more than shoulder-deep, and they often chose to go there. Harland was a strong though not a skillful swimmer; but Ellen swam as easily and as beautifully as a seal, slim and graceful and completely at home in the water; and Harland and Danny watched her with an equal delight.

Sometimes they spent an afternoon sprawled together on a broad ledge beyond the cabin, talking little or not at all, baking in the sun, letting it touch them where it would; and Harland and Danny were soon brown as leather from head to heel, while Ellen's shoulders and legs and back acquired a warm and tawny hue which Harland thought delicious. At dusk they were always sleepy, and as often as not the late sunsets saw them already abed.

Harland was completely happy. Ellen seemed to him more beautiful than ever, and to touch her hand, to hear her voice, to meet her eyes could make his throat fill and his cheeks burn. She wore a sleepy, sultry indolence, smiling at him through half-closed eyes; and whenever he touched her she was warm as a sunned cat, and his days were rich with joy in her. Also, his work went well, and he was filled with a sense of good achievement. Often, after their noonday meal, he read to them what he had written. Danny had always approved what Harland wrote with an uncritical pride. Ellen was less interested, and she listened lazily, watching Harland with hungry eyes, so that if he looked up from his manuscript and met her glance his pulses quickened leapingly. Once, when this happened, he said in laughing accusation:

'You're not listening!'

'I'd lots rather watch you than listen to stories about other people,' she told him in teasing flattery. 'Did you know your ears wiggle when you read?'

Rarely she had comments, but they were always personalized, as though everything he wrote were directed at her. Thus once she said, drawling sleepily:

'You're one of those men who think women's place is in the

home, aren't you? Just good plain cooks? Is that what you want
me to be, Richard?'

He laughed, uneasy under her smiling mockery. 'Well, something besides just a cook!' he admitted.

She touched his hand. 'You're such a boy! See him blushing,
Danny! Mothers too? When I have a baby, will you be happy?'

'I'm happy now,' he assured her, and read on. He made one of
his characters remark that a man needed contact with his fellows
to toughen his fibre, and she said laughingly:

'You're a fine one to preach that, when you hide yourself away
here all summer long, see nobody at all.'

'Oh, a writer's different,' he argued. 'He needs to get away by
himself, to see things in perspective.'

'But mustn't he mingle with crowds to learn to know people?'

'I don't like crowds.' He chuckled. 'People in crowds seem to
me like perambulating eggs. I want to crack a shell here and
there and sample the meat inside.'

'You can't go around cracking human eggs, of course,' she
warned him. 'So often you find them soft-boiled. They'd spill all
over you.'

They had many such drowsy afternoons, talking slow talk together, so absorbed in each other that they sometimes forgot
Danny was listening. If he slept for a while, to compensate for
some unusual exertion, they slipped away like truants, wandering
through the forest or drifting quietly along shore in a canoe.
They liked to go without him to that beach at the pond's farther
end, and Ellen, as she had warned Harland long ago, could be as
pagan as he, so that sometimes as they sported in the clear, warm,
shallow water, their laughter rang through the still hot afternoons
till Leick, busy about his small tasks at the camp far away, might
hear. From these adventures they came demurely home, sleek
and serene.

But there were other hours when it seemed to Harland that a
cloud shadow passed ominously across their world, and there were
hours when he seemed to hear warning thunder far away. Once
when he had been reading aloud to them she said drily: 'Your
hero doesn't think much of women, does he?'

'He hasn't met the right one yet.'

'He'd better do it soon, if you expect women to read your book.'

'I thought women were interested in men?'

'That's what they tell men, but actually they're a lot more interested in other women.' She smiled. 'Poor darling, you don't know much about women, do you?'

'I'm learning,' he assured her. 'You teach me new things every day.'

She looked at him thoughtfully. 'You've a lot to learn,' she said.

He tried to laugh. 'Oh, I don't find women so mysterious!'

'You don't know enough about us — even about me — to know how little you know,' she told him, and there was no smile in her voice nor in her eyes. Harland, uneasy without reason, looked at Danny and saw the youngster watching her with a grave attention, as though trying to appraise her tone.

– VI –

The pond was crescent-shaped, curving around the base of the hill on the flank of which the cabin was set. The ground rose steeply for the first two hundred feet above the water, then ascended more gradually to a ridge that ran southwestward. From the northern base of the hill a narrow point of land, no more than two or three rods wide, littered with great boulders and grown thick with young spruces, extended half across the pond. Late in July, Danny swam from the cove inside that narrow point of land to the opposite shore. Ellen accompanied him in the flat-bottomed skiff, and they told Harland in advance nothing of their plans. They left the wharf one still warm morning two hours after breakfast, and Harland, at his desk in the room above the boathouse, heard them row away; but he was absorbed in his work and did not speak to them, and their voices were hushed so as not to disturb him. He paid no particular attention till, his day's stint done, he realized that they had not returned; and he took the speedboat and went roaring off to find them.

When he emerged from the cove by the boathouse he saw the white-painted skiff a mile or so away, near the northern shore; and he assumed that they were fishing. Then, drawing nearer, he saw that there was only one person in the boat, and he felt a sudden concern; but a moment later he made out Danny's head in the water under the boat's stern, and understood.

When he cut his motor and surged to a stop beside them, Danny was within fifty yards of the shore; and Ellen said reassuringly: 'He's fresh and strong, Richard, not a bit tired. Aren't you proud of him?' And to Danny she called: 'Don't pay any attention to us, Danny. Go all the way to shore first.'

Danny was swimming easily, using a side stroke, his face toward Richard; and he grinned, and Harland said proudly: 'Wonderful, Danny! Ellen, did he swim clear across?'

'From way in the cove,' she assured him.

'That's three-quarters of a mile, easily,' he declared. 'That's swell!'

'I could go on all day,' Danny boasted; and as they neared the shore Ellen — she wore a scant bathing suit, sleek and close — slipped overside and waded along with him, at first throat-deep and then waist-deep, till the bottom steeply shoaled and he could swim no farther. She helped him into the boat and wrapped him in warm blankets against any possible chill; and Harland, his engine throttled down, towed them back to the landing.

Leick was there to meet them, and he and Harland carried Danny up to the lodge, and Ellen insisted that he be put at once to bed, and Harland rubbed him hard with a rough towel, and Leick brought him a bowl of warm soup, and they all celebrated together this grand achievement. Danny was full of a strong excitement, and Harland was as proud as he.

'But you ought to have told me you were going to try it,' he said. 'You might have got into trouble.'

'Shucks, Dick,' Danny said confidently. 'If I'd needed help, Ellen could have taken care of me. Besides, we wanted to surprise you.'

'Just the same,' Harland began, his quick imagination picturing the dark things which might have happened, 'You ought to . . .'

But Ellen interrupted. 'Now Richard, don't spoil our triumph,' she protested. Her eyes warned Harland to silence, and then Danny's eyelids began to droop, and Ellen covered him snugly, and they left him to sleep a while.

He slept all that afternoon, and Ellen and Harland went out of doors so their voices would not disturb him. They climbed to the lookout above the cabin, from which they could see almost the whole crescent of the pond swinging around at their feet in a semi-circle. The view was wide and bold, with a glimpse of Katahdin far away, and of lesser, nearer peaks; and in a weatherproof box nailed against a tall spruce, Harland kept a battered pair of binoculars with which he liked to watch the eagle's nest on a dead stub across the pond, the pair of loons that made the lake their home, the deer that often came out to the waterside to escape swarming summer flies. He spoke of Danny's swim that morning, admitting again his concern, and Ellen protested:

'Don't be absurd, Richard! He wasn't tired, really. This — his sleeping now — is just the reaction from the excitement. That swim was an emancipation for him. Don't you see?'

'I keep thinking what might have happened,' he confessed, and he said insistently: 'Don't ever try it again without taking me along.'

She hushed him, her fingers pressing his lips. 'Don't be silly, darling.' The ledge below the lookout was well carpeted with mosses, soft and springy, and she led him that way and they lay down side by side as they had lain when they watched for turkeys, long ago. 'Besides, my dear,' she reminded him, 'having him sleep all afternoon gives us this time together. We don't have many hours when we're all alone.' She laughed teasingly. 'Even at night, if you turn over in bed, Danny can hear the springs creak.'

'We'll work out something, another year, that will give us a little more privacy.'

'Oh, I don't mind it if you don't,' she declared.

He grinned, turning on his back, shielding his eyes against the sun. 'You don't fool me for a minute!' he assured her comfortably.

'Well, of course,' she admitted, and pressed her lips against his palm. 'I never did believe in chaperones!'

'It's a lot of fun outwitting them!'

She laughed richly, whispered: 'Oh Richard, Richard, I do love you so!'

Leick was too tactful to come seeking them, and Danny slept long, so they had the fine afternoon together; and when they rose at last to go down to the lodge again, Ellen stood with arms outthrown, her bosom rising, her eyes drinking the beauty spread below them. 'Oh, I love it, Richard!' she whispered. 'I love it as much as you do.' She drew close to him. 'Promise me something, darling? When I die, scatter my ashes here. Come up here some day when a high wind blows and throw them to the winds. Promise me?'

He held her hard. 'I'll never live on without you.'

'Oh yes, you will! I shan't live long. I've always known that. I don't want to live too long. I don't want to . . .' She kissed him. 'To outlive my welcome, darling. I don't want to grow old. But you'll live to be an old, old man. Promise me, Richard?'

He tried to laugh her to silence; but she insisted so seriously that she had at last his solemn pledge and nodded in content. 'Now I'll never be unhappy about anything any more forever,' she promised. 'Come! We'll go to Danny together, my dear.'

Summer droned away, and nothing except a change of weather modified the easy routine of their days. Leick twice or thrice a week went to town for mail and for supplies. Harland was not an easy correspondent. He wrote few letters and received few. Ellen wrote once a week to her mother; heard from her — or rather from Ruth — almost every time Leick went to town. Once she told Harland: 'Ruth would like it here. We must ask her to come some time.'

'Sure, if you like,' he agreed.

'Of course we've no guest room.'

'I'll give her my bed, go down with Leick. There's an extra bunk there. I'd like to see her. She's a grand girl.'

She eyed him soberly, but then she smiled. 'On the whole, I think she'd better stay away,' she decided. 'I don't want to share you with the whole family!' And they laughed together.

Fine days saw them much out of doors, but if it rained or were cold they stayed in the cabin with a bright fire going. Harland's work went forward steadily and well. Danny grew stronger every day. Ellen was beautiful and bountiful, and Harland felt like a giant, with unmeasured powers. The sunny days when white clouds sailed in splendid argosies across the sea of the sky and when from their lofty vantage they could look away beyond miles of forest to the heights of Mount Desert and catch far glimpses of the ocean; the days of warm and soaking rain when a pearl-gray screen of falling drops blurred every prospect; the nights when rain pelted on the roof and they lay snug and secure; the days when the wind was crisp with a hint of fall, or raw and cold so that their blood ran quicker; the many days when the air was wine, neither too hot nor too cool; the warm dawns when skeins of mist rose from the still lake; the starlit silent nights; the sound of high winds in the treetops; the bird songs at dusk from the deeper woods; the moonlight mockery of the loons that nested on the lake; the hushed hooting of great owls in the valley; the deer that came to feed on well-salted potato parings which Leick put out for them; the porcupines which gnawed the doorstep; the coon that whistled by the brookside; the whining bark of foxes in the night — all these things, delighting the senses, blended together in a rich draught of which Harland drank deep every hour, fulfilled and at peace, asking for nothing which he did not have.

There was a good store of books in the cabin: a scattering of detective tales and a substantial stock of the old favorites which Harland in the past had read over and over again, as well as a supply of modern publications still in their dust covers which his own and other publishers sent him from time to time; but Ellen cared little for reading, and Harland, except during his working hours, was always with her or with her and Danny, so books were seldom opened. The days passed in a sweet serenity, and every moment was to Harland completely satisfying. He had, except that there were moments when Danny's steady cheerfulness wrung his heart and when he felt a fierce resentment at the youngster's disability, no fault to find with his world at all.

Certainly he found no fault nor flaw in Ellen.

- VII -

One sultry afternoon in mid-August, Harland thought a thundershower was brewing; and Danny said: 'Remember how the trout take at the spring hole sometimes, just before a shower, Dick? Let's go try them.'

Harland was ready enough, but Ellen protested. 'I don't like thunderstorms,' she reminded them. 'This is a good day to stay sensibly indoors.'

'You stay here and Danny and I'll go give them a try.'

'I don't trust you two out of my sight,' she told him smilingly. 'You'd do some outrageous thing, get into some trouble or other.'

Harland hesitated and looked at Danny, and saw a mischievous invitation in the youngster's eyes; and he laughed and said: 'You're afraid we'd talk about you behind your back! Danny and I kept out of trouble other years!' It occurred to him that not once in all these months had he and Danny been alone for any length of time. Ellen was always with them. He and the boy had used to enjoy the long afternoons together, talking as soberly as two men, discussing the problems which bulked large in Danny's mind. Perhaps the youngster missed those hours with him. 'We'll go without you, Ellen,' he told her in a sudden decision. 'You stay here and keep the home fires burning. We'll be back as soon as the storm breaks.'

'Please don't go, Richard,' she begged.

'Why not?' He felt a stubborn resistance rise in him, a determination to beat down her protestations.

'Danny'll get soaked!'

'He's been soaked before.' He laughed. 'We won't melt, you know, darling. We're not made of sugar.'

Danny, as though he sensed the tension between them, said: 'I'll go get the rods into the canoe, Dick.' The fishing tackle was kept in the boathouse. He took his crutches and stumped away down the path; and Ellen came to Harland, touched his arm.

'Don't, Richard,' she urged.

'Aren't you a little unreasonable?'

'Am I? Perhaps. Women are, sometimes, you know.'

He said: 'Let Danny and me have this hour or two together, Ellen. We have a lot to talk about, and a boy his age is shy with even two people. You have him to yourself every day. You must let me have him too, sometimes.'

'I know I'm unreasonable,' she admitted. 'But — I'm blue this afternoon. Let Leick take him. Stay with me. We have so little time alone together.'

'We'll be back soon,' he insisted. 'Don't make such a point of it, Ellen. Why shouldn't Danny and I go adventuring sometimes?'

Without answering, she turned away into their room and closed the door. Harland felt astonishingly and absurdly guilty, and therefore angry too. His jaw set in firm lines, and he left her with no further word.

He and Danny had fine sport for a while, keeping enough trout for breakfast, releasing the others as quickly as they were landed; and Danny shouted with delight at the hard smash and tug of every rise. Harland looked often toward the landing, hoping Ellen would relent and join them, but she did not. Yet when they came home drenched and dripping, she met them with a smile, had dry clothes ready, helped Danny change. Except that she was quiet, she was as tender and attentive as she had always been; and there was no reproach in her at all. The evening was a merry one, and Harland forgot the discordant note which the afternoon had struck. That night when they were alone she clung to him in a passionate repentance, and had his bountiful forgiveness; and next day was for them all as serene, at least on the surface, as the days that had gone before.

The rain brought no lasting break in the heat. Still, sullen days continued, and the pond lay brazen in the sun; and when they swam, the water was as warm as the air. The second evening, Danny discovered a hummingbird which had apparently been hurt or had sickened, perched on top of the low wall outside the cabin, and he called them to see it. They approached within arm's length, and when it did not fly, Ellen gently picked it up. It had no visible hurt, but though alive it lay passive in her hands. She carried it indoors and warmed it and gave it a drop of sugared brandy water, and they admired the beauty of its coloring, and made a nest for it of cotton batting, and hoped it would recover.

But in the morning it was dead, its wings extended, its tail spread like a lovely small fan, and it was so beautiful that their eyes dimmed. 'It's just as if it had flown away,' Danny murmured. 'Had gone soaring and sweeping away and left its body here.'

Leick was to go to town that day, and Ellen as though on sudden impulse said: 'I'm going to ask Leick to bring back father's field kit, and I'll mount it for you, Danny, in flight, just the way it is.'

Harland turned to protest, remembering his distaste for the arsenic the kit presumably contained; but Danny's quick delight forestalled him, so he did not interfere. Leick, having prepared their early breakfast, departed with this mission on his list for the day.

Harland, at his desk in the pleasant room above the boathouse, worked for a while almost indolently, till as his imagination warmed to its task his pen ran fast and faster and he became completely absorbed. Toward mid-morning he heard Ellen and Danny depart in the skiff. They rowed away, moving quietly, not speaking, careful to avoid disturbing him; but presently from a distance Harland heard Danny's voice, singing one of his favorite songs:

> 'Oh a capital ship for an ocean trip
> Was the Walloping Window Blind.
> No wind that blew dismayed her crew
> Or troubled the Captain's mind . . .'

The song, as the receding skiff rounded a distant point, faded and was gone, and Harland smiled and returned to his work again. This was one of those mornings when what he wished to say was completely clear to him, and for a while he forgot his surroundings as the words flowed from his racing pen. But after a time his thoughts drifted, following Ellen and Danny who had gone away up the lake together. She was never so completely perfect as when she played companion to Danny; and he thought how charming she would be when their own babies came to them, how tender and how sufficing. The instinct for paternity was stronger in him all the time, but there was a reluctance in Ellen which he had not till now sought to overcome. He must wait till she was as eager as he, and he thought how natural it was for her to be a little afraid of this great enterprise.

He turned back to his work again, and after a moment the steady fury of composition filled him once more. He wrote rapidly, speaking now and then a phrase aloud to test the sound of it, changing here and there a word. Sometimes he sat for long minutes staring at the pad before him, and sometimes he wrote and scratched out a line a dozen times before he was content. He lighted a fresh cigarette, unconscious of the fact that others, from each of which he had taken no more than a single puff, lay ranged along the edge of the broad desk of smoothed boards which was his worktable. The forgotten cigarettes smouldered beside him, wisps of smoke rising blue in the still air.

He came to a pause at last, and thrust the pages together, and his eyes were shining, for he knew the work was good; yet after a moment his shoulders sagged wearily. He had written till his vision blurred, and he had smoked so much that his senses were reeling, and his hand ached from its grip upon the pen. He left his desk and stumbled up the path to the cabin, still so absorbed that he forgot that Ellen and Danny had not yet come down the lake again.

At the open door he called Ellen's name and had no answer. He wondered what time it was, but they were often careless of time at Back of the Moon. The sun was the only clock that mattered. But if Ellen and Danny were on the pond, he would be able to see them from the lookout above the cabin, so he turned that way.

When he reached the spot, he saw at once the white skiff, off near the end of the point that extended from directly below where he stood halfway across the pond. He looked at the little boat for a moment with puzzled eyes, and then abruptly he snatched the binoculars from the box where they were kept. Someone had changed the adjustment of the lenses; Ellen perhaps, since she was a little shortsighted. In his haste he was clumsy, and it was a moment before he brought into focus the skiff, and Ellen, and the water beyond.

When he could see clearly, his heart stopped. He watched for a breathless instant, and then with a low choking cry he flung the glass aside and plunged headlong down the path past the cabin to the boathouse, terror strangling him.

6

ELLEN, until she and Harland were married, had not looked beyond that consummation. The first morning at Taos, when she remembered Danny, faint doubts disturbed her; but they were forgotten in the rapturous days that followed, when she and Harland were always together, when the sound of his voice, or the accidental contact of their hands, could wake in her faint quickenings that came and went like heat lightning across a distant horizon. Swift glorious storms of tenderness overwhelmed them both as warm spring rains pelting on frozen ground thaw it to a fertile softness.

But just as such showers, passing by, leave the earth washed and clean and the air limpid and clear, so Ellen saw her world with a lucid and crystalline awareness; and she was piqued by the fact that the tumultuous delights of their ardent hours together reawoke in Harland the creative instinct which had made him the novelist he was. It perplexed her to discover that the impulse which she roused in him she herself could never wholly satisfy.

'Does writing mean so much to you, Richard?' she asked once.

'Of course! It's the way I make my living.'

'I've plenty for both of us.'

Harland nodded cheerfully. 'And I don't mind living on my wife's money,' he admitted. 'But — well, I don't write for money, really.' He kissed her. 'Writing's just one of my ways of saying how much I love you!'

She smiled up at him, mischievous challenge in her eyes. 'There are ways I like better,' she assured him, but her laughter was not genuine. She resented everything which stole from her a part of Harland. At Sea Island she saw how easily he and Ruth were friends, and driving back to Warm Springs he spoke of Ruth so often that she said at last, smiling carefully: 'You know, Richard, you ought to have married Ruth instead of me. You'd be perfectly congenial.'

He chuckled. 'I haven't noticed that you and I have any trouble getting along.' And he asked teasingly: 'Jealous?'

'I've always been jealous of Ruth,' she assented. 'Everybody has always liked her, and practically no one ever liked me! She's so — so —' She exploded helplessly: 'So darned good!'

He laughed, a great gust of laughter. 'And you're a regular Jezebel, of course,' he cried, and braked the car to a stop and took her in his arms; and she whispered:

'I'm jealous of anything that touches you, Richard! Of your garments, of the chair where you sit and the bed where you sleep and the ground you tread on!' Her voice was hoarse and shaken, her eyes hot and burning; and he held her close, profoundly moved, whispering many reassurances.

But not often did she let him thus see the intensity of her desire to exclude every thought save of her from his mind. She dared not, for when Harland felt the curb, he laughingly or sternly shook it off; and she would not willingly teach him the habit of resisting her. She won no victories, but she avoided any outright defeats. Even in her careful campaign to leave Danny behind at Warm Springs she worked by indirection, seeking to influence Doctor Mason or Danny himself rather than to persuade Harland. Thus by refraining from making an open issue she escaped abject surrender.

When at Joe Severin's farm she saw the strong bond between him and Harland and the affection between Harland and Leick, she hated them because they had a part of him which she could never share. At Back of the Moon, directing Leick and working with him while she brought the camp nearer her desires, she set herself to win him, thinking she might separate him from Harland either by herself capturing his devotion or by provoking

Harland to send him away; and by an easy familiarity, a deliberate yet subtle coquetry in manner and in dress which if it moved him to any overt word or act she could instantly disavow, she sought to play upon him. She led him to talk about himself, and he told her about the shore farm where he had lived with his father and mother till they died. She asked why he had never married.

'Well, Mom liked to keep the house just so,' he explained, with a smile in his tone. 'And I never found anyone that was a good enough housekeeper to satisfy her; and Pa wa'n't so well, the last few years, so I had the farm work to do and couldn't leave them.' She declared it was a pity and a shame that he should have sacrificed himself for them; and he said: 'Well, ma'am, I've most generally noticed I get the most fun out of doing things for other folks and not worrying too much about myself.'

She laughingly insisted that many a girl must have set her cap for him; and he grinned. 'Well, if they did, I didn't know it,' he declared. 'I never did know much about women anyway.'

He was so steadily himself that she began to suspect he was wiser than he seemed, began to fear his thoughtful watchfulness. He made an inconspicuous fourth in their small world, always at hand yet never intrusive. She knew that though Richard's morning hours at his work were sacred, not to be interrupted by her or by Danny, he sometimes took a recess to join Leick on the wharf for a few minutes of quiet talk; and when from the cabin above she heard their voices, she envied Leick this companionship with Richard from which she felt herself excluded.

But most of all she envied and hated Danny. He was always with them. At night his bed was separated by only a single thickness of boards from Harland's. He was actually nearer Harland than she, for despite the dividing wall their beds were only inches apart, while between hers and Harland's there was a lane three or four feet wide. When, as on warm nights was usually the case, they slept on the screened veranda, their beds lay end to end with Harland's between hers and Danny's; and if she were wakeful — sometimes she lay long with wide eyes, her ears attuned to the night sounds in the forest — she could hear Danny's soft breathing almost as easily as she heard Harland's.

She saw that not only physically but spiritually the bond between him and Danny was maddeningly strong. If at night Danny sat up in bed, or in his sleep touched the partition between their two rooms with his elbow, or even if he slept restlessly, Harland was apt to rouse and call in a low tone:

'All right, Danny, old top?'

And Danny would answer sleepily: 'Sure, Dick, I'm fine.'

But she herself could leave her bed, move about the room, go into the living room, and she might even go out of doors, without waking Harland at all. There were nights when she slept as lightly as a cat, waiting for the hateful moment when Danny would stir and Harland would call to him in instant and tender solicitude; and when this happened, she lay biting her lip in the darkness. More than once, when Danny and Harland had exchanged a low-spoken, reassuring word and were asleep again, she deliberately got up from her bed and walked to and fro and made small unnecessary noises just to see whether Harland would wake and call to her; and the fact that he did not left her to lie in a storm of shaking rage till dawn.

The rare hours when she and Harland could be alone together, to recapture those tempestuously beautiful moments which once had been so freely theirs, had a clandestine character which she hated; and yet she planned for them hungrily, for when Danny was about, Harland was always restrained. If she came to kiss him, he was likely to say in amused warning: 'Careful! Danny can see us!'

'But darling, after all, we're married!'

'I know, but you'll embarrass him!' He was only half-serious, laughing at her protests; but as time passed there began to lie under her jealous longing a desperate alarm. Danny was an incubus of which she might never be free!

Defensively, she wooed the boy as one woos a rival, spending long hours with him, winning him completely. They conspired together to surprise Harland, as for instance when Danny swam across the pond; and after that day they began secretly to plan that he would presently try the longer swim, from one end to the other. He was eager to do it, and she encouraged him; but they would not tell Harland, Danny insisted, till the great deed was done. She never confessed that Harland had forbidden their trying such another adventure alone.

They intended to stay at Back of the Moon till September; and as August drew near its end, Ellen began to believe she could endure the short time that remained. Then — on the heels of a series of sullen hot days which had frayed her temper thin — Danny proposed to Harland that they go to fish the trout hole before an approaching thunderstorm, and Harland — despite her protests — agreed. The idea that these two must never be alone together, implanted by her mother's word at Sea Island last winter, had assumed an extravagant importance in her eyes, and she wished to go with them now; but some stubborn despair restrained her. She was weary with the long struggle, and she let them go.

When they were gone she lay dry-eyed on her bed alone and faced what seemed to her the truth. This was the beginning of the end. Danny today had won a little of Harland away from her. He would win more and more. She recognized the fact that she must, as long as Danny lived, share Harland with the boy.

As long as Danny lived! As long as Danny lived! The phrase repeated itself over and over in her mind, as a cracked record repeats itself on the phonograph.

— II —

From that hour, like a figure lurking in the shadows, too dimly seen to be recognized, the thought of Danny's death — or of her own — was in Ellen's mind. There was in her, from some forgotten ancestor, the emotional intensity of the Slav, which knows no halfway ground between keen exuberance and abject hopelessness; and despair overwhelmed her now. Her passion for her father had transferred itself to Harland, but Harland did not

readily submit to it. She felt in him always something that was
held back from her, some inner self which she could neither touch
nor move; and there had been hours when, even in his arms, conscious that he was not so completely surrendered to her as she
was to him, she had hated him and sought to beat and buffet
him — and she hated him the more because he laughed in tender
delight at her violence.

Now, like sand from a clenched fist, he was slipping through her
fingers. She had lost a little of him, never to be recaptured as
long as Danny lived. But — Danny might die; and surely, if
Danny were gone, Harland would forget him and be wholly hers.
When — on pretext of stuffing the dead hummingbird — she
asked Leick to bring her father's field kit from Bar Harbor, it
was not with any fixed design. But — there was a bottle of arsenic in the kit, and arsenic was death.

Leick that day departed soon after breakfast. The morning
was breathlessly quiet. The oppressive heat which had persisted
for days still lay in a smothering blanket across the land; and even
Danny, usually completely good-natured, confessed:

'I've had about enough of this, haven't you, Ellen? If it
keeps on we'll begin to snarl at each other.' She made no reply,
and he said: 'I'm going to stay in the water as much as I can today.' And then in sudden inspiration: 'Listen, Ellen, why don't
I swim the lake the long way?' His tones lifted. 'We'll never get
a better chance. There's no wind, and the water's warm as milk,
and I can do it! I swam over an hour yesterday in the cove,
without getting tired at all.'

'It's all right for you. You'll be in the water,' she reminded
him. 'But for me it means sitting in the boat in the hot sun for
hours.'

'You can swim along with me some of the time, and push the
boat,' he argued. 'That will keep you cool. Come on, Ellen,
let's, and surprise Dick. It will tickle him so.'

She felt a stirring of anticipation in her, a sense of something
imminent, terrible and yet welcome. 'You'll be in the water a
long time,' she said doubtfully. 'You may get chilled.'

He laughed. 'Say, if there ever was a day when it would be fun to get a chill it's today!'

She agreed at last, but she took dutiful precautions against mishap to him. When they went down to the boathouse, he in scant trunks and she in her bathing suit with a light robe to protect her from the searing sun, she carried blankets and a jar of vaseline, the blankets in case he had to be taken into the boat before the swim was finished, the vaseline to grease his body thoroughly before he entered the water. They planned that he should start at the farther end of the lake, in that cove where there was a sandy beach, and finish his course here at the boathouse. Danny hoped he might reach the cove about the time Harland was done with his morning's work.

'Just the right time to surprise him,' he exulted, and he anticipated what Harland would say, and planned his proud reply.

They embarked in silence, taking the skiff, Ellen at the oars. When the boathouse was out of sight she said rebelliously: 'This is the clumsiest boat to row.'

He laughed and began to sing that song about the Walloping Window Blind; and — secure now from Harland's observation — he made ready for his undertaking. He unbuckled the braces which supported his shrunken legs and took them off. He sat in the stern facing Ellen, and she tried not to look at his thin and knobby limbs, hating with a strong and almost nauseating violence his malformation. She rowed steadily, and Danny began to rub vaseline on his legs and arms, his shoulders — broad and brawny as those of a boy years older than he, the muscles well developed as though to compensate for the weakness of his legs — and his chest and stomach and sides. Watching him, she admitted grudgingly that he had a beautiful head, with a noble brow crowned by soft light curls, and wide intelligent eyes, and a flexible and tender mouth. His head seemed too large for his body, yet seeing only his countenance, one forgot his physical imperfections. His very beauty made his shrunken legs the more repellent to her eyes.

'I'll do your back before you go into the water,' she told him, and he nodded. His body glistened in the sun, and small drops of sweat forced their way through the oily film which covered his skin and trickled down his chest and his arms. She saw these tiny globules with a fastidious distaste. His greased body seemed to her hideous. She felt toward him that profound revulsion which makes the wolf pack turn upon the wounded member.

Danny talked steadily, wishing they had brought a watch so they might know exactly how long it took him to swim the full distance. They had as always breakfasted early, for they habitually rose with or before the sun, and Danny guessed it was even now no more than half-past nine. 'Dick nearly always works till noon or later,' he reminded her. 'I think I can surely get in sight of the cove, at least, before he leaves the boathouse. Don't you?' She answered inattentively, smiling as though amused at his eagerness, while she was thinking: He'll take Richard from me! Richard will never cease to love him. I can't fight him. I shall never have all of Richard, never as long as Danny lives!

When they came to the far beach, the boy, babbling happily, turned and swung his limp and ropelike legs over the skiff's stern, presenting his back to her to be anointed. She spread the vaseline evenly and thickly. 'There!' she said at last. They were in shallow water, and he slipped overside, supporting himself by holding to the stern of the skiff while he turned to face the open lake, beginning at once to swim.

As he moved slowly away from the shore, she kept abreast of him. Danny set as his immediate goal the tip of the point which extended out into the lake. When he reached that spot he would have covered half the distance. She saw that he guided himself by watching landmarks on the shore they had left, and after a time she said quietly: 'Don't worry about your direction. I'll keep you on your course.' She was pushing the oars, sending the skiff stern first through the water. The sun was hot, and toward the point ahead the air shimmered and rose in waves, and refraction produced a blurring of the shoreline, making it seem like a low bluff, like a dark wall.

Ellen marked their progress by a rock on the shore, a blasted tree, the eagle's nest. She wished she had worn a hat, or dark glasses, for the glare upon the water blinded her and made her head ache throbbingly. When she looked toward Danny, his legs, seen through the clear water, were distorted in a way which exaggerated their fragility, making them seem to be soft, boneless things which wavered limply behind him; and she shivered with repugnance at the sight.

He swam steadily, with a long, easy side stroke, floating low in the water, timing his breathing well; but she began to feel trapped, constricted, bound; and, eager to escape, wishing he would hurry, she said once: 'You're not making very fast progress, Danny. You're not halfway to the point.'

He looked ahead. 'I'll have to speed up a little,' he agreed.

'If you're too long in the water you'll get cold, maybe take a cramp.' Her thought found words.

He laughed confidently. 'Today? Not a chance! The water's soupy!'

The minutes drifted tediously by. To her eye it seemed they scarce moved at all; but the shores on either side began to withdraw. She watched the point still far ahead, impatient for him to arrive within easy reach of land again. Danger hung in the sullen air, danger lay like an oily film across the mirror of the water, danger tinted with a brassy hue the arched and silent sky; and she felt the oppression of fear. But it was for herself, not for Danny, that she was afraid.

They reached the widest part of the lake, the point which was Danny's immediate goal no more than a quarter-mile ahead. He had been swimming on his left side, but now he changed sides; and she watched the back of his head and the movements of his arm and shoulder and his fluttering, trailing legs. In a sharpened attention she saw that he swam more slowly now; and after a moment he turned again to face her, said apologetically:

'I was getting a little tired, so I shifted, to rest up.'

'Float for a while,' she suggested. A pulse beat in her throat.

'Oh, I'm all right.' His mouth twitched as though with pain. 'I had a kink in my side,' he admitted. 'But it's gone.'

He began to swim again, and she watched him alertly. An expert swimmer herself, she knew that he should give up, should come into the boat; and she thought: Suppose I were not here. Suppose he were swimming alone, and caught a cramp which left him helpless. How deep, she wondered, was the water where they were? How deep down would he sink, slowly, slowly, whitely, in the dark depths?

'I think I'm getting tired,' he confessed, pausing, treading water, turning on his back to float, looking to her for advice.

If she told him to abandon this attempt, he would do so; but she did not. 'Rest,' she advised. 'You don't want to give up when you've come so far. There's no hurry. We've all day.'

He nodded obediently, but when he began to swim again, there was a roughness in his stroke which testified to his fatigue. She should take him into the boat, wrap him in blankets, hurry him back to camp.

But — if he wanted to stop, let him say so! Let his be the decision!

'I'll get my second wind in a minute,' he promised, a little breathlessly; but in the effort of speaking he swallowed a mouthful of water and choked and coughed and grinned. 'Better keep my mouth shut,' he said, and swam on. The point drew slowly nearer.

She saw presently that his lips were faintly blue. Her heart was pounding hard, and she gripped the oars so tightly that her fingers ached. Danny changed to a breast stroke again.

'It rests me to change,' he said breathlessly. 'We're almost to the point, aren't we?' The tip of the slender neck of land was in fact no more than a hundred yards away.

'Almost,' she agreed. 'Once around that and you'll be on the home stretch.'

He swam a few strokes more, then paused again, treading water in a flurried way. 'I ate too much breakfast,' he confessed, with a twisted, sidewise grin. 'I've got a stomach-ache. It's a peach too. I guess ——'

Then he began to flounder helplessly, making some wordless

s und; and then his head seemed to be pulled forward on his chest and without a word he went under. She had seen turtles, seals, loons, sink thus, not diving but just allowing themselves to settle into the water. She could still see him, see his white form, a few feet below the surface, drawn into a knot like a ball, his knees up, his head down; and after a moment he drifted to the top of the water again, and one of his arms flung out as though he tried to call to her. But then the water covered his open mouth and silenced him and he went down once more.

Ellen in this moment made no conscious decision. She knew that Danny was drowning, and with the knowledge came a tremendous, billowing, exultant comprehension. If Danny drowned, then she could make Richard wholly hers! She did not think: 'I will let him drown!' But neither did she think: 'I can save him!' Nor did she make any move to do so. A frozen paralysis held her, and she submitted to it. Like a disinterested spectator watching the playing out of a tragic drama which is about to end contentingly, she sat utterly still, making no movement at all.

Danny came to the surface a last time, his eyes wide and beseeching, eloquent to say what with his lips he could not say; for he was choking, coughing, strangling, fighting to raise his face and head clear of the water, struggling toward the skiff not twenty feet away — where Ellen sat like stone, watching him almost unseeingly.

In one of his gasping inhalations his mouth submerged, and she saw his eyes roll upward. Water entering his lungs, he lapsed into unconsciousness.

Then he sank. This time he did not come to the surface again at all.

– III –

For a moment — a minute, minutes, she did not know how long — Ellen sat motionless in the white skiff on the still water, staring at the spot where Danny had disappeared. The sun was scorching hot, but she felt cold, and she began to shiver terribly. A few bubbles broke the surface, burst and disappeared; and she saw the faint flash of prismatic color as the sun struck them for an instant before they vanished. There was a great sound in her ears, a rushing and a roaring that seemed to rebound from the steep hillsides everywhere walling in the little pond. One of the oars slipped from her slack grasp and floated beside the drifting skiff, but she did not move to pick it up again. She could not think, she could not even feel. One great hammering fact filled the world with clanging. Danny was dead!

Then, above the din which seemed to be outside her, pressing down upon her crushingly, she heard another sound; and she hearkened to it, and after a laborious moment she knew what it was. She had heard it under similar circumstances once before, that day when Danny swam across the lake and Richard came in the fast little motorboat to join them. This sound she heard was the metallic buzz of the outboard. So Richard was coming!

Richard was coming, the roar of the little engine louder all the time; and panic seized her. She dreaded to face his grief, to face perhaps his blame! Till now this tragic hour had been unreal, like a poorly-played drama on the stage; but full comprehension drove her to belated action. Danny had been in her charge. Richard would say she should have saved him. Instinctively, as though it were not already too late, she threw off her light robe and dove overboard, swimming down and down through the pearly water, peering into the shadowed depths. When her lungs were bursting, she struggled up for air, hearing the motorboat draw nearer, making a surface dive to descend into the deeps again. Danny had been a little away from the skiff; and she swam under water in that direction, and saw a pale brown shadow and felt the ridge of a great rock and set her feet against it and drove herself to the surface once more. But she knew now that the lake here was not deep enough to make her search for Danny hopeless. She dove again and again, trying desperately to find the boy and bring him back to a chance of life before Richard came.

She was so intent that when on one of her brief moments at the surface she failed to hear the motorboat, the significance of this did not at first come home to her. She dove again and came up again and saw Richard swimming toward her from the point not far away; and a red mask covered his face. She swam to meet him, crying: 'Richard! Richard! You're hurt!' From an open cut on his brow, blood streamed.

He wiped it wetly away. 'Where is he?' he demanded, his voice hoarse and strained.

'Right here!' she cried. 'Very near here.' He dived, and she followed him down into the depths, seeing by the tawny hue of his body in the water that he had stripped off his clothes. A moment later they came together to the surface, but without pause he dived again, and so did she.

They continued for a long time this frantic search, expelling all the air from their lungs to make it easier to reach the bottom. The water was deep enough so that her ears rang painfully, but again and again she touched boulders or soft mucky sand; and in the depths there was still light enough dimly to see. She and Richard separated, covering different ground, working in silence, each nearing the exhaustion point.

Till at last, swimming along the bottom, she saw a pale brightness and knew it was Danny. She caught his arm, and his body rose easily, pressing softly against hers. His arm was slippery in her grasp, so she laid hold of the belt of his swimming trunks, and his arms curled softly around her neck. As though in tender welcome because she had come at last to save him, he nestled close and gratefully. Kicking toward the surface, she felt his frail legs intertwined and entangled with her own, and she came up to the brightness of the sun, and supported herself and him, and then Richard's head appeared thirty feet away and she screamed:

'I've got him, Richard!'

Harland came splashing toward her. The white skiff had drifted away, so he took Danny and swam for the point. She followed, terribly weary, remembering the touch of Danny's arms around her neck as he seemed to cling to her, and his cold cheek against her own. She saw Harland wade ashore and lay Danny's body on the ground. He began artificial respiration, compressing

Danny's lungs and releasing them again in a steady rhythm.

Forgetting her own part in what had happened, her heart ached for his grief; and she made haste to his side and caught his shoulder pleadingly. 'It's no use, Richard, darling,' she urged. 'He was under for so long!'

But without speaking, he shook off her hand; so she drew aside and lay down, her face in her arms, and she wept terribly, for a long time, not from remorse nor from sorrow but from simple weariness. When she was drained dry of tears, she looked toward Harland again. His wound had ceased to bleed, but his face was a mask of drying blood, and blood had dripped on Danny, darkly speckling his shoulders and back. She murmured, without moving:

'Tired, Richard? May I try for a while?' He shook his head and she urged: 'It's no use! Oh my dear, my dear, it's no use at all!'

He did not speak, and she drew her arm over her eyes against the glare and looked across the lake and saw that the white skiff had drifted almost a quarter mile away. She rose and swam slowly to recapture it, thinking how easy it would be to sink and breathe deeply of the soft sweet water and never come up again, thinking how Richard would grieve for her. She reached the boat and climbed in. It held only one oar, and she stood up and looked all around and discovered the other, and paddled toward it and recaptured it.

She was beyond the tip of the point, toward the northern shore, and when she looked back she saw the motorboat in which Richard had come up the lake. It was half out of water, canted to one side, not far off shore on the opposite side of the point from where he and Danny were; and Ellen remembered a ledge there of which Richard more than once had warned her. He must have run into that ledge at full speed. The shock had thrown him forward, out of the boat. This would account for the cut across the brow.

Pushing the skiff stern first, she rowed slowly that way, wondering in dull surprise why Richard had forgotten that ledge which he knew so well. She guessed gropingly that he had finished his morning's work and set out to find them; but if that were all, he would have remembered the rock was there. He must have remembered it was there — unless something happened to make him forget!

Then her confused conjectures came into sudden focus. He had raced up the lake in such desperate haste that he forgot the ledge; but only one thing could have swept him so completely out of himself. Her eyes lifted in instant understanding to the rocky outcropping on the hill above camp, to that outlook from which it was possible to see almost all of the pond. Richard, his morning's work done, must have climbed the hill to look for them, and he had seen Danny in distress, had seen her sitting idly by while Danny drowned!

She whispered through trembling lips: 'Oh no, no, no!' Yet she was sure this was the truth. Harland's manner was confirmation, if she needed confirmation; his blind and headlong race up the lake till he rammed that familiar sunken ledge was by itself proof enough.

So she knew that Richard, whose love she held above all the treasures of the world, had seen her let his Danny drown.

– IV –

Ellen, in that first dreadful understanding, chilled with fear; and she sat idle, with trailing oars, watching the steady movement of Harland's brown and naked body as he compressed and released Danny's ribs in hopeless refusal to surrender hope. Her instinct was for flight; but flight would mean confession, and also, if she fled, Harland would be lost to her. Then if not flight, denial? But she could deny nothing till he accused her, and the accusation itself, once it was put in words, would part them forever. She was tenaciously determined not to let him go; and while she sent the skiff slowly nearer, she sought in her thoughts and found at last a way to silence him, to bind him to her side.

Unhesitating then, she thrust the skiff resolutely on till it touched the beach. Along the water's edge she saw Harland's garments lying scattered where he had thrown them when, after plunging ashore from the wrecked motorboat, he raced across the point to swim out to where she was. She picked up his dungarees on the beach, his shoes half in the water. One sock evaded her search. His shorts were in the water, a few feet from the shore, and she salvaged them.

Then she came near him, and Harland, without ceasing his manipulations looked up at her with empty eyes, sweat dripping from his brow and streaming down his chest. Then his head drooped as he concentrated on this task again; but she had seen the blankness in his eyes and knew she need not yet speak the word she planned. So she drew away and waited, till after what must have been hours he accepted defeat. Too weary to rise, he crawled on hands and knees away from Danny's body; and he lay down with his face buried in his arms, his shoulders heaving with fatigue.

She rose then and brought one of the blankets from the skiff and spread it over him, and she sat down by his side, touching his head caressingly. 'Rest, Richard,' she said softly. 'Rest, my dear.'

He lay for a long time without moving, but at last he turned on his back and looked up at her, his eyes searching hers; and she fetched water cupped in her hands and washed the dried blood off his face, and dipped a corner of her robe in the lake to bathe his cheeks and brow.

'It was too long before we got him,' she said, her voice tender and low. She sat beside him, stroking his cheek, touching the cruel gash in his forehead. 'I love you so, Richard,' she told him. 'I love you so.' There was no movement in him except the laboring of his chest as he breathed; but he would presently burst into fierce, contemptuous accusations, and she must speak before he did. She asked gravely:

'Richard, will it comfort you to know that we are going to have a child?'

She knew he had heard, for the pupils of his eyes expanded, as though he had come from light into sudden darkness. 'We're going to have a baby, Richard,' she repeated. 'A son, I hope. Our own!'

His head, at that, flung sidewise suddenly to look toward where Danny lay; and she saw his eyes dry and burning. She rose and took the other blanket and wrapped Danny in it; and kneeling beside him, she said over her shoulder: 'When I found him, he put his arms around me.' She remembered so keenly that embrace, surrendering, completely trustful. 'He always loved me, you know, as I loved him.'

Harland slowly sat up, the blanket falling across his knees. She said hurriedly: 'Your clothes are in the skiff, except one sock I didn't find. You'd better put them on. We must take him home, and I must tend that hurt on your forehead.' If she could lead him to obey her, to yield to her will, then perhaps he would not believe what his own eyes had seen.

He rose, submitting silently, and pulled on his dungarees, belting them around his waist. Then, still not speaking, he came to lift Danny into the skiff. 'I'll hold him,' she said, and sat in the stern and cradled Danny's head and shoulders between her knees. He dragged the skiff off the beach and stepped into it and lifted the oars.

She wished he would say something, for this waiting was hard; but he did not even meet her eyes. He rowed the long way home without a word; nor for a while did she speak at all. If he were lost to her forever, then she too was lost, and there was no help for it. She could do no more than she had done.

Except, she remembered lucidly, that she must do one more thing. She had told him they were to have a baby. That was not true, but she must make it true, and at once. If he ever came to know that she had lied, then she was destroyed most certainly. But the thought did not dismay her. He could deny her nothing now. To remind him of his bonds she said softly: 'I've thought so for days, Richard; but I wasn't really sure, in my heart, till now when you need me so — need us both so. Baby and I will make up to you for losing Danny, darling.'

Not looking at her, he rowed slowly on. This had been a long business — Danny's swim, the endless diving for his body, the hopeless hours of the effort at resuscitation. The day was waning, and the lofty hill above the cabin shut off the descending sun so that they moved in shadow, and the shadow thickened about them even while on the other shore the sun still lay. Since he was rowing, he faced aft, but she could look ahead; and when they rounded the last point she saw a figure on the wharf and knew Leick had returned from his trip to town, and terror swept her. Leick was shrewd and wise and not easily befooled, and she dreaded facing him. She had decided long ago that he was her enemy, persuading herself that he resented her coming between him and Harland; and he might somehow guess the truth. Holding her voice steady, fighting down her fears, seeking Harland's protection, she said:

'Leick's there waiting for us. He's back early.'

Harland's eyes met hers, and he let the oars trail and looked this way and that, searching the opposite shores of the lake as though seeking something he could not find. Then she saw his eyes fix and go blank with hard thought, and then he began once more to row toward the boathouse, and she knew that his decision, whatever it might be, was taken. When they came to where Leick was, Harland would speak; and when he spoke she would know whether she had won. Her arms tightened around Danny's body, clinging to him as though for sanctuary.

They drew alongside the wharf, and Leick stood just above them, looking down at that blanket-shrouded burden in Ellen's arms. He met her eyes, then Harland's; and he uttered some low word of question. Harland spoke, his voice husky. He coughed to clear it, said then carefully:

'Danny's drowned, Leick.' Leick grunted as though under the impact of a heavy blow, and Harland wetted his lips and explained, picking his words. 'We went to swim on the far beach, and he took the motorboat, cutting circles, taking his own waves. He hit one wrong, and it threw him out. Before we could get to him — we were up at the beach with nothing but the skiff — he had drowned, trying to swim ashore.' He added, to complete the lie: 'The motorboat ran wild and cracked up on that ledge off the point. I guess it's ruined.'

Ellen's heart quickened its beat. For a long time no one spoke. Then in a heavy tone Leick said: 'You cut your head.' The word was a question, and Harland after an instant's hesitation answered it.

'We had to dive for him. I hit a rock.'

Leick nodded, but Ellen saw his eyes rest for a moment on Harland's dungarees; and — her perceptions were always acute — she read his mind. If she and Harland and Danny had indeed gone to swim on the beach, then Richard would have worn or taken his bathing trunks; and Leick must know this. So Leick would not be thus easily deceived.

Yet she knew his devotion. While Harland protected her, so would Leick too. She did not speak, but there was a singing triumph in her blood. Harland was hers! He had made her cause his own; and with him beside her, she could face the world.

- v -

Harland lifted Danny's body up to Leick who held it as he might have held a baby while they climbed out on the wharf. Harland secured the skiff, and Ellen said in a low voice: 'Bring him up to the cabin. I'll go make ready.' It was important that she should act in what would seem to Leick, and to the world — and even to Harland — a normal fashion. She was perfectly sure that Harland knew the truth, knew she had let Danny drown. His headlong race up the lake was proof enough of this; his lie to Leick confirmed that proof. But she was equally sure that as long as he thought she was carrying his child — and perhaps forever — he would hide his knowledge of her guilt from her and from the world. He and she would play a grim farce, he pretending he did not know what she had done, she pretending she did not know he knew. Yet her part must be well played; since if it were not, if once he realized she knew he had seen her, then the ugly truth would come to the surface, and dark words would be spoken, and the tragic farce would end.

So now her part must be that of the affectionate and sympathetic wife, grieving for Danny but more concerned to comfort Harland in his deeper grief, bravely forgetting her own sorrow in her effort to assuage his. She hurried ahead to the cabin and held the door for them; she moved on to turn back the covers on Danny's bed so Harland could lay him there; and when he had done so, Leick standing silently, she put her arms around Harland's neck, drew his face down, kissed him, said like a pledge:

'I'll take care of him, Richard. I'll do everything.' She told Leick: 'Take Mr. Harland outside. Be good to him.'

Harland submitted, and Ellen closed the door behind them; and now at last alone she fought for self-control, her hands pressing her cheeks, shivering as though she were cold. Then, dreading what Leick might say to Harland, she hastily opened the door again; but she saw Harland on the veranda, heard Leick busy in the kitchen. She went to the sink to dip water into a basin; and she was tensely armed to meet Leick's accusing word. But he did not speak and she took basin and cloth and returned to bathe Danny. Sand and spruce spills had adhered to the vaseline on his body during those hours while Harland tried to bring him back to life; and she cleansed him, forcing herself to the shuddering task. She put fresh sheets on his bed, and ordered his stiffening limbs and his countenance, and so at last covered him over and left him.

Harland was still on the veranda. Leick said supper was ready; but she begged time, since she still wore her bathing suit, to change. In their room she saw her father's field kit, which Leick had brought from Bar Harbor that day, set on her bed; and she remembered the arsenic in it. If Richard had denounced her to Leick she would have been glad now to have the poison at her command; but he had not, so she could live.

When she joined Richard at the table, he was already seated; and she went behind his chair, taking his cheeks between her hands, turning his face up to meet her kiss.

'I know your grief, Richard,' she whispered. 'But we'll make it up to you, baby and I.'

His arm after a moment encircled her waist, and she read his thoughts. He must be gentle with her, gentle and tender, always remembering the burden of another life which she bore. To make his rôle clear to him she said in his ear: 'I blame myself so terribly, Richard. I shouldn't have let him try it, but he was so happy, wanting to surprise you. I'll never forgive myself. Please be good to me!'

'It's all right,' he told her heavily. 'Just one of those things.'

'You're so sweet to me.'

They ate little, and almost in silence. When they were done, Leick spoke to them. 'I thought I'd go out to Joe Severin's tonight,' he explained. 'Telephone to Cherryfield, have someone come in, first thing in the morning.'

Harland did not reply. Ellen hesitated, half dreading to be alone with Richard; but then she said, eager to separate these two:

'Yes, Leick. Go tonight. We'll expect you early in the morning.' And since Harland did not raise his head, she caught Leick's eye and led him outside. 'He's dreadfully broken, just now,' she said sorrowfully. 'You and I must attend to whatever is to be done. I think we'll plan to take Danny to Boston. Find out about trains, Leick. Make all the arrangements.'

Leick spoke without expression. 'Yes, ma'am,' he agreed, not meeting her eyes. 'I'll start soon as I've cleaned up the supper things.'

'I'll do that,' she assured him. 'You go along while there's still light enough to see the trail.'

So Leick departed, and Ellen and Harland were left alone. He went out to sit on the rock wall beside the path, and she busied herself in the kitchen; but she saw the glow of his cigarettes, lighted one after another in swift succession, gleaming in the increasing darkness. Before she finished, he came in again and set the lamp going and went to the small room where Danny lay; and she did not disturb him there. Instead she turned to their own room, and at once she prepared for the night, brushing her hair long and carefully to steady her hand, to quiet her throbbing pulses. When she was ready, she lay down; but since Richard did not come to her she went at last to him.

She found him sitting by Danny's bed, and she stood behind him and drew his head against her breast. 'I know! I know, my darling,' she murmured. 'I know, my dear.' He was passive in her arms, and she asked: 'Darling, are you blaming me? I can't stand it if you are!'

He did not look up at her, his eyes on Danny, his word a hard challenge. 'Why should I?'

'You told me not to let him try it unless you were along. But he wanted to surprise you, Richard! He was so happy, planning to surprise you. Yet I shouldn't have let him do it! I'll always blame myself!'

His lungs filled with a long breath of resignation, and he shook his head. 'No, no,' he said, and she felt his surrender. 'It's all right, Ellen. You couldn't do anything.'

'It was terrible,' she cried wretchedly. 'Without any warning at all, he was just gone. He'd been all right a second before, and I was watching the eagle flying over, and when I looked back, Danny was gone, Richard!' Her teeth began to chatter. 'He never came up even once, no cry, no struggle. I took a quick pull at the oars, and one of them slipped out of the oarlock, and I dropped it and almost fell backward in the boat, and I couldn't reach the oar, so I had to paddle, and I must have gone to the wrong place, because when I dove down he wasn't there! Oh Richard! Richard! I'll never forgive myself.'

'It wasn't your fault.'

'I could have made him wait,' she insisted, 'But he was so sweet, wanting to surprise you.' She shivered at a sudden memory. 'When I found him, on the bottom, he put his arms around me. He seemed to be trying to tell me how glad he was I had come, and that he loved me, and forgave me. Do you forgive me, Richard? Do you love me?'

He nodded, still not looking at her. 'Of course I do.'

She tugged at his arm. 'Come to bed, my darling. You must sleep. Come, let me give you sleep and rest and peace.'

'I guess I'll stay with him,' he said heavily.

'You mustn't! You needn't stay here. He'll always be with us, now.' And she said: 'We need you, too, you know. Baby and I.' And when he rose, holding him close, pressing close to him, she whispered: 'We need each other now, Richard. We've nobody but each other now.' While he stood passive in her arms she urged: 'Life never ends, darling. Danny's gone, but our own baby's coming. There's always a new life, to fill the empty place. They go together, death and birth, my dear.'

He let her lead him away, and while he undressed, she went back to turn down the lamp in Danny's room so that it would burn all night. Returning, she found Richard in bed, and she extinguished their lamp and came to his side.

'Make a place for me, darling,' she whispered, and he obeyed. She lay down beside him in the sultry night, her body along his, and she began to shake with silent sobs. Tears filled her eyes and overflowed, till he said at last, helplessly:

'It's all right, Ellen. Don't cry.'

She clung to him. 'We loved him so, Richard.'

'Don't, Ellen. Please!'

'You're blaming me,' she wailed. 'It was my fault!'

'Hush, dear.'

'It was! It was! It was! I can feel you blaming me!' She entwined her arms around him hungrily. 'But oh, Richard, I need you so! I need you so! Don't ever let me go.'

'I never will.'

Her lips, wet with tears, found his beseechingly. 'Hold me tight, Richard! I'm afraid, afraid!' Even while she played her part she thought exultantly that she need not guard her tones. Danny, though he lay so near, could never hear her now.

H ARLAND during these hours had been driven near
madness by what he saw from the lookout above the cabin,
rendered for a few seconds actually unconscious by the blow he
suffered when the motorboat crashed into the ledge, physically
exhausted by the long struggle to recover Danny's body and
then to revive him, overwhelmed at last by the knowledge that
Danny was dead and that Ellen had let him drown. But when
Ellen said they were to have a baby, her words were like a dash
of water in his face. They began to bring him back to sensibility
again.

Still half dazed, he did passively what she bade him; but while
he rowed the laden skiff slowly around the point and turned
down the pond toward the home cove, he groped toward comprehension. The motorboat, cocked on the ledge, gave his
thoughts — as mariners say — a true departure; and he remembered, little by little, all that had happened before, and
after, and so came back to the inescapable fact. Ellen, whom
he had held so high, had let Danny drown.

But even though he knew this was true, yet it was still incredible, till remembrance came to him. Women in their first pregnancy might — so he had read, or heard — suffer psychological
changes so that for a while they were completely irresponsible;
and he clung to this suggestion and even welcomed it, because it
was in some slight degree not only an explanation but a justi-
fication.

For certainly — he was from the moment of Ellen's revelation clear on this — no matter what she had done, he must for her sake and for the sake of their baby keep her blameless before the world.

So when they came back to the boathouse, he told Leick that tale of Danny's circling in the motorboat: yet he saw less than full belief in Leick's eyes, and recognized the flaws in the fable he had contrived. Leick, after his return from Joe Severin's, would have gone up to the cabin, so he must know that they had eaten no lunch; and he knew they would not have set out for an afternoon at the far beach without eating. Also, Harland had said that the motorboat when it hit the ledge was empty, running wild; but if Leick went up to the point, his woodsman's eye would mark where Harland had waded ashore, dripping blood upon the strand, and he would see where Harland had crossed the point and so would know that Harland had been in the motor-boat, would know he lied.

Those betraying traces must be removed before the other found and read them; so when Leick departed for Joe Severin's, Harland was relieved. But he could not do his errand at the point in darkness. It must wait till morning. He and Ellen were left alone at the cabin, and at her insistence he assumed the part he would henceforward play; but at first gray dawn he left her sleeping and took a canoe and paddled swiftly up the lake.

The wrecked motorboat was fast on the ledge, and he loosed the clamps which held the motor in place and transferred it to the canoe; then, stepping out in the shallow water, he lifted the boat free, and although since the bow was smashed it filled quickly, he towed it to the near-by shore and beached it there. In the dimness of early dawn he found drops of dried blood and his own tracks in the sand, and he obliterated the brown stains and smoothed out the footprints and sprinkled spruce spills over them till he was sure that not even Leick could read the story which had been so plain.

Then he paddled back to camp again. It was still early, and the bright hues of coming day tinted the whole dome of the sky. Unready as yet to face Ellen, he climbed to his workroom over the boathouse and watched the sun lift above the wooded ridges to the east, and the mist rising from the lake assumed a golden hue as it began to thin and disappear. The sun was a red ball still sufficiently veiled so that the eye could look upon it boldly, and it laid a red ribbon on the water, and the lake was so calm that the edges of this ribbon, broken by no least ripple, were straight as ruled lines.

Harland watched this spectacle unseeingly. Danny was dead, and Ellen had let him drown, and Back of the Moon, which had been so beautiful, was become an accursed place which after today he would never see again. He could turn his back on it forever; but he could not turn his back on Ellen — and on their baby which she would bear. While he watched the sunrise, he remembered how persistently she had sought to persuade him to leave Danny at Warm Springs, or at Bar Harbor with Ruth. If he had yielded, Danny would be alive today; and Harland grimly blamed himself because he had not yielded, blamed himself for marrying Ellen, blamed himself for disregarding Glen Robie's unspoken warnings, and Mrs. Robie's appraisal of Ellen, and his own instinct to escape from her.

He shook his head, staring at the angry ribbon of the sun's reflection in the water. Blame was useless now. To blame himself — or to blame Ellen — would not bring Danny back to life. He began even to defend Ellen, fighting for her against himself, arguing that she had acted from a primitive instinct to prepare in the world a welcome for this child she was to bear. She had let Danny die because he filled a place in Harland's life, and even in her own, which she wished to pre-empt for the child which was to come.

He found excuses for her; and yet he knew that regardless of excuses, he must — if only for their baby's sake — protect and shield her and keep her blameless before the world. He could never say in years to come to that child yet to be born: 'Yes, your mother murdered my brother.' He alone in the world knew this was true, and — not even Ellen must ever know he knew.

Thus he set his life in order. accepting the future which she imposed upon him; and when from the cabin above he heard her call his name, he answered and went back up the trail — to bondage.

- II -

Ellen — Harland thought wonderingly that she was this morning more beautiful than he had ever seen her, as bright and fair as the dewy dawn itself, with radiant cheeks and eyes washed clear — prepared their breakfast. Before they rose from the table, Leick and Joe Severin arrived, with a hush-voiced man whom Leick had summoned from Bar Harbor and who would do for Danny all that was needed now.

'And I telephoned your house, ma'am,' Leick soberly reported. 'I thought probably you'd want they should know. I talked to your sister.'

Ellen thanked him and turned to Harland. 'There's nothing we can do here, Richard,' she said. 'Why don't we start before it gets too warm, leave them to follow us to Bar Harbor?'

'I'd like to stay.'

'I wish we needn't, darling.' Her eyes touched Leick. 'It's hard for me.'

So he yielded, thinking he must always yield to her now. They set out at once, leaving the others here, following the trail through the silent forest; and the brook that was the outlet of the pond chuckled over its small cascades beside them. Where the path was narrow, Ellen went ahead, striding easily, grace and beauty in her every movement; and Harland watched her, his eyes searching her from crown to heel, remembering that whatever she had done, she bore within her slim body their child who would one day assume form and flesh and features, with the gift of laughter and of love. Just as she had taken life — for she had killed Danny as truly as though she had beaten him under with an oar — so was she giving life as well; and he knew wonderingly that even now he loved her for her partnership with him in this task of reproduction.

They came to the beginning of the wood road and saw Joe Severin's cart there, the horses contentedly switching flies; and they went on, now side by side, and they spoke sometimes of the things they saw by the road — an occasional wild flower, the track of a coon in a wet spot in the ruts, the porcupine that watched them from a hemlock as they passed, the moss carpet on a sloping ledge. So they arrived at Joe Severin's farm — Harland was grateful to find the house deserted — and took the car and drove on.

When they reached Bar Harbor, Ruth met them at the door; and though she said nothing, Harland felt her fine unspoken sympathy. Ellen asked where her mother was, and Ruth said: 'I've kept her abed today. She's not so well, this summer, and I make her rest as much as she will.'

They went to see her. The old woman gripped both Harland's hands in hers, looking up at him, saying crisply: 'Don't try to say anything, and neither will I. I don't know what happened and I don't want to know.'

Ellen bent to kiss her dry cheek, and Harland saw Mrs. Berent's eyes blaze with anger under that caress; and he felt the breath of danger and spoke in quick precaution.

'It was tough on Ellen,' he said loyally. 'It was she who found him.' Despite the old woman's prohibition he explained, wishing to be sure Ellen would remember this story to which they must hold: 'He was cutting circles with the outboard in the middle of the lake and it threw him out. He went down before we could get to him.' And he added: 'We kept diving — it wasn't very deep — till Ellen found him, but we were too late.'

Mrs. Berent had not released his hand, and her clasp tightened now as though she knew the truth, knew Ellen's guilt and was grateful to him for protecting her daughter. Then Ruth led them away, suggesting that they rest. Ellen went with her, but Harland walked down to the shore; and he was for a while alone, with the slow beat of the sea on the rocks below him, and the deep rhythm of the surges entered into him in ponderous, clumsy comforting. When Ruth came down the lawn to summon him

to lunch, they stayed a moment in quiet talk together, and he
felt understanding in her, and solicitude, and affection, and was
heartened and made strong.

– III –

Mrs. Berent was not well enough to go with them to Boston,
and Ruth must stay with her; so it was only Harland and Ellen
and Leick, who had loved Danny almost as well as Harland
himself, who made that sombre journey. Afterward Ellen
wished to stay on in Boston; but Harland decided to go once
more to Back of the Moon with Leick to pack their belongings.
She protested with a surprising urgency that Leick needed no
help, could do whatever needed doing; and when Harland held
stubbornly to his purpose, she said she would accompany them.
But at Bar Harbor she tried again to dissuade him. 'You'll only
torture yourself, going back there,' she pleaded, and at the last
she clung to him, crying: 'Please, Richard! Please! I won't go
with you!'

'Then stay here,' he assented. 'I think you're wise. I'll be
back tomorrow.' So he set out with Leick alone.

They made a silent journey, saying little; and they arrived at
the cabin too late to do anything that night. On the way, and at
the supper table, and while they washed the dishes afterward,
Harland felt in Leick something like an unspoken accusation, as
though the other knew the truth and waited for Harland to
justify his forbearance. These two were so close that it was hard
for either to be secret from the other; and when they sat for a
while on the veranda, Leick with his pipe, Harland smoking
many cigarettes, though for a long time they spoke only an occasional word, their thoughts ran together.

So it was like answering an insistent unuttered question when
Harland said at last: 'Leick, Ellen and I are going to have a baby.'
He said only this in words; but behind the words there was an
appeal for understanding. It was as if he cried: 'Oh, I know you
know that Ellen killed Danny, and I know you're wondering

why I don't accuse her. But I can't, Leick! My hands are tied!'

Leick spoke in instant understanding. 'Is she so? Why —
that will make a lot of difference to you.'

'It makes a lot of difference in — my feeling for her.'

'Course it does!' There was a frank relief in Leick's voice.
'Well now!' He puffed deeply on his pipe, and after a time he
repeated: 'Well!' The word was little, but Harland found it
contenting. Leick almost at once rapped out his pipe and rose,
saying easily: 'Well, I guess we'll sleep tonight.' But though
this was all he said, he seemed to say: It's all right. You'll do
what you have to, and I'll stand by.

In the morning, Harland rose early, and he climbed the hill to
the lookout to search for the binoculars which he had there thrown
heedlessly aside. He found them in the bed of moss below the
ledge; and he remembered with a sick sense of loss the afternoon
when he and Ellen had lain on that soft couch while the white
clouds sailed smiling overhead.

When he returned to the cabin, Leick called cheerfully from
the kitchen; and over breakfast they planned what was to be
done that day. Harland said they would need to patch the
motorboat before towing it down the lake; and Leick said: 'Oh,
I brought it down before Joe and me left here. It can be fixed
up as good as new.' Harland, even though Leick knew the truth,
was glad he had been ahead of the other at the point to oblit-
erate the footprints there.

They worked all morning, packing up everything Harland
wished to take away. There was not much. In their room
Harland noticed Professor Berent's field kit, which Leick had
brought so that Ellen could mount the dead hummingbird for
Danny. Danny too was dead now; and Harland remembered the
beauty of the dead bird, its shimmering throat, the jewelled
colors on its outspread wings and wide-fanned tail; and he
thought, turning for comfort to a simple, childlike faith, that
Danny too was complete and perfect now, his deformities all
healed. So, suddenly, his eyes were drenched with tears; and
he lay across the bed in quiet weeping, and found refreshment
and strength in this surrender.

At lunch he said to Leick: 'I'll never come here again. I'll make you a present of the place, if it's any use to you.'

'I ain't likely to use it unless you do,' Leick replied, and Harland was grateful for this oblique assurance of the other's affection.

'I'll make it over to you anyway,' he insisted. 'You can get a fair price for it, some day. Or let it go for taxes if you like.' For a moment his tone was hard with bitter grief. 'When I walk out of here this time, I never want to think of it again.'

He left that afternoon. Leick would stay behind; and Harland promised to bid Joe Severin come next morning with the cart to transport the things they had packed. That last walk through the forest alone seemed to him long and haunted, and sometimes he broke into a jog trot, in haste to leave the shadowed woods behind.

When he reached Bar Harbor, the dinner hour was past and dusk was near. Ruth came down the stairs to greet him, and he asked: 'Where's Ellen?'

'She's in bed,' Ruth told him. 'She's had one of her upsets. Indigestion. Acute gastritis, the doctor always calls it; but she'll be all right again in a day or two.'

'I've never known her to be ill,' he said in sharp alarm, remembering that Ellen's health was all-important now.

'She's had these spells ever since she was a child.'

'How is she?'

'She's not very comfortable,' Ruth admitted. 'We've got a nurse for her, and they've given her a sedative.'

'What made her sick?' he insisted.

Ruth hesitated, trying to smile. 'Why, I suppose she'll blame my cooking,' she said lightly. 'Yesterday was Mrs. Freeman's day out, and I got dinner.' Then she added honestly: 'But Mr. Quinton was here yesterday afternoon. He'd been talking to Doctor Hamper.' Harland knew the name but not the man. Leick had arranged all the routine details of the procedure necessary after Danny's death, and Doctor Hamper had signed the death certificate. 'He made Ellen tell him all about Danny,'

Ruth explained. 'That was terribly hard for her. I suppose it upset her.'

Harland quickly lighted a cigarette, intent upon this task so that he need not meet Ruth's eyes. He had forgotten Quinton; but Quinton was State Attorney now, and he had the reputation of being one to hold a grudge, and certainly Ellen had treated him shabbily. Harland remembered a conversation between them all last June, when Mrs. Berent had warned Ellen not to give Quinton a chance to even the score, and Ellen had said drily: 'I'm not planning to murder anyone, if that's what you mean.' But now — she had murdered Danny, and if Quinton began prying into the circumstances of Danny's death, he might find evidence of the truth.

'Did he come just to see her?' he asked guardedly.

'No, he was driving through to Augusta, stopped on his way.'

'I suppose Ellen's asleep.' He wondered whether this weight of guilty knowledge would forever ride his shoulders.

'She was, a while ago,' Ruth told him. 'But she may wake again.'

He said he would go sit with her, in case she woke and wanted him, and Ruth led him to her room and the nurse came at Ruth's light touch on the door and spoke with them in the hall and agreed that Harland might take her place for a while, bidding him call her if any need arose.

So Harland sat for hours by Ellen's bed. She lay all composed, her dark hair framing her face, and he thought he had never seen anyone so lovely in her every aspect; and thinking of Quinton, who threatened her now, he became fiercely her defender. Sleeping here, she was so completely childlike that it was impossible to imagine any guilt in her, impossible to believe her anything but good. One of her hands lay on the coverlet; and he leaned down and touched it lightly with his lips. She was his wife, and between man and wife there was a bond which never could be broken. He might condemn her utterly — and love and defend her still.

She slept for hours unmoving, but then her lips began to twist and writhe distressfully, and to utter low tormented sounds, and he called the nurse.

'She'll wake and be sick, Mr. Harland,' the woman predicted. 'But I'll take care of her. You'd better go to bed now. I've had my rest. It's almost two o'clock, you know.'

He said in helpless solicitude: 'She's been through a lot, these last few days.'

'She'll be fine,' she assured him, and — as Ellen began to wake — turned him toward the door.

Ellen was ill for three days, weak and shaken, able only to smile and cling to his hand as though she would never let him go. When she was well enough, with a sense of escape, Harland took her away to Boston. It was a relief to leave Quinton so far behind.

8

ELLEN, explaining to Harland her reluctance to have a baby, had always pretended this feeling was temporary, assuring him that it arose from her fond wish to keep for a while all his devotion. But actually she was determined never to submit to the folly of long months of discomfort, to a climactic hour of torment, and then to further years of slavery when she would be bound down to the service of a helpless infant.

But in the half-panic of those hours after Danny's death, she reached out for motherhood, sure it would bind Harland to her. She was right. Whatever his thoughts, he was always during the months that followed solicitous and attentive. When they returned to Boston, he urged her to consult a physician at once; but since she could not yet be sure of her pregnancy she insisted that there was no hurry. Even when she knew certainly, she still delayed for weeks. Completely uninformed about this mystery in which she now would play her part, she was afraid her condition might somehow betray to the doctor's expert eye that the history she meant to give him was untrue. Only when she was doubly certain did she consent to make an appointment.

She chose when the time came a man she did not know except by reputation. Harland had suggested Doctor Saunders, a general practitioner of the old school, who had been his mother's and his father's reliance in times of stress. Ellen knew him, for it happened that he was also her mother's family physician and had been called for her own occasional indispositions; but she dared not go to him, remembering more than one occasion when he had accused her of malingering. There had been a time, before she learned to rely on subtler weapons, when to get her own way she often vowed that she was sick; and she had suffered more than one defeat at his hands.

But she did not explain this to Harland, said instead: 'He's not an obstetrician.'

'He can tell you who to see,' Harland argued.

'Oh, I know who to see,' she assured him, and went to Doctor Patron.

He was a tremendous, bushy-browed man with sleepy eyes; and as though he saw the nervous tension under which she labored, he began by telling her a mildly bawdy story, chuckling like jelly as he did so. She smiled politely, and he held her in casual talk until she began to feel at ease before he came to the business in hand.

She answered his questions warily, but he accepted her statements at face value, and dismissed her at last with a reassuring word. 'Tell your husband I've read his books,' he said. 'I look forward to meeting him.'

That frightened her. What would he say to Richard? And also, she had after that day another concern. Doctor Patron had told her that her baby would be born in May. She knew he was wrong. It would arrive a few weeks later than he thought. But — if the baby were born in June instead of May, would not that fact tell Harland she had deceived him? How surely could a birth-date be fixed? Were babies ever born too soon, or too late? She wished to ask Doctor Patron, but dared not risk rousing his curiosity; so she went to the library and sought information in unfamiliar volumes there, guiltily and secretly, afraid of meeting some acquaintance, afraid her purpose might be read.

She found no sure answer to her questions; and as the months passed the baby within her began to wear in her thoughts, like a character in an old Greek play, the mask of Danger. Doctor Patron had told her to see him at regular intervals, but — fearing he would suspect the truth — she did not go to him again until the baby quickened. His questions seemed to her alarmingly

persistent. Also, as the baby assumed a life of its own she saw in
it an approaching peril from which there was no escape, and she
was afraid; and because it was Harland's discovery of her deception which most of all she dreaded, she was afraid of him, too.
When the shape of her body began to change, she sought to avoid
him. After lunch she might bid him leave her and seek enter-
tainment elsewhere; and if he proposed that they go together to
call on her mother and Ruth, she refused. She knew he went
frequently to see them; yet she felt no resentment, glad of any
diversion which took him for a while away from her.

So as winter drew toward spring she spent many hours alone
— alone except for that living presence in her womb which was
implacably preparing the ultimate betrayal. Nameless terrors
haunted her, and the child growing in her body came to personify
them all.

– II –

Mrs. Berent's health that winter rapidly failed, but in mid-
March she came with Ruth one day to see Ellen. To climb the
half flight of steps which led from the street up to the front door
made her breath come pantingly, and when they were admitted
she was still trembling. Ellen saw her exhaustion and protested:

'You ought to be in bed, Mother; not paying calls.'

'You hadn't been near me for six weeks,' Mrs. Berent retorted.
'People were beginning to wonder why. If you wouldn't come
to me, I decided to come to you!'

'I don't go anywhere,' Ellen assured her. 'I don't care to see
anyone.'

She waited, hoping they would accept this rebuff and depart;
but Mrs. Berent sat down — without invitation — and she
asked sharply: 'Why not? What is it you're ashamed of? Are
you afraid to face people?'

Before Ellen could speak, Ruth said with a quick, appeasing
smile: 'Now, Mother! Anyone would think you'd come to
quarrel!' And she told Ellen: 'It was such a pleasant day, the

first day that's really felt like spring, I thought it would do Mother good to get a little fresh air.'

'The air in this old house is always stale,' Ellen commented. 'No matter how many windows you open.' She walked restlessly across the room, feeling that they had come to spy upon her and wishing to drive them away; but to do so might excite her mother's shrewd curiosity, so she put a curb on her tongue, forcing herself to play a welcoming part. 'But I'm glad to see you,' she said.

'We might all go for a drive,' Ruth suggested. The big car was waiting at the door.

Ellen shook her head. 'I don't go out.' She spoke to Mrs. Berent. 'I remember your saying, Mother, that in your time, when ladies were going to have babies, they never went out of doors in daylight.'

'You show it surprisingly little.' Mrs. Berent examined her with an appraising eye. 'Considering that you've only two months to go.'

Ellen felt a quick constriction at her heart, for this was almost like an accusation. She tried to speak easily. 'Doctor Patron says I'm built for it.'

Mrs. Berent cleared her throat with a mumbling sound, and Ruth said gently: 'You're more beautiful than you ever were, Ellen, it seems to me.'

'Don't be idiotic! I've still a mirror, you know.'

'I think there's always a special beauty in a woman who's going to have a baby.'

Ellen laughed shortly. 'You sound like Richard. I had to have one, to keep him in love with me.'

Mrs. Berent tossed her head. 'Richard's a fine young man, Ellen! You were lucky to get him.'

'You tried hard enough to prevent it!'

'For his sake, not for yours.' The old woman's tone was harsh. 'You're not good enough for him!'

Ruth spoke quickly: 'Hush, Mother!' She smiled. 'You always were a barking dog. You don't fool us, you know.'

'Richard's like a simple, decent boy,' Mrs. Berent remarked, half to herself. 'Completely trusting and credulous.' Ellen looked at her in sharpened apprehension, but the older woman only said, half pleadingly: 'See that you keep him so, Ellen. Don't ever mock the things he cherishes.'

'I'd do anything for Richard,' Ellen assured her. 'You know that!' She met her mother's shrewd eyes, but she could not support that searching glance, turned hurriedly to Ruth. 'You mustn't let Mother get too tired,' she suggested, hoping they would go. But Mrs. Berent said:

'Fiddlesticks! Where's Richard? I'd like to see him.'

'At the club, I think,' Ellen told her. 'He's never here in the afternoon.'

Ruth said: 'He sometimes drops in on us. We're always so glad to see him. He does Mother good.'

Ellen did not speak, but Mrs. Berent said crisply: 'And we do him good, too. You're making him pretty unhappy, Ellen, by the way you're carrying on. I've given him some good advice, but he doesn't take it!'

Ellen's voice hardened and her cheeks were hot. 'I can just hear you all talking me over, over your teacups, like three old gossips!'

'It isn't that, Ellen,' Ruth assured her. 'Dick's just a bewildered young father-to-be, you know.' Her tone was affectionate. 'Imagining all sorts of dreadful things. And he can't talk about them to you.'

'Why not?' Ellen's eyes were icy. 'Why can he say things to you he can't to me? Whose husband is he, mine, or yours and Mother's?' Abruptly her simmering rage at them and at the world overflowed. 'Of course I know you were always in love with him yourself!'

Mrs. Berent came furiously to her feet. 'You ought to be smacked!' she exclaimed. 'You insufferable little . . .'

But Ruth hushed her, and she said to Ellen gravely: 'You're right, Ellen, but not in the way you think. Mother and I are both fond of Dick. We love him dearly. And Ellen — we all — all three of us — love you!'

Ellen bit her lip. 'I'm sorry,' she said. 'I'm — I don't know what I'm saying, half the time.'

Mrs. Berent adjusted her fur piece, turning toward the door. 'Come along, Ruth,' she said indignantly. 'Good-bye, Ellen!'

'Wait,' Ellen urged. 'I'll give you a cup of tea.'

'Thanks, I can get tea at home!'

Ellen looked appealingly at Ruth. 'Make her stay,' she begged. A moment ago she had wished to be rid of them, but now she was suddenly afraid of being alone. 'I didn't mean it Ruth. Make her stay. Richard will be here soon.'

So at Ruth's intercession Mrs. Berent was persuaded to sit down again, and tea came, and they talked polite commonplaces for a while; but Ellen was appraising Ruth with a thoughtful eye, remembering something half seen in the other's face a moment ago. When Harland presently appeared she watched Ruth greet him, and she caught her lip between her teeth, her fingers digging at her palms. She had flung the bitter taunt blindly, seeking only to hurt at any cost. 'You were always in love with him . . .' She had spoken without thought, but her own words produced the thought. Perhaps they were true! Perhaps Ruth had always been in love with Richard — and was in love with him today!

When they departed, he went with them to the waiting car, and Ellen from the open door above watched him hand Mrs. Berent into her place. He leaned in to kiss her wrinkled cheek, turned to grasp Ruth's hand. 'Good-bye,' he said. 'We're mighty glad you came. See you soon.' They drove away, and he climbed the steps to Ellen.

'Ruth's sweet, isn't she?' she said, watching him secretly.

'They're swell people,' he agreed, his eyes on the departing car.

'I always seem to quarrel with Mother, but no one can quarrel with Ruth.'

He laughed. 'Your mother has a sharp tongue, but it doesn't mean anything!'

'Ruth's wonderful, always so good to her.' She persisted, studying him with narrowed eyes. 'Her life will be pretty empty, when Mother dies.'

'I think Ruth will always have a rich, full life,' he said thoughtfully. 'She's that kind of person.'

Ellen, in sudden terror at his tone, desperate to please him and make him content with her, laughed and caught his hand. 'Come, darling,' she cried. 'I feel like being gay this evening. Let's have a celebration.' She led him away upstairs, made merry love to him, said he must dress for dinner. 'We'll be festive,' she insisted. 'Just to humor me.' She put on her most becoming gown, and went downstairs on his arm, and even though she would not share it she insisted that he have a cocktail, and herself mixed it for him; and at dinner she was very gay, and afterward at her suggestion they played piquet together till because he won every game she declared she would play no more, and turned on the radio and found dance music and made him dance with her. He caught the infection of her gaiety, and she thought she won him to a deeper fondness than he had felt since Danny died. It was late, well past midnight, when they went upstairs together, and when after she was abed he came to kiss her good night, wishing to be reassured, she asked:

'Was it fun this evening, Richard?'

'You bet.'

'Have you liked me?'

'I've loved you,' he told her gently.

She brushed this assurance almost indifferently aside. 'I know. I know you love me. But I want you to like me, too.'

He bent to kiss her again. 'Don't you ever worry about that,' he told her heartily. 'Good night, Ellen!' He turned away. 'Sleep well,' he called from the door.

But she lay long awake, remembering that he had not answered her, trembling with recurrent waves of terror, feeling terribly alone.

– III –

After that day, Ellen's solitary thoughts gnawed at another bone. Richard had loved Danny, and Danny was dead; but

now Richard turned to Ruth — who called him Dick, as Danny
had used to do — and who had always loved him! Thus thinking, as a flagellant courts the lash, she urged him to see as much
of Ruth as possible, herself avoiding him. For weeks now she
had had breakfast in bed, and she began to have her lunch from a
tray in her room, refusing to join him at the table, till Harland
in a rising concern insisted she must be ill and would have summoned Doctor Patron. But at her last visit to the doctor's
office she had suspected some unspoken question in his eyes, as
though he were puzzled by what he saw, and she was unwilling
to face him; so she consented to join Harland every day at lunch.
Yet she still sent him away each afternoon, and she began to
urge him to go out in the evening, to his club, or wherever he
chose.

'Go see Ruth,' she suggested more than once, watching him
jealously. 'You like her, and I'm not good company for anyone,
not even for you.'

Because she insisted, he sometimes left her even after dinner;
and she imagined him with Ruth, and not infrequently she was
proved right in this suspicion, because he brought her messages
from Ruth or from her mother.

But one April evening when she asked where he had been he
said that he had gone that afternoon to see Doctor Patron, and
in a quick anger born of terror she demanded:

'Why did you do that?'

'I've been worried about you,' he evaded. 'You're not looking
well.'

She thrust her hand out of his sight below the table, clenching
her fist hard, forcing herself to smile, exclaiming: 'Darling, don't
you know you must never tell a woman that? I feel half-sick
already, just from hearing you say it!' She was breathless with
terror.

'As a matter of fact,' he admitted, 'his nurse called up to ask
why you hadn't been to see him. You're supposed to go every
month, you know, but you haven't done it.'

She tried to speak lightly. 'Oh, I can't be bothered! He's a

regular old Miss Nancy, always giving me pills and things.'
She laughed carefully. 'Don't worry, darling! I'm just as
anxious as you are to have our baby perfect, you know.'

'It's you I'm thinking about, not the baby.'

'Liar!' She smiled. 'You know that's not true!'

'It is, Ellen,' he insisted. 'You see — the baby's not very real
to me yet; but you are! I see you every day, and you're thin,
and you look so tired and dragged.'

'I'm fine,' she insisted, but her nerves were in jangling revolt
and she wanted to scream.

'He says exercise would be good for you. We might take a
walk, on nice days.'

'There haven't been any nice days yet! Either it's freezing
cold, or it's all mush underfoot!' She laughed, fighting for self-
control, hating him, hating his solicitude. 'I shall see to it that
we have our next baby in the fall.'

'Fine,' he agreed. 'But that's the next one. This one is our
job now, Ellen. You've got to take care of yourself.'

She could endure no more. 'I'm sleepy,' she said, forcing a
yawn. 'Maybe you're right. I'll begin right now by going to
bed.'

He went upstairs with her. She had elected, since the turn of
the year, to have a room of her own; and at her door she kissed
him, said: 'There, Richard. Good night!'

'Let me help you undress.'

'For Heaven's sake!' she cried in a sharp exasperation, 'I can
take care of myself!'

'I'm worried about you.'

Her voice rose in shrill hysteria. 'Oh, let me alone! For God's
sake, let me alone!' He stared at her in hurt bewilderment, and
she went into her room, and banged the door hard in his face,
shutting him out, standing with her hands braced against the
door as though afraid he would force his way in to her. He said
at last, humbly, through the heavy panels:

'Good night, Ellen!'

'Good night!'

'I'll stop on my way to bed, see you're tucked in!'

Her lips were red and bitten, but she controlled her voice. 'All right, but don't wake me up!' she told him, and heard his reluctant footsteps move away.

She crossed to her dressing table and sat down, looking at herself in the mirror in a long appraisal. What he had said was true. The smooth roundness of her cheeks was gone, and her sleek hair was lifeless, and her eyes were shadowed. Her own thoughts during these months had clawed at her, till there were faint lines like scars at the corners of her mouth; but she told herself now — even though she knew it was not true — that it was her baby which thus ravaged her, draining her strength, tormenting her nerves, haunting her dreams. She hated it, and she was near hating Richard too; and at the realization her head dropped in her arms and she wept long and rackingly, pitying herself because life had thus betrayed her. It was to hold him that she was bearing him this child; yet now because to do so the beauty he had loved must pay a heavy price, he was turning against her, mocking her who was become in his eyes an ugly, swollen thing. She wept, alone and loveless in the bitter, heartless world, hating him, hating her mother and Ruth, hating herself.

The baby in her stirred and she beat at it with her fists, crying through tight teeth:

'Oh, I hate you, too, you little beast! I hate you, hate you! Oh, I wish you'd die!'

Then, as though her own words had been a revelation, she sat for a long time, staring into her glass, her thoughts a turmoil. The baby had served its turn, averting Harland's first reaction to Danny's death; but now the baby which had helped her hold him was making her lose him. Yet if she were herself again, her beauty restored, she could surely win him back to her side.

She looked intently down at her heavy body, remembering her own wish, wondering how she could make that wish come true.

9

RUTH had long since found that Mrs. Berent and Ellen — allowing for the difference in their ages — were frighteningly like each other, united by a sort of psychic understanding as a result of which the older woman often foresaw what Ellen would do, or interpreted what she had done, with astonishing accuracy. Remarks she made which at the time seemed to be simply ill-tempered explosions were as likely as not to prove in retrospect to have been shrewd prophecy. When Harland and Ellen were married, Mrs. Berent predicted disaster, but till the day of Danny's death they were so obviously happy together that Ruth sometimes smilingly reminded the older woman how wrong she had been, and Mrs. Berent was, if not convinced, at least silenced. But the day Leick telephoned that Danny had been drowned, she said, not with her old violence but in a broken submission:

'Ruth, Ellen had something to do with that! She always hated that young one.'

Ruth, remembering how often the other had been right in such harsh guesses, felt an instant terror. 'Mother! What a horrible thing to say!' She fought down her own fears. 'Don't be ridiculous! Ellen loved Danny for Dick's sake — and for his own.'

'Ellen never loved anyone but herself!'

Ruth, an amiable ferocity in her tone, retorted: 'She's exactly like you! Now mind your tongue, or I'll send you to bed!' The older woman's health that summer had begun to fail, and Ruth, in a concern she tried to hide, watched over her tenderly.

She wished to make Mrs. Berent forget her suspicions, but the other clung to them stubbornly. After Harland and Ellen returned to Boston, Leick one day came to the house in Bar Harbor with some of Ellen's things from Back of the Moon. Ruth, returning from an errand, found him with Mrs. Berent. He seemed glad to escape, and when he was gone the older woman said grimly:

'He's the biggest liar unhung, Ruth. I tried to get the truth out of him about Danny, but he just says the same thing over and over, like a parrot.'

Ruth spoke almost in anger. 'Mother, you're acting like a spiteful child!'

'Well, I'm not the only one,' Mrs. Berent argued. 'Leick says Russ Quinton went up there to Back of the Moon and asked a lot of questions, so he doesn't believe that story either.'

'Mr. Quinton's a busybody, but there's no excuse for you!'

'I can think what I please!'

'Then see to it you think the right things,' Ruth warned her with tender severity. 'Or you'll make me out of patience with you.' She heard her own words with a sudden sorrow, recognizing the fact that Mrs. Berent, who had once made every decision, now accepted her domination; and the realization filled Ruth with a wistful sadness, telling her more clearly than words that the other was aging, that behind the older woman's sharp tongue there was now a quavering uncertainty which she sought to conceal.

They too, a little later, returned to Boston, and winter settled down. One day Harland came to tea, and as he left he said to Ruth: 'I'm worried about your mother.'

'She's not well,' she assented. 'She won't let me call Doctor Saunders, but I've talked with him. He says it's just that she's getting old, says there's nothing to do except keep her quiet, make her rest a lot, not let her get excited.' She smiled a little. 'That's not as easy as it sounds. Mother enjoys getting excited.'

He chuckled. 'She's a grand old dame!'

'She's scared,' Ruth confessed, her eyes shadowed. 'She knows — what's happening to her, of course; and she scolds all the time just to keep her courage up.'

'Don't you need some help, taking care of her?'

'Heavens, no!' Ruth laughed. 'She wouldn't let anyone come near her but me. Mother and I always got along, you know.' Her eyes filled. 'Only sometimes I want to cry, it's so pathetic when she lets me boss her around.'

As winter drew toward spring she saw that he too had his anxieties, that he was concerned for Ellen; and she tried to reassure him, reminding him what a proud young father he would be, bidding him think of the happy hours he and Ellen and the baby would have together. Sometimes she succeeded, but one day in April she saw in him an accented concern, and asked for Ellen, and he confessed his fears.

'I ought not to leave her alone,' he said. 'But she likes to be rid of me, says I make her nervous, says I'm always mooning around.' He laughed uneasily, and added: 'She sent me out after dinner last evening, and when I came home she wasn't there! She came in just about the time I was ready to call the police, dripping with perspiration. She'd gone for a walk, Ruth; had tramped up and down the Esplanade for an hour, worn herself out.'

Ruth hesitated, blaming Ellen but unwilling to let him see this. 'I expect the exercise was good for her,' she suggested.

'I suppose it was.'

'Is she all right today?'

'Oh yes. I guess it didn't do her any harm.'

'These last few weeks before the baby comes seem like an interminable time to her, of course.'

He nodded, grinned ruefully. 'They seem like a long time to me, too,' he agreed.

– II –

Ruth next day, thinking she might be helpful, went to see Ellen. For pretext, she turned first to the shopping district, and she arrived at the house on Chestnut Street with an armful of bundles. Harland was not there, but she found Ellen in the pantry painting one of the cupboards, while old Mrs. Huston who had cooked for Harland's mother and still served him and Ellen now, looked on in severe disapproval.

Ellen welcomed Ruth with a smile. 'Hello there! Get another brush and take a hand!'

'I thought it was about time I brought some baby presents,' Ruth explained. 'Whatever are you doing?'

'Put them on the dining room table,' Ellen directed. 'I can't touch anything now. I'm all daubed up with paint. This dark old pantry has always bothered me. Just thinking about it took my appetite. Enough white paint will make it look bright and clean.'

'A painter would do a neater job,' Ruth said smilingly. 'You've as much paint on the floor — and in your hair — as on the shelves.'

'I got tired of doing nothing all day.'

'Isn't that — painting, I mean — supposed to be bad for you?' Ruth suggested, and Mrs. Huston said triumphantly:

'There, ma'am, haven't I been telling you so!'

Ellen laughed at them both. 'Old wives' tales!' she declared. 'Besides, I'm almost done!'

'You'll be done altogether if you don't stop it,' Mrs. Huston cried.

'Oh pooh!' Ellen said laughingly: 'Go open your packages, Ruth, and show things to me while I finish this shelf.'

She was very gay, her eyes bright, her cheeks flushed, her hair in a pretty disorder; and Ruth, deciding her own doubts were absurd, obeyed, displaying a pair of little blankets, a satin quilt, a collection of small knitted things. Ellen, splashing paint along the shelves, the gifts heedlessly approved. She finished her task, and made Mrs. Huston — vocal in protest at this new recklessness — pour a trickle of turpentine over her hands while she washed them. When she and Ruth were alone, Ruth said laughingly:

'Mrs. Huston's like a hen with one chick over you, isn't she?'

Ellen smiled in agreement. 'Richard says she's always loved taking care of sick people,' she explained. 'If she had her way, she'd put me to bed and keep me there! I keep telling her I'm not sick, that having babies is perfectly healthy; but she'd make an invalid of me if she could.'

'You certainly don't look like an invalid!'

'I'm not,' Ellen assured her. 'I'm wonderfully well. I took a long walk last night, and it was just what I needed. I feel better today than I have for months!'

She had to see and to admire the presents all over again; and Ruth, watching her, listening to her quick, delighted laughter, decided that Richard's concern, though probably natural enough, was reasonless. Kissing Ellen good-bye she said happily: 'I'm so darned glad I came. You're doing a grand job on this baby, Ellen. I know it's been hard for you, all winter, but the end's in sight now.'

Ellen nodded gaily. 'Yes, only a month more,' she agreed. 'Give Mother my love. Maybe Richard and I will walk up and see you this evening. Exercise seems to be good for me!' She was so jolly and so affectionate that Ruth went home completely reassured.

Harland and Ellen did appear that evening, and Mrs. Berent received them in her sitting room. Ellen's happier humor had infected Harland, so they were all merry together. Even Mrs. Berent's tongue lost its roughness, and when they were gone, she said:

'Well there! Ellen was nicer tonight than I've ever seen her!'

Ruth nodded. 'She acted like someone with a lovely secret she wasn't ready to tell. And of course Dick was happy too.'

'She may settle down and make him a good wife after all,' Mrs. Berent reflected. 'I guess I'm getting old and soft, Ruth. I've almost hated Ellen, ever since she was a girl. You're more like my own daughter than she is. But she was real sweet tonight.' Then, in her old harsh tone she added: 'If she ever makes Richard unhappy, she — well, I hope she gets what she deserves.'

'Men are so helplessly dependent, in so many ways,' Ruth reflected. 'I suppose that's why so many wives are tyrants.' She laughed a little. 'We women are natural bullies, aren't we?'

Mrs. Berent said in an unaccustomed, gentle tone: 'You'd

never bully a man, my dear.' She chuckled. 'You're too ready
to let me bully you!'

Ruth did not see Ellen again during the next two or three days.
Then one morning while she was helping Mrs. Berent make ready
to receive her breakfast tray, she was called to the telephone,
heard Richard on the line.

'Did I wake you, Ruth?'

'Oh no, I've been up and dressed long ago.'

'Can I come to breakfast?'

'Of course.' Her breath caught, for his voice was hollow with
pain. 'What is it, Dick? Is anything wrong?'

'Why — Ellen's lost her baby,' he said heavily. 'She's all
right, but she lost the baby.' Ruth for a moment could not speak,
and he added: 'I'm at the hospital, but she's asleep now. I'll get
a taxi, come right along.'

- III -

Ellen was a month in the hospital, and at Ruth's suggestion,
Harland during these weeks took many of his meals with them.
That first morning when he reached the house she thought he was
emptied, like a collapsed balloon, all the life gone out of him. He
talked much, repeating the same things over and over as though
seeking some comfort in empty words. Ellen, he said, had walked
in her sleep during the night, had fallen downstairs. Her cry woke
him, and he was quickly at her side. She insisted she was unhurt,
but almost at once they knew harm had been done, and Harland
summoned Doctor Patron, who took her to the hospital. The
baby — a lusty boy — was dead.

Ruth and Mrs. Berent comforted Harland with empty commonplaces and persuaded him to lie down for a few minutes on the bed
in Professor Berent's room. Ruth, full of maternal tenderness,
went to show him the way. She made him remove his coat and
tie, loosed and took off his shoes and covered him over.

He slept till noon. When he woke, Ruth thought he would go
at once to the hospital, but he made no move. She proposed to

telephone Doctor Patron. He agreed, and she did so; but the doctor said Ellen was sleeping, under a sedative.

'She's perfectly all right.' Ruth wondered why he spoke so curtly. 'But she won't know any of you for a day or two.' He added: 'Of course, Mr. Harland can see her.'

Ruth reported this to Harland, and he nodded in a dull way. 'I'll go tomorrow,' he said. He had lunch with them, then went out, promising to return for dinner; but at dinner time a message was telephoned from the club that Mr. Harland would be unable to come.

Ruth was almost relieved, glad he would not see Mrs. Berent; for after his departure she had spoken of Ellen with a bitter anger which Ruth dared not understand. The older woman was so dis turbed that Ruth wished to call Doctor Saunders, but the proposal roused Mrs. Berent's wrath again, so Ruth was glad when she fell fitfully asleep.

Harland appeared for lunch next day, tired and drawn. 'I couldn't come last night,' he confessed. 'I tried playing bridge, thought it might give me something to think about; and before I realized it, I'd had too many highballs. I slept at the club.'

Ruth nodded understandingly. 'I don't wonder,' she said. 'I hope it did you good.' Her concern for Mrs. Berent had kept her from too much thought of Ellen, and when Harland now asked how the older woman was, thinking that to distract him might serve in his case a like end, she confessed: 'Why, she was pretty sick last night, and she's exhausted today.' She gave details, anxious to help him forget Ellen for a while; but she saw that he listened without attention, his thoughts still his own, his mouth set in grim lines. 'I wish I could go with you to see Ellen,' she said at last. 'But I can't — and it's you she'll want to see, anyway.'

'I don't want to go,' he admitted; and when she looked at him in surprise he said evasively: 'I hate hospitals, always did, even when Danny was at Warm Springs.' His voice caught and he hesitated, said grimly: 'But I'll go, of course.'

During the weeks Ellen stayed in the hospital, Ruth was frightened by the settled hopelessness in him, refusing to guess its cause. The loss of their baby must have been a heavy blow, but other men had suffered thus and still kept a high heart; and it was not like Harland to surrender so completely to despair. He breakfasted at home, and worked every morning. 'Or at least I try to,' he told Ruth drily. 'But I don't accomplish anything. I'm like a boy watching the clock, waiting for school to let out.' Every day he walked up the hill to lunch with her — Mrs. Berent, from the day Ellen lost her baby, never came downstairs, and Doctor Saunders was a regular caller now — and in the afternoon, if Ruth had an errand to do, Harland took her place at the older woman's bedside. Ruth sometimes came home to find him reading aloud while Mrs. Berent drowsed contentedly, or they might be talking quietly together. But always there was in Harland that profound, surrendering dejection, and she wished to challenge him back to bold strength again, but dared not, dreading his reply.

She often took advantage of these free hours when he stayed with Mrs. Berent to go to the hospital to see Ellen. She found the other frail and thin; but she saw too that Ellen was animated by some inner excitement. She talked a great deal, and was extravagantly gay. There was something desperate and frantic in this gaiety, as though Ellen threw out a screen of laughing words to ward off thoughts of which she was afraid.

She asked always for news of Harland; and Ruth was puzzled by this, since he now saw Ellen almost every day. But when she said so, Ellen exclaimed:

'I know. He comes to see me, but he's just — visiting the sick! You know, the heavy smell of flowers and the funereal air!' She laughed in a brittle way. 'When he's here, I feel like a corpse all laid out in her coffin. He's so persistently cheerful that it's worse than if he cried all the time!'

'He doesn't like hospitals,' Ruth remembered. 'But he'll be fine when you're able to go home.'

'I know you're taking good care of him. He tells me every day how wonderful you are.'

'Yes, he has lunch and dinner with me every day.'

'With you and Mother?'

'Mother's not coming downstairs much,' Ruth explained, keeping her tone as casual as possible so that Ellen need not be worried about Mrs. Berent. 'He's with her now.' She smiled. 'Mother always liked him, you know. She's perfectly happy for me to leave her, if he's there.'

'Be nice to him,' Ellen urged. 'Poor man! I've failed him completely, but I'll make it up to him by-and-by.'

Mrs. Berent, during this time while Ellen was still in the hospital, changed in a frightening way. She who had been so vocal now seldom spoke; and when she did, it was in a flat and spiritless tone. It was as though she withdrew behind a wall of silence; and Ruth sometimes thought her silence was like Ellen's vivacity, that each of them erected a protective barrier against something of which they were afraid.

She had her own forebodings, for it was clear that Mrs. Berent's strength was failing. When Ruth more and more often insisted upon summoning Doctor Saunders, the older woman now received him unprotestingly. After half an hour with her, on one of these visits, he said with hollow professional cheerfulness:

'All you need is rest and plenty of it, Mrs. Berent. You'll be right as rain presently.'

Ruth thought that doctors were sometimes wrong to treat their patients like ignorant children, who could be soothed with fairy tales; and Mrs. Berent answered him with some of her old spirit. 'Teach your grandmother to suck eggs, Doctor! I know what's happening to me.' Then in a different tone she added: 'It's all right. I've lived longer than I wish I had, already.' Ruth standing by, pressed her hand to her throat to quiet the beating of her heart there.

'Pshaw!' he protested. 'You'll live to bury the lot of us.'

'Bury?' she echoed. 'I thought cremation was the latest style!' Ruth knew she was thinking bitterly of Ellen's insistence at the time of Professor Berent's death. So often nowadays, when Mrs. Berent spoke of her daughter, it was with something implacable and unrelenting in her quiet tones. Today, after the doctor was gone, she said, apropos of nothing:

'You know, Ruth, there's never been a sleepwalker in our family!'

Ruth did not answer, remembering guiltily that she too had had this ugly thought. Ellen, as far as she knew, had never walked in her sleep till that night she fell; but even though this were true, the implications were intolerable. Ruth was glad now that she had never told her mother about Ellen's painting the pantry, about Ellen's slipping out of the house at night to walk herself into exhaustion.

There were other occasions when Mrs. Berent's words suggested more than they said. 'I'd like to see Leick again,' she remarked one day, and Ruth guessed she was remembering Danny and blaming Ellen for his death.

'You'll see him when we go to Bar Harbor,' she said reassuringly.

'I don't think I'll go to Bar Harbor this summer,' Mrs. Berent murmured. 'I think I'll be happier staying quietly in one place.' And Ruth felt a cold touch on her heart.

Ellen in due time left the hospital, but she still stayed abed all day. Ruth would have gone to see her, but Mrs. Berent grew weaker all the time, and she refused to have a nurse, so Ruth was bound to her side. Harland came less often to the house on Mount Vernon Street, and Ellen came not at all.

One night after Ruth had prepared her for sleep, and had turned out the bed light, Mrs. Berent said: 'Ruth, be good to Richard. He'll need you.'

'Of course,' Ruth assented. 'Good night, now, Mother.'

'Good night, my dear.'

In the morning when Ruth went to her, Mrs. Berent seemed still asleep, breathing a little heavily; but Ruth could not rouse her, and she did not come back to consciousness during the three days more before she died.

- IV -

Their home, Ruth and Ellen agreed, should be sold. It was much too big for Ruth alone, and they quickly found a buyer. Ruth was to give possession on the first of July, and since this meant they must make some disposition of the furniture, Ellen, as soon as she was strong enough, came one day to go over everything with Ruth. Many things would go to the auction rooms. A few pieces Ruth wished to keep for the small apartment into which she planned to move; but Ellen claimed nothing. Only in that upper room where she and her father had worked together did she hesitate; but then she said:

'You'll have to do this room, Ruth. I can't bear to — see these things go. But of course they must.' Yet she elected to stay in that upper room for a while alone. 'I guess I'm sentimental,' she confessed. 'I want to stay and say good-bye to Father, all by myself.' When she joined Ruth downstairs, a few minutes later, she suggested that the museum might like some of the specimens, and Professor Berent's notes and papers, and Ruth promised to have a man come and select what he chose. The auctioneer could take the rest.

A week later Ruth moved to the Hotel Tarleton, not far from Harland's Chestnut Street home, to stay while she chose an apartment. She thought Harland and Ellen might wish to go to Bar Harbor for the summer, and dining with them a day or two later, she proposed this. Harland looked doubtfully at Ellen.

'Would you like that?' he asked. It was the first time since the baby's death that Ruth had seen them together, and she could not blind herself to the change in their relationship. Ellen was outwardly as she had always been, but Harland showed no trace of tenderness.

'No, no!' Ellen told him sharply. 'No, I don't want to stay in any one place.' And she said wistfully: 'I'd like to go back to New Mexico, but we can never go back, can we, Richard? Never recapture what was so perfect once.'

'No, we can't go back,' he assented. 'When a thing's done, it's done.'

His tone was sombre, and Ruth saw Ellen look at him with something desperate in her eyes. 'No, we must do something exciting!' she cried. 'Something we'll both enjoy.' Then, as though on sudden inspiration: 'I know! Ruth, when we went through the house, I saw Father's fishing rods and things. Did you let them go?'

'No,' Ruth assured her. 'They're in storage. I kept all his personal things, and Mother's.'

Ellen spoke quickly. 'Well, listen, Richard. There's a salmon river up in Canada that Father and I used to plan to fish, sometime. The Miminegouche. Darling, let's go there. Father and I found out all about it. We can take our canoes to a town on a lake at the headwaters and go downstream, fish as we go, trout and grilse at first, and then salmon. Father and I met a man in Newfoundland who had done it. He said the upper river's beautiful.' She went on, giving details, speaking more and more rapidly, in a rising animation. 'We can take a week, or two weeks, or a month,' Ellen urged. 'Oh, Richard, it would be wonderful!'

Harland hesitated. 'I'm not sure you're well enough,' he objected. 'Not sure you can stand it.' He looked at Ruth. 'What do you think?' he asked.

Ellen said angrily: 'You two! Don't you suppose I know what I can stand, Richard?' Then, before Ruth could speak, she cried in an eager tone: 'I know! We'll take Ruth along! Then if I play out, she can take care of me. Not that I'm likely to. I'll be fit as can be, once I get away from here. Ruth, you'll be lonesome without us, with Mother gone. I think that's the perfect idea. We'll all go.'

Ruth laughed. 'I'm no fisherwoman, Ellen.'

'You'll learn! I caught a salmon the first day I fished.' She persuaded them with many urgencies, and Ruth thought she was like a teasing child, her eyes flashing from one of them to the other, alert for any sign of yielding in either, pouncing on the first hint of surrender, driving hard through the least breach in their defenses, winning her way as she always had.

Ruth let Harland make the decision. She saw deep weariness

in him, and it seemed to her that his need was greater than Ellen's. Ellen, even in anticipation, was stimulated, full of eagerness; and Harland in the end agreed for Ellen's sake. Ruth
agreed for his.

– v –

They alighted from the train, one early morning in July, at a
well-kept little station labelled Hazelgrove; and Leick — he had
come ahead to secure guides — was waiting to meet them. Of the
guides, one was a fair-haired, lean youngster whom Ruth guessed
to be still in his teens and whose name was Tom Pickett. The
other, older than Leick, was Simon Verity; a cheerful, small man
with shoulders so heavy they seemed almost deformed. Both
dwelt here in this village in the wilderness, and Jem Verity,
through whom their services had been engaged, assured Harland
they were good men.

'Sime has been poaching deer and salmon down the river all his
life,' he said, 'and lumbering in the winter, and if he can't find
you a few salmon, there ain't nobody can. Tom ain't so way wise,
but he can handle a canoe and an axe, and he's a good camp cook,
and he learns quick. Anything you want done, you tell him.
He'll pick up the know-how in no time.' He added, like a good
merchant: 'I been over your outfit with Leick. Might be a few
more things you'll need. I've got anything you've a mind to ask
for, at the store.'

From the station, only a scattering farm or two was visible; but
Jem's car took them to the village. The houses seemed to Ruth
neat and attractive, bright in white paint, each with its cropped
lawn; and most of them had flower beds that gave a splash of
color. The presiding genius of the store was Mrs. Verity, an
enormously fat woman with a merry, understanding eye, and
Ruth liked her at once. Harland and the guides and Jem discussed their needs; and watching Harland speak with these men,
Ruth saw that there was already a change in him. It had begun
when they stepped off the train and the sweet scent of the dew-

wetted forest met their nostrils. He seemed suddenly at home.

After their purchases were made, Leick took Harland to secure licenses and forest permits, Ruth and Ellen waiting with the other guides at the wharf; but when Harland returned, the boatman who would run them down the lake had not appeared, and Harland and Jem Verity had to fetch him. Before they came back, the gear was loaded, the canoes harnessed for towing, and at once they were away.

In the motorboat bound down the lake, Ellen stood in the bow and Ruth and Harland sat in the stern; and Ruth asked many questions. How did people live, in a town like this: by farming? Hunting? Trapping? How many people were there in the village? What did their futures hold?

'You're as full of questions as Mrs. Barrell, our boatman's wife,' he said, amused. 'When Jem and I went to get him, she kept up a rapid fire as long as we were within hearing.'

'I know how she feels.' Ruth smiled. 'It must be terrible to be filled with lively curiosity — and at the same time to know everything about all your neighbors, so that there's nothing about which to be curious. Probably seeing someone she didn't know went to her head!'

Tom Pickett and Sime sat on the load of gear and sucked foul pipes in relaxed silence. Ellen stood beside Wes Barrell at the wheel, her head bare, her dark hair flying; but after a while she turned to watch Ruth and Harland and saw them laughing together. Ruth became conscious of her steady scrutiny and was uneasy under it, for no reason except that Ellen's eyes never left them. She rose at last to pick her way forward, and she asked Ellen:

'Glad we're on our way?'

'Of course.'

'Did the train tire you?'

'Heavens, no! I'm never tired except in cities.' And Ellen said: 'You and Richard were having such a good time back there. I enjoyed watching you.'

'I'd never seen at close range a little town like that one,' Ruth explained. 'And he was telling me about it.'

Wes Barrell beside them grinned and said there was darned little to tell. 'Nothing ever happens there,' he declared. 'Drives my old woman crazy!'

Ruth began to ask him about his family, but she found herself presently answering questions rather than asking them; and Ellen left them together, going back to join Leick and Harland, who now in the stern were talking quietly.

When they reached the foot of the lake, the dam tender, an asthmatic old man who continually panted, like a dog on a hot day, came from his cabin to greet them. It was the driest June he could remember, he said; and Ruth, going with Harland and Ellen to look at the dam while the men built a luncheon fire, saw the stream bed almost completely bare. Leick joined them.

'He's going to give us enough water to get down the first piece,' he reported. 'It'll save us the carry, and the drive's over long ago, so he can spare the water.' He grinned. 'The old man just stays here out of habit anyway. He don't have any place else to go.'

'What does he live on?' Ruth asked. 'I saw a little garden up by his cabin, but it's not enough to raise anything.'

'That's just to fetch the deer around,' Leick explained. 'Then he can shoot one, whenever he's a mind, to keep it from eating up his peas or whatever. He lives mostly on venison and pork and soda biscuits and potatoes.' He looked toward the fire where young Tom Pickett was tending to the cookery. 'Thought I'd give the boy a chance,' he told Harland. 'See what he can do.' And he said: 'I figured Sime Verity would handle Miss Ruth's canoe. I'll take Mrs. Harland, let Tom paddle you.'

Ruth saw Harland's surprise. 'It won't seem natural, not to be with you.'

'Tom's no fisherman,' Leick explained. 'But you can tell him what to do. Sime'll see to 't Miss Ruth gets her share, and I'll help Mrs. Harland all I can.'

So Harland assented, but when lunch was done and they turned to the canoes and he told Ellen the plan she objected. 'You're used to Leick,' she pointed out. 'You'll be miserable with anyone else.'

Ruth supported her for Harland's sake. 'Yes,' she agreed. 'Don't worry about me, Dick.'

'It's Leick's idea,' Harland told them. 'Let him run the show. Besides, we'll all be together.'

'Not while we're fishing,' Ellen argued. 'You and Leick can go off exploring together.' Ruth had a puzzled certainty that for some reason Ellen did not welcome the thought of long days alone with Leick. But Harland said decisively:

'We'll try it his way. Sime knows the river, and I want Ruth to have good fishing.' He saw the canoes below them loaded and ready. 'Come along,' he said, and led the way down the bank.

They took their appointed places, and when they were ready Wes Barrell and the dam keeper opened the sluices to give them a start, and watched them out of sight. Ruth and Sime led the way, and the wilderness received them.

– VI –

They planned to travel slowly, and they stayed several days at their first camping-place a few miles below the dam. Ruth, after a night when she slept ill, began to enjoy to the full this new experience, this complete release from contact with the world. She found Sime Verity, during the long hours when he and she were alone on the river, a good companion. She led him to talk about himself, and he said he was married but childless.

'We had one but it died,' he explained. 'Never made out to have another.' His farm was a mile or so from the village. 'I got everything planted before I left,' he told her. 'The old woman will keep the weeds down till I come home.' He said Jem Verity was the business man of the town. 'It takes a greasy dollar to get away from him,' he declared. 'Once't he gets his hands on it. But Jem's all right. He's a real good man.'

She came to feel that Sime too was a real good man. He had a profound knowledge of every aspect of the wilderness, and he showed her many secret beauties which without his guidance she would not have seen. One day he took her up a tributary brook to a beaver dam and tore out the dam, and they hid and waited till the beaver came to repair it. On another day when toward dusk they fished a wide pool below camp, two bank beaver played together along the waterside, going ashore to nibble bark from poplar twigs; and after his supper one of them sat up on his haunches like a squatting old man and washed his face and ears and forearms and his fat belly with such vigor that Ruth laughed aloud, so that he slipped reproachfully back into the water again and disappeared.

Sime was forever pointing out tracks along the bank: an otter slide, a muskrat's traces, the skeleton of a fish which a mink had eaten; and when she asked him about sounds heard in the silent nights, he imitated for her the whistle of a coon, the whining bark of a fox, the squealing of a porcupine, the whistle of a deer — sounding ridiculously like the whir of a salmon reel — which had scented you and wondered what you were. She came to love the still nights broken by faint forest sounds, and she often lay long awake, acutely listening. Sometimes she thought she did not sleep at all, yet she always woke rested and fresh.

There were three tents, a large one which Ruth and Ellen shared, and two smaller. Leick and Harland slept in one, and Ruth sometimes heard their low voices as they talked together long after she had gone to bed. Tom and Sime had the other. Tom was the clown of the party, full of a boyish pleasure in this expedition. Sime had a quiet humor and an easy smile, but when Tom laughed, the woods rang; and if Harland took a good fish the boy's shout of delight sent the news broadcast up and down the river. Sime said Tom was to be married upon his return. 'Going to marry Alice Morrow,' he explained. 'That's why he's feeling so good.' Ruth one day led Tom to talk about Alice; but after painfully admitting that she was a nice girl, he lapsed into red and grinning confusion.

They caught at first only trout, small eager fish fit for the pan; but when later they moved downstream the river assumed more substantial proportions and they took many grilse, and then some salmon, keeping only the grilse to eat. Tom usually split them and broiled them with wild onions for garnishing; but Leick one night seared three fish in hot grease and then baked them in the reflector oven with slices of onion and strips of salt pork for flavoring, and Ruth thought she had never tasted anything so delicious.

She found new reason every day to appreciate Leick's qualities. Till now she had seen him only when he came to Bar Harbor on some errand from Back of the Moon. She liked his obvious loyalty to Harland. In camp, these two forever drew together; and she thought Leick watched over Harland as a proud father watches over a child. He was equally scrupulous in serving Ellen, but there was a difference which Ruth tried to analyze. Sometimes she saw him watching the other girl with eyes she could not read, and she sensed a steady vigilance in him.

Ruth was disturbed by what she saw of the relationship between Harland and Ellen. The constraint between them was clearly Harland's doing. It was he who had insisted, on the train, that Ruth and Ellen should take the drawing room while he occupied a lower berth in the same car. Here on the river, if they finished dinner while the light still held, Ellen sometimes led him to the canoes and persuaded him to take her to try the near-by waters, leaving the guides behind. On such occasions Leick's eyes were apt to follow them, and if they went out of sight down river or up, he was ill at ease till they returned. If they fished near, Ruth could sometimes hear the murmur of Ellen's voice, and Harland's brief replies; but when they returned they came silently. Sometimes if Harland drew apart alone, Ellen went to him; but Ruth, watching from a distance these two whom she loved saw that Harland did not welcome her. In the morning when they met, and before parting for the night, Ellen might kiss him; but his response was half-hearted, lacking any warmth at all.

So though on the surface their days were pleasant ones, there was an undercurrent of tension. Ruth came to recognize, too, that the guides were uneasy, for reasons of their own. Sime every day commented on the low water, the continued dry weather; and he and the others took pains to extinguish every spark of fire.

Once, smoking a cigarette after she and Sime had lunched beside the river, she finished it and tossed the butt toward the water and it fell short. Sime went to stamp it out, and she said: ' I'm sorry.'

' It's all right,' he assured her. ' We get in the habit, that's all. Specially a summer as dry as this. Fire ever get started in the woods the way they are, and there'd be no stopping it.'

Second-growth spruce as dry as tinder clothed the steep hill-sides to the water's edge. ' I'd hate to see these woods burn up,' she agreed.

' You wouldn't want to,' he assured her. ' It'd be bad.'

— VII —

Toward the end of the second week they moved farther down-stream, below the mouth of the Sedgwick, and camped on a high bank in a bend of the river, close against the forest. The spot was a pleasant one, a tumbling brook coming steeply down from the hills to sing in the night beside the tents; and while the guides made camp, Ruth and Ellen drew apart together, and Ruth said appreciatively:

' This would be a beautiful place to set a house.'

Ellen looked at the hills which came steeply down behind them and shivered with distaste. ' It's too cramped,' she said. ' The hills try to push you into the water. I like space around me, level places.'

' Was it level at Back of the Moon? '

' No, but the hills were friendly, not too steep and high.' There lay suddenly a tragic sorrow in her tones. ' We were so darned happy there,' she murmured. ' I don't suppose Richard will ever want to go back — but I want to, some day.'

Ruth wished they might go back together. Perhaps there or in some like retreat they could recapture what they had lost; and after the next day's fishing — she and Sime had gone down river — she came back to camp in a fine excitement.

' I've found a place where someone really ought to build a cabin,' she told them at dinner. ' Down where Sime and I fished today. It's an old intervale, I suppose; a level tract shaped like a triangle, running way back from the river. But it's high enough to be dry, and there are a lot of elms along the water, beautiful great trees; and the forest is so open it's almost like a park.' She proposed that they move camp down there. 'It's ever so much nicer than this,' she said; and she called to Sime: 'How far is it down to where we fished today?'

'Four-five miles.'

Ellen listened indifferently, but Harland asked questions, and Ruth saw his interest was caught, and thought he might create another Back of the Moon where he and Ellen could be happy together as they once had been. She elaborated her description. 'I didn't explore it, of course, but even from the river we could see its possibilities. It could be made into a regular Garden of Eden.'

Harland smiled at her enthusiasm. 'Only Adam and Eve need apply?' he suggested; and he said: 'We'll look it over. Plenty of fishing for all of us, down there, Sime?'

'Plenty of fishing,' Sime assured him. 'But I don't know as there's many fish. They wouldn't do anything today, with this danged low water. What we need's a good rain, to raise the river.'

'Well then, we'll pass up the fishing and go exploring,' Harland declared; and Ruth, realizing that Ellen had asked no question, had taken no part in their conversation, said eagerly: 'You'll love it, Ellen.'

'Oh, I'll stay here,' Ellen told her. 'You two go. Leick and I will keep camp, maybe fish a while in the afternoon. I want to try the big pool up at the mouth of the Sedgwick.'

'You go with Dick and I'll keep camp,' Ruth urged. 'Sime can tell Leick and Tom the place I mean. You'll want to see it, Ellen.'

But Ellen persisted in her decision; and in the morning Ruth and Sime, young Tom Pickett and Harland, set off down river together. The day was still, and promised to be hot, and Sime said: 'There was smoke in the air yest'day. I could smell it.

Fire somewhere off to the south of us, I'd judge.' There was in
fact a faint haze between them and the sun.

They fished a pool or two on the way downstream, and Ruth
got into a fine salmon of twenty pounds or better. She lost it
after fifteen minutes, and Harland — he and Tom had paused
to watch her — called his sympathy; but she was more relieved
than otherwise. 'I love it when they take the fly, and while
they're fighting,' she said. 'But when they're tired out and it's
just a question of hauling them in, I'd rather see them get away.'

'You're not like Ellen,' he commented. 'She hates to lose
them.'

She laughed. 'I guess I just haven't got the killer instinct,'
she confessed, and was puzzled by the sudden shadow in his eyes.

The salmon took that morning, though half-heartedly. Ruth
got fast to another, Harland to two; but they all rose short,
were lightly hooked, and so escaped. While he played the last,
Ruth and Sime went on to the spot she remembered; and Sime
set a fire going, and when the others arrived to report the salmon's
escape, he was ready to serve broiled grilse and canned peas and
toast and marmalade and good black tea.

The haze across the sky had thickened, and the sun itself
was a red and angry ball, and Sime said thoughtfully: 'There's a
fire not far off. I can smell smoke plain. Looks like the wind's
coming up from the south, too. If it does, that fire'll move this
way.'

But a rampart of high hills walled the river on the south, and
any wind that blew was high above them. The air here by the
water scarce stirred at all, so Ruth and Harland were unconcerned; and after lunch they went exploring, plunging into the
forest, breaking through the fringe of small, close-grown young
spruces which above their luncheon ground bordered the river.
The little trees, their tenacious branches interlaced, formed a
stubborn barricade; but these two fought their way, scratched
and panting, to larger growth, to more open ground. Ruth lost
her hat, and when she stooped to recover it her hair became
entangled and Harland came to free it.

'"Absalom, my son, my son,"' he said laughingly. 'Say, you're a wreck! I thought you said this place was like a park! Some park!'

'It opens out farther on,' she promised. 'You'll see!' And when they had gone a few rods more she cried triumphantly: 'There! Now you can see down river.'

This was true. Tall hardwoods, beech and maple and an occasional oak, grew here more sparingly; and between their trunks he caught at some distance the gleam of water. 'It's pretty good at that,' he admitted. 'And it's well above flood level too.' But the ground was a tangle of underbrush, and the rotting trunks of trees fallen long ago made many a barricade, and he pointed this out.

'Well, I couldn't see them from the river,' she admitted. 'But they could all be cleared away, and you'd cut some of the standing trees, to make vistas.' She was eager, for Ellen's sake and for his too, to impart to him her enthusiasm; and she said in gay challenge: 'Come on, don't keep finding fault! Let's pretend we're pioneers, choosing our own land in the wilderness. If pioneers were discouraged by a little underbrush they'd never get anywhere!'

He laughed agreeably. 'Well, it has some possibilities, at that,' he assented. 'Now let's see. Where would we build our cabin?'

'We must look for just the right place,' she reminded him, and they explored, floundering through boggy pockets, clambering over windfalls, brushing aside the tangle of young growth, till they found a knoll with drainage on all sides. She was sure this was the perfect spot, but he pointed out that they must build near water. So they pushed on, and discovered a hidden brook where the tiny pools were alive with small trout, and they dropped twigs on the water, laughing when the fingerlings struck at them hungrily; and Ruth declared she could almost see the disgusted disappointment on their little fish faces.

'Let's not tease them any more,' she begged. 'Come on.'

So they went deeper into the forest till they reached steeply rising ground, and Harland estimated that they were half a mile or more from the river, that there were here sixty or seventy acres of level, fertile, well-drained soil.

'There's enough for a real farm,' he exclaimed. 'A man could raise his own corn and beans and peas, everything he'd need, and a couple of pigs, and a cow or two.' His eyes were shining, and Ruth saw that he was happier than he had been in these months — almost a year now — since Danny's death; and she wished Ellen were here in her place. But since Ellen was not here, she shared his pleasure.

They wandered for an hour or two, playing this game of make believe together as gaily as children, forgetful of time. Ruth saw everything through his eyes, and Harland was increasingly pleased with each new discovery. The brook plunged down from the hills over a cascade a dozen feet high. 'There's your water power,' he cried. 'If there's as much current as that even in a dry season, there'd always be plenty for light and heat and cooking, all you'd need. You know, Ruth, a man really could make a fine place here, with a little time and work.'

'It's a long way from everything,' she suggested, seeking by raising objections to stimulate his eager imagination.

'It's not a long way from a salmon river,' he reminded her gleefully. 'Nor from a trout brook! Nor from good hunting! And besides, there's room to put in a runway long enough for small planes. Run it toward the river and you could take off over the water. The fair weather wind here is apt to be that way.'

His word reminded them that the wind was stirring in the tops of the trees above their heads. They had been till now too absorbed to notice this. 'It's getting dark, too,' he said, and looked at his watch. 'Only half past three. Must be clouding up! Maybe we'll get a rain to raise the river.'

'I smell smoke pretty strongly,' she remarked, remembering Sime's concern. 'Do you suppose that fire is near us?'

'I guess not,' he said, and he lay prone to drink from the brook. In this moment's silence she heard, or thought she heard, a distant call. When he stood up, wiping his wet lips, she asked:

'Did you hear anything?'

'No. Say, that water's cold as ice.'

'I think I did. Listen!'

The call did not come again, but the wind blew harder, and a thread of warmer air came searching through the trees. She felt it on her cheek, and she saw that Harland felt it too; for he turned sharply, looking toward the river. But he did not speak of it. Instead, so casually that she knew he was uneasy, he said: 'Well, the boys will be wondering where we are. We'd better be getting back.' He looked around almost wistfully: 'But I hate to leave this place. I'll come here again some day.'

He turned to retrace their way, and she followed him; but at once he stopped. 'I heard someone calling then,' he declared, and listened, and cupped his hands and halloed and listened again. The distant cry was repeated, but the freshening wind shredded the sound and tossed it every way. He shouted once more, had this time no answer.

'They can't hear us,' she suggested. 'The wind's from them to us.'

He nodded and set out again, this time at a fast pace, but then he slowed. 'I guess I'm excited,' he confessed. 'We'll be a little careful, take a straight line.' And as they went on, he explained how to do this. 'Take two trees in line in front of you. Then when you come to the first one, get another in line beyond the second. I think the yelling was off this way.'

But within two hundred yards, they came back to the brook again. He laughed. 'That must have been an echo I heard,' he decided. 'But the brook will bring us back to the river.'

She followed him easily, keeping far enough behind so that branches displaced by his passing would not hit her when they swung back. The brook meandered, and there were alders and cedars along its bank, but Harland would not leave it now. Once she thought she heard distant, shouting voices; but they could do no more than they were doing, so they did not speak.

After a long time, fifteen or twenty minutes, the brook brought them to the river. They were both hot and panting from their haste, and from the dry and stifling air; but when they came into the open by the waterside, they stopped still, startled into silence by what they saw.

For the sky to the south and east was all one pall of smoke; and against that dark mass, along the crest of the ridge that walled the river, not a mile away downstream, they saw the red flicker of hungry flames.

Ruth, drawing near him, was the first to speak. 'That's bad, isn't it, Dick?' she said quietly.

'Look!' he cried. 'The fire's flowing down that hill like lava. It's halfway down to the river already, just since we've been standing here.'

'I can feel the heat of it,' she agreed.

He took her arm. 'Come along,' he said. 'The boys are upstream, around that first bend.'

They hurried that way, half-running, silent, side by side.

— VIII —

When Ruth and Harland came to the canoes, the men were not there; but they saw Sime a quarter-mile away up the shore and shouted, and he heard and called in turn to Tom and then came running. From the fire down river, smoke rolled swirling toward them, so thick it made them choke and cough; and Harland wetted his handkerchief and told Ruth to tie it across her mouth and nose.

'Better wet your hat, too, and tuck your hair up into it,' he advised. She wore an old soft felt, and she obeyed him; and then Sime reached them, and bade her get into the canoe.

'We'll start,' he told Harland. 'Fire's coming fast! Tom'll be right along. He's in the woods, looking for you. We thought you was lost.'

Ruth, wise enough to do as she was told without protest, stepped into the canoe, and Sime pushed off and began to pole upstream along the north bank, the canoe surging under his strong efforts. Ruth turned to look back to where Harland stood, watching for Tom Pickett to appear; and she saw that the fire down river had reached the stream side. The strong south wind, pouring over the ridges like a waterfall, created a tremendous pinwheel of racing drafts above the river itself, smoke and sparks and an occasional burning fragment flying high as though flung by an explosion; and she saw a tall tree on the north bank suddenly flare like a torch. The great fire had passed so easily the barrier of the river! Then thickening smoke, flowing up the deep channel among the hills where the river ran, hid the flames from her, and a moment later Harland's figure too was obscured.

She protested to Sime: 'We can't leave Mr. Harland. Something may have happened to Tom.'

'Tom's all right. They'll catch up with us,' he promised, and made the canoe bound with his strong poling.

She was astonished that the fire could have come upon them so quickly, and said so; and Sime grunted, between thrusts with the pole: 'Wind — came up — strong! — It'll outrun — a horse!'

She removed the handkerchief, bone-dry now from the hot air, and wetted it again, and secured it across her mouth and nose. Over the ridges south of the river and abeam of them heavy smoke came rolling down the slopes, and she saw that they were racing across the face of the fire. Escape down river, since the flames had bridged the stream, was cut off. She wondered how far they must go to get out of its path.

It seemed a long time — it may have been half an hour, a mile or more of distance — before she heard behind them the clack of paddle against gunwale and looked back and saw the other canoe almost upon them, Harland paddling, Tom using the pole. She reached back in the canoe and took her own paddle and tried to use it; but she was awkward at it and Sime after a moment said shortly — for he was short of breath:

'Leave be! I'll handle her.'

So Ruth put the paddle down, feeling the haste in him, trembling with excitement but unafraid. The other canoe kept its place just behind them, but Harland was no longer paddling now, and she saw that he too had something tied across his face. Then Sime began to cough uncontrollably, and he poled the nose of the canoe ashore while he fashioned a mask to protect his mouth and nose, and Tom held his canoe beside them and Harland asked her quietly:

'All right?'

'Fine. But I'm no help.'

'We'll be out of this soon,' he promised.

But the smoke was thicker, and her eyes were smarting, and her hands were parched by the heat. She dipped them in the water; and Sime took his pole and they raced upstream for another mile or so, till Ruth began to think — as though of a safe refuge — that they were nearing camp. The campground, she remembered, was close against a spruce wood where the fire might run; nevertheless instinctively she felt they would find safety there.

Then they rounded a bend in the river and saw flames atop the ridge that flanked the stream. The ridge was well back from the water, but already the fire began to flow down the slope toward them, the wind casting brands like scouts ahead. Sime after a moment once more nosed the canoe ashore.

'We'll go overboard, soak our clothes,' he directed. 'Wrap a sweater or something around your head, ma'am. It's going to be hot, the next half mile, till we pass the front of it; but then the river swings north again and we'll have it behind us.'

She obeyed him, as did Harland; and then they went on, racing past that nearing mass of fire. Before they were clear of its path, embers that hissed as they were extinguished began to drop in the water all around them; and once a small red spark fell into the canoe itself and was lost in the water which, draining from her wet garments, lay half an inch deep under Ruth's feet.

They rounded the point and put the fire behind them and for a few minutes followed this northward reach of the river, till in a wide easy curve it began to swing westerly again. They could see no great distance now, for smoke was everywhere; and the roar of the fire was in the air like the rumble of an earthquake, shaking them. West and then southwest the river swung, and so did they;

and Ruth recognized this great bend and knew the camp site was
not half a mile ahead. Soon, even through the smoke, they would
be able to see the dingy white of the tents.

But when they came nearer, she saw where the tents had stood
the hot licking glare of flames; and a moment later she uttered a
low cry. For ahead of them the fire had crossed the river, its skir-
mishers seizing a bridgehead on the north bank, from which the
forces of destruction spread up and down stream and went racing
on through the forest to the north.

Without a word and without hesitation, Sime turned the canoe.
Ruth asked no questions. Back in the wide bend, a gravel bar well
away from either shore divided the channel. Sime poled toward
this, and Tom followed him. They landed on the bar. The hot
and smothering air seemed to sear her lungs, and — holding her
breath — Ruth wetted Harland's handkerchief again and replaced it.

Sime said hoarsely: 'We've got to stay here. We'll keep mostly
under water, wait it out.' He stepped overside in the shallows.
'Out you come, ma'am. We'll sink the canoes, keep 'em wet, so
we'll have 'em when we can travel again.'

The water around her legs was deliciously cool. Ruth waded
deeper and sat down on the bottom, only her head above the
surface. She soaked her sweater and made of it a sort of turban
that was also like a tent, covering her head completely. After a
moment, relieved by breathing the cool, filtered air, she looked
to see what the others were doing. The three men scooped rocks
and gravel into the canoes, then waded to waist depth and filled
the canoes and sank them, and Sime said to her:

'Now you come sit in this one, ma'am. Help hold it down.'
He shifted the canoe into deeper water till, seated on the thwart,
she had only her head above the surface.

'There,' he said with a dry humor. 'Well, we've got grand-
stand seats for whatever's coming, anyway.'

Harland drew near, squatting beside her, his face hidden under
the heavy flannel shirt he had stripped off to wrap around his
head. 'Real adventure,' he said cheerfully.

'I wonder where Ellen is.'

'Leick will take care of her.'

'They're probably worried about us.'

'We're all right, and so are they,' he insisted.

She said frankly: 'I'm scared to death. I guess I'm not a great big outdoors girl.'

He touched her arm, his hand groping under water to find hers. 'You don't sound scared!'

'Probably I'm not, really. But I will be tomorrow after it's all over.'

He laughed. 'You can be as scared as you damned please, tomorrow,' he agreed.

Thus began for them long hours of passive endurance. They were in a backwater by the bar, where no current flowed at all; and the water was their fortress. With only their heads above the surface, they crouched like animals, warily watching their enemy.

The fire, as though sure now of its prey, approached them with a certain deliberation. Ruth opened a slit in the folds of her sweater so that she could see. The wide bend of the river where they had elected to stay drew a half circle around a bold hill which rose steeply three or four hundred feet above the water. Its bulk acted for a while as a shield in that quarter, and just here the river was too wide for the fire to cross. But downstream and upstream the barrier had been passed, and on the north bank, working across the wind, these flanking fires crept nearer. Presently too the main conflagration topped the hill on the south bank and rolled down toward them. Smoke, whirling and eddying, at one moment black as night, at the next shot through with the red glare of the flames, walled them in; and by the increasing heat they knew the fire drew close on either side. More and more often they dipped completely under water to wet their headcoverings, thus winning brief respites from discomfort.

The smoke was so heavy that except for the red glare of the flames, day was already almost as dark as night and they did not know when dusk came down. By that time the two fires on the northern bank had met, and on the other side the trees along the water were ablaze. The fire fed hungrily on the heavy stand of second growth spruce and hemlock. Once when the swirling, scorching wind for a moment swept the smoke aside, Ruth saw that the whole face of the hill on the south bank was a towering wall of flames up which swept serpent torches roaring to the sky; a wall so steep it seemed about to topple down on them. Then the smoke shut in again, sucking and shuttling in the terrific drafts generated by this blast furnace all around.

Even through the soaked sweater which covered her head, the heat was almost unbearable; and when she dipped under water and lifted her head again, the water in the sweater began at once to turn to steam. The river itself, here in the shallows where no current ran, was milk warm, and she wondered if it would grow hotter and hotter till they were boiled alive like so many lobsters. The notion made her laugh, near hysteria, and Harland asked what the matter was and she told him her thought and he said sternly:

'Stop it! Don't think about anything! Just keep down, keep wet, be passive. It can't last long as bad as this.'

Yet time went on, and the thundering, crackling roar of the fire seemed to fill the world; and the swirling fumes came chokingly. Only by bringing her nostrils close down to the surface of the water, could she breathe clear, sweet, smoke-free air. The fire was like a great herd of cattle stampeding, in whose path they lay while the heavy hooves went pounding by their ears. When now and then she parted the sweater's folds to peer out, the murky darkness all around them was shot with falling sparks and brands; and sometimes these burning branches were large enough so that even after they struck the water, upward-thrusting twigs and stubs which had not been submerged continued to wear small flames, like candle-torches dotting the surface of the stream. Some of these floating brands were astonishingly large, giving her a measure of the powerful suction of the updraft from the fire, which had lifted them into the tornado of the upper air.

Eventually it seemed to Ruth there came a lull, as though the fires were dying; but when she spoke of this, Harland said: 'Fires always quiet down at night. This will start up again in the morning.'

'Must we stay here all night?'

'Yes, and half tomorrow probably, till it burns down.'

The immensity of that prospect stunned her. She lost all sense of the reality of this experience. The lightness of her body, almost completely submerged and upborne by the water, made her seem to float, and she clung to the sunken canoe in which she sat, grateful for this firm grip on the substantial world. Once Harland suggested that in shallower water she might lie down with only her face exposed; but Ruth said she was all right as she was. Yet a sort of stupor crept through her, and the warm water made her sleepy, so that sometimes she nodded. He stayed beside her, and after a while he gripped and held her hand, and it was good to know she was not alone. Time stood still — yet somehow the long night passed.

– IX –

They knew the coming of day by a quickening of the fire, by a new tempo in its song; and Ruth slowly roused from the half-consciousness which had helped her endure the night. Long since, the water which seemed so warm had chilled her through and through, so that more than once she had stood erect, Harland's hand steadying her while the hot blast set her clothes to steaming and warmed at least the surface of her body before the heat drove her to take cover in the water again. The coming of day found her not so much tired as drained of strength by long immersion; she felt the skin on her fingers puckered and wrinkled, felt herself emptied and flaccid; and she confessed this to Harland, and he moved to sit on the gunwale behind her, his arm around her, holding her body against his. If he had not done so, she might have toppled drowsily forward. To sleep would have been blissful; to sink lower in the water and accept oblivion was easy and inviting.

They had talked little through the night. Sometimes she remembered Ellen, but remotely. Leick would see Ellen safe; and if he did not, there was nothing, for the present, they could do. Ellen was no longer reality; she was no more than a faint memory far away. Ruth knew Ellen must be concerned for them, and must be wishing Harland was with her; and she sympathized with this longing which Ellen must be feeling. Yet she was glad Harland was here with her, keeping her company, enduring with her this long ordeal, supporting her with his arm around her waist, receiving her sagging weight against his strong body. Once she remembered how pleasant it had been to explore with him that woodland tract downstream, remembered how youthful and eager he had seemed; but the fire had now swept all that beauty away, leaving only a waste of embers behind, and a crushing sense of intolerable loss made her shoulders sag.

The fire, rejuvenated by the new day, burned fiercely for hours that drifted slowly by. Ruth was so near insensibility that she recognized no change in its fierce roar and crackling, knew no thinning of the smoke, no slackening of the heat. But the time came when she heard Sime, standing in the water beside her, speak to Harland, and she tried to hear his words but could fit no sense to them. Then he and Harland were helping her to her feet, their hands under her arms, making her stand erect; and her knees refused to lock, threatening to give way under her, while the two men led her carefully into shoaling water, making her walk between them.

When she could go no farther and collapsed at last, Harland sat down in the shallows and cradled her head and shoulders across his knees and in his arms. He parted the sweater still bound around her head, and she opened her eyes and saw through gray-blue smoke a rift of clear sky overhead.

'It's burning out,' Harland told her. 'North shore's still pretty hot, but we've moved farther out on the bar, away from it. On the south bank it's beginning to cool off a little.' And he asked: 'How are you?'

'Awfully tired and weak,' she confessed. 'I'm sorry.' And after a moment she said: 'Being in the water seems to take it out of you.'

'We'll move up on the bar pretty soon,' he promised. 'As soon as things ease up.'

Sime and Tom loomed through the smoke, towing between them one of the still submerged canoes, returning afterward to bring the other. Then, as their garments dried and the heat became oppressive, they all lay down to soak their clothes again.

An hour later they made another move, nearer mid-river, nearer the cooling southern bank; but the gravel on the bar was still so hot that water thrown on it quickly began to steam, so they stayed in five or six inches of water, and Harland now and then splashed Ruth, scooping up water with his hands to moisten her drying clothes.

She asked once what time it was. He did not know, for his watch, long submerged, had stopped; but Sime guessed it was mid-afternoon. 'Hungry?' Harland suggested, and she nodded, and Sime went to investigate the canoes and reported that there was a can of beans, and some tea in another can, and sugar in a jar, and condensed milk. Everything else was wet and spoiled. He found a few embers and bits of charcoal and started a small fire to boil the kettle and warm the beans. The strong tea brought back some strength and life to her, the beans were life itself. By that time the bar was cool enough so that they could stand on it. Sime said they might as well stay the night there.

'No use starting up river,' he pointed out. 'All our gear is gone, and we'll have to head downstream tomorrow, first thing, anyway. We could start tonight, but I'd as soon wait for Leick and Mrs. Harland. They'll be coming, soon's they can.' Swirling smoke set him coughing, and the ground on which they stood was hot through their shoes, so that now and then they stepped into the water again. 'We'll be warm enough here,' he promised grimly.

Harland asked: 'Any chance camp wasn't hit?'

'Not a chance,' Sime confessed. 'Anyway, we can't get to it.'

They decided to keep a watch for Leick and Ellen, in case the others elected to travel during the night; and soon after dusk the gravel on the bar had sufficiently cooled so that they could lie down in some comfort. Sime found a rift of sand tossed up by the flood currents in the spring, and in this he and Harland scooped a bed for Ruth, with deeper holes to receive her hips and shoulders; and when she relaxed in semi-comfort there, Harland lay down beside her. After a while she slept, deeply and dreamlessly in the completeness of her weariness; but once during the night she roused enough to know that she was cold, and she pressed nearer Harland, and in his sleep his arm came around her, drawing her body against his.

She woke to full daylight, and looked up to see Ellen standing over her, looking down at her with steely eyes. Ruth cried gladly: 'Oh Ellen, darling!' She moved, sitting up, thrusting aside Harland's arm which still encircled her. Harland did not stir.

Ellen laughed in a brittle way. 'You'd better wake Richard, too,' she said. Ruth's gladness faded in puzzled wonder at her tone.

10

HARLAND had felt no actual fear for Ellen, sure that Leick would keep her safe. These two had in fact been able to outrun the fire, and to camp at last, though without tent or blankets, beyond its flank. Leick reported that everything they owned — tents, food, gear — was destroyed, so there was left for them nothing but a return to civilization. A long day's journey down river would bring them to the railroad; and after breakfast — Leick had saved a salmon killed by Ellen before the fire drove them into flight — they started downstream.

For seven or eight miles they ran through the burnt land, and thinning smoke clouds made them cough, and along the shore standing trees still burned feebly, flames like mice gnawing at their blackened trunks. Upon the charred slopes, great boulders that had been cracked and bleached by the fierce heat shone white as bones. The level tract which Harland and Ruth had happily explored was a waste of smoking embers, pricked over with blackened tree trunks as a cushion is pricked with scattered pins; and Harland saw it with a surprising sadness, astonished to discover how strongly that dream of turning it into a forest paradise had attracted him.

The canoes travelled in line, following the most useful current, and little conversation passed between them. Tom Pickett's high spirits had survived the ordeal — once he said that a hill beside the river, where the fire had unaccountably left some scattered patches of timber untouched, looked like a man after his wife had cut his hair — and he was full of words; but Harland answered him little or not at all. He sat low in his seat, relaxed in a stupor of fatigue, dreading to return to the world again, dreading the necessity of resuming his life with Ellen, thinking that just as the fire had turned the wilderness into a desert, so was his life become a hopeless waste.

The death of his unborn son had been the end of any lingering tenderness in him toward Ellen. He might never of his own accord have blamed her for that second tragedy; but Mrs. Huston, the rattle-tongued old woman who had loved him since the days when as a child he came teasing for forbidden goodies in her pantry, in her sorrow at his grief viciously declared that Ellen had never wanted the baby, had tried to be rid of it.

'Haven't I seen her hating it; yes, and pounding at it too, when she didn't know I was about,' she told him hotly. 'And walking herself into a lather, and running up and down the stairs when you weren't at home, and painting all day in the pantry, as if any fool didn't know the smell of turpentine was bad! Yes, and reaching up, and hanging from doorjambs, and dosing herself with castor oil, and I don't know what all. Walk in her sleep, my foot! You can't tell me!'

Harland hushed her, sure she spoke not from any real conviction but out of her love for him and her grief at his bereavement. But when on their return to Boston she took Ellen jealously under her wing — though he knew this was no more than the instinctive tenderness to which weakness in others always could provoke her — he felt an unreasonable resentment. The newspapers had reported their adventure, and as she opened the door of the Chestnut Street house to them Mrs. Huston swept Ellen into her capacious arms.

'My dear, my dear,' she cried. 'You must just be worn to a frazzle, to be sure! You come right along till I put you to bed!' She glared at Harland. 'I said all the time no one with any sense would take you off into the woods, as weak as you were, to sleep on the ground with snakes and frogs and I don't know what all!'

Harland protested: 'Nonsense! We'd have been fine if it hadn't been for the fire.'

'Fire indeed!' she retorted. 'If it hadn't been a fire it would have been something else!'

He saw the twinkling mirth in Ellen's eyes, and she said in an elaborately helpless tone: 'You're so good to me, Mrs. Huston! I don't think I could even get my clothes off without you to help me!' They disappeared together, leaving Harland feeling angrily at fault and ashamed.

Ellen kept her bed for three days, and by allowing the older woman to serve her won Mrs. Huston completely. When Harland moved around the house, Mrs. Huston was apt to hush him with fierce whispers, bidding him let the poor dear sleep while she could; but if he went out, she reproached him as bitterly, accusing him of heartlessness in thus going off to have his own good times while his sweet wife lay weak and suffering! He saw a certain humor in the situation, but he was not amused. Rather he was angered by Ellen's willingness to play invalid in order to win this simple loyalty.

When in the end he told her so, the result was to precipitate the utterance, by both of them, of words Harland had hoped would never be spoken. The third evening after their homecoming, Ellen smilingly insisted that he have his dinner on a card table in her room while she had hers in bed. Mrs. Huston served them, bustling contentedly up the stairs with laden trays, bidding Ellen ring if there was anything else she wanted. When they were above, Ellen said with mischievous delight:

'She's having the best time, taking care of me.'

'Why do you let her?'

'Why not, Richard?' she drawled teasingly. 'You surely don't want me going up and down stairs in my weakened condition!'

'You're a damned sight better able to take care of her than she is to wait on you! The poor old thing can't climb the stairs without panting like a horse with the heaves.' He met her eyes. 'And you're perfectly strong and well. You're simply imposing on her.'

She nodded. 'I know it,' she assented. Her eyes were mocking. 'But she loves it!'

'I'm going to put a stop to it!'

Ellen shook her head. 'Better not try, darling. She already thinks you're rather a brute, you know. You don't want her to think you a monster!' He looked at her with hard appraisal, and she said: 'There, let's change the subject. How's work going, Richard?'

'I haven't written a line since — in months.'

'Really? Oh well, you'll get back into your stride when we settle down to normal again.' And she said smilingly: 'When I'm well enough, we'll have your bed put back in here, darling.' They had had separate rooms for long now. 'You need me, Richard,' she assured him. 'I want to help you, so much.'

Her tone was light, so that he might if he chose read in it mockery; yet he felt too that she was pleading with him, begging him to help her rebuild their broken lives. He took a cigarette, uncertain what to say, wishing to cry out the truth, to tell her that even to sit near her now was almost intolerable. But Mrs. Huston's return to clear away their used dishes made it impossible for him to speak; and in the old woman's presence Ellen asked, politely making conversation, what he had done that day, where he had gone.

'You missed seeing Ruth,' she told him. 'She came in for tea. She's planning to go to Bar Harbor for August and September. She's found an apartment, and she's getting it settled before she goes away.' He made no comment and she added: 'Or perhaps you've seen it?'

He nodded. 'Yes. I went to look at it before she decided. She wanted me to pass judgment on it.'

'She didn't tell me that,' Ellen remarked in a level tone. 'Nor consult me, nor ask my opinion.'

Mrs. Huston had left them alone again, and he rose. 'Well, you'll be wanting to settle down for the night,' he said. 'And I promised to sit in on a bridge game. See you in the morning.'

'Will you look in when you come home?'

'Oh, I may be late,' he said evasively, moving toward the door.

She extended her arms to him. 'Then — kiss me good night,' she suggested, and he returned toward her, hating this necessity he could not easily avoid. When he leaned over her, her arms locked around his neck, and she insisted: 'Put your arms around me, Richard! Lift me up! Hold me close!' His posture was strained and awkward, and her arms, tugging his head down, made his neck muscles ache. She whispered: 'Remember that night you first kissed me, when we'd come through the canyon, Richard?' He did not answer, and she insisted: 'Do you? Do you remember?'

'Of course!'

'Remember I told you I'd never let you go?' In sudden passion her arms tightened and her lips pressed his, and he was pulled off balance and down atop her, entangled in her arms, till the sense of being trapped ran through him like fire through dry grass, and in a rough, desperate haste he wrestled free and backed away, angry and revolted and half-afraid.

She lay relaxed, with half-closed eyes, smiling up at him. 'Scared, darling?' she murmured. 'It's all right! I'll have your bed moved back in here tomorrow.'

He cried out hoarsely: 'No, don't do that! It's no use, Ellen. Don't do it!'

'I want you to come back to me.'

'I'm not coming back to you!' That shrinking terror which had run through him a moment ago was in his tones now. 'Never!' he cried, his voice almost shrill.

Still lying half on her side, exactly as she had fallen when he flung free of her, she watched him with eyes that now were clear and hard and still. 'Never?' she echoed softly. There was no hint of any emotion in her tone.

He wiped his mouth with the back of his hand, feeling the sticky waxiness of her lipstick there, taking out his handkerchief to scrub it away. 'It's no use, Ellen!'

'No use?' She was still an echo, nothing more, lying there like a woman asleep, yet with open eyes.

He tried to escape. 'Good night,' he muttered, and turned toward the door and reached it before she spoke again. Then her clear, soft voice cut him like a whiplash on his cheek.

'You've fallen in love with Ruth,' she said.

That word stopped him stone-still. His back was toward her, and at first he did not turn, and after a minute she said, with no heat or passion in her tones at all: 'Oh, I think I've known from the first. Perhaps I even knew before you and Ruth did, Richard; but I tried to play ostrich, pretended not to see. Yet — that's why I took Ruth on our river trip, my dear; so I could watch you together, so I could be sure.' He swung sharply toward her, and she said: 'I was sure long before I found you in each other's arms that morning on the gravel bar.'

Harland did not hear the word. The impact of her original accusation had set a ringing of great bells in his ears, so clamourous and deafening that he was thrown near madness. He strode back to her, forgetting everything except that which he could never forget; and when he came to her bedside now there was such anger in him that she saw it and was silenced, and he spoke in a quick rush of low words.

'Listen,' he told her breathlessly. 'I can't ever be near you again. I saw you let Danny drown.'

His lips still moved, yet made no sound; his torrential thoughts would not form words — or the words could not be uttered. She lay so passive, and so altogether beautiful, and so completely to be desired; yet all her inwardness was black corruption, from the thought of which he shrank as from an unbearable stench. But he could not tell her so, could not tell her — whom once he had promised forever to cherish and to protect and to defend — that he abhorred her utterly.

She spoke quietly. 'Yes, I know.'

'Know I saw you?' His senses were off balance, his ears not to be trusted. 'Saw you let him drown?'

'Yes, of course,' she said calmly, and she asked in an impersonal tone: 'Why didn't you kill me, Richard? Why don't you now? You could, so easily, you know.' He felt as though he were himself on the defensive, and she went pitilessly on: 'It was you who lied to Leick, you know. It was not I. It was you who protected me.'

'I had to.'

She smiled a little. 'You thought you had to, darling.' Her tone mocked him. 'Because I was to become a mother!' And she said: 'I lied to you about that, but we made my lie true.'

He pressed his hands to his eyes, trying to clear them; and his knees let go and he sat down weakly, and rubbed his eyes and took his hands away and stared at them.

'I didn't mean to let Danny drown, Richard,' she said, not defensively but as though anxious to set the record straight. 'I didn't plan it. But when the cramp caught him and he went under, I thought that if he never came up, I'd have you all to myself.' She smiled again. 'I'm a jealous lover, Richard,' she said. 'I thought if he were gone you'd love only me, and suddenly, while I was thinking that — he was gone! I was sorry then, and frightened, and I tried to find him, tried honestly, tried hard; but we were too late. That's all.'

And she said in serene and level tones: 'But you lied to protect me, so — we share the guilt. That binds us together. We can never escape that now.' After a moment she added: 'So we must go on together, wearing a mask for the world, being honest only with ourselves.'

He whispered a word that was half oath, half prayer.

'If we don't, there will be wondering and questioning,' she reminded him. 'We must pretend all's well with us, Richard.' When he did not speak she added, her lips twisting in a derisive smile: 'It's too bad about you and Ruth, but you'll see her often. She's invited us to dinner Friday evening, in the new apartment. For both your sakes, I'm going to make an effort to be well enough to go.'

He rose and came to stand above her and to speak. 'If you ever link Ruth's name and mine again,' he said in a low tone, 'I'll leave you forever!'

Her eyes met his for a moment in long question, and then her eyes filled with tears and she buried her head in her arms. 'So it's true!' she wailed, in muffled despair. 'You do! It's true! It's true!'

– II –

Ruth's pleasant, small apartment overlooked the river; and when Harland and Ellen arrived she had cocktails ready for the ice. 'I've made a curry, Ellen,' she explained. 'With plenty of rice. Dick, I hope you like curry.'

He said he did. He had not seen Ruth since Ellen's accusation, and he wondered if there were any least truth in what Ellen had said. Just now, her hair a little disordered and her cheeks flushed from her activities over the stove, Ruth was as pretty — or at least as nice looking — as he had ever seen her. But there was nothing in her to awake that hot madness, that longing at once to bruise and to defend, that tempestuous hunger which Ellen had inspired in him. Love — if he had ever loved Ellen — was a continually suppressed excitement; it was a hunger which could never be satisfied. But — if that were love, why, then certainly he did not love Ruth, and never would.

While he watched her, she and Ellen chattered together, and she served them the dinner she had prepared, refusing any help; and she was jolly and gay as Harland had never seen her, leading them both to be merry with her. The curry was perfection, and Harland and Ellen too accepted second servings, and Ruth beamed with pleasure as good cooks do when their viands are appreciated; till at last they could eat no more, and she let them help clear the table away. A maid would come to do the rest. Then they had to admire her new quarters here in detail, and finally they sat a while in her pleasant living room.

She said she meant to go in a few days to Bar Harbor. 'I've lots to do there,' she explained. 'I suppose we'll sell the big house, Ellen, if we get a good offer; but what would you think if I remodelled Father's study and made it into a little summer place for me? It really doesn't have to go with the big house, stuck away in the woods on the point as it is, and I'd buy your share of it from you.'

Ellen said Ruth was welcome to do this. 'I used to work with Father there, but I'll never want to go into the place again,' she confessed, and she asked: 'What did you do with the things out of his workshop in the house here in town?'

Ruth said the Museum of Natural History had been delighted to have his skins and sets and his notebooks. 'And the rest — the instruments and things — I packed into a barrel for Morgan Memorial. There was nothing of any value.'

Ellen laughed faintly. 'Mercy, I hope you didn't send the arsenic to them. They might not know what it was.'

'No. I threw that in the furnace. I started to empty it down the drain, but I was afraid it might kill the fish in the harbor or something.' Ruth laughed at herself. 'I was scared even to handle it,' she confessed.

She asked what they planned for the rest of the summer; and Ellen said she did not know, remarking: 'It's the first time in my life when I've had really nothing to do. Richard's busy at his desk all morning, and sometimes half the afternoon too.' Harland thought lies came easily to her. 'I may take up collecting again,' she reflected. 'Carry on Father's work where he left off.' And she said: 'You see, Ruth, Doctor Patron says I dare never have another baby.'

Ruth's eyes filled with a quick sympathetic grief. 'Really, Ellen. Oh — I'm so sorry, for both of you.' She looked toward Harland, but he was watching Ellen in a sort of fascination, grimly admiring the guile which led her thus to forestall any future questions.

'So I shall have to find some way to keep busy,' Ellen explained. 'And that might be the very thing. I'm sure I can get collector's licenses from the Federal authorities, and from Massachusetts, and probably Maine. The museums to which Father and I sent specimens all know me. They'd give me references.'

'Father had a full outfit in his workshop at Bar Harbor,' Ruth reminded her. Her tone lifted on sudden inspiration. 'Why don't you both come up there, as soon as I have the place settled, and you can select the things you want, Ellen, get them packed up. Or perhaps you might want to keep his workshop there.'

Ellen said emphatically that she would never want to work

there. 'But we may come up for a week or so in September,' she agreed. 'If I can persuade Richard to leave his work for a while.' She smiled at him, made a little face at him. 'He's such an old stick-to-his-desk; he's hard to move, sometimes.' And she asked challengingly: 'What do you think, dear?'

Harland indifferently agreed that a few days at Bar Harbor might be pleasant, and before they said good night, the visit was arranged.

– III –

Ellen had that night an attack of the digestive disorder to which, since her childhood, she had been subject. Her cry woke Richard, and he went to her.

'I'm sorry,' she said apologetically. 'It hurts so, as if I were on fire!' Her head twisted on the pillow in a paroxysm of pain. 'I ought to be used to it by now, but it just seemed to squeeze that scream out of me.' She shuddered, gasping and retching; and he tried to help her to her feet, but she was limp in his grasp. Helpless as any man under the circumstances, he called Mrs. Huston; then at Ellen's painfully whispered direction he telephoned Doctor Saunders.

'He's — seen me like this before,' she told Harland. 'He'll know what to do.'

The doctor when he arrived seemed sure of his ground. He sent Harland out of the room. 'It's not pleasant to watch,' he explained. 'Mrs. Huston can get me what I need.'

Ellen was for hours in acute distress, with pain and nausea and an intense thirst which she could not satisfy, since her stomach refused to retain even a teaspoonful of liquid. When Harland was permitted to see her at last, her features were sunken, her brow wet, and she lay limp and utterly collapsed.

'But she's all right now,' Doctor Saunders assured him. 'Only she'll not want to eat anything for two or three days, just a little weak barley water.'

'I hear she's had these attacks before?'

'Yes, ever since she was a child. I've seen half a dozen of them.'

'What's the answer, doctor? What causes them?'

'Well, you might call it nervous indigestion, I suppose.' Doctor Saunders chuckled. 'Her mother used to say they were the result of an ingrowing disposition; that she always got sick when she couldn't have her own way. That was sometimes true when she was a baby. I've caught her at it before now. She used to pretend to be sick to discipline her parents, just as grown women sometimes pretend to have headaches to discipline their husbands. But this attack was the real thing. Of course, curry's hardly the best dish to put into a nervous stomach.' He picked up his hat. 'And after all, Mr. Harland, she's been under tension for several months now. This will help her relax, do her good. Give her a week and she'll be as well as ever.'

'She looked pretty sick to me.'

'She was,' the doctor agreed. 'Medically, it's a semi-acute gastritis, something of the sort.'

'Dangerous?'

'Well — it might be. There's a good deal of collapse attendant on a severe attack. Yes, it might be; but I'm sure she's on the high road now. She's asleep. That's the best possible sign. However, I'll drop in this afternoon. And of course, don't hesitate to call me if you think best. But Ellen's been through it before.' He chuckled reassuringly again. 'She knows her own condition as well — perhaps better — than I.'

That afternoon he was again unconcerned, and next day he dismissed his patient, saying Ellen could get out of bed as soon as she felt able to do so. But it was a week before Ellen came downstairs. Mrs. Huston cared for her, and Ruth delayed her departure to Bar Harbor and was in the house every day, helping Mrs. Huston, talking with Ellen, reassuring Harland.

'I've seen her this way more than once,' she told him. 'She blames my curry, but I don't, because it wasn't curry the other times. Ellen is high-strung; and after a long strain she goes to pieces this way, that's all. This has been a hard year for her, of

course.' She touched his arm in quiet comforting. 'Just be good
to her, Dick,' she said. 'That's the best medicine she can have.
As long as she's happy with you, she'll be fine.'

Ellen herself said the same thing to him, and in almost the same
words, the day after Ruth left for Bar Harbor. 'Sorry to be such
a nuisance, Richard,' she told him, faint mockery in her tones.
'But I've always had such spells when things didn't go to suit me,
whenever I was unhappy. Someone told me once about conditioned reflexes. Maybe it's a conditioned reflex with me. Whenever I don't get my own way, I stage a stomach upset.' She
smiled at him. 'So if you don't want a sick wife on your hands,
you'll have to treat me indulgently, my dear!'

He thought a new chain was added to his bonds. Since they
were forever fettered together by a common guilt — for she was
right; by concealing her crime, he shared it — they must find
some formula for amicable association. So he showed her day by
day every thoughtful consideration.

Through August, Ellen looked forward to their Bar Harbor
visit, her spirits rising as the set day approached. At dinner the
evening before they were to start, she was more beautiful than
she had ever been; and while Mrs. Huston served them — for
Harland knew the old woman was now Ellen's stout partisan
and would approve the compliment — he told her so.

'Sweet!' she said gratefully, and Mrs. Huston beamed. 'I suppose it's because I've had such a lovely afternoon.'

He knew she had been out. 'Where were you?'

'At the bank, fondling my bonds like a miser. I love the rich
feeling of them, Richard. And I had some business with Mr.
Carlson.' She was prettily mysterious. 'Don't you wish you
knew what it was? You will know some day, perhaps.'

'Who's Mr. Carlson?'

'He's the man at the bank. The bank's our trustee, mine and
Ruth's. He's a darling, so grumpy and disapproving and dusty-
looking. He must be a hundred years old, and he grunts at you,
and smokes tremendous cigars — he eats one end as fast as he
smokes the other — and lets the ashes fall on his vest, and seems

half-asleep all the time. He doesn't like me, I'm afraid, but I adore him. He's a sort of lawyer, too. That's another reason I went to him. You see, I made my will, Richard. Are you excited? You ought to be, because you're in it.'

'I ought to do that myself,' he reflected. Even though he had not published a book since his marriage, the continuing success of *Time Without Wings* had stimulated popular interest in his earlier novels; and his royalties were substantial. Moving picture sales added large sums, and his living expenses in proportion to his income had always been small. His surplus funds he had from the first put into stocks, and though he chose them at random, the market for several years had been moving upward at an accelerating pace, giving him a treacherous sense of infallibility. He was on the road to becoming a wealthy man. 'I will,' he said, 'as soon as we come home.'

'It gives you such a settled feeling,' she assured him. 'Father told us all to do it, but I never bothered till Mother's dying reminded me. Then I put it off till now. You must put me in your will, Richard. You're in mine.' She was charmingly insistent. 'You'd better! I'll claim my dower rights anyway, so you needn't try to cut me off!'

He said gravely: 'I'll never cut you off, Ellen. You're my wife, and I'm your husband.'

'Till death us do part?' she asked, tenderly teasing. 'But death won't part us, Richard! If I die, I shall haunt you always. I promise you that! I've my plans all made!' She added smilingly: 'Remember, long ago, after our first kiss, I told you I would never let you go? I meant it, you know. Don't ever think I've changed my mind, my dear!' Her tone was light, but her eyes held his, something in them which he could not read.

– IV –

Harland dreaded the drive to Bar Harbor, but Ellen when they set out was as jolly as though between them no dark shadow lay. The day was fine, the countryside was fair, and Harland's spirits responded to this beauty all about till he could laugh with her and find her charming and half forget the past. They debated where they would stop for lunch till Ellen proposed a picnic and he agreed; so they bought a can of chicken and a loaf of bread, butter and jelly and a bottle of milk, and beyond Wiscasset they followed byways toward the sea and parked the car and tramped down across a field of stubble to an oak-studded point beside one of the long, narrow bays which thereabouts indent the rocky coast. Beneath the oaks the turf was close-cropped, and they laid out the provisions they had brought and made a feast together.

They had forgotten they would need knives. 'But never mind!' Ellen cried. 'The bread's already sliced.' She dug off a bit of butter. 'Mind my fingers?'

'Not a bit.' He laughed at the mess she made as she worked the butter into paste to spread the bread. She picked slices of chicken out of the can to make a sandwich and extended it to him, licking her fingers.

'M-m-m! Good!' she declared. 'Open the milk.'

When he tried to do so, the cap betrayed him; and his thumb, plunging down into the bottle, sent up a geyser of milk that splashed them both. But they laughed at this mishap, and with his handkerchief she wiped the white drops off his coat and off her sweater, and made a sandwich for herself and a second for him. For dessert there was bread and jelly. 'But you'll have to scoop out your own,' she confessed. 'My fingers are all over sand. Mercy! What did people do before they had knives? Here, put some on my bread too.'

So before they were done they were both well besmeared, and they descended to the waterside to wash their hands. Afterward Ellen was reluctant to depart, lying at length on the firm turf beneath the oaks, laughing at him because he urged they should be on their way.

'You act embarrassed, Richard, as though you were afraid someone would find us here,' she protested. 'Look around, my darling! There's not a sign of a house in sight in any direction. No one's going to see us. You won't be compromised!'

The beat of a motorboat's engine approached from seaward, and he said: 'Don't be too sure. Hear that! We're not as alone as we seem!'

'Lie down here by me, and they won't see you,' she invited. 'I'm out of sight. We'll be hidden by the bank.' The tide was low and they were well above the water. He did not obey till the boat was about to round the point just below them. 'Quickly!' she urged. 'You'll look awfully foolish, sitting there alone! They'll know you've a girl here somewhere, and suspect the worst!'

He smiled and lay down beside her.

'This is like the day we watched for the turkeys,' she reminded him, and she asked: 'Richard, why didn't you make love to me that day? I wanted you to.'

The boat drew abeam of them. 'Hush,' he said. 'They'll hear you.'

She pressed nearer, threw her arms around him. 'Kiss me, Richard,' she demanded; and when he did not, she whispered in merry warning: 'If you don't, I'll scream, and I can scream a piercing scream! They'll come to rescue me!'

He yielded hastily, and she held him tight, drawing him close against her, and the boat was well past before she let him go. He lifted his head to peer cautiously after the departing craft, saw a small cruiser with half a dozen summer folk aboard.

'Probably they can go through from here to Bath somehow,' he guessed, trying to ignore what had happened, pretending to himself that his heart still held its measured beat, steadying his voice to prove to her — and to himself — that he was unmoved by her nearness, by the warm sweet wind that drew across the meadow above them, by this secret hour, by that long embrace. She did not speak, and he turned and saw that she was lying quietly on her back, watching him. The boat was not yet gone out of sight so he lay down again, and her hand clung to his and she rubbed it against her cheek and kissed it, and then she pressed his hand against her bosom till he freed it, drew it away.

She said in light reproach: 'After all, we're married, Richard.'

He was silent, fighting for self-control; and she asked in a low tone: 'Will you never love me?'

'We ought to be moving on, Ellen.'

'Have you no — bright memories?' she challenged. He sat up, staring at the dark water below them, and she pleaded: 'Have you nothing left for me at all?'

He spoke, not to bruise nor to wound but to put his own thoughts in order. 'I remember the night you left off Quinton's ring,' he said. 'I knew — it was in your eyes — that you would marry me if I asked you. I went to my room and thought for hours, and I decided not to marry you, Ellen.'

She laughed teasingly. 'Decided?'

'It was my head that made the decision,' he admitted. 'But that day in the canyon, that night by the fire, something overruled my head.' He felt an almost tender pity for her, yet he was bound to lay this matter plain. 'You're very beautiful. No one could be more so. And you're wholly desirable. That made me forget what my head had decided.'

'Let it make you forget again, Richard.'

'Do you want me on those terms?' he challenged.

'I want you on any terms. I want all of you that you can give me.'

He shook his head. 'No, Ellen.' He added honestly: 'Oh, I'm human, and — masculine. The day may come when you'll win part of me again — but if you do, it will be a hollow victory — and perhaps a defeat in the end. We can go on side by side. I can do that — as long as you don't ask more. But — if you win more than that, you'll have less than you have now.'

Lying beside him she turned her head away, and her breast rose in a deep inhalation, and his pulses pounded hard and he thought it would be easy to surrender; yes, and blissful, too. Yet he knew the self-scorn which would follow, and held himself in bounds. She did not speak, but her very silence was an assault on his defenses; and he said hastily, blurting out the words: 'You've got to know this. When I let myself think of what you've done, I'm sick, nauseated, I feel like trampling you. I want to — vomit! And —

the Hell of it is, I can still want you! But I'd despise you and
myself too. Only this way can I even respect myself. For God's
sake, Ellen, let's keep what we can!'

For a moment more she lay motionless; but then she sat up
quickly, and stood up, and gave him her hand to rise, and she
was smiling, accepting his decision.

'Thank you, Richard,' she said calmly. 'I know your whole
mind now. We'll go on to — Bar Harbor.'

So they took the road again, and a sense of guilt rode with him,
and he spoke gently to her, and laughed with her when she invited
him to do so. But he drove more swiftly, as though in haste his
only safety lay.

– v –

Ruth greeted them happily, and she showed them to a room
that looked toward the sea. Harland in that room with twin beds
felt Ellen's amused eye upon him, felt her waiting for him to
speak; and his jaw set stubbornly. Mrs. Huston, on the fact that
they kept separate rooms, had been easily reassured. Mrs. Harland, he had told her, slept ill unless she was alone; and the old
woman nodded understandingly, agreeing that Ellen needed all
the rest she could get, poor thing. But — he could make no such
suggestion to Ruth, and Ellen offered no word.

'Come down when you're ready,' Ruth said. 'I expected you
hours ago, and Mrs. Freeman's fuming for fear her dinner's
spoiled, but we'll take time for cocktails anyway.'

'Give us five minutes,' Ellen promised. Ruth left them alone,
and Ellen came close to him and asked in mock solicitude: 'Can
you stand it, Richard? Or shall I tell Ruth to put me somewhere
else?'

'It's all right, of course.'

'I hate having you distressed.'

'It's all right,' he insisted curtly.

She turned swiftly away, pressing her knuckles to her lips, and
he suspected guiltily that her eyes had filled with tears. She went

to brush her hair, but when he met her glance in the mirror she smiled and threw him a kiss and he decided he had been a fool.

They had coffee on the terrace, watching the afterglow bright and beautiful across Frenchman's Bay; but at full dark, Ellen rose to go to bed. 'I'm tired,' she confessed. 'The long drive, all day in the open air. But don't you hurry, Richard. Sit with Ruth a while.'

He was grateful to her for this consideration, but while he talked with Ruth in the starlit darkness with the fragrance of phlox coming from the garden below them, he imagined Ellen preparing for sleep, following the routine he knew so well, pulling her dress off over her head — once he had liked to wait to catch her close and kiss her the moment her face appeared, pinioning her arms still entangled in her gown — slipping out of her undergarments and into sleek silk or satin, sitting long at the dressing table to brush smooth her hair, waiting till the last moment to peel off her stockings and toss them across the foot of the bed where they would catch and reflect the first rosy light of dawn. His nostrils remembered the scent she wore, the fragrance of her hair. She always seemed so astonishingly small, and so soft and warm in her delicate night garments.

He stayed an hour or more with Ruth, but when he went upstairs, he found Ellen still awake, her bed light burning.

'Couldn't you sleep?' he asked.

'No, but I've rested, half-drowsing, listening to the murmur of your voices.'

He felt her watching him while he took pajamas and dressing gown and went to the bathroom; but he avoided her eyes. In bed at last he asked, as casually as possible:

'Mind if I read a while?'

'No, Richard.'

He forced himself to concentrate upon the book, feeling her eyes upon him, refusing to look at her; and presently she said:

'Good night, Richard.'

'Good night, Ellen.'

She turned on her side, her back toward him; and though he

was sure she did not sleep, she did not speak again. After a long time he laid his book away, switched out the light.

But to sleep was difficult. There were too many doubts in him. Surely a lifetime of this would be intolerable, alike for each of them. Were it not better to make a clean break, to confess their rupture to the world? Or if not, then to yield, and by yielding perhaps to recapture something of the beauty and the bliss which she had shown him life could hold?

During the next two days and nights this dilemma still tormented him. Ellen made no new attempt to break down his defenses, yet when they came to their room at night and when they lay wakeful in the morning, he felt a waiting in her, as though she knew the question were still unanswered, still open, still at issue. She waited, without urging or pleading, for his decision. He had thought that decision made long ago, made and announced to her that day by the waterside where they paused for lunch; but a decision which consisted merely of words was not enough. Either he must surrender — and he came to understand that if he did yield it would be completely — or he must escape forever from her nearness.

The third morning, he was near capitulating. He had waked before dawn and he lay watching the dark shadow of her hair on the pillow opposite his own, and following with his thoughts every familiar curve of her body under the light bed-covering, till as the light increased he saw that her eyes were open, that she was watching him. That waiting which he had seen before, patient and submissive, as though she put her life completely in his hands, was in her eyes. Their glances held for a long silent moment, and she said at last, smiling drowsily:

'Good morning, Richard.'

'Good morning.'

'It will be a fine day.'

'Fine,' he agreed. They had planned to go today to Leick's farm on the shore off to the eastward, a two hour drive. They would take lunch, and Leick would have lobsters to boil. 'A good day for our picnic,' he said.

She stretched white arms above her head, yawned deliciously, lay watching him — and waiting; and suddenly his breath quickened with a sense of imminency, of immediate necessity. He swung his feet to the floor between their beds, stood a moment beside her, leaned down to kiss her. Her cool lips met his.

'Why, thank you, Richard,' she said. Then she laughed a little, her voice husky. 'It's a long time since you've kissed me without being asked.' There was a wistful, hopeful quickening in her tones.

He forced himself to turn away, as a man forces himself back from the lip of some steep declivity. He crossed to the windows toward the sea and stood there looking out, yet at first unseeingly. It seemed to him that powerful hands were tugging at him, drawing him back to her; he wished to turn and yield.

But then his unseeing eyes focussed on something in the water offshore. A seal was swimming there, the sleek dark head cutting the water like the head of a human swimmer. A lobsterman's tender, a small white boat, was fast to its mooring, the lobsterman gone since before dawn upon his rounds. As the seal approached the white boat, it dived, its head disappearing without a ripple.

And Harland remembered another day when from the lookout at Back of the Moon, focussing the binoculars, he had seen another white boat, had seen Ellen sitting idly in it, had seen Danny's head disappear under the surface as the seal's had disappeared, never to rise again.

So was his decision made. He turned strongly back from the window. 'I've made up my mind, Ellen,' he said. 'We can't go on this way! I've got to leave you forever. We can't go on!'

For a long moment that seemed longer than it was she did not speak. Then she said, with a laughing grimace: 'Well, don't be so serious, Richard! It's a fine day for — a picnic, just the same.'

— VI —

Since there was no haste upon them, they took the road from Ellsworth through Sullivan and along the shore of Frenchman's

Bay, and so by the long way to Cherryfield and on; and the day was perfection, and Ellen had never seemed to drink so fully and completely the beauty of sea and shore and distant hills and radiant sky.

Byways brought them to Leick's home. It had been his father's farm, close along the water; but his father and mother were dead years ago and Leick — except when he was with Harland, or at winter work in the woods, or on some other business of his own — lived here alone. He came to greet them in the yard and bid them in. Harland had known this pleasant small house since he was a boy; but Ruth and Ellen wished to see and to admire.

They would picnic by the shore, half a mile away. Leick had lobsters ready, packed with ice in a wooden box, and he brought a wash boiler from the shed, and they tramped down through the pasture to the rocky beach. A sea wall here was a shield against erosion, and a massive crib work of logs weighted with huge boulders extended seaward, submerged now by the rising tide. Ellen cried:

'Why, how funny! A sea wall and a breakwater, but there's no house anywhere near! Who built it, Leick?'

'I did,' Leick admitted.

'How far out does the breakwater go?'

'To low tide.'

'But what a lot of work for nothing!' Ellen protested. 'What did you build it for?'

Leick, filling the boiler with sea water, adding salt for savor, setting the boiler on two rocks and beginning to build a driftwood fire below, said in mild amusement at himself: 'Well, I don't rightly know. Only I get a lot of satisfaction out of looking at it and knowing it'll still be here a long time after I'm gone.'

Ellen laughed, but Harland saw her bite her lip. Ruth said understandingly: 'Of course! Every man likes to leave some permanent mark on the world if he can.'

'Yes, ma'am,' Leick assented with a chuckle. 'Even a useless old breakwater.'

Ellen said restlessly: 'Come on, Ruth. Let's take a walk.'
They strolled away, and Leick, feeding his fire, remarked that
Ellen was looking well, and Harland assented, saying:

'She had a stomach upset a while ago, but now she's fine.'
Then some constraint fell upon them both, and the water boiled,
and Leick put the lobsters in, and Ellen and Ruth presently
returned.

Ruth, in that fine hamper which Russ Quinton had given Ellen
long ago, had brought potato salad; and the thermos bottles were
full of coffee, and there were bread and butter sandwiches, and
chocolate doughnuts, and ice cream in the cool compartment.
When the lobsters were done, Ruth made a sauce of tamale and
melted butter in equal parts, juice of a lemon, salt and pepper, dry
mustard and a dash of Worcestershire; and they cracked the
claws with rocks, and dug the sweetest morsels out of the body,
using finger and thumb or gnawing teeth, and they were merry
in the sun. Ruth produced the thermos bottles, uttered a regretful
exclamation. 'Oh, Leick, I meant to bring tea for you but I forgot. There's plenty of coffee if you'll have some.'

'Never touch it,' Leick cheerfully assured her. 'It's all right.
I don't drink tea either, middle of the day, only if I'm in the
woods.'

She began to pour the coffee into paper cups. 'Here's your
sugar, Ellen,' she said, and drew an envelope from the hamper.
'Dick, I know you like yours without, and so do I.'

Ellen took the envelope and put it for safekeeping into the
pocket of the soft leather jerkin she wore. 'Don't pour mine yet,'
she said. 'I'm not ready.' When later she asked for coffee Ruth
poured it, and Ellen tore off the corner of the envelope and tilted
sugar into her cup. Ruth served ice cream and distributed
doughnuts; and when they were done, they threw used napkins
and paper plates and cups into the fire, and the two girls went to
lie on the turf above the rocky beach, watching dark squall-
ripples scud across the water, drowsing in the hot September sun.

Leick and Harland stayed behind, and Leick scoured the sooty
boiler with soap and sand, and Harland filled his pipe and sat

near, and slow words passed between them. Leick said he would leave next week to begin a winter's work in the north woods. 'So you came just in time,' he said. 'Three or four days more and I'd be gone.'

The gentle afternoon drifted indolently away. The sun was well down the sky and Harland was thinking he must presently give the word to start for home when he saw Ellen, yonder on the bank above them, suddenly sit up; and he heard her speak to Ruth in a strained tone. Her word he did not catch, but the sound of her voice alarmed him; and he rose and went toward them. Ellen, looking up at him, her face white and contorted, said with a wry smile:

'Isn't it silly, Richard? I'm going to be sick again!' Before he could speak she bent double, hugging her arms across her stomach. 'Oh!' she gasped. 'Oh! Oh! It's like being burned up inside! As though I'd swallowed fire!'

Ruth knelt beside her. 'We'll get her to the house, Dick,' she said. 'Put her to bed.'

Ellen cried out again, twisting with pain, and Harland and Leick made a chair, hands clasping wrists, and took her up between them to carry her to the house. At first she sat erect, her arms around their necks; but her grip was slack, and Ruth walked close behind, ready to support her. Ellen groaned and sobbed, and suddenly nausea racked her so terribly that they had to put her down and she lay retching on the turf, her head — after the first paroxysm — cradled in Ruth's arms.

Leick said: 'I'll get something so we can carry her better.' He loped away toward the house, and Ellen cried between choked spasms of vomiting:

'I'm burning up, Ruth. I've got to have a drink!'

Ruth soothed her. 'Hush, dear! We'll have you comfortable in no time.'

'Water!' Ellen gasped, and Harland started at a run toward the house to find and fetch some; but Ruth called him back.

'She couldn't hold it down,' she said. 'Wait for Leick. We'll get her to bed.'

Ellen's eyes were swimming and she was perspiring with pain, her parched lips drawn back from her teeth; and Harland stood miserably by, all his old tenderness for her awake again, blaming himself for what had passed between them in these days. Leick returned, carrying precariously on his shoulder a door which he had lifted bodily off its pin-hinges, and under the other arm two blankets and a pillow; and they laid her on this rude stretcher, and wrapped her warmly, and bore her to the house and to the great bed in what had been Leick's father's room.

Ruth asked: 'Can you get a doctor, Leick? We'll undress her, make her comfortable.'

'Yes, ma'am,' Leick assured her. 'I'll get Doc Seyffert. I'll have to go fetch him. I don't have no telephone.'

'Take the car,' Harland directed, and Leick hurried away. Harland helped Ruth remove Ellen's garments — sometimes her tormented spasms interrupted them — and Ruth found one of Leick's mother's nightgowns for her, and they gave her water to drink; but Ellen gagged, rejecting every drop, alternating like a woman in labor between agony and torpor when she lay as though stupefied.

Dusk descended and Harland found lamps and lighted them; and at last Leick returned. 'He's coming,' he reported. 'Right behind me. I had to chase all over Hell's kitchen to find him. He was clear out at Pitcher's, the other end of town. How is she?'

'Mighty sick,' Harland admitted. 'I've seen her this way before, but I don't think she was this bad.'

'I'll cook up some supper,' Leick volunteered. 'You can stay all night. There's room enough.'

'We'll have to,' Harland agreed. 'She can't be moved.'

Harland went back to Ellen, and she met his eyes and for a moment seemed about to speak; but then her teeth set on her lip to bite back the word she had meant to utter, and she turned her head away, her eyes closed. He heard her quick, panting breath and looked at Ruth miserably. She whispered: 'She'll be better when the doctor comes.'

Doctor Seyffert drove into the yard. He was a tall, raw-boned, dogmatic man in his fifties, practicing here upon a subsidy from the town, used to tending ailing children or old men and women with failing hearts or kidneys. Leick had told him what to expect. When he came in to where Ellen lay he said, in a loud, bruising tone: 'Well, you summer folks will learn some day that lobsters and ice cream don't mix. One of your lobsters must have been dead; decomposing, full of ptomaines! We'll soon get rid of them — mustard, white of egg. That'll do the trick!'

Ellen, for the moment more comfortable, looked up at him with hollow, empty eyes. 'Leick won't like your blaming his lobsters, Doctor,' she protested with a twisted smile.

He barked like a dog. 'Hah! What of it? Let him like it or not, it's the truth!'

Harland suggested: 'It might not have been the lobsters. She's subject to these attacks, has had them before.'

'Allergic to shellfish, perhaps,' Doctor Seyffert portentously conceded, laying aside his coat, rolling up his sleeves. 'Never mind, we'll get her cleaned out!' He went into the kitchen to seek the remedies he needed, and Ellen whispered:

'I don't think he's much of a doctor!'

Harland gripped her hand, and Ruth said reassuringly: 'He'll fix you up, darling.'

Ellen turned her head on the pillow to look at one of them and then the other. 'You wouldn't let anything happen to me, would you?' she murmured. Harland felt like a stab the ironic derision in her tone.

Then the doctor returned. 'Now we'll see!' he said brusquely.

During the hours that followed, while Leick stayed in the kitchen and Ruth went to and fro, Harland held his post by Ellen's bedside, feeling in himself her every pang, seeing her beauty fade before his eyes, wishing he had been kinder. She was continually drenched with perspiration, and her countenance assumed as time passed a bluish hue, and her breathing was increasingly labored. The doctor inexorably administered a succession of emetics which racked her terribly, till she choked and sobbed with pain, convulsed and writhing. Harland at last was driven to question the wisdom of this treatment, but the doctor bore him down.

'She's full of poison. We've got to get rid of it.' His loud voice was like the blow of a cudgel. 'She can't recover till we get the poison out of her.'

Ellen in a strangling voice echoed his word. 'Poison!' she whispered feebly, and seemed to try to rise, and clutched at nothing and fell back again.

The doctor persisted till she was in complete collapse, unable to swallow his harsh remedies, equally unable to reject them. He was himself by that time almost as exhausted as she. They watched Ellen, lying with eyes closed, panting feebly, her mouth open like that of a hen on a hot day; and Harland spoke to her, but except for a faint movement of her head she did not reply. He said in a low tone to the doctor:

'I'm sure it wasn't the lobsters. She's always had these attacks. Her own doctor calls them nervous indigestion, a sort of semi-acute gastritis.'

Doctor Seyffert snorted. 'Semi? Damned acute, if you ask me,' he declared, and Harland suspected bafflement in him; but then the man added with a loud cheerfulness: 'All the same, I've seen sicker cats than this get well!'

Harland wished for a more capable man, but — it was near midnight, and to bring someone from Bar Harbor or Ellsworth or Bangor would take hours. He remembered that by legend these rural general practitioners were often better physicians than the most fashionable specialists; and after all, any doctor ought to be able to handle an attack of indigestion!

But as Ellen visibly grew worse instead of better, he forgot everything else in his distress for her. She was in a stupor, her face blue, and when she retched, a dark slime trickled from the corner of her mouth. At last she sank into what seemed like sleep, and Ruth whispered hopefully:

'There! She'll be better when she wakes.'

But Harland, watching the doctor's face, read a grim message

in it; and he found confirmation in Ellen's empurpled countenance, her light and rapid breathing. No one so small and
tender could endure what she had endured. Sitting beside her
bed in a helpless grief, he remembered the sweet cajoleries, the
pathetic enticements with which she had sought to win his forgiveness and his love. Her own Doctor Saunders, who had known
her since childhood, said nervous strain, or mental distress, might
precipitate these attacks. Suppose that day under the oaks, or
this morning at dawn, he had surrendered? Perhaps she would
not lie dying now.

For he was sure she could not survive, and Ruth presently
seemed to see the truth as clearly as he; and she called Doctor
Seyffert urgently from the kitchen. The big man busied himself
in baffled futility, till at last Harland muttered: 'Oh, it's no use,
Doctor. Let her be.'

So they watched helplessly while Ellen died.

When she was gone, Doctor Seyffert cleared his throat. 'Well,
well!' he said, loudly in the still room. 'Well, there was no help
for her! Nothing anyone could have done. I'll certify it acute
gastritis.' He hesitated, as though half-expecting denial; but
when they were silent, he said defensively: 'If she'd had these
attacks before, she should have avoided eating lobster, sea food,
anything doubtful at all! Absolute folly!' Still they did not
speak, and he said, gruffly: 'Sorry I couldn't save her. I'm sure
everything that could be done was done; but if you have any
doubt, any question, we can get another opinion?'

Ruth, since his word demanded a reply, said wearily: 'Oh no,
Doctor. That would do no good now.' She leaned forward, bury-
ing her head in her arms on the bed where Ellen lay; and Doctor
Seyffert looked at Harland in defiant challenge.

'That's right, Doctor,' Harland assented. Ellen was gone.
Perhaps if they had summoned at once another doctor she might
have been saved; but now — recriminations were an empty business. 'I'm sure you did all anyone could have done. Thank you
for coming. We appreciate it.'

Doctor Seyffert bowed and left them alone with Ellen. They

heard from the kitchen for a time his loud voice as he spoke with
Leick before he drove away.

- VII -

Harland was stupefied by the impact of this tragedy. He sat in
Leick's kitchen with his hands, the palms upturned, idle on his
knees, while Leick and Ruth carried through the sorry routine
that follows on the heels of death. In midmorning Ruth led him
to lie down and try to sleep; and though presently he heard a car
in the yard and quiet movement in the room where Ellen lay,
merciful sleep did come to him at last. When Ruth woke him he
did not at first know where he was, nor remember why.

She told him gently: 'Ellen's gone, Dick. We must go now,
too.' And when his eyes cleared and she saw that he was awake,
that he remembered, she explained: 'We're taking her to Boston.
Leick will drive us to Bangor to catch the same train, so we can
go home with her.'

He nodded submissively, rising to do as she bade, wondering
and grateful because she could be so steady and so strong; and he
wished he could confide in her, could tell her all the truth that
now came crowding into his mind. If he had not been so unrelenting Ellen might now be alive, smiling and beautiful and loving him as he remembered her; and he thought: 'I would have
forgiven her soon. I couldn't have gone on, holding out against
her. She loved me, and she was so sweet, so sweet!' There was
grief in him like a wailing. In sorrow and despair, he held himself
to blame.

He wished to say these things to Ruth, but he could never say
them to anyone. Confession was a weak surrender, a craven appeal for absolution. He must expiate his crime alone. Yet he
thought Ruth guessed a part of his mind; for next morning in
Boston she said, as though to reassure him:

'You made Ellen very happy, Richard. You did so much for
her.'

He bit his lip to hold back the self-accusing word, held his tone steady. 'I don't suppose any two people were ever happier than we were, last summer at Back of the Moon.'

'I know,' Ruth agreed. 'She told me so, only the other day. We were talking about our three lives, about the fact that we were all — getting back to normal. She said she was happy, but she said she could never expect to be as happy again as she had been there last summer with you.' Harland could almost hear the sardonic note that must have been in Ellen's voice. Then Ruth added: 'She told me that you had promised to take her ashes back there.'

Richard looked at her in dull perplexity. 'Ellen's ashes? To Back of the Moon?'

'Why, yes,' Ruth assented, as though surprised at his surprise. 'Had you forgotten? She said it was in one of your happiest hours, when you and she were together one day at the lookout on the hill above the lodge. She said she asked you, made you promise.'

In a dizzying rush, memory of that afternoon came back to him, bitter sweet, poignant and beautiful. They two had been alone for an hour while Danny slept, and the day was fine and the sky as deep as all eternity and the ardent springs of youth and love flowed full flood in them both. He remembered how before they went down to the cabin again she stood with arms outspread as though to embrace the beauty which lay below their high vantage, and he remembered her word: 'Richard, Richard, I love it here.' And he remembered his own sharp sweet terror when she exacted from him that pledge of which Ruth spoke. He saw her in his thoughts as he had seen her then, and he nodded slowly.

'Yes. Yes,' he said in a low tone. 'Yes, I remember now.'

Thus it happened that when the time came, he carried out that almost forgotten promise. Leick, having driven them to Bangor, had brought Harland's car on to Boston, Harland not then expecting to return to Maine; and these two went by train to Bangor together. They parted there; for Leick was to go up river with a crew that would build new logging camps in a tract of spruce ready to be harvested. He would not even take time to return to

his farm. 'Jed Hatcher, lives up the road, will shut the place up
and see it's all right,' he explained. 'I'll write him a post card.'
Harland bade Leick good-bye, and then he chartered a plane to
take him to circle high above the lovely blue crescent of the little
lake so long familiar. The day was crisply clear, touches of au-
tumn color here and there brightening the sweep of forest that extended in all directions, giving way on the south to farm lands
that ran along the sea. While they soared thousands of feet above
the ground, the motor's slip stream swept Ellen's ashes off upon
the wind, and Harland as the hard gale tore them from his grasp
— for he half-wished to cling to them just as now that she was
gone he wished to cling to her — remembered a day long ago when
she had ridden a great circle around that mountain meadow in
New Mexico so that her father might possess forever the spot he
loved. Thus Harland, in full forgiveness, gave Back of the Moon
again to Ellen now.

When the last grain of ashes was gone, he was reluctant to depart. It would be rest and peace to leap from the plane and like a
falling leaf go drifting downward to the blue waters of the pond —
where Danny, and Ellen too, would welcome him. But that was a
coward's way. He signalled the pilot and they swung westward,
to return to the world again.

II

RUTH through those last days with Ellen at Bar Harbor had found a new sweetness in the other; and after Ellen's death, she was gratefully sure that they had never been so close before. Ellen had seemed to seek her company. Once — Harland had gone alone to climb Cadillac — Ruth at her window saw Ellen coming up through the garden from her father's workshop, and called to her, and they had a lazy afternoon, idle and at ease. Ellen said Ruth might do what she chose with the shop. 'I'll never want to use it, I'm sure,' she explained. 'If I ever decide to go on with his work, I'll get a place of my own somewhere. I went down this afternoon just to see how it would seem, but I could never stand it there.'

Their talk inevitably turned to Harland. Ellen said his abstraction, which Ruth remarked, was because he had not yet become reconciled to the fact that they must be forever childless. 'He's always wanted children so,' she explained, and Ruth nodded.

'It's sad and hard that you can't ever have any, Ellen, but you can make it up to him in other ways.'

'Oh I mean to, I want to,' Ellen agreed, half-whispering, tense and yearning; and she said, thinking aloud: 'We were so happy at Back of the Moon.' Her eyes misted as she spoke of their serene and smiling days together there. 'Usually we were with Danny, of course, and he was sweet, and we loved him; but it was always as though Richard and I shared a delicious secret, and when our eyes met, something flashed between us; and now and then we slipped away alone, into the forest, or up to the lookout, or away to the far beach at the end of the pond; and then it was as though great bells were ringing far away, and the air and the earth seemed both to be in tune with them, and so were we.' She looked at Ruth with eyes suddenly full of mischievous mirth. 'But there, darling, I shouldn't say such things to you! Are you shocked at me?' Ruth only smiled, and Ellen said, speaking once more half to herself: 'There was one day — we'd gone up to the lookout above the cabin; and for an hour love and life and death seemed to merge and to be all one, filling us both completely. I made him promise me that day that when I die — I don't expect to live long; I never want to grow old — I made him promise to take my ashes back there. Don't let him forget, Ruth, when the time comes!' She laughed. 'Or I'll surely haunt you both!'

When after doing Ellen this last service Harland returned to Boston, he came from the train direct to Ruth's apartment. She was just finishing breakfast, and she boiled eggs and made fresh coffee for him. Afterward they sat in talk, of what was past and of what was to come, and he said:

'Ruth, I'm going away.' He hesitated, and she felt in him the desire to confide to her; but he went on: 'I can't stand it here — or anywhere else where I've ever been with Ellen. I've got to go to places I've never seen, and among people I've never known.' He shook his head in a dull bewilderment. 'I'm like a sick dog. I want to be alone.'

'Will you be gone long?'

'I don't know,' he confessed. 'I don't even know where I'm going. London first, I think; or perhaps Paris, with Italy for the winter and then England in the spring. I'll stay away till I begin to want to work again.' And he asked, in belated realization that she too had a problem: 'Will you stay here?'

'Oh yes,' she assented. 'If I've got to rebuild my life I'd rather do it on familiar ground, with the materials I know.'

'I expect you'd advise me to do the same.'

'No, no,' she cried, unwilling to influence him in any way at all. 'No, Dick. You'll do the wise, best thing, I know.'

He hesitated. 'I'm sailing from New York Tuesday,' he said in a flat tone. 'Unless you'd rather I didn't go.'

She shook her head. 'No, I'm sure you're wise to go.'

– II –

Harland departed, and a week or two later Russ Quinton, saying that business had brought him to Boston, called upon Ruth. Because he was so closely linked with what her life had been, she was frankly glad to see him. Russ had put on a little more weight, he had lost a little more hair, but he had that same way of walking with his toes thrown out so that he seemed to waddle, and he smiled as easily.

'I just came to pay my respects,' he explained. 'Professor Berent's friendship once meant a lot to me, you know.'

'I'm so glad you came.'

'I was sorry not to be able to offer my sympathy when Ellen died. I was away, knew nothing of it till I came home. That was a shocking thing.' She nodded, and he asked: 'Where's Mr. Harland?'

'He went abroad,' she said. 'He was — terribly shaken, of course.'

'I'd like to write him a line, express my sympathy.'

'He didn't know where he was going,' she admitted. 'Didn't leave an address. I think he's in London, or possibly Paris. He had no plan.'

'I wonder if he'll ever come back.'

She too wondered, but she said steadily: 'Oh, I'm sure he will, some day.'

'I suppose a story writer takes things harder than the rest of us,' Quinton reflected, and he said: 'Someone told me last winter that Ellen was going to have a baby.' She realized that his every statement was in fact a question.

'It was stillborn, last spring.'

'Oh, too bad. Say, Harland's had a tough time. His brother, and then his baby, and now his wife.' She found herself shaken by memories as he went on. 'I talked with old Doctor Seyffert,' he explained. 'He says Ellen suffered a lot.' Ruth nodded and he spoke understandingly. 'It was hard on you, too, seeing her suffer.' Her throat was full, not only with dregs of pity for Ellen's agony, but with a beginning anger at him for his persistence. 'And you lost your mother, too,' he remembered.

'Yes, Mother too,' she assented, wishing he would be done and go away. He seemed almost to relish this talk of tragedy. Some people were like that, rolling bad news like a sweet morsel on their tongues.

'Doctor Seyffert said he'd never seen anyone die just that way.'

'Ellen used to have terrible attacks of indigestion, even when she was a child.'

'Yes, the doctor told me,' he agreed. 'But I'd have been willing to bet Leick would know better than to give you folks a bad lobster.'

'Oh, I never thought it was that,' she declared. 'It was just — well, Ellen was tired, as we all were. She'd had an attack not long before, and I suppose the last one hit her before she was strong again.'

'Then it wasn't anything she ate?'

Ruth shook her head. 'She ate just what we did,' she assured him, and added: 'Not quite so much, perhaps. She never was a hearty eater, and the rest of us were good and hungry.'

'You didn't all eat the same lobsters,' he reminded her, and she wondered at his tenacity which seemed so purposeless.

'No. But she didn't eat all of hers. She left the tail, I remember. The rest of us had two or three apiece.'

'And of course none of you were sick.'

'No. No, I'm sure it was just her condition, her — susceptibility.' Then, remembering and anxious to satisfy him, she added: 'The only thing she ate that we didn't, she took sugar in her coffee, and Mr. Harland and I didn't, and Leick didn't drink any coffee.' She smiled at the absurdity of her suggestion. 'But sugar wouldn't make her sick, of course.'

'You wouldn't think so. I hear Mr. Harland had her cremated.'

'Yes, she had asked him to.'

'Scattered her ashes at Back of the Moon, out of an aeroplane.'

She said in some surprise: 'How did you know that?'

'Oh, it made some talk,' he confessed. 'A thing like that gets around.' He smiled his ready smile. 'Folks'll talk about anything, you know, down in Maine.' And he said: 'It would have been kind of interesting to know just what did kill her, but Doctor Seyffert said you didn't want any other doctors, or an autopsy or anything.'

'I — we couldn't see that that would have done any good.'

'Unless maybe to help doctors know what to do with the next one that got sick the same way.'

'I'm afraid we didn't think of that,' she confessed, feeling herself on the defensive.

'Naturally you wouldn't,' he agreed, and after a little, to her relief, he rose. 'Well, I might see you next summer, if you're coming to Maine.'

'I expect to,' she assured him, rising too.

'Maybe Mr. Harland will be back by then.'

'I'm — I don't know.'

He nodded. 'Well, good-bye.' He extended his hand. 'Nice seeing you.'

She went with him to the elevator; and when the car descended and he was gone she returned to her apartment in a surprising confusion, feeling without knowing why that his call had not been as casual as it appeared, puzzled and wondering and a little afraid. But she could find no reason for that fear. Russ was like a lonely spinster, interested in everything that happened to people in the world he knew, full of human curiosity, and with that marked appetite for morbid detail which so many folk were eager to indulge. She imagined him cross-examining Doctor Seyffert, prying and probing with a grisly persistence; and she shivered with distaste, remembering that — though she readily liked most people — she had always disliked this man.

She was quite sure, suddenly, that he had never forgiven Ellen — nor, presumably, Dick — since Ellen jilted him. He might

even have felt a dreadful satisfaction in knowing the torment
Ellen suffered before she died.

- III -

Harland's first letter reached her in December. It had been
written from Paris, but he said he was leaving at once for Egypt.
'I've been completely idle,' he explained, 'making no friends,
seeing no one except strangers, people met once or twice and then
forgotten. I've no desire to write anything, not even letters.
This, except for one or two matters of business, is my first. A
casual acquaintance the other day spoke of a trip he'd taken up
the Nile. That's why I'm going to Egypt. So you see I'm just a
feather drifting in the wind.'

She found it hard that winter to fill her days. Her life was, for
the first time since her childhood, empty of responsibilities; and
there was upon her no financial pressure. Professor Berent had
already achieved a modest competence before receiving that
fortune from Glen Robie. He had set up trusts for Mrs. Berent
and the two girls, to pass to the survivor or in equal shares to the
survivors upon the death without issue of any one or two of them;
and the remainder of his estate was by his will divided equally
among them. Thus since his death and Mrs. Berent's and now
Ellen's, Ruth — except that under Ellen's will she and Harland
shared equally — was wealthy. But she was unwilling to be
idle, so she took a secretarial course, thinking that when Harland
— as she was sure he would — returned and began to work again,
she might do his typing.

In February a letter came from Calcutta. 'And I'm going on
to China,' Harland wrote. 'There, I'll be halfway around the
world, so whichever way I move, I'll be heading toward home
again. I may backtrack, or I may go on. I'm far from any plan.'

'But I'm beginning to come to life, Ruth. I met a man on a
Nile steamer who interested me sufficiently so that I filled a notebook or two with some of the ideas his talk suggested. If I'd ever
written any short stories, I might do one about him; but I don't

know the medium. Maybe I'll try one anyway. His life would
make a novel, but I haven't the resolution to tackle so long a job.'

All of his letter except this paragraph or two about himself
dealt with things seen and heard. He wrote with an undercurrent
of humor, sometimes tender and full of understanding, sometimes
ironic and harsh, yet always lively and amusing. Ruth as she
read understood his state of mind; and she found reassurance in
this understanding. His scars were healing; he was on the way to
becoming a well man again.

In March another letter, this time from Hong Kong, and
longer than the last, brought her real content. He wrote:

> 'I've reached the stage of appraising and understanding
> myself as I used to be. Do you mind if I put it on paper — if
> only to get my own thoughts clear. My diagnosis of my case is
> that I made some success — a substantial success — much too
> easily. When Father died, and we were left hard up, I felt
> cheated and abused; and other things happened to make me
> feel that I was suffering more than my share of the slings and
> arrows etc., etc. A girl — I thought at the time — broke my
> heart; and my first book came out of that experience. That
> and succeeding books caught on, and I began to think of
> myself as an Olympian figure, sitting aloof from struggling
> little human beings, excessively aware of their frailties and
> only mildly approving their virtues. I thought myself, if
> not a Holier-than-thou, at least a Wiser-than-thou; and the
> world was just a sketchily interesting drama to which for
> fiction purposes I gave an occasional comprehensive and
> frankly condescending glance.
>
> 'I've never been a religious man — and I'm not now — but
> I can see today a certain attraction in religion. Yet I've a
> stubborn reluctance to allow myself to fall into the "Devil was
> sick; the Devil a saint would be" category. I've taken my
> licking, but I'm not yet ready to admit that it has reformed
> me.
>
> 'Yet I can see that I needed a lesson. I had reached the
> point where I had no affectionate or friendly relationship —
> except in the most casual fashion — with anyone except

Danny. I think I always loved him; but perhaps it was merely that his devotion to me was flattering enough so that I treasured and cultivated it. He was the weak spot in my self-sufficiency; so "for my soul's sake," as they say, I was chastised through him. I mean, his illness staggered me. But I still had some of the Olympian in me. When I knew that Ellen was in love with me, I decided quite cold-bloodedly not to marry her. Perhaps, without realizing it, I reached that decision because Danny's illness had showed me that to allow myself to love anyone was to make myself vulnerable to worry and to pain and to tears — like other men.

'So I determined to keep myself free. If it had not been for the fact that she and I shared a common peril in the canyon, which for an hour drew us close together, I'd never have married her. I suspect that in such moments, when death seems a possibility, life's instinct to perpetuate itself becomes infinitely stronger than normal. Probably no man and woman were ever shipwrecked on a desert island for very long without — as we say — falling in love. They surrender to the biological insistence of the life in them that it be perpetuated. Probably imminent and mortal danger is bound to throw two people of opposite sexes into each other's arms.

'Certainly that happened to us — or at least to me. Back at the ranch next morning I might have sought escape, but I was still under the spell of those hours in the canyon.

'So we were married, and I was well content, and pretty complacent about it. Ellen always let me have my own way. She might try little maneuvers, but she never flatly opposed me. It seemed to me that to be happily married was no trick at all. Danny's poor legs, always under my eyes, might have warned me that I was still vulnerable; but I was blind to that warning, sure of myself and of my opinions, arrogant without knowing it, completely self-satisfied.

'And then the lightning struck! Danny, then our baby, then Ellen. Crack, crack, crack, and each blow right on the jaw! Who was it boasted that his head was bloody but unbowed? I was not only bloody, but bowed too; and yet in me there was still a stubborn feeling that I was a pretty fine fellow, wiser than most, cleverer than most, stronger than most!

I was ready to whine that I'd been unlucky, but that was as
far toward humility as I ever progressed.

'Even now I don't claim to be a reformed character; but in
these months I've met many people, and some of them, men
and women too, have been in real ways great. By knowing
them, some of the arrogance has been drilled out of me. Not
all, but some. I've even realized that I've a lot to learn about
writing! Nothing till now had warned me that I wasn't a literary genius; but now, either because I have lost the old facility, or because I've become more critical, I find writing a
slow and fretful and a not particularly satisfying business.
Maybe I'm growing up. Certainly it's high time!'

Ruth read this letter over and over, and she found herself defending him against his own criticisms. She went back to his
novels, already familiar, and decided that he wrote as Kipling
had written in his earlier years, with complete assurance and
complete confidence in his own infallibility, and with an amused
eye for human weaknesses. It was as though he felt himself set
apart upon a pinnacle from which he surveyed the human race
with tolerant understanding.

But after all, Kipling had never written as well in the years
after he lost his juvenile assurance. Let Harland — whether
rightly or wrongly — keep some of his self-confidence. Did any
man ever achieve any great thing without being first sure that it
was a great thing, and without being in the second place sure that
he could achieve it? And she wanted Harland to achieve. More
than anything else in the world she wanted him to become a
great, good man.

She wished to write him, but she could not till, eight months
after his departure, another letter came, this time from Beverly
Hills. He had met in Honolulu a director of moving pictures
who persuaded him to come back to Hollywood and sign a con-
tract — 'It runs to seventeen pages, closely typed,' he wrote in
amusement, 'but all it says is that I will and that they will' — to
do an original story for the screen.

'So I'll be here two or three months at least,' he told her, and gave her his address. 'In case you have time to drop me a line.'

She wrote at once, and thereafter their letters were frequent. His were at first full of interest in his work, of real enthusiasm. He had outlined the story he meant to write, and the studio chief had approved it. 'Now we go into conference,' he told her. 'With the director, the star, the producer, and the scenarist whose job it is to put my stuff into the technically proper shape. There's a strange and ludicrous conviction out here that if one man can write a story, two or three men can write it better. It's as though an aeroplane had three pilots, each with his own ideas. The result, as you can imagine, is that the plane's flight is erratic, and its eventual landing place uncertain.'

Later, he began to be fretted by lack of progress. She went to Bar Harbor in June. The big house had not been rented, so she lived there and supervised the remodelling of Professor Berent's study and workshop into a smaller cottage which she herself could use. During the summer, Harland's letters reflected his increasing sense of frustration, and in August he surrendered. 'I'm licked,' he wrote. 'The producer has talked my story to death. He's as full of words as a hen salmon of eggs. There's nothing left of the original tale but rags and tatters. So I've resigned. They didn't protest! I'll be home in a week or ten days.'

She had meant to stay in Bar Harbor till September, but she cut her summer short and returned to Boston to be ready to bid him welcome there.

– IV –

When Harland went away, Ruth at his suggestion had offered Mrs. Huston a place with her; but the old woman declined. 'I'll work for him when he wants me, as long as I can get around,' she said. 'But with him away, I'll take a rest while I can.' She had at first gone to live with her daughter; but Ruth kept in touch with her, and she knew that this spring Mrs. Huston had returned to Harland's house to dwell there alone, preferring independence and the routine of caring for familiar things to idleness in her daughter's home. So when Ruth returned to Boston now she telephoned Mrs. Huston, and offered to help, if any help were needed, in making the house ready for Harland's coming; but Mrs. Huston said proudly: 'There hasn't been a day for months that he couldn't walk in the front door any time he had a mind and find things the way he likes them!'

With his return imminent, Ruth was increasingly happy at the prospect of seeing him again. It was as though during this year of his absence she had been merely marking time. When the day came, she waited for his call, and in late afternoon her telephone rang and she sped to answer.

'Ruth?' His voice, she thought instantly, was at once stronger and more youthful.

'Yes, Dick. You sound so well!'

'"Richard is himself again,"' he assured her. 'I got in an hour ago. How shall we celebrate?'

'Come to dinner.'

'No, we've a lot to talk about, and I don't want any interruptions. I don't want to share you with your kitchenette. Let's make it the Copley. Seven?'

'Seven, then,' she agreed.

'I'll pick you up,' he said. 'We'll talk for twenty-four hours without a break.'

When she had hung up she was astonished to find her eyes wet with grateful tears, and happiness shook her and made her tremble. By the clock on her mantel, he would not be here for almost three hours, yet she felt that she must hurry, that there were so many things she must do before he came. Her hair, she decided, needed shampooing, so she was happily busy for a while. She used another half-hour in manicuring her nails, and then began to consider what she would wear — not that he would notice what she wore. She assured herself of this, yet hesitated painfully. She did not even know whether he would be in dinner clothes, and wished to telephone to ask him, and could not bring herself to do so, and compromised at last — since the evening was warm — on a print which seemed to her attractive and not unsuitable.

When she was ready, tremulously happy, she laughed at her own reflection in the mirror. 'You idiot!' she exclaimed. 'You're as excited as a girl going to her first dance — and you look it!' And then, with a toss of her head. 'Well, why shouldn't you be glad to see him? And why pretend you're not?'

Then the bell rang and she ran to click the latch for him; and when the elevator stopped at her floor she hurried to open the door. He came in with a cry of pleasure.

'Well!' he exclaimed, and caught her hand and said: 'My, but I'm glad to see you.' He kissed her cheeks, one and then the other; and she felt her eyes fill again.

'Heavens!' she laughed. 'Why should I be crying? You look so well, Dick!'

He was in fact brown from much sun and wind, his eyes bright. He seemed a little heavier than he had been, and she said so.

'So do you!' he assured her. 'Golly! I didn't realize how anxious I was to see you till I left Chicago on the last lap.' And he asked: 'All ready?'

She laughed, remembering her hours of preparation. 'Yes. Yes, I'm ready, Dick,' she agreed. Absurd, absurd, absurd, this torrent of happiness that filled her now!

— v —

That evening they were gay, interrupting their rapid fire of talk only when the orchestra played something that led them to the dance floor; and Harland said approvingly: 'I'd forgotten what a swell dancer you are. Remember Sea Island?'

'I seldom dance,' she confessed.

'Nor I,' he agreed. 'But I'm in a dancing mood tonight. If I'd known what fun it would be to come home I'd have done it long ago.'

They stayed till the tables all around them were empty; and afterward they walked toward the Esplanade, and since the night was pleasantly warm, they clung to these first hours together. The eastern sky was paling before at last he left her at her door.

They saw each other frequently that fall. Sometimes these encounters were prearranged, with a football game or the like as a pretext; but occasionally, without forewarning, he rang her bell and demanded a cocktail, and she always welcomed him. They wished to celebrate Thanksgiving together, so they drove into the country and dined at the Wayside Inn by an open fire, and sat late before the embers there. Christmas too, they shared. She had declined an invitation or two and so had he.

'Christmas is a family time,' he reminded her. 'And we're the only family either of us has, so we'll get together and be as merry as any of them.' But on Christmas Eve, at her suggestion, they joined a group and went singing carols around the hill, stopping here and there for a hospitable eggnog.

In January he departed for a week of skiing and she missed him astonishingly. Ruth had never learned to ski, but he volunteered to teach her; and thereafter they sometimes drove into the wintry countryside and sought an easy slope and he labored with her through the short afternoons, and they were apt to stop somewhere for dinner on the homeward way. They found in this steady comradeship their greatest pleasure. Ruth was happy because she saw the mounting happiness in him, and since he so often came to her without forewarning she kept herself free and was always ready to do what he proposed. He had kissed her, that first evening, as naturally as in the past, in frank brotherly affection; and this straightforward liking — and nothing more — lay on the surface of their hours together. Yet Ruth presently understood that beneath this friendly surface there were depths, and she confessed this to herself and wondered if he knew. She believed he did not, guessing that if he suspected the truth it might destroy this pleasant companionship which she found so contenting.

He was working, once more rewriting that novel begun so long ago. 'I started it before Danny was taken sick,' he told her. 'And I rewrote it after Ellen and I were married, but now it seems to me thin stuff with no meat in it, like a woman who has starved herself to get what she thinks is a good figure.'

She listened while he read parts of it aloud to her; and if he asked, she offered comments. They were seldom favorable. 'But my opinions are just — my opinions,' she reminded him.

'I know, I know,' he assured her. 'Don't worry. If I don't agree with what you say, that's the end of it; but it helps me to talk the thing out with you.' And he told her: 'Argue with me! Fight for your ideas! That's the most stimulating thing you can do.'

To one point she came back again and again. Because he wrote with the derisive intolerance of immaturity, critics had called him a satirist; and accepting their label he had made this novel a catalogue of petty human follies. But she thought his thesis too severe. 'You're forever emphasizing the silly things people do, making fun of them in clever ways,' she urged. 'Of course it's ever so easy to do that. Everyone is ridiculous in some special little fashion. But in other ways everyone is admirable too. It's easy to make fun of people, but it's not so easy to recognize the fine things in them. This just isn't my kind of book, I'm afraid. You're — jeering at the world, but I think most people are pretty nice!'

He protested laughingly: 'My God, woman, look at them!'

She shook her head. 'That's what you do! You look at them! But instead of just looking, you ought to get inside them, see how many of the unattractive things they do are done because they're shy, or embarrassed, or worried, or scared; see how often they're really doing the best job they know how — and usually with not much capacity or ability to do any job at all.' And she said earnestly: 'Why, Dick, the world is full of men who never have an hour free from worry — about their jobs, their families, their homes, money, all sorts of things. But they go ahead, keep their chins up, keep telling their wives that everything is fine; and they make a home, and give their children a better start in the world than they had. Most men are pretty grand, Dick.'

'How about women?' he asked quizzically, and she colored and smiled and said:

'You're making fun of me; but I'm going to say my say! Women are fine too, most of them. Oh, I know we wear funny hats, and go to silly lectures, and play bridge like fiends, and talk and talk; but a lot of us — most of us — are doing our jobs, too. The trouble with you novelists is that you like to write about the unusual people, the extraordinary people. Or you write about the unusual, extraordinary things people do. Why not write about the ordinary everyday things all of us ordinary people do?'

'Because if I did, you ordinary people wouldn't read what I wrote,' he assured her. 'Novels, like newspapers, are built on the unusual, the exciting, the tragic, the dramatic. Such events make news. By your rule, papers would come out with big headlines: "No News Today. A Hundred Million Americans Yesterday Led Perfectly Normal Lives."'

'Well, they did,' she reminded him, laughing, yet holding her ground. 'And a really good novelist could write about them in such a way that they'd love to read it.' She added with a strong sincerity: 'Instead of ridiculing people's ridiculous ways, I'd like to see you glorify the glorious things they do.'

'The other's a lot more fun.'

'I know. Just as there are some critics who prefer to write about poor books, so they can say clever, cutting things. They'll take pages to tell you how poor a book is, just so they can show off their own cleverness in doing so.'

'But see here,' he argued. 'In this book of mine, the hero — he's a good fellow, with sound ideas. At least he has the fundamental virtues.'

'All except the big ones,' she objected.

'What are they?'

'Why — humility, I think, and tolerance, and to be steadfast, and to be friendly. He's too ready to — denounce someone!'

'So was Christ,' he suggested.

'He denounced people for important things! Your young man doesn't care what he denounces. Why should he waste his energies criticizing millinery, for instance?'

'Didn't Christ criticize someone for making broad his phylactery? Aren't phylacteries millinery?'

She felt a deep surprise. 'I didn't suppose you knew the Bible.'

He confessed with a shy grin: 'Oh, an author has to know a little about everything. As a matter of fact I read it through — or almost — while I was away. Started at the beginning and ploughed right along — till I got into the Acts and got bored and lost interest. I skipped through the rest, but the Old Testament's grand.'

'Why did you read it?' she asked, watching him.

'Well, I knew a lot of people had found — comfort in it; and I needed comfort, so I decided to give it a try.' He added honestly: 'It did me good, too; or at least it made me feel better. I kept remembering how many people before me had reverently studied those pages. I even read the history of the Book. It takes me a year or two or three to write a novel, but it took seventeen hundred years to write the Bible. Scores of men collaborated in writing it, and hundreds of other men gave their whole lives to copying it and checking the copies for errors. They were called scribes, and their job was to make the copies, and then they counted every letter in every book, and how many times each letter occurred. That was so they'd be sure to catch any mistakes. A book that has been treasured as faithfully as that, for hundreds of years before the first printing press came along, is bound to have meat in it.'

Listening, seeing the earnestness in his eyes, the quick eagerness in his tones, she knew surely and deeply that she loved him and would always love him; and she smiled in proud tenderness and he saw her smile and asked: 'What is it?'

'I was just — being glad for you,' she evaded.

He chuckled. 'That's a favorite trick of yours,' he remembered. 'Being glad for other people.' Her heart lifted its beat, and he said comfortably: 'You're pretty swell, you know.' She waited, half-breathless — wondering if he too had seen the flash of truth; but he began to put his manuscript away. 'I'd keep you up all night if you let me,' he confessed. 'You'll have to learn to send me home!'

They had, that second winter after Ellen's death, many such

hours together, and the pleasure they thus found insulated them against the world in which they lived. He usually declined the invitations that came his way, and she kept her time free for him. If he had put off an insistent hostess by pleading a previous engagement — only to take Ruth into the country for an afternoon of skiing — they avoided being seen, dining afterward at some little frequented inn; and their hours together assumed a clandestine quality at which they laughed like amused conspirators.

When spring began to come, they planned to have many picnic suppers, to drive down to remote beaches on the shore or to hidden lakes he knew, with steaks or chops to broil over an open fire; but for a while the weather served them ill. Not till the day before Easter did the signs promise a settled fine day for the morrow. Saturday evening he called her on the phone.

'I tried to get you this afternoon,' he said. 'How about Humarock tomorrow? We'll cook our dinner on the beach. If it's as warm as it is today, we might even swim.'

'Oh, I'm sorry, Dick.'

'Can't make it?' There was disappointment in his tone.

'I — like to go to church on Easter Sunday,' she explained. As a matter of fact she went regularly; but this winter, whenever he proposed a Sunday expedition, she had agreed, making no objection.

'That's right; it is Easter, isn't it?'

'Yes.'

He hesitated, and she thought afterward she might have willed his next word. 'See here,' he challenged, 'is there any rule against my going with you?'

Her hand pressed her throat in a quick happy gesture. 'Why no, I don't think so,' she said gravely. 'Churches don't have many rules, you know.'

'What time?' he asked, and she told him. 'I'll pick you up,' he promised, and chuckled. 'I haven't been to church since I was a boy in Sunday school.'

'Then it's high time you did go!' she said lightly, but she turned away from the telephone in a quick gladness so great she found it hard to breathe.

– VI –

That picnic on the beach was only postponed. Ruth was happy in doing with him whatever he chose to do, and there were long afternoons of quiet talk, and still dusky evenings when they sat late by the cooling embers of the fire over which he had cooked their supper, their low tones murmuring under the stars. They drove sometimes for mile on mile, abandoning the traffic routes for unfrequented roads. Often, having no destination in mind, they let chance decide their course, taking the first left turning and then the first right at random, until perhaps they came to a dead-end road and had to retrace their way. Whenever they discovered any particularly attractive spot, whoever was driving at the time claimed — and had — credit for that discovery. Thus Ruth could boast of 'My place in Lincoln,' or of 'My place down back of Sudbury,' or of 'My place by the river out in Sherborn,' and Harland had an equal score.

One such place, for no obvious reason, held for each of them an equal attraction. In Lincoln — Ruth was at the wheel that day — chance led them to follow a road which eventually lost its firm-surfaced respectability and degenerated into sandy ruts, descending at an easy grade through oak scrub and scattered pines to come out at last upon the border of a grassy bog through which the river meandered. Here the road ended, but a blue heron feeding in the shallows heard their voices and rose to fly heavily away, and they watched it follow the stream's course for a while and then settle in again; and Ruth said:

'Why don't we have supper here? I like this place.'

'So do I,' he admitted. 'I don't know just why.'

'It reminds me of the lovely intervales along that river where we — and Ellen — went fishing.'

'We might be just as far from civilization as we were there,' he agreed. 'Except for this road — and it's not much of a road — there's no sign of human beings anywhere.'

They alighted from the car and walked to the riverside, and a fish that was almost certainly a trout — Harland thought it was

a big brown — sucked down a struggling fly. 'Next time I'll
bring my rod,' he said. 'If that fellow shows again, I'll give him
a try.'

Back near the car they found a grassed slope shaded by small
oaks, and sprawled there for an hour or two, Harland talking of
his work and Ruth listening and offering some comment now and
then. At sunset he built a small safe fire, and after their cooking
was done the fire became a smudge to banish mosquitoes, and
they stayed beside it till full dark, reluctant to end this quiet
hour. When it was time to depart and they were in the car, Harland before starting the engine looked at her smilingly:

'You're good company, Ruth,' he said.

'So are you,' she assured him, happily content.

'We get along, don't we?'

'Yes,' she assented. 'We get along.'

Turning homeward, they drove in silence till they came back
to travelled ways again, and Ruth found this silence deeply exciting, like being in a warm, still, friendly darkness with the sense
of a well-loved presence near. It was, she suspected, like being
married and waking in the night and knowing your dear husband
was asleep beside you, and thinking of the strength in him, and
the gentleness, and of his steady, friendly love for you; and she
smiled at herself for the thought, yet treasured it, all the same.

The next time they met, Harland was disturbed about his book.
She had felt in him for some weeks an increasing dissatisfaction
with what he was doing; but now that feeling found words. 'I
think the real trouble is with me,' he confessed. 'I'm — changing, Ruth, in some way not yet clear; changing from day to day.
I realized it today when I went back to begin revising what I've
done thus far, before going on to write the last hundred pages.
If I were writing the first part today, I wouldn't write it the way
it stands.' She said nothing, and he went on: 'I'm afraid the job
is a patchwork. When I began it, I was a cocksure, arrogant
youngster — and I thought myself ever so sophisticated and wise.
Then after Ellen and I were married I was tremendously stimulated, saw — or thought I saw — deeper into my characters;

and I rewrote a lot, and changed a lot. And now this last winter
— after leaving it untouched for months — I've revised it again;
but the result is like the product of those story conferences in
Hollywood. At least three different authors have collaborated
on this job. All of them were me; but they were three different
men, just the same. The boy who began this book might have
finished it and been satisfied with it; or Ellen's husband might
have finished it. But I don't believe I can. I'm about ready
to junk the whole thing.' And he asked helplessly: 'What's
happened to me?' He laughed. 'The world's beginning to seem
to me a pretty fine place, full of fine people. When I read
what I've written, I don't believe a damned word of it.'

'Perhaps you're tired, stale.' Her pulse was firm with pride.

'Tired?' He laughed again. 'Why, I never felt so well in my
life. Not only physically, but mentally and spiritually too.
And I'm not stale either. I'm anxious to finish this book because
there's another one in me all ready to be written and I'm eager to
get at it. It will be the sort of book you want me to write; just a
straightforward story about simple, average, normal men and women. I think I can see them as brave and beautiful, and make the
reader see them so. But damn it, I've got to finish this job first.'

'Why?' she asked, watching him happily.

He grinned. 'Well — I'll be damned if I know,' he said. 'Except that I hate being licked.'

'If you don't want to finish it, that's not being licked. Sometimes it takes more bravery to accept defeat than to fight on to
victory — especially if it's to a victory that should never be won.'

He smiled and touched her hand. 'You're swell,' he said.
'You've a philosophy that can meet just about any problem.'

'Why don't you lay the book aside?' she suggested. 'Get
Leick and go away fishing for a month, then come back and read
it again and see how it strikes you.'

He nodded. 'I may do that,' he said. He added thoughtfully:
'You know, some day I want to go back to that river where the
fire so nearly caught us; but I'll wait till the forest has had time to
grow again.'

She had suggested that he go away, but she was glad he did not do so. He stayed in Boston and they went instead, once and then again, to that road's end by the river in Lincoln; and he tried to cajole the big trout into taking a fly, and never succeeded and did not greatly care. The third time, they were sitting in the moonlit dark beside their smudge fire when another car came down the road and saw theirs and backed and turned and drove away again, and they heard a boy's voice and a girl's laughter; and when the car was gone he said in a puzzled wonder:

'Now there's a sample of the change in me, Ruth. Once I'd have been contemptuous of them and of their cheap flirtation. Now I'm remembering that they're lovers, and that what they do is a part of their search for beauty.'

She nodded understandingly, and the green grass which he had put smotheringly on the fire dried and threw up a little flame; and in its light she saw his eyes turn to her and hold hers, and her heart beat hard.

'Ruth,' he asked at last, in grave inquiry: 'Do you suppose I'm in love with you?'

For a long time, minutes on end, she did not reply, not trusting her voice, feeling herself tremble inwardly with great happiness, knowing — yet still not quite believing — that the moment for which for weeks now she had prayed was thus simply come upon them. She did not speak, yet her eyes met his, and he waited for her answer. His question, even though she had dreamed of the moment when this word would be spoken between them, had surprised her, as a lightning flash surprises, and with an equal illumination. In that sudden brightness, just as in the lightning's instant glare the visible world is all revealed, she saw clearly many things not hitherto clearly seen or comprehended but now completely clear; and in the long silence which followed his word, just as after the flash in the heavens the eye retains for a while a perfect picture of all that was so briefly seen, so did her clear vision persist. When she answered him it was steadily and honestly.

'I think so, Dick, yes,' she said. 'I hope so, because I love you.'

There was a pulse beat in the silence, and the flame burned

brightly and then died, so that half-dark came between them.
He plucked grass and laid it on the embers and darkness was
complete, and in that dark he spoke at last, his question like a
thought finding words:

'What is it to love a woman?' After an instant he went on:
'Did I love Ellen? I knew, one night at the fishing lodge in New
Mexico, that she would marry me if I wished, but I decided I did
not want to marry her. Then she and I went through that adventure in the canyon together, and there were moments when I
thought we'd never win clear; and something woke in me. It
wasn't just — appetite. It was more permanent than that. I
wanted to possess her, not for a moment but forever; wanted her
to be — as the word goes — mine. By the time we reached the
ranch, that feeling was beginning to evaporate; but then, suddenly, we were married and — she was everything I wanted, all
compacted into one small, lovely body.'

Ruth thought he had forgotten she was here beside him as
he went on. 'She made me feel tremendous,' he said. 'Omnip-
otent and omniscient and enormously full of potentialities.
We were congenial as two people equally intoxicated are congenial, each stimulated by the other. We never had a quarrel,
you know; not in the usual sense of the word. It's true we —
parted; but even that seemed normal in our relationship.' He
was silent and she thought there was hesitation in him, as though
he considered saying something which presently he decided not
to say; for he went on: 'But Ruth, I don't feel about you the way
I did about her.'

She said at once: 'I know.' Gladness filled her.

'If I loved her, then I certainly don't love you.' The flame
blazed up again and she saw his sober countenance. 'I'm happy
with you, completely so,' he said. 'With you I feel — good.
Virtuous. And I like that. With you, I like people. With her,
you know, other people didn't count. It was always Ellen who
filled my world. But you — being with you — just sharpens
my appreciation of other people, of places and scenes and things.
Everything is more beautiful or more interesting when I see it
with you. Is that — loving you?'

'Love's just a word,' she suggested. 'Perhaps it's harder than most words to define.'

'I know. You can't get all the connotations. Love means to each one what he has called love in his thoughts. I would have said I loved Ellen. But loving her was an end in itself. Loving you — if I love you — is only a beginning.' He spoke quietly. 'Forgive me, but I want to make you understand. If I embraced Ellen, that embrace was everything, complete in itself. But if I ever hold you in my arms, to do so will be a part of something a great deal bigger than ourselves; no more than an incident in a great plan. My love for Ellen ended in loving her. My love for you would be only one aspect of our life together, important only because it promised the babies we would have some day.' And he said in a low tone: 'You'd be my wife. Ellen was never quite that, Ruth.'

The flames still burned between them as she spoke. 'We will be happy, Dick.'

'Do you want to marry me?'

She said, like a ritual, gravely: 'I want to be always with you, living together, doing what life asks of us together. I want the duties, and the responsibilities, and the tasks; I want the successes and the joys, the griefs and the gladnesses; I want to receive all from you, and to give all to you. I want us to be one person, my dear. If that's marriage, yes, I want to marry you.'

He rose and with his foot scuffed out the little fire, thoughtfully pressing the embers till the last spark was extinguished, taking the coffee pot to the riverside to fill it with water and returning to pour the water on the already cooling brands. Ruth too rose and stood waiting in the shadowed dark, till at last he came to her and faced her for a silent moment and then took her in his arms.

Her blood quickened then to meet the quickening of his, and after an instant she laughed in breathless happiness, and then her laughter ended in a whispering rapture, and when at last their lips parted, he said huskily and reverently:

'Oh thank God! Thank God!'

'I thank you too, God,' said Ruth softly, and their lips and their hearts gave thanks together.

– VII –

They were married a few days later, in the vestry of the church where since Easter Sunday Harland had more than once joined Ruth in attendance. There were no wedding guests. When this question came to be considered, Harland left the decision to Ruth.

'There aren't more than half a dozen people I'd ask, unless we had a mob,' he confessed. 'But we'll do the thing in style if you say the word.'

'If I asked six people I'd have to ask sixty,' she reflected. 'And if I asked two I'd have to ask six.' It was simpler, they decided, to go quietly together and alone to the minister. 'After all,' Ruth reminded him, 'we're the chiefly interested parties.' And she said: 'It's curious, I suppose, that you and I haven't any intimate friends. As long as Mother was alive, I didn't go out much; but I've been in circulation for two years now. Of course, I know dozens of girls — and men too; but I've been a sort of lone wolf!' Her eyes met his. 'Even while you were away, Dick, I think I must have been absorbed in you.'

'Did you suspect it?'

'No, honestly I didn't. Looking back now, I can see that I began to love you that day before the great fire. Remember, when we went exploring in the woods? I was happy with you that day. It was a gay, light happiness, like bubbles in wine held up against the sun, and I'd never felt that way before. But I didn't know what it meant, and I didn't feel it again till the day you came home.' She smiled. 'You'd kissed me before, in just the same way, but when you kissed me that day you came home, it was not just because I was Ellen's sister. It was because I was me.'

He nodded. 'I felt the same way, that day by the river; but I'd felt something like it before.' He added in a thoughtful tone. 'I remember a night in New Mexico, the night Ellen stayed up in the mountains till morning. We were sitting on the veranda — Mrs. Robie and I — and you came in the darkness to tell us not to worry. I felt it then, felt the friendliness and strength in you, and I liked the way you walked.' He asked her seriously: 'Do you suppose I was in love with you then, and all the time afterward?'

'I know what you're thinking,' she confessed. 'But neither of us ever betrayed Ellen in even the smallest thought.'

'She accused me once of being in love with you.'

'She accused me of loving you,' Ruth assented. 'But it wasn't true of either of us, Dick. She was wrong. If she were still alive — we'd never have come to love each other now.' She touched his hand, clasped it strongly, full of a high pride.

He spoke again of that day beside the river and they relived it, remembering each incident. 'We'll go back there, some day,' he said at last. 'After the young green has had a chance to hide the waste left by the fire; next year, perhaps, or the year after.' His eyes lighted. 'We might buy that land and build a home there, as we planned that day.'

'That would be fine,' she agreed. 'You like solitudes — and with you I'd never feel solitary.' The thought pleased her, and she spoke more eagerly. 'And we'd be too busy to be lonely, anyway; you working in the morning, and me — and you in the afternoons — busy with our farming and our flowers.'

'And our dogs and horses,' he amended. 'We'll keep a dozen dogs, and a horse apiece, and some sheep and cows.'

She said doubtfully: 'That sounds sort of — permanent! Or would we take them in every spring and out every fall? We'd need a regular Noah's ark to carry them up the river.'

'And the animals would go aboard two by two!' He laughed. 'I suppose we'll have to keep the menagerie in bounds. Unless we could get a farmer to stay there the year round and take care of them.'

'Would Leick?'

'I don't know. I've never reached the bottom of Leick's

resources; never yet wanted anything he couldn't do.' And he said: 'See here, this thing is getting hold of me. Suppose we go up there this summer and have the place surveyed, see what shape it's in, maybe even buy the land and build a temporary camp there anyway.'

'What about the book?'

He said grimly: 'I'm near a dead end on that. After we're married, we'll take the car and go wandering for a couple of weeks — unless there's something you'd rather do?'

'No, I like just wandering with you.'

'Then I'll come back and take another look at it, and if it still seems as empty as it does now, I'll give it up.' He grinned. 'I like my next idea better anyway.'

'You've put so much work on this one.'

He chuckled. 'I know. I'm a thrifty soul, too. But I've learned a lot, stewing and fussing over it. I've had my money's worth out of it in experience.'

So they were married and departed, leaving no forwarding address; and the fortnight Harland had planned extended itself. At first they drove leisurely westward, avoiding resorts and cities, never hurrying, stopping to admire every pleasing prospect, lingering in talk with farmers by the roadside and with housewives from whom they begged a drink of water and with merchants where they made purchases and with the keepers of the small hotels where they preferred to stay. Since these lodgings were often unattractive, Harland bought sleeping bags and cooking dishes, and they acquired provisions at need, and when the nights were fine they were apt to find some contenting spot and sleep in the open air. The byroads which they followed led them sweetly on, and each day was an adventure, and the world was friendly and serene; and Ruth one night, clinging to him in a soft swift passion, cried:

'Oh Dick, Dick, I've never guessed two people could be as happy as we are; as happy as you and I.' And, begging for reassurance, she asked: 'Will it last, my dearest? Will it always be like this?'

He said, confident and proud: 'Of course. Why not?'

'I hate going back to the everyday world again.'

'There'll never be an everyday world for you and me. There'll always be new wonders to see and to admire.'

On Sundays — this was at her suggestion, but he willingly agreed — they often sought out some small village church and joined the congregation which sat stiff and uncomfortable in unaccustomed 'Sunday clothes,' the men smelling faintly of moth balls, their womenfolk, before the services began, nodding and smiling and whispering, and gathering afterward in chattering groups outside the church doors.

'Why is it I enjoy these churches?' Harland asked one day as they drove away. 'That preacher was just a boy, and his Adam's apple fascinated me, and his sermon was nothing but a collection of familiar quotations. But I liked it.'

'I don't think it's what you get out of church,' she suggested. 'It's what you take into it. But — especially in these little churches — I'm always conscious of the congregations which have sat there in the past, the old people now buried in the churchyards. I feel them around me in the pews; and I picture their strong, kindly, simple, decent faces. The world is so darned full of nice, ordinary people, Dick, doing their daily jobs. They may be tricky or cruel or something during the week, but they turn to church on Sunday.'

'Why do they do it?'

'It must give them something they want, something they can't put into words. Probably in church they feel themselves in a great communion with millions of others like themselves, all over the world.'

'Then why don't more people go to church?'

'I think perhaps it's because they're in-betweens, either too intelligent or else not intelligent enough. I think the little people and the big ones are alike very simple. It's the in-betweens who have lost their simplicity. Cars and radios and rapid communication have enlarged their world — and made it thin and diffuse. There are so many things in their world, and so many ideas in their minds, that they're forever pulled this way and that, have no rock of simple conviction on which they can stand firm. They hear statements made one day and denied the next, so they learn disbelief rather than belief, and fall into the pit of believing nothing. But in the old little world where your farthest horizon was only a day's horse and buggy ride away, the church was the center, and the minister was the fountain of truth, and your life instead of being diffused and confusing was concentrated and simple and comforting.'

He said smilingly: 'Such ministers as we've been hearing certainly weren't fountains of eternal truth! And yet if you just let go and relax and submit, you come out of their churches feeling rested and — well, as though you'd made friends with something fine.'

They had, during these weeks together, long hours of contenting talk; and even though they seldom drove great distances in any one day, they went as far west as Wisconsin before turning homeward. The weather was hot, so they swung northward into Canada, and eastward and then south into Maine. From Skowhegan they wired Mrs. Huston to expect them; and Harland telegraphed to Leick — he had written him before they set out, bidding him make plans — that by the first of August they would be ready to go back to the river to undertake that project of creating a home in the wilderness which now more and more clearly took shape in their minds.

When they arrived at the house on Chestnut Street, Harland swept Ruth up in his arms and carried her across the threshold. Mrs. Huston showed him a pile of unopened letters on his desk, and Ruth promised to help him answer them tomorrow.

'I'm going to be your secretary, you know,' she reminded him. 'We'll turn them off in no time.'

But those letters would wait long for answers. Mrs. Huston reported that Quinton had telephoned that morning.

'I said I expected you home in time for dinner,' she explained, 'and he said he'd come this evening to see you.' Harland started to protest and she said: 'I told him you wouldn't want to see anyone your first night at home, but he said this couldn't wait. He said it was important.'

Ruth saw that Harland was puzzled and disturbed. 'Wonder what that's all about?' he asked her.

'I don't know.' She too was perplexed, full of a reasonless concern.

Harland laughed. 'Oh well, let him come. He won't stay long,' he said.

12

Harland had instructed Mrs. Huston to arrange during
their absence that all Ruth's more personal possessions should
be brought from her apartment to the Chestnut Street house;
and when now he carried their bags upstairs, the old woman
came to show proudly how she had disposed Ruth's garments in
bureau drawers and closets, and Ruth approved all she had done,
and after Mrs. Huston had gone to set their dinner on, Ruth
gave Harland a happy hug and a kiss.

'She worships you, doesn't she?' she said. 'I'll have to be
good to you, or she'll scratch my eyes out.'

He chuckled. 'If she tries to discipline you, you just get sick,'
he advised. 'No matter what you do to me, she'll forgive you
if you're sick enough.'

They made a merry hour of their first dinner at home together,
and Harland fought out of his mind the frightening wonder why
Quinton was here, refusing to remember Danny's death and what
the State Attorney's coming might foreshadow. But almost at
once after they went into the living room the doorbell rang. Mrs.
Huston was busy in the kitchen, so Harland himself, saying im-
patiently, 'Drat it, that must be Quinton,' went to answer.

When he opened the door he saw that Quinton was not alone.
A man and a woman stood beside and behind him. Quinton
stepped briskly into the hall, and the others pressed on his heels,
so that Harland felt himself crowded back. Quinton said, with
importance in his tone: 'Good evening, Mr. Harland. This is
Deputy Sheriff Hatch, and my secretary, Mrs. Parkins.'

Harland, feeling a cold touch on his spine, took the deputy's soft hand, bowed to Mrs. Parkins. Ruth came to greet them, acknowledging Quinton's introductions, bidding them into the living room. She seemed to find nothing unusual in this visitation; but Harland knew she must be as disturbed as he, and he crossed to stand by her side at the hearth, watching Quinton and these others with a wary eye. Deputy Hatch, a large fat man who, it was clear, habitually ate too much, sat down on the couch, turning his hat over and over on his knees, looking all around, obviously impressed by his surroundings. Mrs. Parkins, a grim young woman with a tight mouth, watched to see what Quinton would do; and when he chose a straight chair at one end of the table she drew up another and seated herself beside him, stripped off her gloves, took from her handbag a stenographer's notebook and a pen, and sat waiting expectantly.

Their movements were ominous, but Ruth said in a pleasant tone: 'You're our first callers. We only just got home.'

Harland tried to laugh. 'You were practically sitting on the doorstep.'

Quinton cleared his throat. 'We're here on business,' he said impressively. 'I want to ask you some questions. Your lawyer would advise you not to answer. I warn you that Mrs. Parkins here will take down whatever you say and it may be used in evidence against you.'

Harland, sure now that Quinton had somehow stumbled on the truth about Danny's death, saw Mrs. Parkins's pen begin to race across the first page of her notebook. His palms were moist and he felt a damp coolness on his brow, and his voice when he tried to speak caught in his throat. He asked hoarsely, pretending an uncertainty he did not feel:

'What the Hell are you talking about?'

'I'm not answering questions,' Quinton told him. 'I'm asking them. Mind you, you can refuse to answer; but your refusal will be noted.'

Ruth, beside Harland near the hearth, said seriously: 'Aren't you being unnecessarily mysterious? What is it? We'll gladly

answer any questions you care to ask, I'm sure.' Harland remembered that she — since she did not know Ellen's part in
Danny's drowning — had nothing to hide; but guilt lay heavy
on his shoulders, and he tried to guess how much Quinton knew
— and how he had discovered it. Certainly not from Leick,
who though he had seen the truth from the beginning would never
speak. Yet Quinton must know, or at least suspect. There was
no other possible explanation for his coming tonight.

Harland was so sure of this that the other's first word came as
relief and reassurance, for it did not concern Danny at all. 'I
want to ask you, Mrs. Harland,' the State Attorney explained,
'about that picnic the day your sister died.'

Ruth echoed in bewilderment: 'About the picnic?' Harland
was as surprised as she; and he was for the moment so grateful
to find Danny's death was not in question that his thoughts
failed to focus.

'Yes,' said Quinton. 'Guess you haven't forgotten it.' There
was something so derisive in his tone that Harland, his fears now
banished, spoke in quick anger.

'What's the idea?' he demanded.

Quinton told him, as one silences an obstreperous child:
'Now, now, Mr. Harland! We'll get along faster if you speak
when you're spoken to. I want Mrs. Harland to do the talking.'

Ruth touched Harland's arm to quiet him. 'What is it you
want to know?' she asked Quinton.

'Well, let's start at the beginning,' he proposed. 'Whose
idea was that picnic, anyway?'

'Why, I don't remember,' Ruth confessed. She looked at
Harland. 'Mr. Harland's, I think. He wanted to see Leick,
and we decided to take our lunch over to Leick's farm, that's
all.'

'Did your sister like the idea?'

'Yes, of course.'

In the brief silences after Ruth's every answer, Mrs. Parkins's
pen made a slight scratching sound; and Harland, frowning in a

strained attention, could hear the deputy's heavy breathing, as though the fat man were on the verge of a snore.

'What did you take to eat?'

Ruth hesitated. 'I'm not sure. Potato salad, or possibly potato chips, and some bread and butter sandwiches, and I think some of Mrs. Freeman's chocolate doughnuts, and thermos bottles full of coffee. I don't remember anything else. Oh, we had ice cream, too.'

'Lobsters?'

'Leick was to have some ready for us.'

Deputy Hatch made an audible digestive sound, his eyes opening wide; and Quinton looked sharply toward him and he mumbled something apologetic.

'Who put up the lunch?' Quinton asked.

'Mrs. Freeman and I.'

'How'd you carry it?'

'In one of those fitted hampers,' Ruth said, and then, re-membering: 'It was the one you once gave Ellen, Mr. Quinton.' She added: 'And we took lemons, and mustard, and Worcester-shire sauce, and salt and pepper. I always make a tamale sauce for lobsters, and I did that day.'

'Take along sugar and cream for the coffee?'

'None of us used cream. I took some sugar for Ellen.'

'She'd lost the sugar canister out of that hamper, the time we used it.'

Ruth nodded. 'Yes. I put some in an envelope.'

'She was the only one put sugar in their coffee?'

'Yes.'

Harland watched and listened, his eyes swinging with each question and answer from Quinton to Ruth and back again, as a spectator at a tennis match watches the ball dart to and fro.

'She used the sugar out of that envelope you put it in?'

'Yes.'

'After you'd eaten lunch, what did you do?'

'Ellen and I went up the bank and lay on the grass. Mr. Har-land and Leick stayed by the fire.'

'How long was it after lunch till Ellen took sick?'

Ruth's eyes closed for a moment. 'Quite late in the afternoon,' she said then.

'Where was she?'

'Up on the bank with me.'

'What'd you do?' The questions were coming sharply now.

'Why, Mr. Harland and Leick tried to carry her to the house, sitting on their hands; but she was so sick she couldn't sit up, and Leick went to get a door to carry her on, like a stretcher. Then Mr. Harland and I put her to bed while Leick went for the doctor.'

'What time did she die?'

'Toward morning.'

'You were with her right along?'

'Yes.'

Harland, remembering those hours of Ellen's agony and his, for a little ceased to listen. Quinton had asked some question about Ellen's earlier, similar attacks, and Ruth answered him at length, while Harland lived through again that night of Ellen's suffering and death.

'When did you decide Dr. Seyffert wasn't doing her any good?' Quinton asked at last.

'I don't know. It was late, long after she was taken sick.'

'Did you try to get another doctor?'

'It would have taken hours. I didn't know who to get, nearer than Bangor. Our doctor at Bar Harbor had gone home, gone back to New York.'

Quinton harshly repeated his question. 'Did you try to get another doctor?'

'No.' Ruth's color rose at his tone.

Quinton looked at Harland. 'Did you?' he challenged.

Harland shook his head. 'Damn it, I was distracted!' he cried. 'We all were. We knew Ellen was dying. What's this all about, anyway?'

'You knew she was dying,' Quinton said implacably, 'and you let her die.'

'What's back of all this?' Harland insisted. 'Come out with it, man!'

Quinton said flatly: 'Keep your shirt on, Mr. Harland.' He turned to Ruth again. 'Your father used to kill birds and stuff them.'

'Of course.'

'Had a workshop at Bar Harbor, didn't he?'

'Yes, and one in our house in Boston, too.'

'You've cleared his stuff out, made his study and workshop into a cottage for yourself, haven't you?'

'Yes. I hoped to rent the big house, planned to live in the cottage.'

'What did you do with your father's things?'

'I gave some to the Museum of Natural History, here in Boston; packed some and stored them.'

'Throw anything away?'

'Things for which I could see no use, yes.'

Quinton hesitated. Then he asked: 'When he killed these birds, how'd he preserve the skins?'

'Sprinkled them with arsenic.'

'Any arsenic in his workshop at Bar Harbor when you cleaned it out?'

'Yes, a full jar, and one half full.' Harland saw that Ruth's lips now were white.

'What did you do with it?'

'I took those jars and some other jars and cans down to the dory and rowed offshore and emptied them into the water and then sank them.'

'Empty out the arsenic?'

'Yes.'

'All of it?'

'Yes.'

'Knew what it was, did you?'

'Of course.'

'When'd you do all that?'

'Last summer.' Ruth bit her lips.

'That envelope you put the sugar in, what'd she do with it after she got through using it?'

'Why, I don't know. Put it back in the hamper, I suppose.'

'The rest of you didn't take sugar?'

'No.'

'You knew beforehand that you and Mr. Harland wouldn't take any, didn't you?'

'Yes.'

'Knew Leick wouldn't drink any coffee, didn't you?'

'Why yes. I knew he never drank any on the camping trip we all took together, earlier that summer. I meant to take along some tea for him, but I forgot.'

'So you knew Ellen'd be the only one using that sugar.'

'I suppose so.' Her voice suddenly was weak, and Harland cried furiously:

'That's enough, Quinton! We'll not answer another damned question till you tell us what this is all about.'

Quinton met his eyes, and the chubby man smiled that mirthless smile which always came too easily to him. 'Notice any lies in what she's said?' he asked.

'Of course not. She's told the plain truth.'

'Think of anything she's left out?'

'Blast you, Quinton! What are you up to?'

Quinton looked at Mrs. Parkins. 'Got it all down, have you, Sophy?' he asked. She nodded, and he turned to Harland again. 'I've been talking to her, up to now, but now I'll ask you a question,' he said triumphantly. 'Suppose I told you Ellen died of arsenic poisoning?' Harland sagged under the sudden shock, and Quinton grinned. 'Take your time. We've got all night. Suppose I told you that. What would you say?'

- II -

Quinton's question summoned out of the past into Harland's mind two scenes. He remembered that day they drove north from Boston, and Ellen sought to win him and he told her she could never do so, and she said at last in quiet surrender: 'Then let us go on to — Bar Harbor,' with a faint pause before the last two words. And he remembered too that on the last morning of her life, when the seal's sleek head, sinking out of sight, reminded him of Danny so that he turned to tell her they must part, she had said: 'Well, don't look so serious, Richard! It's a fine day for — a picnic, just the same.' Again that faint pause, not conspicuous then but memorable now, making blindingly clear what her thoughts then had been. He saw as surely as he would ever see it, the truth; that when she knew she had lost him beyond recapture, Ellen chose to die.

He was silent so long that Quinton prompted him. 'What would you say to that, Mr. Harland?'

'I'd say it was absurd!' His thoughts were his own, and loyalty to Ellen bound his tongue. 'It's impossible!'

'It's possible, all right,' Quinton assured him. 'Know anything about the way arsenic poisoning hits a person?'

'No.'

'I've looked it up.' Quinton was almost cheerful. 'There's vomiting, and a burning pain in the stomach, and awful thirst but they can't even keep water down, and cramps, and collapse, and sometimes coma and sometimes not, and then they die.' Harland was shivering uncontrollably, his teeth locked to keep them still. He felt Ruth's hands clinging to his arm, and Quinton asked, 'Isn't that just about what happened to her?'

Harland said doggedly: 'It doesn't prove anything.'

'Any good doctor, seeing her die, would have said the way she died is the way she would have died if someone had given her arsenic.'

'Damn it, no one gave her arsenic!'

'Mrs. Harland here gave her sugar for her coffee,' Quinton pointed out, with a nod toward Ruth. 'She knew no one but Ellen would want sugar, and she brought some along special. That sugar was over half arsenic.'

Harland was beyond coherent thought. His retort was pure emotion. 'That's a damned lie!'

'It's no lie,' Quinton assured him; and he spoke so confidently that Harland accepted the statement. But if it were true, then — Quinton was in so many words accusing Ruth; and in this realization Harland forgot all thought of protecting Ellen, and he cried:

'Well, if she died of arsenic poisoning, she committed suicide!'

'You're a little late thinking up that one,' Quinton drily commented, and he asked: 'By the way, why didn't you have an autopsy? Doctor Seyffert asked if you wanted one.' His eyes turned to Ruth. 'Mrs. Harland here said no, and you backed her up.'

'He never mentioned an autopsy!'

'He offered to get some other doctors.'

'After she was dead.'

Quinton said amiably: 'Oh all right, we'll pass that. But why did you have her cremated?'

'She'd asked me to.'

'*I* hear she'd asked to be buried in Mount Auburn?'

Ruth spoke. 'She wanted to be cremated, Mr. Quinton. She told me so, a day or two before she died. She said she'd asked Mr. Harland to have it done, and she made me promise to remind him.'

'Funny she'd speak of that just before she died. As if she knew something might happen to her.'

Harland cried again: 'Of course she did. I told you, she committed suicide! She knew she was going to.'

Quinton sat forward in his chair. 'Well,' he said crisply. 'The grand jury didn't think she killed herself. They've indicted Mrs. Harland here for murder.' He let that word shudder in the silence, and Harland saw all their eyes — the deputy's, the stenographer's, Quinton's — fixed upon Ruth. His arm encircled her protectingly, but he could find no word.

Quinton rose. 'So there it is. Now I can get the local police to arrest her, and then start extradition proceedings; but that'll take time. If you want to be reasonable, we can all drive back to Maine tonight. Whatever you say.'

Harland turned to Ruth, wondering that she could be — or seem to be — unmoved. 'I'll get a lawyer,' he cried. 'We'll fight this rotten foolishness every step of the way.'

But Ruth shook her head, steady and strong. 'Let's not bother with technicalities, Dick,' she told him quietly. She smiled. 'Besides, I know enough about law to know it wouldn't do any good. He can make us go, so we'll make no fuss. We'll go with him to Maine.'

– III –

Quinton proposed that they make the journey in his car. A sedan, it would accommodate five people readily enough. But this seemed to Harland intolerable. 'I'll take my car,' he insisted. 'Mrs. Harland and I will go in that. You can follow us. We'll not try to get away.'

Quinton said reasonably: 'I don't know as I can stand for that, Mr. Harland. If you did make a break for it, we'd have to do some shooting. No, I'll have to keep my eye on Mrs. Harland.'

Ruth would have submitted. 'He must do what he thinks is his duty, Dick,' she pointed out; but Harland said furiously:

'To hell with that! We're making it easy for him! If we fight, we can hold him up here for weeks.'

'We're not going to,' she reminded him.

'Not if he's reasonable,' Harland agreed; and he told Quinton strongly: 'But if you're not, we'll start fighting right now. Either Mrs. Harland and I travel in my car, and alone, or you'll have to drag us.'

Deputy Hatch roused himself. 'If there's any dragging to do, I guess't I can handle it,' he said heavily; but Quinton intervened.

'Let it go, Joe. We'll trail them.' He told Ruth: 'I don't want to make this any harder for you than I have to.'

'I'm sure you don't,' Ruth assented. She smiled. 'I'm sure, for instance, that you'll let me pack a bag,' she said.

'Sophy can go up with you?' he agreed.

So Ruth and Mrs. Parkins, Ruth calling Mrs. Huston to help her, went upstairs. Harland's own bag was ready — he had not unpacked it since their return that afternoon — so he took this opportunity to telephone Roger Pryde, who handled his legal business, and enlist his aid. Roger did no criminal work, but he promised to locate the best legal talent available, to join Harland in Maine tomorrow.

It was not yet eleven o'clock when they set out, Harland and Ruth in his car, Quinton and Hatch and Mrs. Parkins following close behind. Harland drove slowly, as much because his senses were still confused as out of any consideration for Quinton; and there was in him a stifled, futile rage so that his hands were tight on the wheel, his jaw set, his cheeks hot and stiff. Ruth beside him linked her hands through his arm, and for a while they did not speak at all, till he drew from her a measure of her composure and she felt the hard muscles in his arm relax.

'There, darling,' she said at last. 'You're all right now.'

'This isn't real, is it?' he demanded. 'Isn't it just some sort of nightmare?'

She said, with only a faint break in her voice: 'I feel ever so important, being indicted!'

'That doesn't mean anything,' he assured her. 'Quinton has probably always hated me for marrying Ellen, and of course he could tell the grand jury anything he chose. We'll straighten it out damned quick tomorrow.'

Ruth asked after a moment: 'Even if the sugar did have arsenic mixed in it — how can he know, Dick?'

Harland had had no time for such considerations. 'I don't know. How could he?'

She considered. 'What became of the lunch hamper?'

'I think we left it on the beach. I don't remember anything about it.'

'Leick probably has it.'

'He didn't go home at all after he came to Boston with us, when we brought Ellen. He went off to the woods, left me in Bangor.'

'I expect he went down to the beach and got it, and his wash boiler, that night Ellen died. He had plenty of time, after he brought the doctor.'

Harland thought long before he spoke again. 'If Leick has it, he wouldn't give it to Quinton. But even if he did — didn't Ellen use all the sugar?'

'I suppose not. I put in plenty. It was in an envelope. She tore the corner off and poured some into her cup.'

'She must have put the envelope in the hamper, and Quinton's got hold of it somehow.' Harland added bitterly: 'Or else he's lying. Maybe he planted it.'

'He wouldn't do that.'

He said slowly: 'You know — I believe Ellen killed herself, Ruth.'

She looked at him wonderingly. 'Why, Dick? Why do you think so?'

He hesitated. Upon his tongue he had set a seal so long, but now he was weary of silence. 'I had told her we'd have to separate,' he admitted. 'We'd been discussing it for a long time; and that morning I decided finally to leave her, and told her so.'

She waited, and he was conscious of the white blur of her face upturned to his. He kept his eyes upon the road till her hand at last pressed his arm.

'Why, Dick?' she asked again. 'If you want to tell me.'

So he told her what he had thought he would never tell anyone. He told her how Danny died; and he heard her low murmur of pitying grief. She asked no questions; but his tongue, once loosed, went on, omitting nothing. 'She didn't know, not for a long time, that I knew,' he said at last. 'You see, that day — while I was trying to revive Danny — she said we were going to have a baby. So I couldn't tell anyone the truth, couldn't even let Ellen herself know that I knew. And I tried to — keep our love alive, tried to make life together possible for us. Perhaps if our baby had lived, I could have done it. But it died.

'Then one day we quarrelled. She accused me of loving you,

and — I can see now that I did love you then, because the accusation made me furious. So I told her I knew she had — killed Danny.'

Still Ruth did not speak; and he said at last: 'And after that she tried to win me back, and when she saw she couldn't, she killed herself.'

She lifted his right hand from the wheel with both hers and pressed it against her cheek and kissed it over and over. 'Darling, darling, darling,' she whispered. 'How wretched you've been.'

'Not since I've known you love me.'

'I want to be so good to you.'

'You have been. You are.'

'And now this!' She said miserably: 'I don't mind for myself, but it's terrible for you.'

They drove a while without speech, and she pressed close to him, and the headlights of Quinton's car behind them shone through the rear window, so that sometimes when he turned his head he could see her eyes, deep and steady, and when she met his eyes, she smiled. He said at last:

'What started Quinton digging into this now, I wonder?' She did not answer. 'Maybe he's been at it right along,' he hazarded. 'Or — maybe he just waited till we were happiest, so he could hurt us most.'

'Sh-h! Don't, darling,' she urged. 'Let's stop thinking till we know more about it. Please!'

'You're a wonderful woman!'

'You're a wonderful man!'

'You don't seem to think of yourself at all,' he protested. 'But — it's you he's after! You're the one he's had indicted.'

'You're the one I'm thinking about, darling. I just wish there were some way you needn't have to — suffer so.'

He laughed in a sudden lifting strength. 'Suffer? Me?' he cried. 'Why, Lord love you, Ruth, this gives me a chance to fight for you, to do something for you! Quinton's done me a favor, really. He's giving me a chance to show how much I love you!'

She smiled with him. 'You don't have to show me, darling.
I already know!'

'Then I'll show the world,' he declared, and they came to
Portsmouth and crossed into Maine.

Just beyond the bridge, the car behind suddenly drew alongside and passed and cut in front of them and stopped. Harland
jammed his brakes, and Quinton on one side, the deputy on the
other, came back to them.

Harland asked sharply: 'What's wrong?'

Quinton's smile was like a gleeful shout. 'We're in Maine
now!' he said. 'Mrs. Harland, you're under arrest. I've an
indictment warrant charging you with murder. Harland, the
deputy sheriff will ride with you from now on. You're held as a
material witness. Mrs. Harland, shift into my car. You'll go
the rest of the way with me.'

– IV –

Perry's Harbor is a town — or a city — of two or three thousand people, lying along a steep hillside above the water, most
of the houses strung on roughly parallel streets which eventually
angle together to form the Square. This is a tree-shaded triangle
set with maples and tall elms. Cross streets ascend the hillside,
and the county jail is on top of the hill. The courthouse is a
block beyond the Square.

Harland — the rotund deputy noisily asleep beside him,
Quinton's car ahead showing the way — drove into town toward
ten o'clock next morning. He followed Quinton's car to the jail
where Ruth must be lodged, and he went in with her and Quinton
and stood with her during the brief formalities. They had only
a moment together. 'All right?' he asked.

'Fine, darling! I slept till daylight.' She added smilingly:
'But I'm starved! I hope the food's good here.'

'I'll have you out before night,' he promised; and she touched
his hand.

'Don't lose your head, Dick. We'll need to be patient. It

will take time.' Then Quinton spoke to her, and she kissed
Harland, and they parted. She followed the jailor through the
heavy door, and Quinton and Harland were left together. Harland said harshly:

'I suppose you'll lock me up too.'

'You're on your own recognizance,' Quinton explained. 'I
guess you'll not run away.'

There was something so sleek and sure in the man's bland
countenance that Harland choked with helpless rage, but he
held his tone steady. 'I'll be at the hotel. How can I arrange
bail for her?'

Quinton said calmly. 'You can't. This is a murder charge.'

'Damn it, Quinton, you know that's nonsense!'

'The grand jurors took it seriously, Mr. Harland.'

'What started you on this now? Ellen's been dead almost
two years.'

Quinton said mildly: 'The evidence has only just become available. The news of your marriage led me to make an investigation — and the facts came to light.'

'What facts?'

'A motive, for one thing,' Quinton told him. 'I mean the
fact that Ruth loved you. And I found proof that Ellen died of
arsenic poisoning, found arsenic mixed with the sugar in the
envelope in the hamper.'

'Where'd you get the hamper?'

'I got it; that's enough.'

'The arsenic could have been put there since.'

The other shook his head. 'It wasn't,' he said. 'You'll have
to accept the fact, Mr. Harland. Arsenic was mixed with the
sugar which Ellen put in her coffee that day.'

Harland insisted: 'Then Ellen put it there.'

'Ruth put the sugar in the envelope, gave the sealed envelope
to Ellen at the picnic.' Quinton moved toward the door. 'Now
I've business, Mr. Harland. You can find me at my office. I
may see you at the hotel.'

Harland followed him out to the street. Mrs. Parkins was

waiting in Quinton's car. Deputy Hatch had disappeared, and
Harland drove to the Perry House and registered. When he signed
his name, the little old man behind the marble-topped desk
looked at him curiously; but he said no word, took a key, picked
up Harland's bag and led the way to a room on the second floor.
The room overlooked an area on which backed garages and stores,
and Harland could see the waters of the narrow Bay beyond.
The Perry House was an old hotel, its days of glory past. The
wallpaper was stained, the carpet worn, the brass double bed
sagged in the middle as though it had wearily surrendered to the
burdens it was forced to bear. The pictures on the wall were
familiar, of the sort that were sold by the gross in the years before
the turn of the century, their gold frames permanently spotted
by generations of flies. There was a stale smell of dust and coal
smoke and disinfectant; and Harland opened the windows,
fighting them when they stuck, pounding at the sashes till his
hands were bruised.

Then he threw himself on the bed, his arm across his eyes,
and for a while he lay there unmoving, his thoughts chaos.
His closed eyes burned with weariness, and he wished to sleep
but could not, and discovered wonderingly that he was hungry;
so he splashed his face in the basin and went down to the lobby.
The dining room was closed, but a lunch counter a block away
gave him orange juice, two boiled eggs which should have been
scrambled, and a cup of coffee so bad that though he preferred
coffee black, he added thin milk and much sugar to make it
drinkable. He returned to the hotel, to his room; and almost at
once there was a knock on the door.

He thought this would be Roger Pryde and called a summons,
but instead of Roger a woman appeared; a little old woman, extraordinarily little and extraordinarily old, her face covered with
fine wrinkles like a jockey's, her eyes big behind thick lenses,
her wispy hair straggling under a ridiculous hat. Harland stared
at her, and after a moment he asked:

'Who are you?'

'I'm Miss Batten,' she told him, in a friendly, thin voice.

'I work on the paper here, and send dispatches to the Boston papers.'

Harland had forgotten till now the newspapers, and he had a sudden mental picture of a thousand headlines which the world would read this afternoon and tomorrow morning. His successful books had made his name news, and scores of newspaper men and women had in the past, because he was a novelist, sought to interview him. Recognizing the commercial value of publicity, he had always welcomed them cheerfully and cordially, had done his best to give them usable material, had sympathized with their problems — he remembered his own months on the *Transcript* when he too had been sent out, on more than one occasion, to 'interview' persons of whom he had never heard before — and had appreciated the fact that they were as bored with the necessity of talking to him as he was at talking to them. He had never feared them.

But now this frail old woman woke in him a sudden tremor of alarm; for behind her were legions of editors, reporters, desk men, linotype operators — waiting to spread his story before their readers, to winnow him fine in a fierce blast of nation-wide publicity. 'Novelist's Wife Held For Murder.' 'Mrs. Richard Harland Accused of Poisoning.' 'Novelist in Love Triangle.' His racing thoughts formed a hundred scalding phrases. On the front page of every daily in the country, his tragedy today and tomorrow and for days to come would be spread large.

So Miss Batten, for all she was so weak and small, must not be antagonized, for there was a mighty army at her back. 'Sit down,' he told her. 'Please sit down.'

She did so, with the fussy, settling movements of a hen. 'Mr. Quinton has given out the news of Mrs. Harland's arrest and of the indictment,' she explained. 'I've wired Boston a story on that.' She added apologetically: 'I had to, you know. I'm sorry, but that's my business.'

'Of course. I know.'

She hesitated, and then — Harland saw that she was giving

him time to think, felt a sudden lonely liking for her — she
spoke about herself. 'Whatever money I get for outside stories,
I never spend, you see. It goes into a special fund in the savings
bank; and when I've enough, I'm planning a year's vacation;
a trip around the world.' There was an amazing youthfulness in
her. 'I'll have enough in another year or two, I think,' she said.
'Of course not many news stories break here, but my fund has
been growing for twenty years.'

Harland said with wry humor: 'You ought to get quite a lot of
space on this story.'

'Oh, the city papers will send their own reporters,' she reminded him. 'There'll be a dozen of them here tonight; so I have
to get what I can today.' She seemed, incredibly, to blush.
'That's my excuse for bothering you,' she confessed. 'I hated
doing it, knowing how distressed you must be; but I thought you
might just possibly have something to say.'

He laughed mirthlessly. 'I have,' he agreed. 'I could talk
for a week steady.'

She uttered a little mirthful chirrup. 'Oh, I won't ask you to
do that. But if you're sure you want to say something . . .'

'I say it's a damned ridiculous outrage!'

She shook her head. 'No, I wouldn't say that. Do you mind
if I don't let you say tactless things? "Outrage" suggests persecution, you see. It's — you don't mind my being frank — it's
a cry-baby word! Mr. Quinton and the grand jury — they're
only doing what it's their job to do, you know.'

He looked at her in sudden respect. 'I used to be a reporter,'
he said. 'We were taught to get our — subjects — mad, because
then they'd say things they shouldn't. That's not the way you
work.'

'Oh no,' she assured him. 'If people are already in trouble,
I don't want to make things worse for them.'

'Thanks,' he said. 'Well — what do you think I should say?'

'Well,' she reflected. 'Mr. Quinton gave out a statement.
I'm sorry I haven't a copy, but I put it on the wire. He told
about your first wife's death, and he said new evidence proves

she died of arsenic poisoning, and he said the present Mrs. Harland gave her some sugar for her coffee and that the sugar had arsenic in it.'

'Trying his case in the newspapers?'

'I'll tell you a secret,' she said. 'I think — you see the Attorney General's away just now on his vacation — I think Mr. Quinton wants to get as much personal publicity as possible.'

He smiled drily. 'Is that part of his duty?'

'Don't be unfair,' she warned him. 'His duty is to prosecute criminals; but he's entitled to credit for what he does. And — I think you might try your case in the newspapers too. For instance, do you think Mrs. Harland died of arsenic poisoning?'

'I don't know anything about it.'

'Were you with her when she died?'

'Yes, of course.'

'Did you suspect anything of the kind?'

'No. She was subject to severe attacks of indigestion. This seemed like the others, only worse.'

'Mr. Quinton says there's no doubt what caused her death.'

'That's for the jury to decide, isn't it?'

'Yes, of course. But if she did die of poison — what do you think about that?' He hesitated, wondering whether he should suggest that Ellen had taken her own life; and he foresaw the questions that would follow and which he could not bring himself to answer. But before he could speak, little Miss Batten said: 'I'll take back that question, Mr. Harland. I don't think you should answer it. I think you'd better just say this is all a complete surprise to you, that you can't believe it's true, that you can't even speculate about it, something like that. Don't you think so?'

Harland said gratefully: 'You're right, of course. I can't say anything because I don't know anything. Except of course I know that Ruth, my wife, is completely innocent.'

'Of course.'

'I'll trust you to make me say the right things. Write something tactful.' He smiled. 'And string it out, Miss Batten. Get as much space as you can.'

'You're so nice. I'll be careful. Would you like to see it before I file it?'

'If you think I should.'

She rose. 'I'll see how it sounds after I write it. I don't want to bother you more than I must. Thank you for being so kind.' And she said solicitously: 'You know, I think you'd be wise to go to bed, get some sleep. Just take off your clothes and go right to bed. I'll bring you some pills if you like. I have some at home that I've used for years.'

'Thanks,' Harland told her. 'I'll be able to sleep all right, I'm sure.'

At the door she said: 'Oh, by the way, if anything comes up so that you could give me a story all for myself, it would be ever so nice for me.'

'I will if I can,' Harland promised. When she was gone he was surprised to discover that he was no longer so depressed. She had given him somehow a measure of serenity. He took her advice, removed his clothes and drew the shades and went to bed; and almost at once he was asleep like a man drugged.

– v –

He was still asleep when Roger Pryde knocked on his door. Roger was ten years the older, a gangling tall man with cropped dark hair so wiry that he had long since despaired of bringing it into any order. When he finished Harvard Law School he went into his father's firm — the firm's specialty was corporation and tax law — and married a girl he had known since childhood, and he and his wife had exchanged dinners once or twice with Ellen and Harland. He told Harland at once that he had arranged with Nathaniel Pettingill, the leading criminal lawyer in Maine, to take charge of Ruth's defense. He refrained, and Harland was glad of this, from any questions; but Mr. Pettingill when he arrived was naturally more insistent. He was a big, heavy-shouldered man who seemed half asleep; but his mind never slept, and Harland quickly learned to respect and to like him. Under the lawyer's shrewd inquiries Harland told everything he knew — with one exception. He kept from Mr. Pettingill the truth of Danny's death. Whatever he must do for Ruth he would do, but to admit that Ellen had murdered Danny could not help Ruth now.

When the lawyer asked his opinion as to what had happened, Harland said that Ellen loved him; that knowing him lost to her forever she had killed herself.

'That's no defense unless we can prove it,' Pettingill reflected. 'Would you be willing to go on the stand and testify to the rupture between you — and undergo cross-examination?'

'Listen,' said Harland with a quiet vehemence: 'I'll do anything. I'll carry the courthouse down the hill and throw it into the Bay brick by brick, if that will help Ruth. I'll tell the truth, or I'll lie, or I'll do both. But this is ridiculous, this whole damnable thing. I don't know whether to laugh because it's so ridiculous or to swear because it's so damnable. I want to get Quinton by the neck and kick his teeth in.'

The lawyer smiled. 'None of that,' he said.

'He knows damned well there's no truth in this charge. He's known Ruth for years.'

'Has he any animus?' Mr. Pettingill inquired; so Harland told him the story of his own marriage to Ellen, and Pettingill nodded. 'Quinton wouldn't forgive that,' he agreed. 'But he'd not go this far unless he was sure of his ground. I'll see him, see what he's got.'

'Will he tell you?'

'Oh yes. The State's not supposed to spring any surprises.'

Mr. Pettingill came back from that talk with Quinton grave and thoughtful. 'He's got a prima facie case,' he told Harland. 'For motive, Mrs. Harland's death meant a large inheritance for the present Mrs. Harland — I'd better use their first names. It avoids confusion — and Ellen's death cleared the way for your marriage to Ruth. Ruth admits, he says, that she had

access to arsenic, knew what it was, prepared the sugar with
which Ellen sweetened her coffee, knew Ellen alone would use
that sugar.' His tone implied a question, and Harland nodded,
and he went on: 'He says Leick saw Ellen put the envelope back
in the hamper. He says the sugar in it has been analyzed and
contains arsenic. Ellen's symptoms were those of arsenic poisoning. And he says he found a supply of arsenic hidden in
Ruth's room in Bar Harbor.'

'Oh, that's ridiculous!' Harland made a helpless gesture,
laughing wretchedly. 'It's all just plain crazy,' he protested.

Mr. Pettingill half-smiled. 'I suppose your idea would be to
have the case thrown out of court.'

'No!' Harland cried. 'No, I don't want that. My God, man,
have you seen the Boston papers?' Pettingill nodded, and
Harland said hotly: 'Don't you realize that this story has been
printed all over the country? There are twenty Boston and New
York and Portland and Augusta reporters here in town right
now, badgering me, trying to get me to talk. I don't blame them.
It's their business. But everyone in the United States knows by
now that Ruth has been arrested on a charge of poisoning Ellen.
Throwing the case out would be as bad as the old Scotch "not
proven" verdict. We've got to blow the indictment sky-high in
open court.'

Ruth, when Pettingill made to her the same suggestion —
Harland suspected that he did so in order to appraise their reactions — gave him a like answer.

'I want a trial,' she insisted. 'Even if you could have the
charge dismissed, people would always think you'd pulled some
underhanded legal trick. I want to face it and put an end to it,
so everyone will know the truth.' She added, smiling faintly:
'And the sooner the better, please. I don't care very much for
my lodgings here.'

Pettingill chuckled, said frankly: 'Well, of course there's no
real chance of a nol pros anyway. They've got enough to go to
the jury.' And he asked, looking from one to the other: 'Any idea
what started Quinton digging into this thing now, so long after
Ellen died?'

Neither Harland nor Ruth could hazard a guess, but they were to have the answer to that question, and from two sources. Miss Batten came to Harland one day — Pettingill had moved for an early trial, but there were weeks of waiting — to tell him some gossip she had heard. One of the stenographers in Quinton's office was her friend.

'She gives me stories sometimes,' Miss Batten explained. 'So you mustn't tell anyone how I found this out; but she says Mr. Quinton got a letter one morning, and he was excited, and he called in Mrs. Parkins and Deputy Hatch and they went to his house and got a lunch basket and took it to the state chemist at Augusta; and after that he went off to see Doctor Seyffert and Leick Thorne and Mrs. Freeman — she's the cook at the Berent house at Bar Harbor — and a lot of people, and then he came back and got the indictment.'

'A letter?' Harland repeated, completely puzzled.

She nodded eagerly. 'Anonymous, I suppose. At least no one knows who it was from. But I thought you might like to know about it.'

Harland was grateful, and he told her so; but neither he nor Ruth could guess the author of that letter till a day or two later Roger Pryde, who had returned to Boston pending the opening of the trial, wrote Harland:

'I got some important information today. Old Mr. Carlson of the Security Trust used to be in our office. He's trustee for a lot of estates, and he took care of Professor Berent's business, and of Ellen's after her father and mother died. He came to me this morning with a story, confidential of course, but he'll testify if he's needed.

'He says that a week or ten days before her death, Ellen had him draw her will, and she gave him a sealed envelope and told him to open it if after her death you remarried. When you and Ruth were married, he did so, and found another letter enclosed, addressed to Quinton, with a covering note instructing Mr. Carlson that if you married Ruth he was to mail the letter to Quinton. If you married anyone else,

Carlson was to destroy the letter unopened. He mailed the letter to Quinton that day. He doesn't know what was in it. As I say, he doesn't want it known that he's told me this unless it becomes necessary. He's careful to keep his trustee business confidential; but since I'd been called in by you, he felt he should pass this on. It's all right, of course, to tell Mr. Pettingill where you got the information.'

Harland took this letter at once to Mr. Pettingill. The other read it and looked at him inquiringly. 'Well, what's the answer?' he asked, in noncommittal tones.

'I've no idea.' Harland shook his head, pressed his knuckles against his brow. 'I can't even guess,' he confessed. 'Can't you make Quinton let you read the letter?'

The other shook his head. 'I doubt it,' he decided. 'No such letter could be, in itself, evidence. Unless of course it contains a sworn statement, and even then its admissibility is doubtful. Presumably Quinton would say the letter's not evidence and refuse to let us see it. No, we'll have to wait. Possibly we can force it out of him at the trial.' He looked at Harland shrewdly. 'Unless Ellen might have written something you don't want known.'

'Listen!' Harland cried. 'There's nothing we don't want known!' He hesitated, remembering Danny, but brushed the thought aside. 'We don't want to keep anything back. We want to blow this whole thing wide open.'

Pettingill cleared his throat, and Harland guessed that the other had marked his momentary hesitation; but the big man only said:

'Well, we'll see what Mrs. Harland thinks.'

Ruth, when they consulted her, agreed with Harland. 'We're not afraid of the truth, Mr. Pettingill,' she insisted. 'I know sometimes lawyers try to keep out damaging evidence; but — let's not do that. I don't know what Ellen could have written, but nothing that's true can really hurt us, and if she said things that aren't true — we can prove they're not.'

Mr. Pettingill said thoughtfully: 'Well, it might make a hit with the jury if we show them we're trying to see to it they get all the facts. Juries hate to have us lawyers keep them from hearing things they want to hear. But we'll see how it works out as we go along.'

So the matter rested, and the weeks passed, and the day set for the trial at last arrived.

13

F OR RUTH, those weeks of waiting were made more easily endurable because she found a friendly companionship in the matron at the jail. Mrs. Sayward was a cheerfully voluble woman, widowed some years before, with two children near their teens; and she often came with her knitting to sit outside Ruth's cell, her tongue never still.

'You won't mind it so much after you get used to it here,' she told Ruth the first day. 'It's the same as home to me. My father was sheriff for twenty years, till he died; so I as good as grew up in the jail. It's hitched right onto the sheriff's house, you know, same as a shed and barn. When my husband died it was like coming home, to come to work here. 'Course, I'm only part time, when there's some woman here, and that don't happen often, and mostly they're poor company; but it's a real pleasure to be here with you.' And when Ruth asked whether she found the work depressing, she chuckled heartily and said: 'Land sakes, I find any work depressing, far as that goes. I've got a lazy streak in me a yard wide. But jail's the same as any other place after you get used to it. Half the folks that get locked up are just as nice as most folks outside.' She tossed her head. 'And some of 'em are nicer.' She added cheerfully: 'And I need the money, with two young ones to take care of; and then of course it's real int'resting too, the different cases and all.'

The fact that it was Mrs. Sayward who on the morning of her trial came to summon Ruth made the ordeal more easily tolerable. 'Well, it's time to go,' she said, and added with approval:

'You look real nice, my dear.' She helped Ruth into her coat, keeping up a cheerful flow of conversation. 'Sheriff's going to drive us down, him and Deputy Hatch. Guess't he wants to get his picture in the paper. Don't hold it against him. He's a real good-hearted man.'

When Sheriff Sohier escorted them out to his waiting car, Ruth faced half a dozen photographers. They backed away before her, their cameras half-hiding their faces so that they seemed rather less than human. Deputy Hatch was waiting in the car, in the front seat. The sheriff drove, and Ruth sat with Mrs. Sayward. The photographers leaped into other cars and raced ahead, so that when she reached the courthouse she had to face them a second time; and she came into the dimly lighted hallways with a sense of escape. The sheriff cleared a way for her through the curious crowd, and a moment later she and Mrs. Sayward were alone. They had only a little while to wait before Deputy Hatch appeared to summon them; and with him on one side, Mrs. Sayward on the other, Ruth was ushered into the courtroom.

Her first impression was that there were hundreds of people in the room; and for a moment she hesitated, checked by the solid impact of so many staring eyes. Then the deputy's firm hand guided her, and she saw Harland and went toward him, and took the waiting chair between him and Mr. Pettingill, and Roger Pryde beyond Mr. Pettingill leaned toward her with a smiling word, and Harland pressed her hand. The deputy and Mrs. Sayward took chairs just behind her.

Ruth forced herself to look around. The courtroom was on the second floor of the courthouse, with windows on three sides. Except in the empty jury box, every seat and bench was occupied. Beyond the bar enclosure, facing the jury box, tables for reporters had been set, and she saw there twenty or thirty men and women, some simply watching her, some already writing, two or three busy with sketch pads, their eyes forever lifting to scan her face. Quinton and Mrs. Parkins and Attorney General Shumate and a young man Ruth had not seen before were at a table just beside this one at which she sat. When Judge Andrus took his place upon the bench, she saw a pink-cheeked, white-haired man with kindly eyes beneath heavy black brows that were like a band across his countenance. Beneath his high bench at a long table sat the clerk, and the court stenographer was at the end just under the witness stand on the judge's left.

The selection of a jury was not a tedious procedure. Mr. Pettingill, accepting Harland's insistence that he put nothing in the way of swift progress, used no peremptory challenges. Quinton was more demanding; but an hour after court convened, the jury was completed and Quinton rose to make his opening.

Ruth guessed that he had dressed with care for this occasion. His suit was new, his thin hair neatly brushed, his collar a little too tight. For once his face wore no trace of a smile. He was flushed, and she foresaw that he would soon be perspiring; but he spoke well, in concise and careful sentences. His precision had in it something which despite her courage she found affrighting.

'Ruth Harland is here brought to trial,' he began, 'upon an indictment charging that on September 5, almost two years ago, she deliberately and maliciously planned and carried through the murder by poison of her adoptive sister, Ellen, the former wife of Richard Harland. The defendant herself has since married Richard Harland.'

Ruth heard her own name with no sense of familiarity. It might have been a stranger's. Quinton went on:

'Ellen Berent Harland was the daughter of Professor and Mrs. Randolph Berent, who were for many years summer residents of Bar Harbor. Ruth Berent Harland was their niece, the daughter of Professor Berent's brother. While she was still an infant her father and mother died and she was adopted by Mr. and Mrs. Berent. She and Ellen grew up as sisters.'

At his word, Ruth remembered with sudden clarity the whole panorama of her childhood; remembered Ellen's jealousy of every tenderness Professor Berent showed her, remembered so many hours when Ellen's malice was revealed without conceal-

ment. Yet even through this swift procession of her memories
she heard Quinton's careful phrases.

'Professor Berent treated her in every respect as his daughter.
He was a wealthy man. He set up trust funds for his wife and for
Ruth and Ellen, the survivor to inherit. His remaining estate
was on his death divided among Mrs. Berent, Ruth and Ellen.
After Mrs. Berent's death, Ellen and Ruth shared equally. By
Ellen's death in turn, Ruth's fortune was approximately doubled,
so that it amounted to well over a million dollars.

'Cupidity and greed have led men — and women — to commit
murder in the past; but the State will contend that Ruth Berent
had not only her hunger for more money but another motive for
murdering her sister.

'Four years ago this summer, Mrs. Berent, Ellen, and Ruth
went to New Mexico, as guests of a ranch owner there. Richard
Harland was a guest at the ranch at the same time. At the end
of the two weeks of that visit, Ellen and Richard were married.'

Quinton's voice hardened on the word, and Ruth was conscious
of sharp tension in the man, and she remembered how angry
he had been when he arrived at the ranch too late to prevent —
or even to seek to prevent — that marriage. He poured a glass
of water, swallowed a little, went quietly on.

'The State will present evidence that beginning about eighteen
months after that marriage, Mr. Harland regularly sought Ruth's
company, leaving his wife, who was at that time pregnant with
a child which was later stillborn, alone at his home. There will
be other evidence suggesting a rupture between him and his wife,
evidence which it will be your responsibility to assay.

'Eight months after this increased attention to Ruth on Mr.
Harland's part began, and twenty-six months after the marriage
of Ellen and Mr. Harland, the two sisters, Mr. Harland, and
Leick Thorne had a picnic at Mr. Thorne's farm, some forty
miles west of this town. The four persons present ate, in different
quantities, the same things — with one exception. Ellen alone
took sugar in her coffee. I ask you to remember this fact. It is
also a fact that the defendant knew that Ellen alone would use
sugar in her coffee that day.

'Late that afternoon, three or four hours after eating lunch, Mrs. Harland — Ellen — was taken violently ill. Leick and Mr. Harland carried her to the farmhouse, and a physician was summoned to attend her; but early next morning she died.

'Now in the nature of things, murder by poison often goes long unsuspected. The skillful poisoner uses a drug which produces symptoms that may be mistaken for those of a disease. Ellen had suffered previous attacks of indigestion. Her fatal illness had a surface similarity to those attacks. The doctor who attended her, being informed of this fact by Mr. Harland, made a death certificate giving as the cause of death acute gastritis; and for almost two years, the suspicion of poisoning did not arise.

'When in the case of death by poison suspicion does at last develop, it is customary to order the exhumation of the body and an autopsy. If death was caused by poison, and particularly if death was caused by arsenic, that fact can often be demonstrated by an autopsy, even years after death. In this case, the attending physician suggested having Ellen's body examined by another doctor, but Ruth and Mr. Harland declined this suggestion. They took the body to Boston where at Mr. Harland's direction it was cremated — in spite of the fact that Ellen had requested normal burial — and the ashes were delivered to Mr. Harland, who disposed of them beyond recovery. So an autopsy was made forever impossible.'

Ruth whispered quickly to Mr. Pettingill: 'She wanted to be cremated. She told me so and told Dick so.'

He nodded, lifting his hand to bid her wait, and Quinton went on:

'In June last, Ruth Berent and Mr. Harland were married. Subsequent to that marriage, investigation led to recognition of the fact that Ellen Harland died under circumstances consistent with arsenic poisoning. The picnickers that day ate, as I have told you, the same things, except that Ellen Harland put sugar in her coffee while the others did not. Some of the sugar was left in the lunch hamper. Analysis shows that it contained arsenic.

'Professor Berent died before Ellen's marriage; but his hobby

was the collection of bird skins for museums. To preserve these
skins he used arsenic. To that arsenic, before and after his
death and before and after Ellen's death, Ruth had easy access.

'The State will prove that Ruth Harland, who had two good
reasons to wish Ellen dead, packed the lunch hamper; that she
put the arsenic-flavored sugar in it; that she handed the sugar to
Ellen during the picnic.'

Mr. Pettingill stirred and came awkwardly to his feet. Ruth
noticed with some surprise that — although when they had met
heretofore he had presented an appearance that accorded with
his position at the bar, and had spoken in cultivated tones —
he was today almost shabby, in a suit too large for him and
sadly in need of an iron; and when he spoke, it was in terms
frankly colloquial.

'Your Honor,' he remarked. 'I guess I ought to object to the
way Brother Quinton puts his case. He oughtn't to say he's
going to prove things. He'd ought to say he's going to try to.
It'll be for the jury to decide whether he does it or not.'

Before Judge Andrus could speak, Quinton said quickly:
'Your Honor, my brother is within his rights, and I suggest the
record be amended. These are the facts we propose to try to
prove.'

'Your Honor,' Mr. Pettingill insisted. 'I don't know as I'd
go so far as to say they were facts. Call them allegations.'

'The State accepts that amendment as well,' Quinton assented.
'There is no wish to prejudice the jury against the defendant,
but only to arrive at the truth of Ellen Harland's death.' Mr.
Pettingill sat down again and Quinton turned once more to the
jury.

'The State will further try to prove,' he told them, 'that investigation led to the discovery in the Bar Harbor house, from
which the picnic party that day set out, and in a hiding place
known only to the defendant, a small supply of arsenic — kept
for I know not what purpose, even after Ellen's death.'

Mr. Pettingill rose again. 'Your Honor,' he suggested, 'I
sh'd say the least Brother Quinton can do would be to stick to

things he claims to know. If we started talking about all the
things he admits he knows not, we'd be here till snow flies.'

A murmur of amusement ran through the crowded room and
Quinton reddened, and Judge Andrus said mildly:

'That last phrase, beginning: "kept for I know not" may be
stricken out.'

Quinton — he was perspiring now — proceeded. 'The State
will also try to prove,' he said emphasizing the word 'try'
looking with malicious derision at Mr. Pettingill, 'that Ruth
Berent and Richard Harland were married last June; and the
State will argue from that fact and from other evidence that
she loved him — and had loved him long before their marriage,
and before her sister's death.'

He hesitated, then concluded:

'In order to prove a charge of murder, it is necessary to establish first of all the fact that a murder was committed; second,
that the accused person had the opportunity to commit the crime;
third, that there was a motive; and finally, and most important
of all, it is necessary to prove to the jury's satisfaction that having motive and opportunity, the accused person did the deed.

'The State will prove that the sugar with which Ellen that day
sweetened her coffee was mixed with arsenic; and that the manner of her death, her symptoms and her sufferings, were consistent with a diagnosis of death by arsenic poisoning. Ellen
Harland was poisoned. A crime was committed.

'Ruth Harland, the defendant here, had the opportunity to
commit that crime. She had access to arsenic; she packed the
sugar mixed with arsenic in the lunch basket; she gave it to the
deceased woman at the picnic to use in her coffee.

'Ruth Harland, the defendant, had two motives, either of them
sufficient to lead her to commit that crime. The death of Ellen
Harland made the defendant tremendously wealthy; the death
of Ellen Harland cleared the way for this defendant to marry
Richard Harland.

'Ruth Harland, on the fifth of September, some two years ago,
by treachery and with malice and intent to murder, administered

to her sister the deadly dose from which that night, next morning, Ellen Harland died.'

There was an instant's dreadful hush, and Ruth clenched her
hands hard. Then Quinton turned to the table where his associ-
ates sat, consulted with them for a moment, addressed the court.

'The State calls Doctor Emil Seyffert to the stand.'

– II –

Ruth had not seen Doctor Seyffert since the night Ellen died.
He was older than she remembered; yet his voice, when he spoke,
was the same, loud and bruising. Perhaps his lack of a reassuring presence accounted for his narrow practice in a small Maine
community. It was possible that if he had been more easily
liked, if his voice and manner had given strength and hope to his
patients, he might have become a great physician. There was
the tragedy of unnecessary failure in the man.

He described, under Quinton's questions, his summons to
Leick's house, and Ellen's sufferings; and Quinton led him carefully from one step to the next, till Doctor Seyffert said Ellen
sank into a coma from which she did not rouse.

'Now, doctor,' Quinton asked. 'Did you have any conversation with Mrs. Harland before her death?'

'No.'

'Did you hear her speak?'

'I suggested she might have been poisoned by a bad lobster,
and she said Leick Thorne would resent my saying that.'

'Did she say anything else — then or later?'

Doctor Seyffert hesitated, and his face was red. 'She said one
word.'

'What was the word?'

'"Poison."' Ruth, her spine cold, remembered.

'She said the word "poison"?'

'Yes.'

'Thank you. Now was there at any time any question of
calling in another doctor?'

'Not till after she died.' Doctor Seyffert spoke more easily, as though in relief. 'Then I suggested they might want another doctor's opinion as to the cause of death.'

'You were yourself uncertain?'

Mr. Pettingill started to rise, but before he could do so Doctor Seyffert shouted: 'I was not!' So Mr. Pettingill, with a twinkle in his eyes, sat down again.

'When she spoke the word "poison" did that suggest to you the wisdom of getting another opinion as to the cause of her death?'

'It did not. I knew what was the matter with her.'

'What reply did your suggestion that another doctor be called receive?'

'Her sister, the defendant, said, "No!" Mr. Harland backed her up.'

Quinton nodded. 'That is all,' he said. Doctor Seyffert seemed about to leave the stand, but Quinton checked him. 'Wait,' he directed. 'Mr. Pettingill may wish to ask some questions.'

Pettingill spoke to Ruth and to Harland beyond her in a whisper. 'Did she say "poison"?' he asked.

Ruth said breathlessly: 'Yes. Doctor Seyffert kept giving her emetics, and Dick wanted him to stop, and the doctor said she was full of poison and Ellen just said the word after him.'

The lawyer's eyes went blank with thought. He rose heavily, a big, slightly stooped, helpless-seeming man. 'Well, doc,' he said in casual and friendly tones, 'I can see you're a man has had a lot of experience taking care of sick people. How old are you?'

'Fifty-one.'

'Been a doctor all your life, since you grew up, likely? Seen a lot of people get well, and seen a few die?'

'Yes, of course.'

'You signed a death certificate that Mrs. Harland died of indigestion, didn't you?'

'Yes. Acute gastritis. It's the same thing.'

'That was your opinion?'

'Yes. It still is!' The man's voice rang on the words, and Ruth almost smiled. Quinton must prove that Doctor Seyffert had made a mistake, that what he called gastritis was actually arsenic poisoning; but Doctor Seyffert had the stubbornness of ignorance, and he would never admit that he had been wrong. Mr. Pettingill, knowing this, was presenting Doctor Seyffert to the jury of farm folk — some of them were perhaps his patients — as a man of their own sort, and thus winning for the doctor their sympathy, and preparing them to resent Quinton's next move.

'That's still the way you figure it,' Pettingill agreed. 'It looked to you like indigestion — and you've been taking care of sick people for twenty or thirty years?'

'Yes, I have.'

'You thought something she'd eaten had made Mrs. Harland sick? Tainted lobster or something?'

'Yes.'

'Thought she was poisoned by it?'

'Yes.'

'So you gave her emetics?'

'Yes, to get the poison out of her.'

'Anybody object to that?'

'She became very weak and her husband asked if it was necessary.'

'What did you say to that?'

'I said she was full of poison and we'd have to get it out of her.'

'Was that when she said "poison"?'

'Yes.'

'What'd you think she meant?'

'She didn't mean anything! She was delirious.'

'So you didn't take her seriously.'

'She didn't know what she was saying.'

Mr. Pettingill nodded. 'Much obliged, doctor. That's all.'

But before Doctor Seyffert could leave the stand, Quinton was on his feet. 'One question, doctor,' he said sharply. 'After she said "poison" did she say anything else?'

'No.'

'"Poison" was her last word before she died?'

'Yes.'

'That's all.' Quinton turned away and, as the other left the stand, called Doctor McGraw.

Doctor McGraw had a head like a lion, with a great mane of tawny hair. Quinton addressed him respectfully.

'Your name?'

'Robert Winston McGraw.'

'Your occupation?'

'Medical examiner of Suffolk County, Massachusetts.'

'For how long have you held that position?'

Mr. Pettingill came to his feet. 'You don't have to qualify Doctor McGraw, Brother Quinton,' he said in a friendly tone. 'Everybody knows he's the best there is.'

But Quinton, ignoring this interruption, proceeded with his questions, leading Doctor McGraw to recite his years of experience with death by violence.

'Now, Doctor,' he said at last. 'I want to present you with a statement of certain symptoms.' He lifted a sheet of paper from his desk and began to read a careful catalogue, based upon Dr. Seyffert's testimony, of the phases through which Ellen passed before she died; and when he finished he asked: 'Could you, doctor, on that statement, determine the cause of death?'

Doctor McGraw hesitated, and Ruth was surprisingly certain that he disliked Quinton; that he thought Quinton an incompetent blunderer. She guessed that he had so often been a witness in such cases as this that he knew better than Quinton how his testimony should be conducted. His tone was full of dry scorn as he answered.

'No,' he said.

Quinton flushed as though under a sharp rebuff. He stepped back to the table, hesitated, turned again to the witness.

'If you had been in attendance in this case,' he asked, 'and the symptoms were as stated, what would your procedure have been?'

Mr. Pettingill climbed to his feet. 'Your Honor,' he said agreeably. 'Brother Quinton's trying to keep within the rules and

having a hard time of it, but I guess what we all want to know
is what Doctor McGraw thinks Mrs. Harland died of. The
defense wants the jury to have all the facts we can give them, so
as far as we're concerned, the Doctor can go ahead and tell us,
without all this beating around the bush.'

Judge Andrus' eyes twinkled under his black brows. He said
to Quinton: 'The defense will offer no objection if you allow
Doctor McGraw to discuss Mrs. Harland's death in his own way.'

Quinton was crimson with humiliation, but he accepted the
opportunity. 'Doctor,' he directed, 'give us your opinion as to
the diagnosis suggested by the facts stated.'

Doctor McGraw's voice when now he spoke was deeper; it
rumbled in the quiet room.

'On the facts as stated,' he explained, 'it is certain that this
woman died of an acute digestive irritation. That might be
gastro-enteritis, gastritis arising from natural causes, ptomaine
poisoning, something of the sort. Or it might be from arsenic
poisoning, or from some other artificial or mechanical irritation.
In all such cases, where death results from a sudden onset of
indigestion without known cause, an autopsy is indicated.
Superficial indications are seldom conclusive without a post-
mortem. Examination of the rejected contents of the stomach,
even before death, would probably reveal arsenic if it were
present. A post-mortem would certainly do so. But without
an autopsy, it's impossible to state positively the cause of death.'

Quinton asked insistently: 'It might have been arsenic poisoning?'

'It might have been, yes, certainly.'

Quinton dismissed him and when Pettingill asked no questions,
Quinton called Doctor Rowan of Augusta, whose testimony
paralleled that of Doctor McGraw. Then a Mr. Martinsbury
whom Ruth had never seen testified to the cremation of Ellen's
body and the delivery of her ashes to Harland; and the morning
session ended.

Ruth spent that noon recess in a room in the courthouse,
where she and Deputy Hatch and Mrs. Sayward were served

lunch on trays. The deputy — he was a ponderous and bulky man — ate enormously and in silence, and having done so he relaxed in a semi-somnolent condition to submit to the laborious processes of digestion; but Mrs. Sayward chattered while she ate, and afterward she produced a half-knitted sock and set her needles clicking; and she talked cheerfully about herself and her affairs. Her tongue rattled as amiably and as tirelessly as her needles, and Ruth found herself listening, interested and sometimes amused. The hour passed quickly.

– III –

When Judge Andrus once more took his place on the bench, Quinton called Leick to the stand. Ruth had not seen Leick since her arrest, and his eyes met hers in loyal greeting. Quinton, to her surprise, asked Leick nothing about the picnic on the shore. Instead, omitting preliminary questions, he came at once to that moment when Ellen uttered her first cry of pain, and he made Leick tell how he and Harland tried to carry her to the house, how she collapsed on the way.

'So I fetched a door — took it off its hinges — and I brought some blankets,' Leick explained. 'And we carried her up to the house on that.'

'What then?' Quinton prompted.

'They sent me to fetch the doctor.'

'How soon did you return?'

'Soon's I could, but it was all of two hours. I had trouble finding him. It was getting on to dark.'

'What then?'

'Doctor Seyffert went to work on her, and I fixed them up some supper.'

'They ate it?'

'Yes. They took turns, one at a time, the others staying with her.'

'Did you at any time go into the room where Mrs. Harland was dying?'

'I don't know as I did. She was in bed.'

'Did you hear her speak?'

'No.'

'Now, after she died, what happened?'

'Well, Mr. Harland was wore out. After the doctor left, he went to sleep. Come daylight, Mrs. Harland had me go telephone to the undertaker and we got ready to take her to Boston.'

'The jury may not understand you. Mrs. Harland was dead. The defendant was not then "Mrs. Harland." You wish to say that the defendant took charge, and that you arranged to have Mrs. Harland's body sent to Boston?'

'Yes.'

'Did you at any time go back down to the beach, the scene of the picnic?'

'Yes, just before we left the house to drive to Bangor.'

'For what purpose did you go to the beach?'

'We'd left some stuff down there. I was going up into the north woods, the next week, to help build a logging camp and swamp out some roads, so I wouldn't be coming home again till spring; so I went down to get my wash boiler, that we'd boiled the lobsters in, and the lunch basket.'

Quinton turned to Mrs. Parkins. From beneath the table where she sat, she produced a wicker hamper, and Quinton showed it to Leick. 'Have you seen this before?' he asked.

'That's the lunch basket,' Leick agreed. 'Or anyway, it looks like the same one.'

Quinton addressed the bench. 'Your Honor, I ask to have this hamper marked for identification.' He looked toward Mr. Pettingill. 'Unless there is some objection?'

Pettingill brought the hamper to where Ruth and Harland sat. Ruth told him quietly: 'It's ours. I remember that scratch on the handle.' She opened it, but it was empty. 'It's ours,' she repeated.

Pettingill spoke to Judge Andrus. 'No objection, Your Honor.'

Quinton asked Leick: 'Did you on that occasion open the lunch basket?'

'No.'

'Had you opened it before?'

'We'd used some forks to eat the lobster. I scrubbed them with sand and put them in the basket, put the thermos bottles back in, and the leftover lobster and things. That was right after we et lunch.'

'Did anyone use sugar in their coffee at that picnic?'

'She did.'

'The deceased?'

'Yes.'

'Was the sugar in a container?'

'In an envelope. She tore the corner off.'

'Did you see that envclope at any time after she last used it?'

'She put it back in the basket.'

'Now what did you do with the basket?'

'I brought it up to the house and put it and the wash boiler in the shed.'

'When did you next see it?'

'Here, a minute ago.'

Quinton turned to the bench. 'Your Honor, if there is no objection, I should like to excuse this witness at this time and recall him later. My present purpose is to establish a corpus delicti, to present the complete chain of evidence that a crime was committed.'

Judge Andrus looked inquiringly at Mr. Pettingill, and the big man stood up. 'If the court please,' he suggested, 'Leick Thorne was one of the three people — outside of Ellen — who saw what happened at the picnic. We'll want to hear him tell all about it.'

Quinton explained: 'I propose to recall him for that purpose.'

Pettingill addressed the court. 'All right, we'll let Brother Quinton put his case his own way, Your Honor.'

Judge Andrus nodded, and Quinton said: 'Then for the present, that is all.'

'No questions, Your Honor,' Mr. Pettingill announced. 'But we reserve the right to cross-examine on all this witness's testimony later.'

Leick left the stand. Quinton sat down, and after a whispered word, Attorney General Shumate rose. His movement hushed the courtroom; and he said quietly:

'Your Honor, the State calls Russell Quinton!'

– IV –

At the sound of Quinton's name, there was an instant quickening attention across the crowded benches. Quinton took the stand, was sworn. Mr. Shumate stood facing him, put the preliminary questions. Ruth, watching them both, felt the pounding of her heart, and she wondered what was now to come, what testimony Quinton could possibly give, and she listened in a still attention as the quiet interrogation got under way. After the preliminaries, Mr. Shumate asked:

'Now, Mr. Quinton, were you at some time informed of the death of Mrs. Ellen Harland?'

'I was.'

'Did you, as a result of that information, do something?'

'I did.'

'Will you tell us what you did at that time?'

'At the time of her death,' Quinton explained, 'I was in New Brunswick, duck shooting. I heard about her death a few days after my return. I had known her — and her father before his death — for years, and I felt a deep and sincere grief. I called on Doctor Seyffert to learn the details.'

'Go on, please.'

'After talking with him, I went to see Leick,' Quinton continued. 'He was not at home, but his shed door was open and I stepped inside. I saw a copper boiler and a lunch hamper on the floor near the door that led into the kitchen.'

'I show you the hamper here marked for identification.'

'It is the same one.'

'Had you ever seen it before that day?'

'I had presented it to Ellen Berent, before her marriage to Mr. Harland.'

'Under what circumstances?'

'We were — friends.' Ruth wondered why he did not say they were engaged, but he went quickly on. 'I had gone to Boston to see her after her father's death. We went for a picnic on the shore north of Boston, and I bought the hamper and gave it to her for that occasion.'

'When you recognized the hamper, in Leick's shed, what did you do?'

'I opened it.'

'How long was this after Mrs. Harland died?'

'Ten days or two weeks.'

'What did you see in the hamper?'

'The ice compartment was half full of water; and a lobster, and some claws, were floating in it. There were thermos bottles, forks, salt and pepper shakers, a bottle of Worcestershire sauce, a can of dry mustard, a sandwich covered with blue mold, some chocolate doughnuts.' He added: 'Maybe I didn't notice all those things at the time. I just looked in. I didn't touch anything.'

'What did you then do?'

'I took the hamper out to my car.'

'Why?'

'I had known Ellen for many years. It had been my gift to her. I knew she would be glad for me to have it.'

'You took it out to your car?'

'I took it home. On the way home I threw away the stale food, the moldy sandwich, the lobsters.'

'Did you put anything in the hamper?'

'No.'

'You took it home?'

'I put it away up in the attic.'

'Did you first clean it, or have it cleaned?'

'No. I decided that I had had no right to take it, so I hid it behind some trunks, under the eaves.'

'When did you next see it?'

'On the eighteenth of last June.'

'Under what circumstances?'

'Deputy Hatch, Mrs. Parkins, and I went to my house. I pointed out the hamper to the deputy. He drew it out from where it was hidden. At my direction, without opening it, Mrs. Parkins sealed it with gummed paper. We drove to Augusta and delivered it, still sealed, to Mr. Catterson there.'

'From the time you put the hamper in the attic till at your direction Deputy Hatch picked it up, did you touch it or see it?'

'No, sir.'

'Did anyone else?'

'Not that I know of. I'm sure no one saw it.'

'Now Mr. Quinton, did you at some time go to the Berent house at Bar Harbor?'

'Yes.'

'Under what circumstances?'

'On June nineteenth, I went there with Mrs. Parkins, Deputy Hatch, and Mrs. Freeman, the housekeeper.'

'For what purpose?'

'I had a search warrant. I went to make a search of the house.'

'In the course of that search, did you find anything?'

'I found a bottle containing some white powder.'

The Attorney General turned back to the counsel table, and Mrs. Parkins from a suitcase under the table produced a bottle with a wide mouth and a glass stopper. Ruth recognized it. It had once contained bath salts, had been in her bathroom cabinet.

'I show you this bottle,' said Mr. Shumate.

Quinton took it in his hands. 'It's the same one,' he said.

The bottle was marked for identification, and Mr. Shumate asked: 'Where did you find this bottle?'

'Behind a loose section of baseboard, in the bedroom in the southeast corner of the second floor.'

'What did you do with it?'

'I picked it up carefully, with a handkerchief around my hand.

Without touching it with my bare hands, I wrapped and sealed it, in the presence of Mrs. Parkins and Deputy Hatch, and in their presence I delivered it to Mr. Catterson, the state chemist.'

'Do you know what he did with it?'

'At my suggestion and in my presence, he had it examined for fingerprints by Mr. Norton. He then analyzed the powder it contained.'

'By the way, what did Mr. Catterson do with the lunch hamper when you took it to him?'

'In my presence, he broke the seals, took out the things in it, listed them, and then analyzed the contents of an envelope he found in the hamper.'

The Attorney General nodded and turned to Mr. Pettingill. 'Your witness,' he said.

Mr. Pettingill, before rising, spoke in a low tone to Ruth and to Harland. 'No use trying to break him down on that story,' he said. 'He'll have his secretary and Joe Hatch to back him up. But you notice he left it open for me to ask him why he went to get the hamper when he did, and why he searched the Bar Harbor house. If I ask him, he'll say it was because he had that letter from Ellen, and then I'll have to ask him about that. But if she could have put anything in that letter that we can't handle, I'll keep clear of the whole thing. What do you say?'

Ruth said quickly: 'I don't know what's in the letter, but I remember that bottle. It had bath salts in it. I kept it in my bathroom cabinet. It was a birthday present, but I used the salts only once or twice, and I never missed the bottle. Ellen discovered that loose baseboard when we shared that room as children, and she called it her secret hiding place and made me promise never to look in it. I hadn't thought of it for years. The carpenters forgot to nail the end of the baseboard, and you could pry it out two or three inches from the wall.'

Pettingill nodded. 'What about the letter?'

Ruth looked at Harland, asking his agreement. 'We don't want to keep anything hidden, Mr. Pettingill. I want to know what's in the letter.' Harland whispered his assent.

Pettingill hesitated. 'Well,' he said. 'I'm taking your word for it that the letter can do no harm.' They were silent, and he reflected: 'All right, I'll walk into Brother Quinton's trap.' He rose in that laborious way which was his courtroom habit, like an uncertain, feeble old man; and his manner was humble and confused. 'Well, Mr. Quinton, this about the lunch basket is all news to me,' he remarked, in an interested tone. 'I want to be sure I've got it straight. You stole the hamper full of rotten lobsters because you'd given it to Mrs. Harland as was, and you wanted it to remember her by. Is that it?'

'You can have it so!'

'I don't want it any way only the true way. Is that the way it was?'

'I didn't consider it stealing.'

'Well, we all have our ideas about that,' Mr. Pettingill suggested. 'Most of us country folks have gone off and left our houses unlocked, one time or another, and come home and found something missing; and most generally, unless we know the neighbors have borrowed, we get kind of mad, call the folks that did it thieves. Sometimes summer folks pick up little things for souvenirs, or boys break in and see some gimcrack they want. Course, it's hard on the folks that own the things; but I can see how it might not seem like stealing to the ones that take them.'

Quinton did not answer. Ruth understood that he must have known his testimony would lay him open to this attack, must have hardened himself to endure it. He held his tongue and his composure; and Mr. Pettingill said shrewdly: 'I judge you had some doubts about it yourself, hiding it away in the attic.' But Quinton held his silence, and the big man asked: 'Don't you have spring house cleaning at your house, Mr. Quinton?'

'My mother used to go over everything with a fine-tooth comb, but she's dead. The attic hasn't been touched since she died.'

'Well, I don't hold much with house cleaning myself,' Mr. Pettingill agreed. 'Anyway, far as you know, no one touched

the hamper, or put anything in it, from the time you stole it out
of Leick's shed till the time you went and got it.'

'I'm sure no one even saw it,' Quinton repeated.

'So!' the other assented. 'Now, Mr. Quinton, about that
bottle you found behind the baseboard in the Berent house in
Bar Harbor, you wrapped a handkerchief around your hand
before you touched it?'

'Yes.'

'Why did you do that?'

'So I wouldn't spoil any fingerprints there might be on it.'

'And so you wouldn't get your own fingerprints on it?'

'Yes, of course.'

'Well now, if you could handle the bottle that way and not
leave any marks on it, then whoever put it in behind the baseboard could have done the same thing, couldn't they?'

Quinton hesitated. 'If they thought of it.'

'Anybody that didn't want their fingerprints on it would
likely think of it, wouldn't they?'

'They might.'

'And if they did, their fingerprints wouldn't show, would they?
And whoever's fingerprints were on it before it was put behind
the baseboard would still be there, wouldn't they?'

'I suppose so.'

'Put it this way,' Mr. Pettingill suggested. 'Just for instance,
suppose that bottle belonged to Mrs. Ruth Harland, so's her
fingerprints were naturally on it, and then supposing Ellen
wrapped a handkerchief around her hand and picked up the bottle
and went and hid it, then the bottle would still have Ruth Harland's fingerprints on it, but it wouldn't have Ellen's. That
right?'

Quinton's lips were tight. 'I suppose so.'

'Well, you're a pretty good supposer,' Mr. Pettingill said
cheerfully. 'Now, Brother Quinton, about stealing the hamper.
I sh'd judge you're telling the truth about that. Nobody'd
own up to a thing like that only if it was the truth. But there's
one place where you left out something. I don't know what it

was you left out, but we want to find out all we can about this
business. The more truth comes out, the better we like it. So
here's the point. You put the hamper away in your attic, and
for nigh on to two years, far as you know, there it stayed. You
didn't go up and look at it, to remind you of Mrs. Harland; didn't
do anything like that. And then all of a sudden, you took Deputy
Hatch and your secretary, and rushed off and got that hamper,
and carried it clear over to Augusta and gave it to Mr. Catterson.
Now, Mr. Quinton, why did you do that?'

Quinton said readily: 'Because I received information that
Mrs. Harland had been poisoned, and I thought the hamper
might contain some evidence one way or the other.'

'Well, now we're getting somewhere. Go on. Tell us about
that information. Where did it come from?'

Ruth realized that her hands under the edge of the table were
so tightly clenched that the nails hurt her palms. She tried to
relax, and Quinton said: 'I received a letter.'

'Got it with you?'

'Right here.' Quinton produced from his pocket a sealed
envelope; and Mr. Pettingill took it and examined it, turning
it in his hands.

'Your Honor,' he said then, 'maybe I'm a little out of order.
This is sealed and it bears certain signatures across the flap.
Maybe Mr. Quinton intends to put this letter in evidence later?'
His tone was an inquiry addressed to Quinton.

'I intend to offer it,' Quinton agreed, 'after the groundwork
has been properly laid.'

'Well now,' Mr. Pettingill declared, 'I want to let you put in
your case your own way. Maybe this isn't the right time. I
don't want to push you. What say if His Honor and you and
me take a minute to talk it over?'

Judge Andrus interposed. 'Court will recess for fifteen minutes,' he directed; and as the jury filed out he called Mr. Pettingill
to the bench, and Quinton too. They followed him out of the
courtroom, and Attorney General Shumate went to join them
in the judge's chambers.

– v –

That recess, while Pettingill and Quinton and the Attorney
General were closeted with Judge Andrus, lasted for thirty-five
minutes instead of fifteen. Ruth stayed seated at the counsel
table, Harland beside her, Deputy Hatch somnolent in his chair
at her back; and behind her, waves of whispering ran along the
packed benches where the spectators sat. Ruth might have
found the waiting more bitter than she did but for the fact that
Harland needed her reassurance. He mopped his damp brow,
constantly shifting his position; and she wished to take him in
her arms, to bring him peace. Since with so many eyes upon
them she could not even touch his hand, she whispered her en-
dearments, leaning toward him, murmuring:

'Darling, pretend we're just talking about the case, but I do
love you so!'

He said helplessly: 'What do you suppose is in that letter?'

'Hush, my dear! Don't torment yourself. Look at me, into
my eyes; feel me loving you. This will all be over, soon, and we
can be happy again.' And to distract him she said: 'Then we'll
go back to the river, as we'd planned, buy that land we liked so
much. We'll make a world of our own there, Dick.'

'It's too late to go this year.'

'It's never too late, darling. We'll stay till snow flies, till the
river freezes. We'll get a crew of men to work there all winter.
We'll clear the ground and level it, and transplant some trees,
and plant lawns and flowers and shrubs, and build a house.
There'll be so much to do, years of work and planning. We'll
start as soon as this is over.'

He said wretchedly: 'We don't know how this is going to come
out!'

'Of course we do. It's all mumbo-jumbo, darling; but two or
three days will see the end of it.'

She poured her own strength into him, winning him at last to
some composure; and presently Mr. Pettingill came back to them.

'Smile,' he directed in a low tone. Ruth saw agitation in his eyes. 'Look happy while I'm talking to you.' Ruth obeyed, and Harland tried to. 'Ellen wrote the letter all right,' Pettingill told them. 'She says in it that you'd tried to poison her twice before, once with apple pie at Bar Harbor after Mr. Harland's brother was drowned, and once with curry in Boston; and she says she expects you'll try again, and that if she dies and you marry Mr. Harland, Quinton can be sure you killed her.'

Ruth held her meaningless smile, looking at Harland. 'Those were the two times she was sick,' she reminded him. He nodded, unable to speak. Quinton and Mr. Shumate returned to their table; and Pettingill chuckled — for the benefit of whoever might be watching.

'I can keep the letter out,' he suggested. 'It's not admissible as evidence. The judge will exclude it if I ask him to.'

Harland whispered: 'For God's sake, yes, do that!'

But Ruth said: 'No. Whatever she says, it isn't true, and we're not afraid of lies.' She touched Harland's hand. 'It's all right, darling! Please.'

He met her eyes, turned after a moment to the lawyer. 'She's right, of course,' he agreed, more steadily. 'I can't think straight, but she always sees the truth. We'll do what she says.'

The jury filed back to their places, and Judge Andrus returned to the bench. 'All right,' Mr. Pettingill assented, doubt in his tones. 'I'll go ahead. But this is going to be bad. It'll hurt.' Quinton once more took his place on the stand, and the big man rose to face him.

'Now, Mr. Quinton,' he said, 'you were telling us that you received a certain letter. Has anyone besides you read it, up to now?'

'No.'

'Tell the jury what shape it is in now.'

'When I had read it, I sealed it up, in the presence of witnesses. It is still in that sealed envelope.'

'Who were the witnesses?'

'Deputy Hatch and my secretary, Mrs. Parkins.'

'You figure to have them identify this sealed envelope later?'

'Yes.'

'And then you will offer the letter?'

'Yes.'

'All right,' Mr. Pettingill agreed. 'We'll wait for that. That'll do for now.'

Quinton, upon leaving the stand, called first Mrs. Parkins and then Deputy Hatch, leading them to identify their signatures on the still-sealed envelope containing Ellen's letter, and to describe the recovery of the hamper and the finding of the bottle. Their stories paralleled Quinton's as exactly as though they were made from the same master record, and Pettingill let them go without questions. 'Never does any good to butt your head against a stone wall,' he told Ruth over his shoulder.

'Mrs. Parkins is in love with him,' she whispered. 'It sticks out all over her.'

He said drily: 'That'd be a first-rate match. They're a pair.'

Then Quinton said: 'I now propose, Your Honor, unless there is an objection, to offer this letter.'

Mr. Pettingill rose. 'Well, Brother Quinton,' he said, 'I'll have to read it before I know whether it's good evidence or not.' Quinton hesitated, uncertain how to proceed; and Mr. Pettingill said: 'Go ahead and open it.'

Quinton obeyed him. Mr. Pettingill took the letter, and stepped to the bench. He and Judge Andrus read the letter, and this was a slow business. Ruth, watching them, shook with the thudding of her heart, and the crowded courtroom lay under a breathless silence. Then Mr. Pettingill returned to the counsel table, but without sitting down he asked:

'Brother Quinton, for what purpose do you offer this letter?'

'To answer your question as to why I investigated the circumstances of Mrs. Harland's death.'

Pettingill nodded. 'Your Honor,' he said, 'this letter, so far as what it says goes, is not competent evidence.'

Quinton spoke quickly: 'Your Honor, on my cross-examination I was asked why I investigated Mrs. Harland's death.

That letter is the answer. The answer is responsive to the question, and the letter for that purpose is competent.'

'Your Honor,' Mr. Pettingill explained. 'My brother is a little previous. We do not object to the admission of this letter. We want all the facts in the jury's hands. But we request that the jury be warned that nothing in the letter is evidence of the truth of any statements the writer makes. With that stipulation we agree to its admission, to show what started Brother Quinton into action.'

Judge Andrus hesitated. 'If there were an objection,' he said at last, addressing the jury, 'I should exclude this letter.' He looked in doubtful surprise at Mr. Pettingill, then went on: 'Since there is none, I will let it be read. But gentlemen of the jury, I instruct you that nothing in this letter is evidence, and you are neither to believe nor disbelieve anything it says. It contains some accusations which you will ignore and disregard. It is to be taken as explaining why the investigation leading to this indictment was begun.' He spoke to Quinton. 'You may read the letter to the jury,' he said.

– vi –

Quinton took the letter, but he turned back to·his seat and spoke for a moment to the Attorney General. Mr. Shumate rose.

'Your Honor,' he explained. 'To complete the foundation, I desire to recall Mr. Quinton for redirect examination.' Quinton once more took the stand. 'Now, Mr. Quinton,' the Attorney General said. 'I show you a letter. Do you recognize it?'

'I do. It is a letter I received last June, the eighteenth.'

'Addressed to whom?'

'To me.'

'What is the signature?'

'It is signed "Ellen."'

'Did you — do you recognize the handwriting?'

'I do.'

'Whose is it?'

'Mrs. Ellen Harland's.'

The Attorney General hesitated, turning to Mr. Pettingill as though expecting an objection; and Mr. Pettingill sighed and — as though to do so were a burden — went to take from Quinton's hand one page of the letter, returning to show it to Ruth and Harland.

'I suppose there's no doubt she wrote it,' he suggested in a low tone.

They looked at the single sheet, Ruth's eyes racing down the lines; and Harland said chokingly: 'It's her handwriting.' Ruth nodded, unable to speak, and the lawyer returned the sheet of paper to Quinton. Attorney General Shumate looked at him inquiringly, but Mr. Pettingill shook his head, and the other asked Quinton:

'Is that letter dated?'

'It is.'

'What is the date?'

'August twenty-ninth, two years ago, six days before Mrs. Harland's death.'

'Now will you read the letter.'

Ruth felt Harland stiffen in his chair beside her, and she wished to touch him, to give him strength; but as Quinton began to read, she forgot Harland, forgot everything in the anguish of that listening. Quinton read slowly and carefully, his voice pitched to carry to every ear; and though he spoke quietly, the silence was so complete that his each syllable was audible throughout the silent room.

'Dear Russ:

'I am writing this letter to you because we once meant a great deal to each other, because perhaps you still love me, because unless you do, there is no one who does love me now. Richard and I are driving to Bar Harbor tomorrow or the next day to visit Ruth. They love each other, and wish to be rid of me. Ruth has tried twice to kill me. Perhaps next time she will succeed.

'Oh, I may be wrong, may be doing her a terrible injustice; but if I am, you will never see this letter. For I am leaving it with Mr. Carlson at the bank here, enclosed in a sealed envelope on which I shall write:

"'This is to be opened if after my death my husband remarries."

'Inside the envelope I shall put a note to Mr. Carlson instructing him that if Mr. Harland marries Ruth, he is to mail this letter to you; but if Mr. Harland marries someone else, Mr. Carlson will destroy this letter unopened, for I will be proved to have been wrong.

'So if you ever read this letter, you will know that I was right, and that Ruth poisoned me.

'Ruth was in love with Mr. Harland almost from the beginning, but at first he loved me. Your know my father's hobby, so there was arsenic in his workroom at Bar Harbor, and also in the house at home. After Mr. Harland's brother was drowned, I stayed at Bar Harbor while Mr. Harland went to Back of the Moon. You remember you came to see me there. That was "maid's day out" and Ruth cooked dinner, giving us trays. Mother was in bed, and we all ate in her room. Ruth and I had our trays on the card table, but when I was about to sit down she caught my arm and said: "No, that's my place. This is yours." Yet the trays were, as far as I could see, exactly alike; lamb chops, salad, and apple pie sprinkled with confectioner's sugar. I think there was arsenic in the sugar on my pie, for that night I was taken sick. I seemed to be burning up inside, and I was terribly thirsty, and yet I could not even keep water down.

'But I recovered. We were to have a baby, and Mr. Harland and I — even though we grieved for Danny — were happy that fall. But little by little I saw him turning from me to Ruth, going almost every day to see her.

'In the spring I lost my baby, but I lost Mr. Harland too, for after that he put me out of his life. I tried to win him back, and we planned a fishing trip together, but he insisted that Ruth go with us; and even the guides must have noticed that he preferred her company to mine. During the forest fire which caught us on the river they were together, and they slept that night in each other's arms.

'A few days ago, Ruth tried again to poison me. We had dinner at her apartment and she made a curry, and served our plates in the kitchen and brought them in to us. I saw traces of white powder on my curry but thought nothing of it. She must have used too much, or not enough, because though I was sick for days, I did recover.

'I suppose she will try it again, and perhaps succeed, but I can't seem to care, for Mr. Harland no longer loves me, and I'm tired, tired, tired. If I die during this visit in Bar Harbor, I think it will be because she gave me arsenic. I think she must have kept some of Father's when we sold our Boston home after Mother's death, or she can get it from his workshop in Bar Harbor. When we were girls, we shared what is now her bedroom, in the southeast corner of the second floor of the Bar Harbor house; and the baseboard was loose in the corner by the east window, and we pried it out and dug into the wall behind it and made a secret hiding place there. If she has arsenic hidden, it may be there. Here in Boston, of course, she doesn't live with us, so she could hide it anywhere.

'If I die, and if Mr. Harland does not marry Ruth, I may be mistaken. But if he does, then you will read this letter, and you will be able to find some way to punish them. I've told Mr. Carlson I want to be buried in Mount Auburn. The book says you can always detect arsenic poisoning even years after death. If she does kill me — she's always hated me, as adopted children often do hate the real sons and daughters — please try to punish her, if only for the sake of the promise I once gave you. I've wept many times because I let Richard persuade me to break that promise.

'Goodby, Russ. I always loved you.

'Ellen'

Quinton finished; and he let his eyes run along the double row of jurors, then looked toward the spectators, and then toward the Attorney General, who while he read had stood quietly before him.

Mr. Shumate took the letter, handed it to the clerk. 'This

should be marked,' he said. He spoke to Quinton. 'That is all.'

Quinton waited, and Mr. Pettingill approached the witness stand. 'By the way, Brother Quinton,' he remarked. 'You said, when you were telling about giving her the hamper, that you and Ellen were friends. Pretty good friends?'

'Yes.'

'How friendly were you?'

'We were engaged to be married.'

Ruth looked quickly at Mrs. Parkins. Her eyes were downcast, her cheeks blazing.

'When was that?' Pettingill asked.

'We became engaged immediately after her father's death.' Quinton's face was white, his tones like ice.

'What happened to break it up?'

'She decided to marry Mr. Harland.'

'You mean she was still engaged to you when she went to New Mexico?'

'Yes.'

'Did she let you know she was going to marry Mr. Harland?'

'Yes.'

'Invite you to the wedding?'

'No.'

'Did you go to New Mexico?'

'Yes.'

'To the wedding?'

'They were married and gone before I got there.'

Mr. Pettingill nodded contentedly and sat down. Quinton left the stand. He consulted for a moment with the Attorney General, then addressed the court.

'We call Joseph Catterson,' he said.

– VII –

As Mr. Catterson came in from the corridor, a sigh, as though each spectator had been holding his breath, rose from the crowded courtroom. The chemist was a frail-seeming man with timid fair hair thin across his scalp, and pale eyes behind his spectacles; and as though forever afraid of contradiction if he said too much, he spoke in compressed sentences as compact as his own formulae. Ruth, still half-stunned by Ellen's letter, heard Quinton, prolonging the suspense, elaborate his early inquiries, making Mr. Catterson describe his professional qualifications, the circumstances under which the lunch basket was delivered to him, the procedure he followed in opening it, the objects it contained. Eventually Mr. Catterson came to the point; to that envelope in which he said a small quantity of sugar had been found.

Quinton echoed: 'Sugar?'

'My assumption.' The chemist's clipped sentences were like bullets.

'Was that assumption correct?'

'No. I tested — your suggestion — for arsenic. I...'

'Describe those tests,' Quinton interrupted, and Catterson did so. 'What did those tests reveal?' Quinton asked, when he was done, and the chemist answered:

'Assumption wrong. Apparent sugar tested sixty per cent arsenic.'

Quinton nodded. 'Do you remember another occasion, a few days later, when I came to you?'

'Yes.'

'Tell the jury what happened.'

'You delivered sealed parcel. Contents: bottle half-full of white powder.'

'I show you a bottle.'

'The same.'

'What did you then do?'

'Called Mr. Norton — your suggestion — to test for fingerprints. Then analyzed contents.'

'What was it?'

'Arsenic. Pure.'

Quinton waited a moment, then turned toward Pettingill. 'You may inquire,' he said; but Pettingill shook his head, and the chemist left the stand.

Norton, the fingerprint expert, followed him. He was a calm, heavy man with an absurdly large and dark mustache, like a defiant gesture at an unfriendly world. There were fingerprints on the bottle, he said, and he had compared them with the fingerprints of the prisoner, found them identical. He produced photographic copies, duly marked, of the fingerprints on the bottle and of Ruth's, and they were put in evidence. But when his testimony was done, him too Mr. Pettingill allowed to go unquestioned.

And court adjourned for the day.

Ruth, when Mrs. Sayward touched her shoulder to summon her to rise, wished she need not leave Harland, for his cheek was drawn, his eyes sunken with fatigue. She said in a low tone: 'It's all right, darling. Sleep well. You'll be fine tomorrow.'

'We'll see you tonight,' he promised. 'Mr. Pettingill and I.'

She shook her head. 'Don't come, Dick. It's too hard for you. Get Leick and go for a drive out into the country somewhere.' And when he would have protested, she urged: 'Please. I'm a lot more worried about you than I am about myself.' She appealed to Mr. Pettingill. 'Make him be sensible. I'm all right. You don't even need to come yourself unless you want to.'

The lawyer said agreeably: 'Probably I won't. I think it much better for you to sleep, rest as much as you can. The State expects to close by noon tomorrow, and I will at once put you on the stand.' He smiled reassuringly. 'Quinton made his effect today. We will make ours tomorrow. I shall keep you on the stand, in my hands, till the hour for adjournment.'

Harland asked despairingly: 'Does she have to take the stand?'

'Oh I want to, Richard,' she assured him, and laughed almost gaily. 'It will be my first chance to answer back, you know.'

But when she was alone in her narrow cell in the jail above the town, her courage for a while deserted her. She knew well enough the damning effect which Ellen's letter, read aloud in that crowded court, must have had; and she had seen the flying pen-

cils of the reporters, seen them after court crowd around Quinton
to seek copies. For a while a deep anger at Ellen burned in her;
at Ellen whose whole life had served herself and none other, who
now in her death had sought to do an irreparable injury. She
remembered that Ellen too had suffered, loving Harland as she
did, knowing him irrevocably lost to her. It was always easy
for Ruth to find excuses for others, and she could have forgiven
Ellen the injury to herself; but she could not forgive her for hurt-
ing Harland so grievously.

– VIII –

Quinton's first witness that second morning was Mrs. Freeman, who had been for many years at once housekeeper and cook
in the Bar Harbor home. Compressed into shiny black, a little
red in the face from tight lacing and from excitement, she was
during Quinton's first inquiries so nervous that her voice broke
like an adolescent's, shrill and piping. Quinton, till she was more
at ease, made her answer questions completely unimportant,
about her winters at home, her family, her husband. Only when
she was reassured did he lead her to speak of her long service with
Professor and Mrs. Berent. By that time, becoming sure of herself, she was answering almost indignantly, as though resenting
this waste of time on matters so familiar.

'Mrs. Berent is now dead?' Quinton suggested.

'Of course she is!'

'And did her death end your employment by the Barent
family?'

'It did not! Whenever Miss Ruth is there she always sends
for me.'

'Was the big house kept open?'

'She lives in it summers, but she's had her father's study fixed
over for a cottage in case she ever rented the big house. She
wanted to, but she never did.'

'Did Mr. and Mrs. Harland ever visit her there?'

'Yes, they did.'

'Do you remember an occasion during that visit when they planned a picnic, took lunch, went away for the day.'

Mrs. Freeman's voice, when she realized that Quinton had come at last to the point, rose to a squeak, so that she had to stop and start again. 'It was the time — That was the day Ellen died.'

'Who prepared the picnic lunch on that occasion? If you remember.'

'I'll remember everything that happened that day, long as I live!'

'Suppose you tell us, in your own way,' he suggested; and she took a deep breath.

'Well,' she began, and smacked her lips, 'Well, Miss Ruth told me the day before that they'd all be away for lunch, and that morning she came out to the kitchen with a lunch basket.'

'Excuse me,' Quinton suggested. 'Is this the basket?'

'That's it,' she agreed. 'So she told me to make coffee, and some bread and butter sandwiches, and she got some of my chocolate doughnuts and wrapped them up in oiled paper, and she'd had me make some potato salad, and I wrapped up the sandwiches, and filled the thermos bottles, and she packed the things in the basket.'

'Did she put in anything you haven't mentioned?'

'Worcestershire sauce and mustard and butter and lemons for a tamale sauce she always made for lobsters.'

'Any other seasoning?'

'There was salt and pepper shakers in the basket, and she put some sugar in an envelope for Miss Ellen's coffee.'

'Did you see her put the sugar in the envelope?'

'Yes.'

'Tell us what happened?'

'Why she just fetched an envelope and poured some sugar into it. Dipped it up with a scoop, out of the firkin.'

'What kind of an envelope?'

'One from the desk in the library, kind of gray, about so square.' She illustrated with her hands.

'Like this?' Quinton asked, showing her the envelope which he had led Mr. Catterson to identify.

'That's the same kind. It's the same one for all I know.'

'What did she do with it, after she'd put the sugar in?'

'She put it in the hamper.'

'Did you seal the envelope?'

'Yes, I mind she did.'

'Lick the flap?'

'No, just wet her finger and ran it along on the glued part.'

Ruth, her wits alert, understood what was in Quinton's mind, caught the suggestion that her failure to lick the flap was a precaution against getting even a few grains of arsenic on her tongue; and she was about to whisper to Mr. Pettingill, but Quinton's next question checked her.

'Now, Mrs. Freeman, do you remember Professor Berent?'

'I'll say I do!'

'Do you know whether he had a hobby?'

'You mean collecting bird skins and stuffing them?'

Quinton nodded. 'Do you know how he preserved the skins?'

'He'd put arsenic on them.'

'How do you know that?'

'I've seen him and Miss Ellen working at it, down at his shop on the rocks by the shore below the house. He had bottles of arsenic there.'

'What did it look like?'

'Like flour, or fine sugar.'

'Do you remember a day last June when I came to you?'

'The time you asked me questions, same as now?'

'A later occasion.'

'When Mrs. Parkins and the fat man came with you?'

'Deputy Hatch, yes.'

'Yes, I remember that day all right.'

'Tell the jury what happened on that occasion.'

'Why, I had a key to the house, and you had a search warrant, and I went and let you in.'

'Did you go with us through the house?'

'I'll say't I did!' She tossed her head.

'Do you remember our taking anything away?'

'You pried out a piece of the baseboard in Miss Ruth's room and took a bottle from behind it.'

'This bottle?'

'It looks like it.'

'Had you seen it before?'

'It had bath salts in it, first time I saw it. Miss Ruth had it in her bathroom.'

'Had you known there was a hiding place behind the baseboard?'

'No.'

Quinton considered, stepped back. 'I think that's all,' he said.

Mr. Pettingill spoke in a low tone to Ruth beside him. 'Was that the way it happened? Packing the lunch, I mean?'

She nodded. 'Except that Ellen reminded me about the sugar.'

'Did Mrs. Freeman hear her?'

'I think so. Ellen came into the kitchen.'

'Did you wet the flap of the envelope as she described?'

'Yes. I always did that. I hate the taste of the mucilage. We had a glass roller — one of the kind that picks up water when you revolve it — on the library desk to wet envelopes and stamps.'

'I judge you used granulated sugar.'

'Yes. Mrs. Freeman couldn't find the lump.'

Pettingill nodded and stood up. 'Well, Mrs. Freeman, I guess we've got that all straight,' he said. 'Only I was wondering, did Miss Ruth always pack the lunch baskets for these picnics?'

'Either she did or I did.'

'Not Miss Ellen?'

'Ellen never came fussing around the kitchen.'

'Never? Didn't she come into the kitchen that morning?'

Mrs. Freeman said in a quicker fashion, as though suddenly interested: 'Why yes, I mind she did. She was in the kitchen when I came downstairs.'

'At what time?'

'I always get down at seven sharp.'

'You found her in the kitchen so early?'

'Yes. She had a kettle on to boil, and she was looking for the coffee. She said Mr. Harland was down on the shore and she wanted to make some for him.'

Ruth listened intently. That Ellen should have gone to the kitchen so early was almost incredible, and Mr. Pettingill seemed to guess this, for he remarked:

'You said Ellen never came fussing around the kitchen. Did finding her there that morning surprise you?'

'I'll say't it did! First time in her life she ever set out to do anything like that in my kitchen.'

'Where was she when you came down?'

'In the pantry looking for the coffee. It was right in front of her eyes, but she couldn't find it.'

'Did she come into the kitchen again later that morning?'

'Why yes, come to think of it, she did. When Ruth was packing the lunch, she came in and offered to help. I had to laugh. She never helped Ruth do anything in her life.'

'Her offer was so unusual that you noticed it?'

'Yes, it was.'

'Did she help?'

'No, the job was mostly all done by then.'

'Make any suggestions, did she?'

'Why —' She hesitated, thinking back. 'Yes, she reminded Ruth not to forget the sugar.'

'Was it in response to that suggestion that Miss Ruth fetched the envelope?'

'Yes, I guess 'twas.'

'Did Ellen see her do it?'

'Yes, because I mind she kind of teased Ruth for using one of the special envelopes marked with the name they called the house. Grayledges, it was! Ellen said Ruth was extravagant, using up the envelopes, and Ruth said there were more envelopes than there was paper, and she'd have to use them up or else throw them away.'

'So there were other such envelopes in the house?'

'Yes, sir, plenty of them!'

'Could you tell one of them from another?'

'Not unless there was writing on it.'

'Where were they kept?'

'In the desk in the library.'

'Was it a part of your work to dust the library?'

'Sometimes I did it, but Ruth did it too. She was always a help around the house.'

'Did you sometimes dust the desk?'

'Whenever I did the library, I did.'

'What kind of desk was it?'

'Flat-topped, only with pigeonholes along the back.'

'Do you remember the desk furnishings, the things on top of the desk?'

'Well, I sh'd say I did! I had to move 'em every time I dusted it. There was paper and envelopes in the pigeonholes, and some post cards, and most generally some letters stuck away; and there was a glass inkwell, with a glass ball for a stopper, big as an egg; and pens in a tray; and a little glass box they kept stamps in; and there was a ground-glass thing like a rolling pin set on a little pan that had water in it — they used it to wet stamps with — and there was a blotter on a rocker like the rocker on a rocking chair, and a big blotter to write on.'

'A roller to wet stamps with? Why didn't they just lick them?'

'Mrs. Berent hated the taste of the glue, and the others the same.'

'I see. Now you said Ruth scooped up some sugar out of the firkin. Why didn't she use lump sugar?'

Mrs. Freeman, reluctant to admit any flaw in her housekeeping, exclaimed: 'Somebody'd hidden it.'

Ruth was by this word electrified into new attention. She had forgotten the missing lump sugar, seeing in the fact of its disappearance no importance. But you couldn't mix powdered arsenic with lump sugar without detection, and Ellen would have known that!

'Hidden it?' Mr. Pettingill echoed. 'That must have annoyed you.'

'I'll say't it did!'

'When had you last seen it?'

'I'd used up the last of a box two days before that, so I ordered two boxes and they came the day before. I put them on the pantry shelf, and that morning they were gone. The place where they'd been was empty.'

'Wasn't there any in the sugar bowl?'

'No. Ruth went to get some and came back and said the bowl was empty; and it was, too. I looked myself, because it had been half-full the night before.'

Ruth, remembering, understanding to the full the malignant deliberation with which Ellen had acted, was physically sick, feeling waves of nausea in her cheeks and throat. She swallowed hard, and Mr. Pettingill went calmly on:

'Did you ever find those two boxes of sugar? The ones that were missing.'

Mrs. Freeman nodded vigorously. 'Yes, the next spring when I cleaned the pantry they were in behind the flour barrel, in the bottom cupboard.'

'They couldn't have got there by accident?'

'I'll say they couldn't! They were stuffed in out of sight, so you couldn't see them without you moved the barrel. Whoever put them there had to get down on their hands and knees and reach around behind the barrel.'

Mr. Pettingill shook his head. 'Too bad. Well now, Mrs. Freeman,' he asked. 'Did you notice what Miss Ellen wore that day?'

'She wore a print,' she said after a moment's thought. 'Sort of pale yellow, with flowers on it.'

'Any wrap or coat?'

'Yes, she wore an old suède leather jacket she used to have. It was a sight to behold. She used to wear it on trips with Professor Berent. She'd had it made special, with pockets, because she always took along scissors and knives and cotton and things in case he collected a specimen.'

'Plenty of pockets?'

'Two big ones on each side in front, and another, a lot bigger, in the lining in back,' Mrs. Freeman explained. 'She used to get it all bloody and I'd have to wash it out for her. It was like chamois, and you could wash it in soap and water.'

Pettingill considered, and he caught Quinton's eye. 'No more, I guess,' he said, and Mrs. Freeman, dismissed by Quinton too, stepped down.

Quinton recalled Leick, and he led him to tell of his long association with Harland, of their many excursions together, of their summers at Back of the Moon, emphasizing the man's devotion. Then he came to the picnic on the shore.

'Now with regard to the lobsters,' he suggested. 'Where did you get them?'

'Out of my traps,' Leick assured him. 'Where would I?'

'Who boiled them?'

'I did.'

'When they were ready, what happened?'

'We opened some of them to get out the tamale for the sauce, and Mrs. Harland —'

'Which Mrs. Harland?'

'Miss Ruth. She mixed the sauce.'

'What then?'

'Why, we et lunch.'

'Did you have anything to drink?'

'The three of them had coffee. I didn't drink anything.'

'Do you remember anything that happened with regard to sugar for that coffee?'

Leick said, half reluctantly: 'She asked for the sugar, and Mrs. Harland gave it to her.'

'Please refer to the ladies by their names at that time. Mrs. Ellen Harland asked for the sugar and Miss Ruth Berent gave it to her?'

'Yes.'

'Was it in a container?'

'In an envelope. She tore off the corner and poured some into her cup.'

'Mrs. Harland did?'

'Yes.'

'Did she later have another cup of coffee?'

'I didn't notice.'

'What became of the envelope?'

'When we were through eating, she folded the corner down so's the sugar wouldn't spill out, and put it back in the basket.'

'Was it an envelope like this one?'

'Near as I can tell.'

Quinton changed his tone. 'Now referring to the last summer of Mrs. Harland's life, did she and Mr. Harland and the defendant take a trip together?'

'They went fishing on the Miminegouche.'

'That's in Canada.'

'Yes.'

Quinton led him to describe the trip, and the forest fire which cut it short, and he asked: 'Now, Leick, you took tents?'

'Yes.'

'What was the sleeping arrangement?'

'Mrs. Harland and her had the big tent, and Mr. Harland and me had one, and the guides the other.'

'The two ladies slept together, so that Mr. and Mrs. Harland did not share the same tent?'

'No.' That Leick spoke unwillingly was plain.

'Referring to the summer Mr. and Mrs. Harland spent at Back of the Moon, were their relations that summer affectionate?'

'Yes.'

'Were they equally affectionate during those days on the river?'

'Why, with Tom Pickett and Sime Verity along, naturally they wouldn't ——'

'You needn't explain,' Quinton said curtly. 'Were they equally demonstrative?'

'Allowing for the guides ——'

'Please let the jury make its own allowances. Were they less openly affectionate than they had been at Back of the Moon, or more so, or the same?'

'Well, if you put it that way, less.'

'You said you guided Mrs. Harland? How did you and she escape the fire?'

'Went up river out of its way.'

'Where were the others?'

'Down river in the middle of it.'

'When did you rejoin them?'

'Why, when the fire burned down so we could travel, we started down river till we came to where they were.'

'Where were they?'

'On a gravel bar in the middle of the river.'

'Awake or asleep?'

'The guides were awake.'

'Mr. Harland? Ruth?'

'They were asleep.'

'Did you see them asleep?'

Leick looked helplessly at Harland. 'Why yes, I did,' he admitted.

'What was their position?'

'Curled up in the sand.'

'How near each other were they?'

'Why, it'd been a cold night. They was keeping warm.

'How near each other were they?'

'Right together.' Leick's lips were tight, his eyes dark with anger.

'Describe their position.'

Leick hesitated, then said in a rush of words: 'Mr. Harland had his arms around her, keeping her warm.'

Quinton half-smiled; he nodded, gave the witness to Mr. Pettingill, and the big man came slowly to his feet. 'Ever sleep out on a chilly night, without blankets, Leick?' he asked.

'Yes, sir.'

'Anyone with you?'

'Sometimes there was.'

'How did you sleep?'

'Close together as we could get.' There was relief in Leick's tone. 'It's the only way to keep even half-way comfortable.'

Mr. Pettingill nodded. 'Before the fire that day, where were you and Ellen Harland fishing?'

'Upstream from camp.'

'Where were the other two canoes?'

'Downstream.'

'How did that happen?'

'Why, Mrs. Harland — Miss Ruth — had found a sightly spot down river, and she wanted them all to go down there that day. The other one said she'd stay at camp. They tried to get her to go but she said for them to go without her.'

'So it was at Ellen's insistence that Ruth and Mr. Harland went downstream together.'

'Yes, it was.'

'I see. Now Brother Quinton has had you tell us twice about that envelope with sugar in it, but I want to go over it once more. Who poured the coffee?'

'Mrs. Harland did.'

'Miss Ruth?'

'Yes.' Ruth half-smiled, touched by Leick's persistent refusal to speak of Ellen as 'Mrs. Harland.'

'Did she pour all the cups at once?'

Leick frowned, trying to remember. 'Why no, come to think of it, she said she wasn't ready for hers.'

'You mean Mrs. Ellen Harland said that?' Mr. Pettingill was patient.

'Yes.'

'Was anything said about the sugar?'

'Yes. She asked if Mrs. Harland had brought it, and Mrs. Harland took the envelope out of the hamper and gave it to her.'

'Ellen asked for it and Ruth gave it to her?'

'Yes, sir.'

'Was that after Ruth poured Ellen's coffee?'

'No, before.'

'Do you remember what Ellen did with the envelope till she was ready to use it?'

'Why yes, I mind she put it in her pocket.'

'In her pocket?'

'She had on an old leather coat with some big pockets.'

'When she was ready to use the sugar, what then?'

'She took the envelope and tore the corner off and poured some into her cup and put the envelope back into her pocket.'

'You testified that she put the envelope back into the hamper. When did she do that?'

'After she had all the coffee she wanted, when we were cleaning up the beach. We threw the lobster shells and the paper plates and napkins that we'd used and all that rubbish into the fire, and what they wanted to keep went into the basket.'

Ruth listened in puzzled attention, wondering what was in Mr. Pettingill's mind.

'Who repacked the basket?'

'I guess I did, much as anybody. Mrs. Harland and her went up and sat on the bank, and Mr. Harland and me set there talking some, and I scrubbed the wash boiler, and I scrubbed the forks with sand and put them in.'

Quinton on redirect examination asked only one question. 'But you saw Miss Berent give Mrs. Harland the envelope, and you saw Mrs. Harland put it in the basket?' he insisted.

'Yes,' Leick assented, and Quinton let him go, and he called to the deputy at the door:

'Simon Verity.'

Ruth had not seen Sime since they left the river, and she almost smiled now at the difference in his appearance. In comfortable old clothes he had been at ease, his every movement inspiring confidence in his capacities; but now he wore a stiff suit and a white collar and he was shaved pink, his hair slicked down and then brushed up in a barber's curl above his left eye. She suspected that the strain of this elegance might at any moment prove too much for him, and she wondered how Quinton had persuaded him to come so far from home.

Quinton drew from him the story of their days on the river; and at length he asked: 'Now did you during those days see any affectionate gestures or caresses between Mr. and Mrs. Harland?'

Sime said readily: 'Sure. They'd kiss each other, most every morning.'

'She kissed him? Or he kissed her?'

'Well, I most generally tended to my own business, figured not to look. B'en my experience two's enough for a kiss.'

A murmur of amusement ran among the spectators, and Quinton said drily: 'I suppose your experience has been a wide one.'

'Well, wider than some folks, I judge,' Sime retorted, and Judge Andrus rapped for order. Quinton asked:

'What was the apparent relationship between Mr. Harland and Miss Ruth Berent?'

'Friendly.'

'During the forest fire, while Mrs. Harland and Leick were elsewhere, was Mr. Harland attentive to Miss Berent?'

'He took care of her.'

'Stayed near her?'

'Yes. We all stuck together.'

'Did you see him touch her?'

'Why, she got pretty tired,' Sime assented. 'He sat and held her, the way anyone would.'

'Never mind what anyone would do. What did he do?'

'Being in the water so long takes it out of you,' Sime explained. 'She couldn't hardly keep her head out of water, so he set behind her with his arms around her, kind of bracing her and holding her up.'

'He held her in his arms?'

'Yes, to keep her from drowning.'

'The jury will judge for themselves his reasons. He did hold her in his arms?'

'Yes.'

'How long?'

'Most all the last part of the time we was in the water.'

'Now as to the night you all spent on the gravel bar, did you sleep?'

'Why yes. We hadn't had a chance to sleep for a long time.'

'Where did Mr. Harland sleep with relation to Miss Berent?'

'We scraped away the ashes and all from a patch of sand, and they slept there.'

'How far from where you slept?'

'Maybe a couple of rods.'

'Who waked first in the morning?'

'I did. Then Tom.'

'When you waked, what was their position relative to each other?'

'I sh'd judge she'd got cold during the —'

'Never mind what you judged.'

'He had her hugged up to him to keep her warm.'

'You don't know the reason. You say he had her hugged up to him. Describe their position.'

'Why, they was both laying on their left sides, and she was backed up against him and he had his arms around her.'

'Both arms?'

'Yes.'

Ruth, feeling the whispering interest of the crowded spectators, held her head high and steady; but she remembered Ellen's coming in the morning, and the anger in Ellen's eyes when she found them thus. Then Quinton turned to Mr. Pettingill. 'Your witness,' he said triumphantly.

Pettingill leaned nearer Ruth. 'Did Ellen see you that way?' he asked.

'Yes.'

'Well,' he decided, 'we'd better get that in.' He rose and led Sime to describe Ellen's arrival, then let him go.

Quinton called Tom Pickett. Tom, awkward and embarrassed, obviously friendly to Ruth as Sime had been, nevertheless told the same story. Him Mr. Pettingill allowed to go unquestioned.

There were three more witnesses. Mrs. Huston, resentful and angry not only at Quinton's questions but because he kept her under a curb, forever checking her runaway tongue, nevertheless admitted that during the months while Ellen waited for her baby, Harland left her alone almost every afternoon. 'And why wouldn't he?' she demanded. 'With her forever . . .'

'Wait,' Quinton warned her. 'Just answer the questions, please. Now when was the baby expected to be born?'

'The doctor said May; but if you ask me . . .'

'The doctor said May. Did Mr. Harland in March and April spend more time at home?'

'I tell you, she wouldn't let him. And at the last of it, when she was trying to . . .'

'How often did he leave her alone in April?'

'Right along. She got rid of him because she was trying to . . .'

'Twice a week? Four times? Every day?'

'She got him out of the house so she could paint, and run up and down . . .'

'I'm asking you only what he did.'

'Well, I'm a-telling you what she did; and I ain't told the half of it. Walking herself into . . .'

Quinton interrupted, himself angry now. Harland understood completely what the old woman was trying to say; and he found himself for the moment on Quinton's side, hoping the State Attorney would be able to silence her eager tongue.

'You'll tell me only what I ask you,' Quinton insisted. 'Nothing more.'

'Sleep-walking my foot!' the old woman exclaimed, and tossed her head, and Quinton said:

'You leave it that up to the day the baby was stillborn, Mr. Harland left the house practically every day. Is that correct?'

'I said so, didn't I? But she . . .'

Quinton said curtly: 'That is all.'

'You mean you ain't going to let me . . .'

'That is all,' Quinton insisted, and looked at Mr. Pettingill, and the big man came to his feet. But before he could move away from the table, Harland caught his sleeve, and Mr. Pettingill turned back. Harland whispered:

'Let her go.'

Pettingill looked doubtful. 'She's trying to tell something. The jury wants to hear it.'

'Let her go,' Harland insisted. From this at least Ellen could be saved. 'She blamed Ellen for losing the baby,' he explained. 'But don't let her say so, please.'

Pettingill caught Ruth's eye, and she agreed. 'Yes, let her go.'

So Pettingill, though with obvious reluctance, said: 'No questions.' Mrs. Huston started to speak, but caught Harland's eye and was silenced; and Quinton called:

'Alice Murphy.'

She was the maid who had served Ruth and Mrs. Berent in Boston, and she said Harland came regularly to see them, that he did not always see Mrs. Berent, saw sometimes only Ruth.

Then Mr. Carlson, grunting and grumbling at the necessity of thus openly discussing the private affairs of his clients, took the stand to explain in detail how Professor Berent's estate had come almost intact into Ruth's hands.

'Now, Mr. Carlson,' Quinton asked at last. 'When did you last see Mrs. Harland before her death?'

'August thirty, two years ago.'

'Five or six days before her death?'

'Yes.'

'Under what circumstances?'

'She came to me on business.'

'What was that business?'

'To sign her will. Some other matters.'

'Who was to be executor under her will?'

'I was named executor.'

'Did she have other instructions for you, not included in her will?'

'She gave me a sealed envelope.'

Quinton drew from him the story of that envelope and of what he eventually did with it; and he asked: 'Did she give you any other instructions?'

Mr. Carlson's big chest filled; he seemed to sigh. 'We had some further conversation,' he admitted.

'What was the purport of that conversation?'

'She wanted to arrange for perpetual care of her mother's grave at Mount Auburn. I said Ruth had already done that.'

'Did she say anything else about the lot in Mount Auburn?'

'She said she'd told Mr. Harland she wanted to be buried there.'

'Where were you at the time of her death?'

'Trout fishing in the Laurentians.'

'When you returned and found she had been cremated, did you do anything?'

'No. Mr. Harland had gone away around the world. It was too late to do anything. In any case, I'd not have interfered. She gave me no instructions on the point; simply said she had asked him to have her buried there.'

'Asked him or told him?'

'Told him,' Mr. Carlson admitted. Quinton dismissed him, and Mr. Pettingill had no questions.

Then Quinton called Mr. Pettingill to the bench; and the big man returned to the table to say with a chuckle: 'Brother Quinton offered to prove that you two are married, but I said we'd admit that,' he explained.

Quinton, after a moment's whispered conference with Mr. Shumate said: 'That's the State's case, Your Honor.' Judge Andrus recessed court for fifteen minutes.

- IX -

When Mr. Pettingill faced the jury after court reconvened, Ruth thought he looked more like a farmer than ever, shambling and awkward, humbly anxious to get at the truth, doubtful of his own powers; yet she felt in the crowded room liking for him, just as she had felt the rows of spectators disliking Quinton.

He began in a groping and uncertain fashion. 'Well, gentlemen,' he said, 'maybe you're a little puzzled, so far, about this business. What we've all got to do is sift out the facts that nobody denies, and put them together, and see what sort of a picture they make.

'But the thing we've got to be careful about is to separate what we know is true from what someone says is true. Just to show you what I mean, take that letter Brother Quinton read to us. The judge told you not to pay any attention to anything that letter said. Some of it was true, and some of it was just notions that the poor woman had got into her head. I want to go through it, just to show you the difference between things you can believe and things you can't pay any attention to.

'For instance, Mrs. Harland — Ellen — says in that letter that she and Mr. Harland were coming to Bar Harbor to visit Ruth Berent. Well, there she's stating a fact, and it happens to be true, and if it mattered, it could be proved. Mr. Harland and Mrs. Ruth Harland and probably other people could come in here and tell you it was true.

'But right after that she says they're in love with each other. Well, there she's not stating a fact, but an opinion. Maybe it wasn't even that. Maybe she didn't write it because she believed it, but because she wanted someone else to believe it. Maybe she was mad, and hitting out, the way a woman will. One way or another, it can't be proved; and so you and I, being sensible, take it with a grain of salt, as they say.

'She goes on to say that she wants her letter destroyed unless Mr. Harland and Miss Ruth got married. If they did get married, she wanted to get even with them. That's what she says in the letter. There again she's saying something that can't be proved; but it sounds reasonable. She knew why she wrote the letter — as well as a woman ever knows why she does anything — and the letter sounds enough like a piece of spite work so you can believe that was her reason.

'She goes on mixing facts and opinions. She says they loved each other, but she doesn't ever claim to prove it. She says there was arsenic in Bar Harbor and in Boston before her father died. Well, that's a fact, and that can be proved. She'd used it, and knew about it, and could get at it if she was a mind to. But then she goes on to claim that Ruth poisoned her dinner, but she doesn't even claim she knows that. She just says she "thinks"

there was arsenic on her piece of apple pie. There's a sample of
the sort of thing you can't pay any attention to in trying to figure
out this case. Even if she was here in court, His Honor wouldn't
let her tell you what she thought. All she could tell you was
things she knew.

'Same way with that curry, where she says she saw white powder on it — and she says she "thought nothing of it." Well now,
I put it to you, if you believed someone had tried to poison you
once, and then saw what might be poison on something else
they'd cooked for you, I sh'd judge you'd think something of it.
I know I would.'

A whisper of amused agreement ran across the room, and he
went on. 'Same way with everything in that letter. His Honor
told you the letter isn't evidence, and I'm just using it to show the
way you have to be careful to stick to the facts. The proved and
certain facts.

'Now I'll just run through the proved and certain facts —
facts we don't question — in this case.' He proceeded methodi-
cally to do so, beginning with Ellen's marriage to Harland, coming to the day of the picnic and to Ellen's death. Ruth, listening,
felt a sick emptiness within her. This recital of uncontested facts
made a damning catalogue. Quinton himself could have painted
the picture no more blackly. Mr. Pettingill's measured words
were like blows, and she began to believe he would never be done.

'Well, those are the things you can be sure are true,' he said at
last. 'They're in the testimony, and we don't deny them. But
when the State says those facts prove that Ruth put arsenic in
that sugar and gave it to Ellen, there's where Brother Quinton
and I part company.

'Because I know she didn't; and when we've given you the
rest of the facts, you'll know it as well as I do.

'What happened was simple and plain enough. Ellen Harland
killed herself. Before we get through we'll tell you why she
did it, and we'll tell you how she did it, and you'll see the whole
thing straight and plain.'

He glanced at the clock, turned to the bench. 'Your Honor,'

he said. 'Mrs. Ruth Harland will be our first witness, but maybe we'd all better get a bite to eat first. It's only five-six minutes till time to recess anyway.'

Judge Andrus nodded, and a moment later the jury filed out of the courtroom.

14

F OR HARLAND, the waiting before the trial had been long. He stayed in Perry's Harbor, seeing Ruth regularly, maintaining for her a confident and cheerful air; but his hours alone were desolate and haunted. Mr. Pettingill came more than once to consult with him; and Leick, except for an occasional day's absence to attend to necessary tasks on the farm at home, lodged at the hotel and was always ready to be silent with Harland or to talk with him as Harland chose, offering a steady comradeship. Roger Pryde came twice; and little Miss Batten somehow managed to see Harland almost every day, cheerful and friendly. But despite these contacts, Harland was desperately alone; and when on the day before the trial the witnesses from a distance began to arrive — old Mrs. Huston, loyally indignant at this whole proceeding; Mr. Carlson, coming with Roger Pryde, grunting angrily; Doctor McGraw, grave and frightening; prim Mr. Catterson; and finally Sime Verity and Tom — Harland saw them in the hotel dining room with an uncontrollable tremor, just as a patient waiting for an operation watches the cheerful preparations of the nurses, tries to read the mind of the surgeon.

The hours in court while Quinton made his case were hard to endure; and when Ellen's letter was read aloud Harland felt stripped naked before the world. He suffered for himself; but just as a pleasure shared is doubly sweet, so is pain, by sharing it with one beloved, intensified, and he suffered even more for Ruth. At lunch on this day when Quinton finished, Harland could neither eat nor speak; but Mr. Pettingill and Roger Pryde agreed that Quinton had made a good presentation of the State's case.

'He's got the makings of a lawyer,' Mr. Pettingill conceded, and he reviewed the evidence. 'First he proved she might have died of arsenic, and that she said "poison" and it was the last word she spoke. He'll say she realized that she'd been poisoned and tried to say so. He traced the sugar she used back into the hamper, and to the chemist, and proved it had arsenic in it. He proved Ruth packed the sugar and gave it to Ellen. He put in evidence that you and Ellen, Mr. Harland, were at outs, and that you and Ruth were friendly, and that you neglected Ellen for Ruth during Ellen's pregnancy. He'll remind the jury over and over that you and Ruth slept together, that night on the river; and they'll remember the ordinary connotation of that phrase "slept together," and forget it was innocent if he can make them. He proved you had her cremated, and he proved she said she'd told you she wanted to be buried in Mount Auburn.

'And our defense has got to be that she planned her own death, planned Ruth should be blamed, hid the lump sugar, planted evidence against Ruth, contrived an elaborate, fantastic scheme. She couldn't plan for Quinton to steal the hamper, couldn't know he would do that. There were plenty of holes in the plan we've got to argue she made. It's going to be hard to make the jury believe our theory of her death.'

Roger said hopefully: 'We've one thing on our side. All the witnesses who knew her, even the State witnesses, obviously disliked Ellen and liked Ruth. The jury saw that.'

'And the jury'll like Ruth too,' Mr. Pettingill agreed. 'I'll see that they do. That's our real defense — to make them like her, and dislike and distrust Ellen.' He laid aside his napkin. 'Well,' he said, 'time to go.'

When a few minutes later, at Mr. Pettingill's summons, Ruth walked from her chair across to the witness stand in that fluent, indescribably lovely fashion which was so much a part of her, Harland's throat filled and his eyes burned with sorrow because he could not protect her from this ordeal she must now endure. But he was presently able to forget himself in listening. Mr.

Pettingill's questions were so simple and reassuring and he spoke so slowly and quietly, no haste in him or in Ruth. He began by asking her name.

'Mrs. Richard Harland,' she said. Her tone at first was low, but as the questions continued she pitched her voice so that it carried easily to every ear.

'What was your name before your marriage?'

'Ruth Berent.'

'What was your father's name?'

'Stephen Berent.'

'Is he alive?'

'He died when I was two years old.'

'Is your mother alive?'

'She died when I was a baby.'

'Was Stephen Berent, your father, related to Professor Berent, the father of the first Mrs. Harland?'

'Yes, they were brothers.'

'When your mother died, what happened?'

'My father sent me to live with Professor and Mrs. Berent.'

'When your father died, did they do anything?'

'They adopted me.'

'Was Ellen Berent older or younger than you?'

'Two years older.'

'You grew up as sisters?'

'Yes.'

'When did you first know that you were not actually sisters?'

'I've known for as long as I can remember. I remembered my father — or seemed to.'

'Professor Berent lived where?'

'In Boston. In the summer at Bar Harbor.'

'Were you fond of him?'

'Yes. I loved him dearly.'

'Fond of Mrs. Berent?'

'Yes.'

'Of Ellen?'

'Yes.'

Mr. Pettingill went quietly on, leading her to tell of her girlhood and adolescence. By skillful questions, as an artist with a stroke here and a stroke there produces his effects, he made the jury understand what Ruth's life had been; and somehow, without leading her into any word of criticism of Ellen, he showed the jury Ellen too, in all her youthful ways, till they knew how she had devoured her father, flouted her mother, subordinated everyone's wishes to her own. Yet he did this so deftly that Ruth seemed always to be defending Ellen, defending her against the jury's crystallizing ill opinion. Once Quinton, seeing what was happening, objected; but Mr. Pettingill argued that the jury in reaching a verdict would have to estimate Ruth's character, insisted that it was relevant to let the jury hear everything about her from her own lips, and won his point. Harland, seeing Ruth through the lawyer's questions more clearly than ever before, loved her more and more.

Mr. Pettingill came eventually to Professor Berent's last years, and so to his death.

'Where was he buried?' he inquired.

'His ashes were scattered across a mountain meadow in New Mexico.'

'Why was that done?'

'He had asked Ellen that it be done.'

'Did you and Mrs. Berent know this?'

'No. He told only Ellen.'

'Did Mrs. Berent wish his ashes taken there?'

'No. Ellen said that was what he wanted, but Mother didn't believe her. But Mr. Quinton had heard Father say the same thing, and when Mother told Ellen she didn't believe her, Ellen sent for him and he came to Boston.'

'Did anything happen between Mr. Quinton and Ellen at that time?'

'They became engaged.'

'What was done about taking the ashes to New Mexico?'

'We all — Mother and Ellen and I — went out to Mr. Robie's ranch.'

'Did you meet anyone there?'

'Mr. Harland was a guest there at the same time.'

'Did anything happen between Ellen and Mr. Harland?'

'They were married before we left there.'

'What was your mother's attitude about that?'

'She asked Ellen to wait, to treat Mr. Quinton with more consideration.'

'Yes?'

'Ellen refused. Mr. Harland's younger brother was ill in Georgia. He was going directly there. Ellen told Mother she wished to be married at once, to go with him.'

'Tell us only what you know, Mrs. Harland. Did you hear the conversation between Ellen and Mrs. Berent?'

'Yes.'

'Did you have any part in that discussion?'

'Ellen asked my opinion. I encouraged them to be married at once. I said they were the ones to decide.'

'After their marriage, when did you next see Mr. Quinton?'

'He came to the ranch. Ellen had telegraphed him, breaking their engagement and saying she was to be married.'

'Did he say anything you remember?'

'He said he would have prevented their marriage if he had arrived in time.'

'Did he say how he would have done that?'

'No.'

Harland, looking from Quinton to the jury, saw that they watched Quinton for a moment with blank eyes. Then Mr. Pettingill made Ruth describe her trip back to Boston, and the winter there; and in every word the story of her loyal attendance upon Mrs. Berent was manifest. He came to the weeks at Sea Island, to the day when Harland and Ellen joined them.

'What was then your mother's feeling about the marriage?' he asked.

'She liked Mr. Harland, and she saw that Ellen was happier and nicer and gave him credit. She told him so.'

'In your presence?' Mr. Pettingill suggested. 'You can only tell us what you know.'

'I heard her tell Mr. Harland she liked him, and that he had been good for Ellen. She also said the same thing to me.'

Pettingill went quietly on, coming at last to Danny's death, and to Ellen's sickness afterward, and to Ellen's pregnancy. Ruth said Harland, during those months, came almost daily to be a while with her and with her mother.

'With both of you?'

'Mother was ill, spent much time in bed. If she were asleep or tired — this was frequently the case — he did not see her, saw only me. If she were feeling better, we sat with her. Sometimes if I had an errand to do he stayed with her while I was gone.'

She told of the loss of Ellen's baby, and of Harland's grief. She told how she sought to comfort him, keeping nothing back, answering readily and frankly every question; and for Harland the past came alive through her words, and he suffered again those remembered torments. Then she spoke of the river trip, and described the forest fire, and her own exhaustion, and how for hours only Harland's arm around her held her erect.

'Did you welcome his support, his arm around you?'

'Yes. I was so tired it would have been easy to give up.'

'The night before Ellen and Leick rejoined you, where did you sleep?'

'Beside Mr. Harland, on the sand bar. I was cold in the night and pressed closer to him. I don't know whether he woke — we didn't speak — but he put his arms around me.'

'When did you wake?'

'When Ellen and Leick got there. When I woke, Ellen was looking down at us.'

'You were in Mr. Harland's arms?'

'Yes.'

'Do you know Ellen's feeling at that time?'

'She was angry.'

'How do you know? Did she show her feeling in any way?'

'In her eyes and her tone.'

'Did she say anything?'

'She said I had better wake Mr. Harland too.'

'Did you and she have anything like a quarrel?'

'No. Almost at once, she was herself again.'

She described their return to Boston, and her own subsequent departure for Bar Harbor; and he asked:

'Now, at some time later that summer, did Ellen and Mr. Harland come to Bar Harbor to visit you?'

'Yes.'

'Did you have some conversation with Ellen during that visit?'

'Yes, often. She was so sweet, nicer to me than she had ever been. We'd never been so close before.'

'Where did those conversations occur?'

'Why, wherever we happened to be, whenever we were together.'

'Did she ever, during these conversations, refer to the possibility of her death?'

'Yes.'

'When was that?'

'The afternoon before the picnic.'

'Under what circumstances?'

'I was in my room, relaxing. I looked out of the window and saw her coming up the lawn and called to her; and she put on a dressing gown and came to my room and we had a long, lazy afternoon together.'

'Where was Mr. Harland?'

'He'd gone to climb Cadillac Mountain.'

'Did she say where she had been before you saw her on the lawn?'

'Yes, she said she'd been in Father's workshop. She had thought she might want to use it, to take up his collecting where he'd left off; but she said that afternoon that she didn't want to do it, that being in his workshop made her miss him too much. She said I could clear his things out and make the shop into a cottage for myself.'

'Did you do so?'

'Yes, the following summer.'

'Now during this lazy, long afternoon in your room, you say
... By the way, where was your bathroom?'

'Off my bedroom.'

'Did she go into the bathroom that afternoon?'

'I don't remember her doing so. Oh yes, I do. She asked for
an orangewood stick ...'

'What is that?'

Ruth smiled. 'It's used in manicuring, to push back the cuti-
cle. I started to get one for her, but she said she'd get it, and I
said there were some in my bathroom cabinet. She went and
got one and came back and lay down again.'

Mr. Pettingill turned to the table where the exhibits were.
'I show you a bottle here in evidence. Do you recognize it?'

'Yes, it was mine. It held bath salts.'

'Where did you last see it?'

'In my bathroom cabinet.'

'When?'

'I really don't know.'

'Was it there that day?'

'I don't know. I hadn't used it for some time.'

'All right, go on with what she said that afternoon about the
possibility of her death.'

'She told me how happy she and Mr. Harland had been at
Back of the Moon the summer before, and she said she had made
him promise that when she died, he would have her cremated and
scatter her ashes on the lake there; and she told me to be sure to
remind him. She said if I did not, she would haunt us.'

'Was that her only reference to the possibility of her death?'

'Yes, except that she said — I'm not sure it was that day, but
she had often said the same thing — that she did not want to live
to be old, that she expected to die young.'

'Now come to the day she died.' Harland felt his muscles
tighten, but Mr. Pettingill's tone remained the same, and there
was in this fact and in Ruth's quiet responses a deep reassurance.
Under the lawyer's leading she described the picnic in meticulous
detail; and she told of the hours of Ellen's agony, and of the sorry

journey to Boston, and of Harland's trip to Bangor with Ellen's ashes, and of his subsequent departure for far places, and of her long months alone, and of Harland's return, and of their many hours together during the winter that followed, and so of their marriage. Harland, listening, relived those happy hours, and he was full of pride and joy in her, and to him she seemed to shine with an inner radiance as she serenely faced the intent and avid crowd.

Mr. Pettingill at last glanced toward the clock on the wall. 'Well, that's about all,' he said. 'But I'll ask you a few more questions. Was Ellen normally a healthy person?'

'She had, all her life, occasional attacks of indigestion.'

'How often?'

'I suppose I remember a dozen, beginning when we were both children.'

'Was she on these occasions seriously ill?'

'Yes, she suffered great pain, nausea, distress.'

'Was a doctor usually called?'

'Yes, always.'

'Do you remember an attack after Danny died?'

'Yes.'

'Was it different from the others?'

'It seemed to me the same.'

'Did she on that occasion have a doctor?'

'Yes, a doctor and a nurse.'

'Had she before that attack eaten food you prepared?'

'Yes.'

'What was it?'

'I cooked our dinner. Mrs. Freeman was out and we had just then no second maid. I broiled chops and made a salad, and Mrs. Freeman had left an apple pie.'

'Did you sprinkle arsenic on Ellen's piece of apple pie?'

The question came so abruptly that despite Mr. Pettingill's easy tone Harland twitched with shock; but if Ruth too was startled, she did not show it.

'No,' she said simply. Harland felt the taut attention in the

crowded room, heard behind him in the silence the racing pencils
of the reporters. Mr. Pettingill asked quietly:

'Did you, in Boston, a few days before her coming to Bar Harbor, prepare a dinner which she ate?'

'Yes, she and Mr. Harland dined with me. I gave them curry.'

'Did you put arsenic in her curry?'

The repeated question was as searing as it had been when Mr.
Pettingill first asked it. To Harland it was like a lash across his
cheek; and he thought Ruth felt this too, for her lips paled a little
and her voice was lower when she answered.

'No.'

'What happened after that dinner?'

'She had an attack of indigestion.'

'Had she medical attendance on that occasion?'

'Yes.'

'With regard to the illness that resulted in her death, was that
different from her previous attacks?'

'It seemed no worse at first, but it persisted — and she died.'

'Let's go back to the picnic, repeat ourselves a little. Did she
eat anything that day which the rest of you did not eat?'

'She had sugar in her coffee. We did not.'

Harland hardened himself for what was coming, for the third
asking of that monotonous question.

'Where did she get the sugar? I want to go over that once
more.'

Ruth clearly was tiring, but she answered steadily: 'While I
was packing the hamper, she reminded me to take along some
sugar for her. I couldn't find any lump sugar, so I put some granulated sugar in an envelope and put it in the hamper. When she
asked for sugar during lunch, I gave her that envelope.'

'The same one in which you had put the sugar?'

'I thought it the same one. It was the same one as far as I
know.'

'Where did you get the sugar?'

'Out of the firkin.'

'Where did you get the envelope?'

'From the desk in the library.'

'Was it the only one of its kind there?'

'No, there were several, perhaps two dozen, in a pigeonhole on the desk.'

'I show you an envelope. Is this the same one?'

Ruth examined it carefully. 'It looks just the same,' she said. 'They were all alike.'

'It has been testified that two years later, this envelope contained sugar to which arsenic had been added. Do you know anything about that?'

'No.'

'Did you put arsenic in the sugar you took to the picnic for Ellen's coffee?'

'No.'

'Did you murder your sister?'

Ruth's lips drained white, but she said quietly: 'No.'

'Did you ever, while Ellen was alive, wish her dead?'

'No.'

Mr. Pettingill nodded, and he spoke more gently. 'Were you in love with Mr. Harland before Ellen died?'

'No.'

'When did you realize that you were in love with him?'

'It was some time after his return from his trip around the world.'

'Did you find, in retrospect, that you had loved him long before that?'

She smiled frankly. 'That is the sort of question lovers ask each other,' she commented, and she said in even tones, looking toward Harland with her heart in her eyes: 'I feel now that I have always loved him, and I know I always will.'

Mr. Pettingill turned away. 'Your witness, Brother Quinton,' he said quietly; but he had timed his questions well. Before Quinton could rise, Judge Andrus announced adjournment for the day.

- II -

Harland had a moment with Ruth, to touch her hand, to say: 'I never loved you so much.' Her fingers, clinging to his, shook and trembled; and he saw that in the reaction from these hours in the box, facing hundreds of curious eyes, she was weak and breathless now.

Then she was gone, Mrs. Sayward beside her, Deputy Hatch moving ponderously on their heels. Pettingill and Roger Pryde and Harland left the courthouse together, and when they were alone, Pryde shook Harland's hand. 'You're a lucky man,' he said. 'She's wonderful.'

Harland laughed brokenly. 'I don't feel lucky,' he said. 'I could kill Quinton — and every spectator, and the damned reporters.'

'Easy,' Pryde warned him. 'You'll have to keep your temper. Quinton will give her a hard time tomorrow, you know.'

Harland's fists knotted, but he did not speak. Before they reached the hotel, Leick joined them; and at Harland's suggestion he stayed to have dinner with them. It was served in Mr. Pettingill's room; and although they ate almost in silence, they sat afterward in talk a while.

'Well,' Mr. Pettingill remarked. 'Mrs. Harland made a splendid witness; and I'm sure she'll stand up under cross-examination. But after all, her testimony is negative; just a general denial, nothing more. Quinton will point out that if she did poison Ellen she would of course deny it. I hope the jury will believe her. My idea was to let her win them, let them come to know her and like her.'

'They did,' Pryde agreed.

'Well, we've made our denial,' the big man went on. 'We can't question that Ellen died of arsenic poisoning, nor that arsenic was found in the Bar Harbor house in a bottle bearing Ruth's fingerprints, nor that Mr. Harland and Ruth — even before Ellen's death — were pretty good friends. So — where do we go from here?'

He hesitated, and they saw that he had forgotten them. 'We

could put in some testimony about Ellen's previous attacks of
indigestion,' he remarked. 'Call her doctors, get their opinions
that in each case — the apple pie and the curry — her illness
seemed to them indigestion and nothing more. But that's still
negative evidence — and Quinton would make them admit that
her symptoms might have resulted from arsenic poisoning.' He
looked thoughtfully at Harland. 'Since we're arguing that she
killed herself, we'll have to tell the jury that you and she were at
odds.' His tone was a question, but Harland did not speak, and
the lawyer said: 'By the way, Ruth tells me Ellen had been warned
she couldn't have any more babies?'

Harland assented. 'Yes. I didn't know it till she told Ruth, in
my hearing. The doctor never told me so.'

'We'll check with him, see if her condition — physical condition — was such as to produce melancholia. What's his name?'

'Doctor Patron.'

Mr. Pettingill said: 'Make a note of that, Mr. Pryde.' Roger
did so, and the big man suggested: 'Better get him on the phone,
see what he has to say.' Roger departed to do so, and Leick, sitting silently by, whittled a fresh fill for his pipe, rolling the tobacco
to crumbs between his palms. Mr. Pettingill said thoughtfully:
'We're arguing she committed suicide; but we'll have to at least
suggest how she could have done so. We can argue that she saw
Ruth prepare that envelope with the sugar in it, and fixed up a
duplicate, and took it along in her coat pocket, and switched envelopes during the picnic, when she put the real envelope in her
pocket; but it's easier to argue that she made the switch at Bar
Harbor, or maybe in the car.'

'Why?' Harland asked, not understanding.

'Because if she'd switched the envelopes at the picnic, she'd
have had to get rid of the one with the real sugar in it; but she had
no chance to do that. She was with you or Ruth all the time. If
she just stuck it in her pocket, it would have been found by now,
by whoever put her clothes away.'

'I suppose so,' Harland agreed. 'Ruth must have cleaned her
pockets out, and she'd have found it.'

'I'll ask Ruth about that,' Mr. Pettingill decided. 'Or Mrs. Freeman might know. But no, you went direct from Leick's place to Boston — took her clothes along, I suppose?'

Harland hesitated, and Leick answered. 'That's right. Mrs. Harland wrapped them up in some paper, put them in the car; and I mind she took everything out of the coat pockets, cigarettes and matches and dark glasses and a little purse and a handkerchief.'

'Well, that's too bad,' Mr. Pettingill commented. 'If we could show she got rid of the real envelope with the sugar in it at the picnic, we could nail the thing right down snug.'

Then Roger Pryde came back, saying quickly:

'Dick, I've got Doctor Patron on the phone, but he wants to talk to you. Professional ethics, I suppose. I told them to switch him up here.'

Harland took the phone and heard the doctor on the line. 'This is Richard Harland, Doctor,' he explained. 'We're working on the theory that Mrs. Harland committed suicide, and I wanted to ask you — was there anything in her physical condition to produce melancholia?'

'No, no,' Doctor Patron told him. 'She was perfectly healthy.'

'I thought possibly — I know of course that you'd told her she could never have a baby.'

'Never have a baby?' Harland heard the indignant surprise in the other's tone.

'She told us so, yes,' he said.

'Nonsense!' Doctor Patron exclaimed. 'She could have had a dozen! There was nothing wrong with her at all!'

Harland hesitated, looking at the others. 'Hold the line a minute,' he said, and cupped the transmitter and spoke to Mr. Pettingill. 'Doctor Patron says she could have had babies all right. I remember now I suspected at the time that she just said that so Ruth wouldn't wonder why we didn't have another.' And he asked: 'Do you want him to come up here, to testify?'

Pettingill hesitated. 'We can tell better tomorrow night,' he decided; and when Harland left the phone, he added, his hand caressing his heavy chin: 'Well, that's interesting. Psychologically at least.' He looked at Harland. 'You say Mrs. Huston thought Ellen got rid of her baby on purpose. Doctor Patron might know.'

Harland said wretchedly: 'He couldn't know surely. Let's not go into that.'

'We're claiming that she not only killed herself, but deliberately tried to throw the guilt on Ruth,' Mr. Pettingill reminded him. 'We'll need to show the jury she was an extraordinarily selfish, jealous, malicious woman.' But Harland did not speak; and after a moment Leick said:

'I b'en thinking, Mr. Pettingill. That other envelope, the one with the real sugar in it, she might have thrown it into the fire.'

'Possibly,' Pettingill agreed, and sat in silent thought, and then suddenly he rose, dismissing them. 'Well, we're all tired,' he said. 'Mr. Harland, go to bed, get a good rest. I want you to follow Mrs. Harland on the stand.'

Harland when he was alone found his brow beaded with moisture at thought of the morrow; but whatever he need do for Ruth's sake he would do. He slept easily, too near exhaustion to stay awake; slept like a man drugged.

– III –

Harland did not see Ruth next morning until in court she came to her seat beside him; he had time for no more than a secret pressure of her hand before she took the stand and Quinton rose to begin her cross-examination. Quinton said at once:

'Now, Mrs. Harland, you have pleaded not guilty to this indictment, so I don't expect you to admit poisoning your sister. But there are a few questions I'd like to ask you. Go back to the time when your Boston house was sold. Your father had a workshop where he sometimes skinned and stuffed birds, on the top floor of that house?'

'Yes.'

'He had there a supply of arsenic?'

'Yes.'

'After your father died, did you enter that room?'

'Yes. After he died, Ellen put his things in order, and ——'

'I asked about you, not Ellen.'

Ruth continued as though he had not spoken: 'And I went in now and then to dust and clean.'

'An unused room? Weren't the windows closed?'

'Yes.'

'Then why did it need dusting?'

Ruth smiled. 'I'm afraid you're not a housekeeper.'

'At any rate, on one pretext or another, you often went into that room.'

'Yes. Several times.'

'After your mother died, you sold the house?'

'Ellen and I. We owned it jointly.'

'But you yourself cleaned out that room?'

'May I tell you just what happened?'

Quinton bowed. 'Nothing would please me more.'

'Very well,' Ruth assented. 'We decided to sell the house, Ellen and I. Ellen came one day to discuss what should be done with the furniture. She suggested that the Museum might like some of Father's things. She stayed in that room alone, saying she wished to "say good-bye to Father," and I went downstairs. She joined me after perhaps ten minutes.' Harland saw triumphantly that Quinton's own question allowed Ruth to remind the jury that Ellen too had access to the arsenic. 'Next day the Museum sent a man who selected what he wanted.'

Quinton said in an ironic tone: 'What we want to hear, Mrs. Harland, is what you did with the arsenic in that room. I trust you will come to the point.'

'Oh, I will,' she assured him. 'After the Museum man was done, I cleaned out everything. The arsenic I put in the furnace, burned it.'

'How much was there?'

'Two jars, quart jars. One full, the other almost empty.'

'I don't expect you to admit that you kept any of that arsenic; but if you wished, you could have done so?'

'Of course,' Ruth assented. 'I could have kept it all, but I didn't.'

'Were you alone when you cleaned the room?'

'Yes.'

Quinton led her to describe the Bar Harbor workshop, inquiring what was done with the arsenic there; and she said she destroyed it the summer after Ellen's death.

'The arsenic was there in the workshop before her death?'

'Oh yes.'

'You had the key to the shop?'

'Yes. It was kept in the back entry, hanging on a nail.'

'Did you at any time take some of the arsenic and put it into a bottle and hide it behind the baseboard in your room?'

'No.'

'You knew there was such a hiding place?'

'Yes. Ellen ——'

'Did any other living person know about that hiding place?'

'Ellen knew about it.'

'But Ellen has been dead almost two years.'

'She and I were — as far as I know — the only ones who knew about that place.'

'How recently have you hidden anything there?'

'I never did. Ellen discovered the loose baseboard when we were children. The carpenters forgot to nail it in place, I suppose . . .'

'Never mind your suppositions. You and Ellen used to hide things there.'

'Ellen did. I came to our room one day when we were children and she had the baseboard pried out and propped open with a book, but she was furious with me for seeing her. I promised never to tell, and she told me never to dare look in there, and I never did.'

'Were you always so obedient to her wishes?'

'We all did what Ellen wanted.'

'But you never put anything in there?'

'No, never.'

'I show you a certain bottle. Do you recognize it?'

'Yes.'

'Tell us about it.'

'It was given to me.'

'When?'

'For my birthday, I think. In August, the year before Mother and Ellen died.'

'Was that the summer you cleaned out your father's workshop at Bar Harbor?'

'No, I did that after Ellen died.'

'About the bottle. What was in it?'

'It was a bottle of bath salts. I used them one or twice, left the bottle at Bar Harbor when we went home to Boston. In the cabinet in my bathroom.'

'When did you see it again?'

'I'm not sure. I came to Bar Harbor in August, the year Ellen died, about two weeks before Ellen and Mr. Harland came. I don't remember seeing the bottle then, but I might have forgotten. I don't remember seeing it till I saw it here in court.'

'When did you first miss it?'

'I never missed it.'

'Did you use some other bath salts?'

Ruth smiled. 'I never had used any before, largely because I normally take a shower. I used these once or twice, as one does, to show my appreciation of the gift; but then I forgot them.'

'When did you last touch this bottle?'

'I'm sure I don't know. I don't remember seeing it since the year before Ellen died.'

On this point Quinton hammered at her; but Ruth remained calm and unshaken. Then he turned to the day of the picnic, leading her to recite her every action that day.

'You took two thermos bottles full of coffee?' he asked.

'Yes.'

'How well did you know Leick Thorne before that day?'

'As well as I do now. I've barely seen him since.'

'You became acquainted where?'

'Mostly on our fishing trip up in Canada.'

'Did you notice on that trip that he never drank coffee?'

'Yes. The other guides drank coffee for breakfast, but even for breakfast he drank tea.'

'Did he use sugar in his tea?'

'Yes.'

'Why didn't you take tea for him to drink that day?'

'I forgot it.'

'Are you always so forgetful of those who serve you?'

'I hope not.'

'By neglecting to take tea, you made sure he would not use sugar that day?'

'I thought nothing about it. I forgot the tea, that's all.'

'But if you had thought about it, you would have known, would you not, that since you took along no tea, and he did not drink coffee, he would use no sugar?'

'I presume so.'

'Mrs. Harland, when your sister, at the point of death, tried to tell you that she had been poisoned, why did you not try to save her?'

Ruth's tones strengthened. 'I do not believe she tried to tell us anything of the sort. And in any case, we tried in every way to save her.'

'You heard her pathetically gasp out the dreadful word "poison"?'

'Yes.'

'What did you believe she meant?'

'I did not think.'

'I see. You thought nothing about the fact that Leick would not use the poisoned sugar, and you thought nothing about your sister's statement that she was poisoned.'

'I did not know the sugar was poisoned.'

Harland, listening, seeing how steadily she met every barb, felt his throat swell with tender pride. Then Quinton shifted his attack, demanded:

'Mrs. Harland, do you love Mr. Harland?'

'Yes.'

'You first met him in New Mexico?'

'Yes.'

'Was it love at first sight?'

'No.'

'You spent two weeks with him then?'

'We were in the same party for two weeks.'

'At the end of those two weeks, did you love him?'

'No.'

'You next saw him — where?'

'At Sea Island.'

'Did you love him there?'

'No.'

Harland, his fists clenched and a sick rage shaking him, spoke to Mr. Pettingill, whispering over the other's shoulder. 'Damn it, can't you make him stop that?'

Quinton asked: 'When you next saw him, at Bar Harbor, did you love him then?'

Mr. Pettingill rose slowly. 'Your Honor,' he suggested. 'I don't want to hinder Brother Quinton from doing the best he can with what he's got to work with; but it strikes me he's asking for an opinion, and that's not competent.'

Quinton addressed the bench. 'Your Honor, love is not an opinion. It's a physical reaction. It's a fact. At one time this defendant did not love Mr. Harland. At some later time, she did. I want to fix the time when the change occurred.'

Judge Andrus allowed the question; but Quinton for the moment turned back to the sale of the Boston house, making Ruth describe again the disposal of the arsenic there. In the middle of this interrogation he asked sharply:

'Mrs. Harland, when you learned Danny was dead, did you love Mr. Harland?'

'No.'

'When you comforted Mr. Harland after the birth of his still-born child, did you love him then?'

'No.'

'How did you comfort him?'

Harland's breath caught, but Ruth answered simply and straightforwardly: 'I tried to find words. I put him to bed, made him rest and sleep.'

'Where did you put him to bed? Whose bed? How? Did you undress him?' The questions pounded quick and hard; but Ruth's quiet answers robbed them of their sting. He went back to the matter of the bath salts, broke off that line of questioning to demand: 'The day Ellen died, did you love him then?' Harland, watching Ruth, saw her color slowly fade, and knew how weary she must be; and he urged Mr. Pettingill to ask a recess so that she might have a respite; but the lawyer whispered:

'She's doing all right. She's licking him.'

Harland began, as time passed, to see that this was true. Quinton skipped back and forth over the whole fabric of Ruth's testimony, attacking with a question here, another there, like a trapped animal seeking some weak spot in the pen in which it is confined, and he pounded hard always on the point of her love for Harland. 'Do you love him now? Did you love him when you married him? Did you love him a week before you married him? A month before? A year before?' Ruth's very serenity drove him to helpless fury. He was red and perspiring, his voice high and shrill. At the constantly reiterated question there were occasional titters from the tense-strung spectators, till Judge Andrus warned them to silence. The newspaper men and women at their long table finally stopped trying to record the testimony, watching Quinton's labors with a dry, amused scorn, till at last he cried:

'Now see here, Mrs. Harland. You've dodged long enough. You can answer a simple question, and I demand that you do so. Just when did you fall in love with Mr. Harland?'

Ruth hesitated, and suddenly she smiled. 'If you had ever loved anyone finely and cleanly, Mr. Quinton,' she said in clear tones, 'you would know how impossible any answer is. Love is not an explosion, an impact, a blow. It begins slowly, in little sweet ways, continuing to grow through many hours and days, continuing through long happy lifetimes to grow and to develop and to become stronger and more beautiful all the time. I love Dick more today than I ever did, and I shall love him more and more every day until I die.'

Quinton was beaten, and he had the wit to know it; yet he could not resist one last word. 'Then you began to love him long ago,' he said, and before she could speak, he added quickly: 'That's all!'

Ruth looked inquiringly at Mr. Pettingill; and he came to meet her and to escort her back to her chair again. The deference in his movements was eloquent beyond any words, and every eye followed Ruth till she was seated. Then Mr. Pettingill turned and said quietly:

'Mr. Harland, will you take the stand?'

— IV —

Harland was surprised at the brevity of his direct testimony. Mr. Pettingill let him speak only a little of his marriage to Ellen, of their year together before Danny's death, of the months of her pregnancy.

'Were your relations during that whole period before your baby died pleasant or otherwise?' he asked.

Harland, remembering the months when the memory of Danny's death lay like a naked sword between them, hesitated; but of Danny he would not speak unless he must. He said:

'Yes, normal and happy.'

'Did those normal and happy relations continue until her death?'

'No.'

'Why not?'

Harland was shaken by a deep dismay. In their private conversations, the lawyer had never pushed his questions on this point, accepting Harland's evasions; and Harland wondered resentfully why the other now insisted.

'Well, we were at odds,' he said slowly, groping for words.

'Can you be more specific?'

'Why, before the baby died, we began to occupy separate rooms, and we continued to live apart afterward.'

'Did you never again share the same room?'

'No, except at Bar Harbor on our last visit there.'

'Did she or did you originate this arrangement of separate rooms?'

'She did.'

'By the way, did you ever discuss the question of having another baby?'

'She told me we couldn't have any more.'

Quinton started to rise, then seemed to change his mind; and Mr. Pettingill asked: 'This arrangement for separate rooms which she originated, did she insist on maintaining it?'

Harland filled his lungs deeply, his hands tightening on the railing of the witness box in which he stood. A grim anger filled him; and it sounded in his tone. 'She did not,' he said hoarsely, damning Mr. Pettingill for his question.

'Did you?'

'Yes.'

'Then this regime, separate rooms, living apart, was originally at her suggestion; but you persisted in it?'

'Yes.' He spoke curtly.

'Did she ask you to return to her room?'

'Yes.'

'You refused to do so?'

'Yes.' Harland began belatedly to understand. If they were to contend that Ellen had killed herself, they must affirm that she did so because Harland no longer loved her. He had not till now appreciated what this affirmation would require of him, had not realized that he would appear in a sorry light before the crowded courtroom and the world; and for a moment he rebelled. But then, remembering that for Ruth's sake the truth must be told, he welcomed the ordeal, and his voice strengthened.

'Why?' asked Mr. Pettingill.

'I was unwilling. I no longer loved her.' He knew, seeing the racing pencils of the reporters, how contemptible his words must sound; yet since it was for Ruth, he accepted this ignominy with a high pride.

'I get a picture,' the lawyer suggested, 'of a situation in which Mrs. Harland wished to resume wifely relations with you and you refused.'

'Yes, that is correct.'

'Were others aware of this?'

'No. We were superficially friendly.'

'Were your servants aware of the fact that you occupied separate rooms?'

'Yes, we told my housekeeper that Mrs. Harland's health made it necessary.'

'How long did Mrs. Harland continue her efforts to secure a reconciliation with you?'

'Till the day she died.'

'Did you always refuse?'

Harland said explicitly: 'I never gave her a flat and final refusal until that day. We had discussed it more than once. I hoped — we both hoped — that — things would somehow straighten out between us.' He remembered that day, driving from Boston to Bar Harbor, when on the bank above the inlet Ellen had been so completely lovely and enticing. 'I thought things — my own feeling — might change,' he said.

'Did you ever give up that hope?'

'Yes.'

'When?'

'The morning before the picnic, the day she died. I told her that morning that I had decided to leave her.' He winced inwardly at his own words, at the role he thus assumed; the character of a man who by a stubborn refusal of his affection drove his wife to suicide.

'Did she express reproach, or distress, or despair?'

'No, she didn't express anything.'

'When had she known of your antagonistic feeling toward her?'

'Months before.'

'Months before she died?'

'Yes. Since a few weeks after the baby died.'

'Could she have foreseen your eventual decision?'

'I don't know. I wasn't sure of it myself.'

'Did you ever — half-surrender, give her any hope?'

'No.' Harland hesitated. 'No,' he repeated.

'Was Mrs. Harland subject to fits of depression?'

'No.'

'Moody? Sullen? Tearful?'

'No, never.'

'Did you have quarrels?'

'Rarely. They were unimportant.'

'Did she ever threaten to leave you?'

'No.'

'Did she ever threaten to kill herself?'

'No.'

'Did she ever refer to the possibility of her death?'

'Yes, several times.'

'Any you recall?'

'I remember her saying once that she didn't want to live to be old. And once she made me promise to sprinkle her ashes at Back of the Moon when she died. And she used to say, laughingly, that if I didn't do something or other she'd haunt me, but she was joking.'

'Joking? In this trial, is she not in fact making good that threat? Is she not haunting you?'

But before Harland could reply, Quinton was on his feet with a furious protest; and Mr. Pettingill withdrew the question. He asked instead: 'When she died, had you any suspicion that her death was not natural?'

'No.'

'Were you grieved by her death?'

'I was sorry I'd made her unhappy that morning.'

'Unhappy? I understood you to say a while ago that she expressed no emotion.'

'I knew what she felt.'

Mr. Pettingill looked inquiringly at Quinton; but Quinton, his countenance bleak and stony, made no move, and Pettingill went on: 'After her death, a few days after, what did you do?'

'Went away, to Europe and on around the world.'

'Why?'

'I never wanted to see a familiar face again.'

'Why not?'

'I was — I hated to think Ellen was dead.'

'Were you in love with the present Mrs. Harland?'

'No.'

'When did you realize that you were in love with her?'

Harland's glance touched Ruth. 'I'm realizing it more completely every day,' he said.

'How long after your return to Boston did you realize your affection for her?'

'Not till a few days before we were married.'

The clock was on the tick of the hour for noon recess. Mr. Pettingill nodded. 'That is all,' he said.

Harland drew a deep breath, but before Judge Andrus could speak, Quinton came quickly to his feet. 'Your Honor, we've half a minute,' he cried. 'I'd like to put two questions.' He strode toward Harland, came face to face with him.

'Now, Mr. Harland,' he said sharply. 'Do you mean us to understand that when she died, your wife loved you, and that you did not love her?'

'Yes.'

'And you boast that your refusal to accept her pitiful efforts to be reconciled with you drove her to suicide?'

Harland wetted his dry lips. He tried to speak, cleared his throat; but before he could reply, Quinton with a gesture of scorn turned to the bench. 'Your Honor, I'll reserve further questions,' he said.

Judge Andrus hesitated, looking at Harland; then he nodded. Court adjourned.

Harland, when he stepped down, found his knees unsteady, his vision confused. Quinton's question had made clear to him the ordeal he must now prepare to face; and he wished for any catastrophe which would make it impossible or unnecessary for him to go on. Ruth gave him one quick handclasp before they parted, and then Pettingill and Roger Pryde hurried him back to the hotel; and Mr. Pettingill when they were alone said reassuringly: 'That was all right.'

'It was hell!' Harland declared. 'Did you have to put me in this position?'

Pettingill looked at him quietly. 'Mr. Harland,' he said. 'The State has made a strong circumstantial case on the theory that Mrs. Harland poisoned Ellen. Unless we present an alternative theory which fits the facts as well as or better than theirs, a conviction is possible. Our theory is, in plain words, that Ellen killed herself because you no longer loved her. You are the only one who can make the jury believe that. For Ruth's sake, I had to ask those questions. Frankly, I was surprised that Quinton did not prevent my doing so; but perhaps, feeling as he does toward you, he's glad to see you put in an ugly position. He'll make you look even worse this afternoon; but the more he persuades the jury that you treated Ellen badly, the more readily they'll believe that she killed herself.'

Harland nodded in reluctant acceptance of this fact. 'I see what you mean,' he admitted. They were silent while their lunch was served, but when the waiter had left the room, as though there had been no interruption, Mr. Pettingill told him gravely:

'Keep it in mind. Remember, Ruth is in real danger; but the more despicable you appear, the safer she becomes. And another thing. Before the jury accepts the suicide theory, they will want to know why Ellen, planning to kill herself, should try to throw the blame on Ruth. They'll ask themselves — what incredible sort of woman was she to write such a letter as that which they have heard read in court? They've been told the letter's not evi-

dence — I'm afraid it was a mistake to let it be read, but we
won't cry over spilled milk — but they'll remember it, and half
believe what it says. So we're in a position where it is necessary
to discredit Ellen, Mr. Harland. Quinton will go after you
hard, this afternoon, demanding the cause of your estrangement.
I didn't press you on that point this morning, but he will.
You've never told me. He'll hammer at you till he gets it.'

Harland swallowed a morsel of food that seemed to choke him.
'I know.'

'I don't normally take a case where my client — or her husband
— refuses to give me his complete confidence,' the big man remarked. 'I took this case because I admired Mrs. Harland and
was sure of her innocence; and I respect you, sir, and I regret that
you must face a hard time this afternoon. But it's inescapable.
I can protect you, somewhat, with objections and interruptions;
and I'll do so if you like, but — I'd rather not. We've let the
jury have everything we know, so far; and that has had a good
effect, I'm sure. I don't want to seem now to have anything to
hide. And remember, if you must say something discreditable to
Ellen, it will at least help Ruth.'

'I'll— stand up to it somehow.'

'Good man,' Mr. Pettingill agreed. 'Now don't eat if you're
not hungry. And on the stand — don't lose your temper. Quinton
will try to make you ridiculous and contemptible. But remember
that it's Ruth, not you, who is on trial. The more he succeeds in
making you appear badly, the readier the jury will be to accept
Ellen's death as suicide.'

– VI –

When court again convened, Harland, though he tried to preserve an outward calm, was nevertheless full of a churning, fluttering sensation as though his vital organs were writhing in his
body. But the ferocious attack he had expected did not come.
Quinton began in the mildest tones.

'Mr. Harland,' he said. 'Let us inquire into your first marriage, your life with the first Mrs. Harland. You met her in New Mexico?'

'Yes.'

'Tell the jury what sort of woman she was. I mean her appearance.'

'She was beautiful.'

'You found her so?'

'Yes.'

'You and she were acquainted how long before your marriage?'

'Two weeks.'

'Were those two weeks your courtship?'

'We saw each other every day.'

'Under what circumstances?'

'We were all together at the fishing lodge.'

'I hope you can be more specific. When did you first see her?'

Harland said, remembering: 'Why, on the train going west.' Quinton required him to give details. There was a smile across the room when Harland admitted that Ellen had gone to sleep over a copy of his own novel. Then under the quiet questions he recited each of his encounters with Ellen; the expedition to kill a turkey, the scattering of her father's ashes, his going to meet her next morning, their moonlight walk together, the ride back from the branding, the ordeal of the canyon. Quinton kept this narrative purely factual, but when it was done, he asked:

'And this was your courtship?'

Harland said slowly: 'Your question gives a wrong impression. I was not — courting her. I was a bachelor, and intended to remain so. After about ten days I realized that we were — drawing together. I knew she would marry me if I asked her to.'

Quinton's tone was only mildly interested. 'Indeed? How did that realization come to you.'

'She had told me . . .' Harland felt a malicious satisfaction in this reply. 'She had told me that she was engaged to you, but that she would never marry you. Later she stopped wearing your ring, and called the fact to my attention. I knew what she meant by that.'

Quinton seemed undisturbed. 'So you suggest that the courtship was on her part?'

'I knew she would marry me if I asked her to.'

'Did you — do anything about that?'

'I decided not to marry her. I preferred to continue as a bachelor.'

'Ah? And what later caused you to change your opinion?'

'That experience in the canyon. That threw us together —
and when we were safe, I knew I loved her.'

'Did you tell her so?'

'Yes.'

'What did she say?'

Harland remembered that moment completely; he perceived
too that Ellen's words now assumed real significance. 'She said:
"I will never let you go."'

'How soon after that were you married?'

'The second morning afterward. At her insistence.'

Quinton asked politely: 'Were you reluctant?'

'I was doubtful. I thought we need not hurry.'

'Now, Mr. Harland — I don't say this critically, nor in mockery, nor to suggest that you are conceited, but simply to be sure
I understand you correctly — you suggest that a beautiful young
woman, engaged to another man, fell in love with you, courted
you, won you, and persuaded you into a quick marriage against
your better judgment. Is that a fair statement of the facts?'

Harland colored, but said doggedly: 'Yes.'

'I see. Now how soon afterward did you begin to regret your
surrender?' Harland hesitated, and Quinton asked in a helpful
tone: 'Were you happy with her for the first month?'

'Completely.'

'The second? The third? The fourth?'

'Yes.'

'You went from New Mexico to Georgia?'

'Yes.'

'Where your brother was under treatment for infantile?'

'Yes.'

'You and your brother were alone in the world — except for Ellen?'

'Yes.'

'When did you leave Georgia and come north?'

'It was almost a year after we were married.'

'Were you still happily in love with Ellen?'

'Yes.'

'In June, you came north to Boston and then to your fishing lodge at Back of the Moon. Were you still happily in love with Ellen then?'

'Yes.'

'You loved her in June. How about July?'

'Yes.'

'How about August?'

Harland had guessed to what Quinton was coming; he had prepared an evasion. 'My brother was drowned in August,' he said.

'That saddened you?'

'Yes.'

'Did it affect your love for Ellen?'

For a moment, his own memories made Harland hesitate. He said, half choking: 'It changed everything. Danny meant a lot to me.'

'But so did she?'

'Yes, so did she.'

'Danny was drowned in August. Come to September. Did your love for Ellen continue in September?'

Harland felt half-stifled, as though constricting bonds were tightening about his chest; but he found an answer. 'In a different way,' he said.

'In what different way?'

'We were to have a baby.'

'Ah! You have testified that at some time your feeling toward Mrs. Harland changed. Do I understand that it changed during her pregnancy?'

Harland hesitated. 'Yes,' he said.

'So!' There was satisfaction in Quinton's tone. 'Now we
come to the point. Your love for her changed during her pregnancy. Describe that change.'

'I suppose I had loved her because she was beautiful, and
because she loved me. After I knew we were to have a baby. I
loved her for that reason.'

'As the prospective mother of your child?'

'Yes.'

'Tenderly? Devotedly? Exclusively?'

'Yes.'

'Then why did you during her pregnancy begin to pay so much
attention to the defendant here?'

Surprised by the question, Harland fought down a confusion
like panic. 'Ellen regularly urged me to go to see her mother
and Ruth.'

'But up till the time the baby was stillborn, in spite of your
attentions to Ruth, you continued to love Ellen tenderly, devotedly, exclusively?'

'I wasn't paying attentions to Ruth.'

'You were seeing her often?'

'Yes.'

'Every day?'

'Almost.'

'But you didn't consider that paying her attentions?'

'I was seeing my housekeeper, Mrs. Huston, every day, too;
but I wasn't paying her attentions!'

'I see. Yet during this period, though you went to see Ruth
almost every day, you still loved Ellen tenderly, devotedly, exclusively?'

Harland said in a hoarse voice: 'Yes.'

'When did you cease to love her in that way?'

'My feeling had changed during her pregnancy.'

'During the period when you were seeing a great deal of
Ruth?'

'No, no!' Harland cried. 'Before that!'

Quinton watched him for a moment in silence. 'I'm afraid

we'll have to start over,' he said then. 'Perhaps you wish to correct your testimony. You have said that till your baby was stillborn, you loved Ellen tenderly, devotedly, exclusively. Do you still so say?'

'I said I loved her as the prospective mother of our child.'

'But no longer tenderly, devotedly, exclusively?'

'I didn't love anyone else, if that's what you mean.'

'We're trying to find out what you mean, Mr. Harland; not what I mean. Have you been quibbling, evading a truthful reply?' Harland did not answer, and Quinton demanded: 'Have you? Answer the question.'

'I may have misled you.'

'Then please lead us aright, Mr. Harland. Before you knew of your prospective paternity, you loved Ellen. Afterward, that feeling changed. What caused that change?'

Harland stared at him blindly. The change of which Quinton spoke had come in an instant, in the instant when he knew Ellen was responsible for Danny's death; but he could not bring himself to lay that crime at her door. Quinton said again, sternly now:

'Perhaps you did not hear me. I asked you what caused that change?'

Harland felt himself half choking. 'I — don't want to answer that question,' he blurted. He knew that Judge Andrus might require him to do so; but to his astonished relief Quinton seemed to yield.

'I don't wish to press you,' he said gently. 'Let us go on. Mr. Harland, was Ellen jealous?'

Harland foresaw the trap. 'She had no cause to be.'

'Was she jealous? Or is this another question you prefer not to answer?'

'She was jealous of my work — in a laughing way.'

'Was she jealous of the defendant?'

Harland, fighting to control his tone, said carefully: 'Mrs. Harland — Ellen — was of a possessive nature. She had monopolized her father's life till he died, and she wished to monopolize mine.'

'You haven't answered my question. Was she jealous of Ruth?'

'She was jealous of everyone, of everything.'

'Of Ruth?' Quinton insisted.

'Of everything.'

'Mr. Harland, may I have a plain answer. Was Ellen jealous of Ruth? Did she ever accuse you of being in love with Ruth?'

'Yes.'

'Ah! And was that accusation true?'

'It was not.'

'What was your reply to it?'

'I told her that if she ever repeated it, I would leave her.'

'I see.' Harland began to find something affrighting in Quinton's steady calm. 'I assume this conversation in which she accused you of loving Ruth took place after the rift between you was obvious to you both.'

'Yes.'

'How long before Ellen's death?'

'Some weeks.'

'But outwardly, up to the time of her death, you and she preserved a normal way of life?'

'Yes.'

'Now, Mr. Harland, I suggest to you that an affection for Ruth, of which you were perhaps not conscious, led you to turn away from Ellen.'

'That is not true!'

'Did Ellen resent your seeing Ruth so often during her pregnancy?'

'No. She used to urge me to go see Ruth.'

'You did go?'

'Yes.'

'Almost every day?'

'Frequently. Almost every day, yes.'

'Leaving your pregnant wife at home alone?'

Harland wetted his lips. 'Yes. She insisted on it. She did not want me with her.'

'Isn't it possible that you did not know what she really wanted?'

'I only know what she said.'

'Women sometimes say one thing and mean another. Perhaps she really wanted you by her side, yearned for your love and your solicitous attendance. Women about to have babies like to have their husbands with them, do they not?'

'Ellen didn't,' Harland wretchedly insisted.

'And you insist that it was not your increasing affection for Ruth which led you to leave your wife so much — almost every day — during her pregnancy.'

'It was not.'

'Your physical and spiritual separation from Ellen had another source — which you will not state.'

'Yes.' Harland was made bolder by the other's forbearance.

'And, refusing her efforts at reconciliation, on the morning of the day she died you told Ellen you had decided to leave her?'

'Yes.'

'Did you reach that decision because she had again accused you of being in love with Ruth?'

'No, she never repeated that accusation.'

'But you did reach that decision — and announce it to her?'

'Yes.'

'What finally led you to that decision?'

Harland remembered with a sudden flashing clarity that moment when, standing at the window of their room at Bar Harbor, yearning to turn to Ellen, he had seen the seal's head disappear under the dark water and so remembered Danny. But this was a thing that could not be explained.

'It came after weeks and months of thought and — suffering,' he said.

'And you suggest that because you killed her hope of winning back your love, Ellen that day killed herself?'

'Yes.' Harland set his jaw.

'You were present when she died?'

'Yes.'

'Did you suspect the cause of her death?'

'I thought she died of gastritis.'

'What was the last word she spoke?'

Harland shut his eyes, for there was a whirling before them and a thundering in his ears. He said in a low tone: '"Poison."'

'Did it not occur to you that she knew she had been poisoned and was trying to tell you so.'

'No. Doctor Seyffert had just said . . .'

'I know. He said she was full of poison, and Ellen, her senses dimmed by the approach of death, heard the word, and in a flash of understanding knew what had been done to her, and tried to tell you, so that you could save her. Is that not true?'

'She was just muttering, almost unconscious.'

'But the word she muttered was "poison" — and to that word you shut your ears?' Harland could not speak, and Quinton's tone changed. 'Now, Mr. Harland, you and Ellen were married for two years or more. Did you feel that you understood her?'

'Yes.'

'I show you a letter.' Quinton stepped to the counsel table, picked up Ellen's letter and returned and gave it to Harland. 'Will you read it, please?'

Harland took the letter, looked at it with blurred eyes. 'Aloud?' he asked huskily.

'No, read it to yourself. Read all of it, if you don't mind.'

Harland obeyed him, his eyes following the lines, reading in a sort of wonder. This was Ellen writing, Ellen whom he had loved and to whom in many intangible ways he felt himself still married; for marriage was a thing which went deeper than ministers and laws, deeper even than death itself. He read with half his mind, the other half remembering so many moments he and Ellen had spent together, moments shared with no one, never to be shared with anyone, when the world ceased to exist for both of them, and the universe of each was the other.

He read slowly, and at last finished, and Quinton took back the letter. 'Now, Mr. Harland,' he asked, 'knowing Ellen as you did, do you think her capable of writing that letter if it were not true?'

Mr. Pettingill, who had foreseen this question, was a wise man. 'Yes,' Harland said. 'Yes, I do.'

Quinton's voice rose sharply. 'You think her capable, while she was planning suicide, of falsely accusing her own sister of causing her death?'

'I do!' There was in Harland a lucid and triumphant comprehension. This was the crisis for which Mr. Pettingill had hoped. He saw that Quinton was surprised by his answer, for the State Attorney suddenly was almost shouting; and as the other raged, Harland himself became calm.

'You mean to say you think Ellen capable of falsely accusing her own sister of murder?' Quinton was black with anger, his own old passion for Ellen making him furious now.

'They were not actually sisters, of course.'

'Don't quibble! We've had enough of that! You think she was capable of this?'

'Ellen was capable of anything.'

'You want us to think she was a monster?'

Harland said simply, sure now of what he meant to do: 'She was a monster!'

Quinton was livid. 'Ready to send an innocent woman to a living death in prison?'

Harland spoke quietly and clearly. 'She had already sent an innocent child to actual death,' he said.

A stir of excitement ran along the crowded benches, and Harland heard the point of a reporter's pencil snap under sudden pressure, heard the scrape of the knife that sharpened it. Quinton recoiled as though he had been struck, his lips working, completely at sea.

'You mean your stillborn baby?'

'I mean my brother Danny,' Harland told him.

Quinton stood silent, digesting this. Then he swung to the table where Attorney General Shumate sat; and while they conferred, Harland, unwilling to meet Ruth's eyes, looked down at his own hands tight clenched on the bar of the witness box. There was a deep peace in him, the peace of submission. He accepted freely this necessity which for Ruth's sake he must accept. Then in the silence Judge Andrus rapped his gavel, announced a recess.

– VII –

As Harland approached the counsel table, Mr. Pettingill rose and went out into the corridor. Harland, alarmed by this departure, asked Ruth: 'Where's he gone?'

'Leick sent word he wants to see him.' She touched his arm, whispered: 'Darling, darling! Why did you tell?'

He smiled at her. 'It's all right.' Quinton and Attorney General Shumate were talking together in low tones, and he watched them as a boxer during the interval between rounds watches his opponent. Ruth's hand pressed his arm, and he touched it lightly, and felt Roger Pryde's scrutiny, and turned to look at the reporters, thinking that tomorrow every newspaper in every city would headline his testimony, strip him naked to the shameful winds. The Attorney General left the courtroom, and Quinton spoke to Mrs. Parkins, and she made rapid notes of what he said.

When the brief recess was done and Harland crossed to resume his place in the witness box, Mr. Pettingill had not returned from the corridor; but at once he did so. Quinton came to face Harland again. He spoke quietly and with complete composure.

'Well, Mr. Harland,' he said. 'Your statement opens a new field of inquiry. We will go back to the time of your brother's death. That occurred when?'

'He drowned in the lake at Back of the Moon, in August, a little over a year after Ellen and I were married.'

'He was how old?'

'Fourteen.'

'He was an invalid?'

'He had had infantile, and his legs were weak and shrunken.'

'Could he swim?'

'He was a strong swimmer. He had swum across the lake that summer.'

'At what time of day did his death occur?'

'Early afternoon.'

'Who was at your camp that day?'

'Ellen, Danny and myself.'

'Where was Leick?'

'He had gone to town for supplies.'

'Let us take things in order. Begin with breakfast. After breakfast, what did you do?'

'I went to work in my study over the boathouse.'

'Did you see Ellen or Danny during the morning?'

'I heard them row away up the lake.'

'At what time?'

'I didn't notice.'

'How long did you work?'

'Till I was tired. We seldom knew the time at Back of the Moon.' Harland was at last serene.

'What then?'

'I finished work and climbed the hill to camp, found no one there. I remembered that they had gone out on the lake, so I went on to the hilltop above camp. You could see most of the lake from there.'

'Did you see them?'

'I saw the skiff, about half a mile away. I took the binoculars we kept at the lookout and focussed on the skiff.'

He hesitated, and Quinton prompted: 'Go on. What did you see?'

'I saw Ellen sitting in the skiff. Danny was floundering in the water about twenty feet from the skiff, obviously in distress. She made no move to help him. I saw him go under. She let him drown.' He was surprised that he could speak so steadily; held himself under an iron control

'Could Ellen swim?'

'She was an excellent swimmer, better than I.'

'What did you do?'

'I ran down to the boathouse. We had an outboard motorboat, a fast one. I took it and raced up the pond to come to them.
It's a mile or so. They were just west of a long narrow point of
land that runs out into the pond. There's a ledge on the east
side of that point. I knew it was there, but I forgot it, ran hard
on to it. I was thrown out, cut my head. I waded and swam
ashore and ran across the point.' He waited for no prompting
now. 'I saw Ellen diving for Danny. The skiff was drifting
away across the pond. I took off my clothes and helped her dive
for him, but the water was too deep for me to get to the bottom,
most of the time. She finally got him, brought him to the surface.'

'What then?'

'I took him ashore and tried to resuscitate him, but he was
dead.'

'What did she do, while you were doing this?'

'She swam after the skiff and brought it back and we took
Danny home to camp.'

'You said, before recess, that she —' He looked at a bit of
paper in his hand. 'That she had sent an innocent child to actual
death. What did you mean by that?'

'Danny had tried to swim the length of the pond. She went
along in the skiff to help him out of the water if he tired. He
caught a cramp and she let him drown.'

'Yet you say you found her trying to rescue him?'

'I saw her let him sink without trying to help him.'

'But she tried to rescue him. It was she who actually brought
his body to the surface.'

'She deliberately let him drown.'

'How do you know?'

'She told me so.'

'At the time?'

'No, months later.

'Did you accuse her at the time?'

'No.'

'Why not?'

'At first the shock stunned me. I had loved her completely, and to find her capable of murdering my brother was like being hit on the head. Then before I reached the point of being able to talk at all, she told me she was going to have a baby. After that, for the baby's sake, I couldn't say anything. I never told her I knew the truth till after our baby died.'

'If she let Danny drown, she must have had a reason.'

'She hated sharing me with him, didn't want him living with us. She had often urged me to send him away somewhere so she and I could be alone.'

'Did you report her act to the authorities?'

'No. I protected her. I couldn't accuse my wife of murder. Certainly not with a baby coming. I made up a lie to tell Leick and everyone else, to explain his death. I said Danny had been running the motorboat and that he fell out and that it cut circles till it ran ashore on that ledge. I said Ellen and I had been swimming on the beach at the west end of the pond and had seen it happen.'

'You say now that that was a lie.'

'Yes, it was.'

'Did Leick believe you?'

'As far as I know. I was afraid he might find my tracks on the point and know that it was I who had wrecked the motorboat, so I went up early next morning — we'd sent him out to Joe Severin's the night before — and smoothed my tracks, so he couldn't find them and know I was lying.'

Quinton asked quietly: 'In other words, you not only failed to report Ellen's crime; you also lied to protect her, and you concealed evidence which would have revealed her guilt.'

'Yes.'

'You are aware that you thus become an accessory after the fact to this crime?'

'Yes.'

'Mr. Harland, are you also an accessory, before or after the fact, to the murder of Ellen?'

Harland flushed under this abrupt attack, but he held his voice steady. He said quietly: 'Ellen was not murdered. She committed suicide.'

'And you say that she caused Danny's death, and that you destroyed the evidence of her crime?'

'Yes.'

Quinton turned away. 'You may have him, Mr. Pettingill,' he said in drawling scorn.

Mr. Pettingill rose, came slowly nearer Harland. 'Well now, Mr. Harland,' he said. 'You told Brother Quinton that Ellen had urged you to send Danny away so that you and she could be alone.'

'Yes, sir.'

'Where did she want you to send him?'

'She wanted me to leave him at Warm Springs for the summer while we came to Back of the Moon.'

'Did she make any other attempt to get rid of him?'

'On the way north, we stopped in Boston. She asked me to leave him there with Mrs. Huston; and later she asked me to leave him at Bar Harbor with Ruth.'

'What was your reply?'

'I said Danny was our joint responsibility; that he would either come with us or we would stay with him.'

'I see. And now you say that when she saw a chance to let him drown and thus be rid of him forever, she seized it.'

'Yes.'

'Thank you. Now we'll just get back to the point again for a minute, keep the record straight. Brother Quinton asked you whether you thought Ellen capable of planning suicide and plotting to have her sister blamed for it, and you answered yes. Is that correct?'

'Yes, sir.'

'He asked you why you believed her capable of such a thing and you said because she'd let your brother drown. Correct?'

'Yes, sir.'

'Referring to that hour in the canyon when you first declared your love, what did she say?'

'She said: "I will never let you go."'

'And now she reaches back from the grave to punish you through Ruth for escaping her.' Quinton rose with an angry haste, but Mr. Pettingill said easily: 'That is all.' He turned away, Quinton made a contemptuous gesture, and Harland. trembling with the reaction from his ordeal, left the stand.

– VIII –

For a moment after Harland sat down, the courtroom rustled and whispered. Then with a glance at the clock, Mr. Pettingill said:

'Well, Your Honor, we've time for one more witness before adjournment. This evidence has just come to my knowledge. It won't take five minutes. I'll call Leick Thorne.'

When Leick took the stand, Harland forced himself to pay attention, wondering what was to come; and Mr. Pettingill began:

'Now, Leick, you've already told the jury about that shore picnic the day Ellen died, but we'll go back to it again. Do you recall anything you haven't told before that might be important?'

'Yes, sir.'

'Suppose you just go ahead and tell us what it is.'

'Well, it's like this,' Leick explained. 'When she finished eating . . .'

'By "she" you mean whom?'

Leick said shortly: 'Ellen.' He began again. 'When she finished eating, she had some napkins — paper napkins — that she hadn't used, and she rolled them up in a tight roll and threw them into the fire.'

'Yes?'

'The outside of the roll begun to burn, and I happened to watch it. After a while a jet of smoke begun to come out of it, maybe three–four inches long and half as thick as a lead pencil. Then the smoke turned to flame, and then some black stuff like tar begun to drip out of the hole the flame was coming out of, and drip down into the fire; and it burned too, in the ashes, sizzling like tar, till it all burned out.'

'Did you know what caused this?'

'No, sir. They were all talking and laughing and I was listening and watching the fire, and I noticed it, and thought it was a funny way for paper to burn . . .'

'Brother Quinton would rather you didn't tell us what you thought. But describe what you saw once more, if you please.'

'Well, it was just like I said,' Leick repeated. 'She twisted up some paper napkins in a sort of roll . . .'

'How big was the roll?'

'Oh, maybe an inch thick and six inches long.'

'Go on.'

'And she threw it into the fire. It lit crossways on a couple pieces of driftwood, and the twisted ends caught fire, and the outside of the paper begun to burn, and then this jet of smoke came out, puffing straight out, steady; and then this black stuff like melted tar — only it was more brown than black — begun to drip out of the hole, and drip into the hot coals, and it caught fire, and kept burning till it all burned out.'

'Had you ever seen anything like that before?'

'No.'

'Have you ever seen anything like it since?'

'Yes, sir.'

'When?'

'Today.'

'Under what circumstances?'

'Why, last night I got to thinking about the picnic ——'

'Never mind what you were thinking. What did you do or see?'

'Well, I went down to the shore here and built a fire, near as I could about as hot as the fire we had that day. I'd bought some paper napkins and borrowed half a cup of sugar, or maybe a little less, and an envelope from the post office. I put the sugar in the envelope and wrapped it in the paper napkins, to look as near as I could like the bundle she threw in the fire, the same size and shape and all; and I put it on the fire as near as I could in the same sort of place.'

'Yes.'

'Well, sir,' said Leick. 'It behaved just the same as that rolled-up bundle she threw on the fire at my place that day. Same smoke, same flames — only there was two jets this time — and the same black stuff running out and burning in the ashes.'

Mr. Pettingill turned to Mr. Quinton. 'That is all,' he said.

Harland, with a strong exultation, understood the significance of this testimony. If Ellen committed suicide by substituting for the envelope Ruth had prepared another containing arsenic as well as sugar, then she must somehow have disposed of the original envelope. Leick's story tended to show how she had done so; and he wondered whether Quinton would recognize this fact. But Quinton faced Leick almost casually.

'You're an old friend of Mr. Harland's, aren't you?'

'Guess't you could say so.'

'Any time he or Mrs. Harland was in trouble, you'd do anything you could to help them, wouldn't you?'

'Yes, I sure would. They're fine people.'

'You'd even remember things that never happened, wouldn't you?'

Leick drawled: 'Don't see how I could remember them if they didn't happen.'

'Invent them, then?'

'If I was smart enough, I might,' Leick assented.

Quinton nodded. 'I thought so. That's all.'

– IX –

Harland was so jubilant over Leick's testimony that he almost forgot what he himself had that afternoon endured. When court rose, he saw in Mr. Pettingill's eyes unconcealed satisfaction.

'You can sleep soundly tonight, Mrs. Harland,' the lawyer assured her. 'We'll go to the jury tomorrow, and tomorrow night you'll be free.'

'I'm a lot more worried about Dick than about myself,' she confessed, and she said to Harland: 'That was terrible for you. I know how you hated it. You'd protected her so loyally.'

Before he could speak, Mrs. Sayward touched Ruth's arm. 'Time to go, ma'am,' she said in her brisk, cheerful tones. 'They can come see you tonight if they want.'

'We'll let you sleep,' Mr. Pettingill told her. 'Sleep with a mind at ease.'

Ruth pressed Harland's hand and turned away, but from the door her eyes sought his. Then he and Roger Pryde and Pettingill went back to the hotel together, and they gathered in Mr. Pettingill's room. The big man was in high humor, producing a bottle and glasses.

'I think the time has come to pour a small libation,' he announced. 'The war's over!' He filled the glasses and said: 'Well, here's to Leick!'

They drank, and Roger remarked: 'Queer, though, that he didn't think of that before.'

Mr. Pettingill looked at Harland. 'Would he lie for you?' he asked.

'I suppose so,' Harland admitted. 'He'd do anything he could for me, I think.'

The big man rubbed his chin. He spoke in an explanatory tone to Roger Pryde. 'Leick says he didn't know this might be important till last night. He heard me say that if Ellen switched envelopes at the picnic she'd have to get rid of Ruth's somehow, so he started thinking back, trying to figure out how she could have disposed of it; and he remembered the queer way those napkins burned. But he didn't say anything to me till he'd tried that experiment of his, to see if the sugar in Ruth's envelope would have acted like that.' He added honestly: 'That's his story and I couldn't shake him. I tried. You notice Quinton didn't even try.'

'I'd hate to think we were using perjured testimony,' Roger confessed, and he asked: 'Why didn't Quinton go at him harder?'

'He didn't dare,' Mr. Pettingill explained. 'If he tried to shake

Leick and failed, it would hurt; so he dismissed him as briefly and contemptuously as possible.' He added: 'If Leick's lying, he's damned clever about it.'

Harland said thoughtfully: 'I'm sure he's always known what happened to Danny. He was different toward Ellen after that day. On the river trip he never let her out of his sight, and I saw him watching her at the picnic. But if he's lying about this, no one will ever know it.'

'If he's lying, I don't want to know it,' Mr. Pettingill cheerfully admitted, and he rumbled mirthfully at his own thought. 'I'd like to follow Brother Quinton tonight, watch him try that experiment himself,' he said. 'He'll be wrapping up sugar parcels and throwing them into fires till daylight.'

'Does sugar really burn that way?' Roger asked.

Pettingill said frankly: 'I don't know.'

Harland remembered one of those fragments of fact with which a novelist's mind is stored. 'I know there's a trick, lighting a lump of sugar with a match,' he said. 'You can't do it unless you touch the corner of the lump of sugar with cigarette ashes. A chemist friend of mine told me. He says the ashes act as a catalyst.'

The waiter came with their dinner; and since Mr. Pettingill preferred to eat in silence — he was as valiant a trencherman as Deputy Hatch — they talked little till they were done. Then when the table had been cleared, the big man filled his pipe.

'Well, we've got our case won,' he said. 'Everything Quinton will argue that Ruth did, we'll show Ellen could have done just as well. But we're one jump ahead of him. We say Ellen fixed up an envelope containing arsenic, exchanged it in her pocket for Ruth's envelope containing sugar, put the arsenic in her coffee, put her envelope back in the basket, wrapped Ruth's envelope in paper napkins and threw it into the fire.'

Roger, his misgivings forgotten, cried: 'And that settles it.'

'That settles it,' Mr. Pettingill agreed. 'Brother Quinton will claim Leick is lying because he likes Mr. Harland; but the jury will believe Leick, and they'll believe Mr. Harland's story about Danny.' He looked at Harland with a sympathetic eye. 'As I said to Brother Quinton when he admitted stealing the hamper, no one would testify to a thing like that unless it was true. Not many men would have had the courage to do it, Mr. Harland.

'But the jury will believe you, and they'll decide Ellen was a bad woman and that Ruth's a good one. They'll find her not guilty. That's sure as rain.'

Roger said contentedly: 'Besides, you're not done yet. You can put on Doctor Patron, and the doctors who attended Ellen on those other occasions when she was sick. And you can . . .'

But Mr. Pettingill interrupted him. 'No, Pryde, when you've got a case won, leave it alone. We'll get an acquittal on the evidence. When court comes in in the morning, I shall rest.'

Roger was doubtful. 'Really?'

'Ruth's all right,' Mr. Pettingill insisted. 'We don't need to worry about her.' He said soberly: 'But I'm afraid you're due for trouble, Mr. Harland. Your testimony would almost certainly have cleared Ruth, even without Leick; but it puts you in a hole. When Ellen allowed Danny to drown, she probably committed a crime. In the case of a person whose duty it is to provide sustenance, warmth, or medical attention to another, if they deliberately and purposely fail or refuse to do so, it's usually been held to be manslaughter, or murder if the circumstances were bad enough.'

And he continued: 'Ellen went along with Danny that day so that if he got in trouble she could save him. That was her job and her responsibility and her duty. But he got in trouble and she didn't try to save him, although she could easily have done so. If he'd tried to get in the boat, say, and she pried his fingers loose, that'd probably be murder. If she just let him drown, that's probably manslaughter.'

Harland said grimly: 'I've always felt she murdered him. She encouraged him to try that long swim — and I had asked her not to do so unless I was with them. I think she hoped something of the sort might happen.'

'Well, say it's manslaughter anyway,' Pettingill assented. 'You knew about it and didn't report it. That made you just a passive accessory, and that might not be so bad. But also you destroyed evidence of the crime. That makes you an active accessory, and that's serious.

'Quinton's going to lose his case against Mrs. Harland, but he's got you on the hook and he won't let you off. My guess is that he'll send his assistant, young Cushing, who's been sitting at his table during this trial, before the grand jury tomorrow, while we're finishing up; and Cushing will take a transcript of your testimony and they'll indict you as an accessory to murder, and probably as an accessory to manslaughter too, just to cover the whole ground. I'd expect you'll be arrested on an indictment warrant some time tomorrow.'

'I see.' Harland felt cold. 'When I told Ellen I knew what she had done, she warned me that I was as guilty as she was,' he remembered. 'I judge she was right.'

'The only fight we can make,' Pettingill explained, 'is on the point as to whether what she did was a crime or not, but we won't get far with that. Your testimony amounted to an admission that you believe she premeditated Danny's death and that you actively concealed evidence of her acts. You can't deny what you did. You've already admitted it.'

Harland's hand clenched hard. 'I'll plead guilty,' he said.

'You might full as well,' Pettingill agreed. 'I'll try to get you off with no jail sentence, or a light one, but I'd expect you'll have to go to jail.'

Harland felt his breath catch; but then he relaxed, and he smiled. 'If Ruth can stand a few days in jail, why so can I,' he said.

'It'll be more than a few days, if it's anything,' the lawyer warned him. 'But I'll see what I can do.'

— x —

Harland had been able to speak calmly; but an hour later,

alone, he felt the oppression of stifling terror, so that his instinct was to burst out of his room, out into the streets, out of the confinement of any walls at all. His thoughts went around and around the same track without pause; he lived in imagination the months of imprisonment which might now await him; he remembered prisoners who had gone mad, or who saved themselves from madness by scuffing a pin into the thick dust on their cell floor and then sifting the dust with their hands till they found it again, or by watching through their narrow windows a single leaf upon a single tree, or by scratching a line each day in the stone wall of their cells. Once as a reporter he had seen in Charlestown State Prison the quarters where Jesse Pomeroy lived out his life in solitary confinement; and he remembered now that he had thought the cell not so bad, long and narrow, with matting on the floor — or was it a rug; he could not be sure — and a high window that admitted ample light, and pictures on the wall. It was a cheerful little slot of a room — except that from it one could see nothing but the sky.

Yet to think of spending a lifetime in that room, unable to leave it if you chose — or of spending a year, or even a day — brought back to his nostrils the sickening prison smell; new paint, human effluvia, antiseptic. He shuddered in an icy sweat, twitching where he lay.

He shrank from the imagined horrors of prison and scanned every possibility of avoiding them. The grand jury might refuse to indict, or the judge might be merciful, or the Governor might pardon him; or with Leick and Ruth to help him he might escape and make good his flight into the wilderness and never look upon the face of any — save these two — again. Through the hours of darkness, when the world at its best looks black enough, he lay in a waking nightmare; and the gray face of dawn peering into his windows was at first like the pallid countenance of a jailor come to summon him. Then the gray turned to brighter hues, and the sun rose and touched him with a friendly warmth, seeming to promise that the thing he dreaded would not come to pass.

Yet with full day this shadowy promise faded, and in a calmer mind Harland faced the truth. He sat on the edge of his bed, thinking what his life had been; and at last, without realizing the strangeness of his own action — it was a thing he had never done before — he knelt, his head pressed on his crossed arms. He prayed no formal prayer, yet his thoughts shaped humble, grateful words. 'I've made as many mistakes as most men. Probably I've made more. But Ruth loves me, so I'm the richest of men. Nothing can take that away from me; and, having her love, I'll go through whatever's coming and never damn my luck. I'll need help — need all the help I can get, to be what I want to be to her; but I'll do the best I can.'

Humility and surrender brought him peace, and he who had lain wakeful through the dark hours, there on his knees beside the bed disordered by his tossing slept for a while as a child sleeps, his head pillowed on his arms.

15

RUTH knew better than anyone what it had cost Harland to tell — to judge and jury, and to the racing pencils of the reporters, and through them to the world — the story of how Danny died; and that night, though they were physically separated, her thoughts and her dreams dwelt with him. In the morning she came eagerly to court, wishing he and she might have one moment alone; but she saw at once in him a serenity of spirit which reassured and comforted her. She spoke a warm and tender word, and they sat side by side, not needing the clasp of hands to feel the bond between them. In the interval before Judge Andrus appeared she looked toward Quinton's table, and she whispered to Harland:

'That young man isn't here today, the one who's been sitting with Mr. Quinton.'

'Mr. Cushing?' Harland asked, remembering Mr. Pettingill's prediction. 'Probably gone fishing,' he said, and smiled crookedly as if at some secret jest.

Then court came in and they spoke no more; and a moment later, to Ruth's surprise, Mr. Pettingill rested his case. She heard him with a tremor of dismay, feeling that something else should be done, some other evidence presented; but she could think of no definite thing he ought to do. Unfamiliar with court procedure, she did not know what now to expect; but Quinton, after a brief consultation with the Attorney General, likewise rested for the State, and the closing arguments began.

Mr. Pettingill spoke in slow and easy tones, and his manner

assumed that he and the jury were already agreed. Ruth, listening, liked him and she felt the liking for him among those about her.

'We're trying a queer kind of case here,' he explained. 'Here's a woman, when she died, everyone — Doctor Seyffert, and her husband, and her sister, and Leick, and everyone that was there — they all thought she'd just took sick and died. If her husband hadn't married again, no one would ever have thought any different. So this is an unusual state of affairs we're trying to get the straight of.

'It's unusual because Ellen Berent Harland was a mighty unusual woman. Our job is to try to figure out just what sort of a woman she was.'

And he began to analyze the testimony from this point of view, reminding the jury of fragments of evidence which Ruth herself had forgotten, putting together bit by bit a biography of Ellen from her earliest childhood, illuminating each fact with homely wisdom and with references to familiar everyday circumstances in the lives of his listeners which would make his meaning clearer. Ruth perceived with appreciative wonder that he — who had never seen her — understood Ellen better than she did herself. He made Ruth see and recognize as true things she had never guessed before, leading her memories down forgotten vistas, shedding light on moments that once had seemed inexplicable. She found herself as he spoke remembering things Mrs. Berent had said, things which had seemed to her at the time meaningless, or meant to be amusing, or simply ill-tempered. When Mr. Pettingill described Ellen's devotion to her father, she seemed to hear the older woman say, at Glen Robie's dinner table: 'Sometimes I was surprised she didn't sleep with him.' When he spoke of Ellen's pursuit of Harland, she remembered the night Ellen asked him to walk in the moonlight with her, and Mrs. Berent acidly commented: 'Quoth the spider to the fly!' A dozen caustic phrases came back to her. In the hour of Ellen's triumph: 'I thought Mr. Harland had more sense.' When Harland said he wished to marry Ellen: 'She'll eat you alive and gnaw

your bones.' When they heard of Danny's death: 'Ruth, Ellen
had something to do with that. She always hated that youngster.' When the baby was stillborn after Ellen's fall: 'There's
never been a sleepwalker in our family.' Thus Ruth, listening
to Mr. Pettingill, seemed again and again to hear Mrs. Berent's
biting tones, seemed to see her nod in angry affirmation of the
truth of all he said.

Mr. Pettingill built out of words and phrases which the jury
had heard spoken on the stand a portrait, so valid, so true, and so
terribly like Ellen that Ruth shivered as she listened, and her
thoughts were lost in the past, seeing through his words truths
to which she had at the time been blind.

She returned to close attention again only when he began to
speak of her, to compare her life to Ellen's; and he said at last:

'So, gentlemen, there's the two women in this case. Ellen
and Ruth. You know as much about what they're like as I do.
Keep thinking about them while we go on and see what happened. Some of the things that were done in this business,
either one of them might have done. It's our job — your job —
to decide which one did them.

'Now let's take, first, what the State says happened. The
State says Ruth, already worth over half a million dollars,
wanted Ellen's money; and the State says she wanted Ellen's
husband. The State says that to get that money and that husband Ruth took some arsenic out of her father's workshop, and
hid the lump sugar, and put arsenic in the granulated sugar she
took along to the picnic for Ellen to use, and hid the rest of the
arsenic behind the baseboard in her room, and gave the sugared
arsenic to Ellen, and saw her drink it, and watched Ellen die.
After that, the State says, she left the extra arsenic behind the
baseboard; left it there for two years, even after she married Mr.
Harland.

'That, generally speaking, is what the State says Ruth did.
Well, you've heard her testify. You've had a chance to size her
up. You know what sort of a woman she is. You don't believe
for a minute that she did those things. She's not greedy enough

to kill anyone for money, not for all the money in the world. She's never done anything selfish or greedy in her life. Nor she's not a sex maniac, ready to kill her sister so she could marry her sister's husband; nor she's not foolish enough, if she did kill her sister, to keep the rest of the arsenic long after she'd ever need it. Gentlemen, she's just not that kind of a girl.

'Now let's see what the defense says Ellen did. Where the men she loved were concerned, she was a greedy woman. She loved her father — and she shut everyone else out of his life, even his own wife, her mother. When he died, her greed fastened on Harland. She set out to get him to marry her, and when she had him hooked, she told him: "I will never let you go." When she found she had to share his love with Danny, she killed Danny — indirectly, it's true, but she killed him all the same. But Mr. Harland saw her do that; and though he protected her against prosecution for the crime, he hated her from then on. Oh, he tried to get along with her, because he's a loyal gentleman and she was his wife; but he hated her just the same.

'Well, she tried to win him back, but she failed. When she knew he was going to leave her, she decided to kill herself. She couldn't bear to live without him; but she'd told him she would never let him go, and she meant it. She planned to reach out from the grave and lay her grip on him again. She planned to kill herself and lay the blame on him and Ruth.

'Well, how did she go about it? She'd handled arsenic, and it was natural for her to decide to use it, choosing a time when Ruth had fixed up something for her to eat. The chance was bound to come during the Bar Harbor visit, so she got ready ahead of time. She wrote that letter, knowing Quinton hated Mr. Harland so he'd do something about it. She told him where to look for arsenic — there'd be time enough to hide it in Ruth's room after she got to Bar Harbor — and she told him she'd asked to be buried. Matter of fact, she'd asked Mr. Harland to have her cremated; but if he did, when it was found out she'd died of arsenic poisoning, his having her cremated would count against him.

'The picnic was her chance. She'd be the only one using sugar
in their coffee, so she decided to have Ruth pack some sugar
and then she could put arsenic in it herself. But you couldn't
mix arsenic with the lump sugar Ruth would naturally use, so
Ellen slipped down to the kitchen early that morning and hid the
lump sugar so Ruth would have to use granulated. Then she reminded Ruth about putting in the sugar, and watched her prepare
it, and then she fixed up a similar envelope and put it in the pocket
of her jacket. At the picnic she took Ruth's envelope — made an
excuse, said she wasn't ready for her coffee — and put it in the
same pocket. Later she took out her own envelope and used the
sugar with the arsenic in it and put it back in the hamper. Then
she wrapped up Ruth's envelope full of real sugar in some paper
napkins and threw it in the fire. Leick saw it burn.

'Then she got sick. Maybe it was just an accident that she
used the word "poison," or maybe at the last minute she was
afraid to die. But I think she wanted to make sure there'd be an
immediate investigation of her death. I think she tried to tell
Doctor Seyffert she was poisoned. She got the word out, but
that's all she could say. Then she died.

'That's what she did. She was a greedy, jealous, sexy, mur-
derous, heartless, shrewd woman. She could do it, and she would
do it, and she did do it.' His voice grew shrill with angry scorn.
'That's the sort of a hairpin she was.'

He went on, summing up; and Ruth found herself trembling
while she listened, and the shocking impact of his harsh and
level words made her senses waver. When at last he finished,
she heard a movement across the courtroom, a rustling and a
stirring as of relief; and she saw the jurors shift their positions,
and knew that he had held them all alike motionlessly attentive.

He came to resume his seat, and Quinton at once was on his
feet. Quinton, from his first word, attacked not Ruth but Harland, and with an unrestrained ferocity, so that Ruth wished to
cry out protest and denial. But when she looked at Harland she
saw him unmoved, and so forgot to be angry; and she came presently to understand that Quinton knew himself defeated, knew

she would go free. Now in pure malignance, he took on Harland
his revenge; and as he raged, fairly foaming with venom, the
naked hate in him plain to see, she began to be almost sorry for
the baffled man.

He argued Ruth's guilt not at all, seeming almost to concede
her innocence, referring only twice, and then obliquely, to the
charge against her. Once he cried: 'Mr. Harland brags that
Ellen loved him well enough to murder Danny and to commit
suicide! Well, the State says Ruth loved him well enough to
murder Ellen! Whichever you believe, you've got to say his
physical charms led to the taking of life, to suicide or to murder.
But look at him! He looks to you and me not greatly different
from other men! He has the same number of features; two ears,
two eyes, a nose, a mouth! What is this mysterious attribute
which he possesses, and which makes him thus irresistible to
women?' And at a later stage of his argument he shouted: 'He
accuses his dead wife of murdering his brother, and admits his
own connivance in that murder! Well, I accuse him of conniving
not only in that murder, but also in this one!'

But except for these allusions, it was Harland, not Ruth, whom
he denounced; and his very violence seemed to Ruth to make him
ridiculous and pitiable. To listen and to watch was like being a
spectator at an outburst uncontrolled and shameful. Not for
herself — nor for Harland — but for Quinton's own sake, she
was glad when he was done.

Judge Andrus, when Quinton finished, looked at the clock.
There was still — for Quinton had been as brief as he was violent — almost half an hour before the time for a noon recess.
The judge's charge to the jury was short, and it seemed to Ruth
frighteningly stern. Once he said: 'You are to remember, gentlemen, that the question of how Danny Harland came to his death
is not here at issue, nor the question of who was primarily or as
an accessory responsible. You are to remember too that Mr.
Harland is not here on trial. It is Ellen Harland's death with
which you are to deal. Nor need you decide whether or not she
committed suicide. Your task is simply this. If you find that

Ruth Harland deliberately led Ellen Harland to take a dose of arsenic, planning thus to kill her, you will return a verdict of guilty. If you have any reasonable doubt that Ruth Harland did this, you will return a verdict of not guilty.'

When he was done and court recessed, Mr. Pettingill told Ruth:'

'Well, ma'am, you're all right. The jury'll eat lunch — they won't want to miss a free lunch on the State — and then they'll take a ballot. You'll be free by three o'clock. Take my word for it.'

She bit her lip. 'I'd forgotten myself, thinking of Dick.'

'You heard what the judge said,' the lawyer reminded her. 'Mr. Harland's not on trial. Quinton knows he's lost his case against you. He as good as admitted it. He was just letting off his spleen.'

She met Harland's eyes; but then at Mrs. Sayward's touch upon her arm she turned away. Over their lunch — Deputy Hatch eating with his usual silent intensity, as though he were a half-starved dog — Mrs. Sayward said cheerfully: 'Well, ma'am, the Sheriff's lost a good boarder, and I'm out of a job again.'

'You think so?'

'No question about it,' the other assured her. 'If Russ Quinton wa'n't a darned fool, you'd never been brought to trial. Anyone'd know to look at you you wouldn't kill a chicken-stealing dog.'

'You've been very nice to me.'

'Why wouldn't I be?' The other laughed. 'Only I'm sorry the trial didn't last longer. I get paid by the day!' Then, in a sharp exasperation, to the deputy: 'For Heaven's sake, Joe, stop shovelling in the food. A body'd think you never had a square meal in your life before!' The fat man grunted comfortably, his mouth full; and Mrs. Sayward said to Ruth: 'It was real hard on your husband, wa'n't it? I could see he hated telling that about her. Men are that way about their wives. They hate to admit they've been fooled. But I sh'd judge he's a real good man.'

'Oh, he is, he is,' Ruth whispered. 'I'm going to spend the rest of my life making it up to him.'

At twenty minutes past two, word was brought to them that the jury was ready to report. Ruth as she walked back into the courtroom felt her knees weak and trembling; but when the time came for her to stand and hear the verdict, she faced the jury with a high head. A moment later she was free.

She had not known her own fears till she was released from them; and she sat down weakly, and her senses swam, and the world revolved before her blurred, uncertain eyes. Then court was dismissed and many strangers crowded around her, spectators eager with congratulations and beaming with good will, and reporters and camera men begging for a chance to take her picture. In this confusion Harland and Mr. Pettingill somehow disappeared. When she missed them and asked where they were, Roger Pryde said evasively:

'They'll join us at the hotel. They're having a conference with Mr. Quinton.'

She looked at him in deep alarm. 'What is it?' she asked. 'Is everything all right?'

'Fine,' he assured her, and he took her arm. 'Come along. We'll go back to the hotel, wait for them there.'

She submitted; but when they reached the sanctuary of Mr. Pettingill's room she insisted on the truth, and Roger told her as much as he knew and guessed. 'Quinton asked Mr. Pettingill to bring Mr. Harland to his office,' he said. 'I'm afraid Mr. Harland has been indicted as an accessory to Danny's death, and they're arranging bail.'

Her hand pressed her lips to hold back her cry of pain, and she asked questions; but he could tell her no more than this. Yet while they waited, she recaptured her mastery of herself; so when Harland, with Mr. Pettingill, presently appeared, without a word she went into his arms.

— II —

They had agreed, Mr. Pettingill explained, that Harland tomorrow morning would face Judge Andrus; and he would plead guilty, offer no defense. When in loyal tenderness she protested against this easy surrender, the lawyer answered her, and in the end she submitted, accepting his decision.

'But they'll let you go, Dick,' she said confidently.

He looked at Mr. Pettingill, and the big man said: 'I'll put up the best argument I can, ma'am; and Judge Andrus is fair, but he's not one to go too easy. Look at it any way you like, Mr. Harland did what they claim. If he was let go, others could do the same and hope to get away with it.' He shook his head. 'No, ma'am, I sh'd judge he'd have to go to jail.'

She thought of Mrs. Sayward. 'Here?' she asked.

'Thomaston.'

'For how long?'

'I wouldn't think it would be long.' Her heart lifted, but he added: 'Maybe one to two years; maybe a hair more.'

One year? Two? More? The blood drained out of her lips and she stared at him with blind eyes, cold with terror; and then her knees sagged and she might have fallen, but Harland took her in his arms.

He held her till she was strong again, and when she was able to look for them, the others were gone and she and Harland were alone. Since not till tomorrow need they part, they had these rich hours together. She gave way for a while to helpless grief, sobbing against his breast. 'I don't mean to make it hard for you like this. I just can't help it, darling.' But he comforted her and as they talked together the time came when she could smile. 'Thomaston's a lovely old town,' she reminded him. 'I shall find a nice house and live there and see you every day.'

He chuckled. 'They'll hardly stand for that,' he predicted.

'Well, as often as they'll let me, then.'

But he shook his head, spoke earnestly. 'No, my darling. I don't want that. I don't want you to see me in prison. Leick can come, sometimes, and bring messages from you. But to see you there would just make my days so much the harder.'

'I want us always to be together.'

'So do I,' he agreed. 'And we always will be, after this.

We'll be together even when I'm there, if thoughts mean anything.' And he said. 'I've had time to think — last night and
today — of just what we must do. You remember that spot
by the river, where we planned to go together, this summer?'

'Where I first loved you?' She clung to him. 'Of course I
remember!'

'I want you to go there,' he told her. 'Take Leick. I'll be
with you in my thoughts, knowing everything you do; and when
I can, I'll come to you there. I want to find you waiting there,
with a place made ready that will be our home.'

She would not at first agree to go so far away, and it was not
till after long discussion, he urging and persuading, her instinctive
resistance slowly giving way, that she came to full assent. Once
she had agreed, they turned to detailed plans, discussing how
much land she should buy, and where the house should stand, and
what its plan and fashion should be, and what trees and what
other growing things when the land was cleared she should plant,
and how that waterfall which they had found together should be
harnessed. They found happiness together in these dreams they
made. She had urged in her first reluctance that the burnt land
all around them there would be ugly and depressing; but he said:

'In one way, yes, of course. But — forests aren't all beauty,
you know. Remember we saw the rotting corpses of dead trees,
and tangled thickets, and lightning-blasted trunks. The forest
there was all surface greenness, but its roots were in corruption
and decay. But the fire wiped away the scars and the decay and
the death and made the land ready for a new birth.' And he said
quietly: 'You and I've been through a fire, Ruth, just like that
land. There were a lot of things in my life, some of them my fault
and some not, that needed to be seared away. They're gone now.
I went down on my knees this morning — I don't remember ever
doing that before — and I felt a lot better afterward.' She pressed
near him, and he kissed her lips and said, half-smiling: 'This
that's coming will leave me burned clean, just like the forest
floor, ready to begin a new growth, to grow straight and tall.'
He kissed her eyelids, gently. 'You didn't need any dross burned

out of you, my dear; but I did. I'm only sorry you had to share this with me.'

'I wish I could share everything, always, with you,' she whispered, and so they passed from words to silence, and were one.

16

J EM VERITY dominated the little village of Hazelgrove, and this was by virtue of a certain force that dwelt in him of which other men, even though they might rebel at his dictation, were conscious. He had the gift of being wisely thrifty and the knack of management and the capacity to recognize opportunity and to seize it; but these qualities in themselves were not enough. There was something more. Sime Verity, who had paddled Ruth's canoe on that trip down the river when the fire caught them, and who was one of the crew Jem mustered to carry through the enterprise which during the long months of Harland's imprisonment she undertook to accomplish, once tried to frame for her an answer. She had spoken admiringly of Jem's ability to lead men and to command them, and she asked:

'What is it in him which makes the rest of you so ready to follow him?'

Sime packed a thoughtful pipe before he replied. 'Well, ma'am, I don't know as I can tell you,' he confessed. ''Course, Jem's smart, and he's able; but that ain't the whole of it. Most things, I can do as well as he can, and so can a lot of others. It's kind of hard to say; but the thing is, when he wants you to do a thing, you can most generally see that it's a good thing to do. And I don't mean just clever, or that it'll earn you some money. I mean — well; I mean good.' He grinned. 'I hate to admit it, ma'am, and I wouldn't say so to his face; but I wouldn't wonder but what Jem's a real good man.'

She remembered Sime had said this long ago, but certainly

there was nothing offensively virtuous about Jem. He was not, for instance, in any sense an altruist; and if he did or proposed what was on the surface a friendly and a helpful — a good — deed, he was usually able to demonstrate that it promised to be profitable too. Jem served himself; but to do so is perhaps the highest form of altruism. Certainly he had thus — as often happens — made Hazelgrove a better place in which to live. Because his house and his store and his garage were kept painted and in good repair — and because when after a job of painting or of building he was apt to give the leftover materials to any man who would use them — most of the buildings in the village were as well-kept as his. Because his lawn was mowed once a week, and because he had some well-tended beds of flowers, other lawns were mowed and other flowers planted. Because of his many business interests, men in Hazelgrove found it easy to earn what cash money they needed. Because he kept a registered bull, and a good draft stallion, the quality of the livestock on the farms within reach of his improved. His crops were an example and an education to his neighbors; and his traits to a surprising degree were reflected in the men about him.

That first fall when Harland in Thomaston began to serve his sentence, Leick and Ruth came to Hazelgrove and to Jem to discuss what they proposed to do; and it was he who found the necessary crew of men and it was his wise counsel which solved for them the many problems which during that winter and the first summer arose. When early in the second summer the time of Harland's release approached, Leick, in order to have his canoe for the trip down river, shipped it to Hazelgrove; and he wrote Jem to tell him the day they would arrive, and asked him to have Wes Barrell and the motorboat ready to set them down the lake.

The post office was in the store, and the night that letter arrived half a dozen men had gathered to receive their mail. Wes Barrell was there, and Sime Verity, and others — all of them had worked on the project down river, and all of them knew Ruth and liked her — and Jem told them the news.

'It's going to make a lot of business for us right along, having them down there,' he suggested. 'We'll be freighting in their supplies, and doing any job of work they want done; so I figure we want to keep on their good side.' Seeing their assent he went on: 'I wouldn't wonder if Mr. Harland'd kind of hate to face people, right at first. It strikes me he did a pretty good job, owning up to all that and taking his medicine; but like as not he thinks everybody is ready to yell bad names at him.' The men facing him nodded in sober agreement, and Jem said: 'I liked him all right when he was here before, the year of the fire; and Sime, you and Tom liked him on the trip down river; and we all know she's a grand woman, so he's bound to be all right. Or if he ain't, he will be, married to her. A woman mostly makes a man the way she wants him, 'fore she gets through, if she's in love with him.

'But he won't want to have to see people first off. My idea would be that when he comes through here nobody'd bother him at all, only them he has to talk to.' He looked at Wes. 'You'll be the one to set him down the lake,' he said. 'And your old woman will want to know all about it when you come home. There's no harm in that; but if I was you I wouldn't say a word to him, only if he starts to talk to you. You can come home and tell her anything you've a mind to, to satisfy her.'

'I'll keep my mouth shut,' Wes agreed. 'The way I look at it, he's had a hard time enough.' He added loyally, 'The old woman don't mean no harm. She's just curious to know everything that goes on. But I'll tell her to keep out of his way, and she'll do it, too. She don't ever go to bother anybody, or hurt their feelings; and she likes Mis' Harland fine.'

'I'd kind of like to say hello to him,' Sime said doubtfully. 'Look queer if I didn't.'

'You could keep out of sight,' Jem suggested. 'He'll be real glad to see you later on, I wouldn't wonder; but in his place, I wouldn't want to have to talk to folks right away.'

Mrs. Verity, perched tremendous on her stool, added her word. 'He won't want a look at your horseface, Sime,' she said in friendly derision. 'He won't want to see anyone. He'll think

we're all watching him and talking about him behind his back
as it is.'

Leick had said in his letter that Harland would want a license
and a forest permit, so Jem spoke to Ed Sullivan, and to Will
Parish, the supervisor. 'I'll fetch him to your house for his
license, Ed,' he said. 'You keep them young ones of yours from
pestering him, and then you can take him on to Will's.'

'Well, my Mamie's crazy to see him,' Ed objected. 'She and
Mis' Harland got to be real friendly. Mis' Harland wants me
to bring her and the young ones down river some time to see
the place, pay 'em a visit; and I said I would.'

'I'd wait till she asked me again, if I was you,' Jem advised.
'I sh'd doubt he'd want anybody down there for a spell; but
she'll know best. And you can well as not make out his license
ahead of time; and you can do the same with his permit, Will.
Save him as much talk as you can.'

'I'll tell Maw to stay in the house,' Will promised. 'She read
all the newspaper stories about the trial, and she thinks he's all
right. She'll want to make over him, but I sh'd judge he wouldn't
want her to.'

'I judge not,' Jem agreed. He added: 'Why don't you and
Ed fetch him right down t' the wharf after you get him fixed up?
I'll have Wes there ready. Best thing everybody else can do is
keep out of sight.' And he reminded them again: 'If we can let
him see nobody here's going to stand around gawking at him,
him and her'll be more likely to do their trading here than if
they felt like they was freaks in a sideshow. Or anyway, that's
the way I'd feel if it was me. And they'll do a good trade in
the town.'

There were no skeptics to suggest that the trading would be
done at Jem's store, that he would reap the major advantage.
It had long been recognized — even though it was not openly
admitted — that what profited Jem also profited the town.

So when Harland and Leick came to Hazelgrove, they were
wrapped in a protective isolation. Only once was this threatened. When Jem drove to the station to meet their train, in

turning his car around, he backed too far — his own sense of the importance of the occasion made him careless — and mired in the ditch beside the road. Since the train was a few minutes late, Jem had time to summon Chet Morrow and his two sons from their near-by farm; but they did not succeed in freeing the car till the train was just pulling in. They too had worked in the crew that went down river to bring Ruth's plans there to fruition; and they could not resist lingering a moment on the platform. The train stopped, and Harland and Leick alighted; and when Leick and Jem went to see to their gear Harland was left alone. Chet and his sons, uncertain whether to go or stay, stood together looking at Harland secretly, till when Jem and Leick returned from the baggage car Jem stopped to speak to them.

'Git along,' he urged. 'Don't stand there gawking.'

'He looks real peaked,' Chet said in interested sympathy.

'So would you,' Jem reminded him. 'Give him a chance, Chet. Go along.' And they obeyed.

In the village, Jem dropped Harland and Leick at the game warden's house and then went to get his truck and with Wes Barrell drove to the station to fetch their gear; but back at the wharf he was uneasy till with Ed and Will escorting them, Leick and Harland appeared. Jem and Ed and Will sat by the gas pumps watching Leick and Wes load the motorboat, and Jem kept a vigilant eye toward the store to be sure no one came this way. Ed — he was the youngest of the three — said in a low tone:

'He takes it hard. You can see to look at him.'

'He'll come out of it,' Will predicted. 'He's got good courage, or he couldn't have gone through that business the way he did.'

'If it'd been me,' Ed strongly declared, 'I'd have knocked that first wife of his over the head the day she let the kid drown. I never could stand to see anyone harm a young one.'

'Nobody'd blame him if he had,' Will agreed.

Jem said thoughtfully: 'He'll be all right, give him time.' He added: 'He hasn't said a word to me. Have anything to say to you boys?'

'Leick did the talking,' Ed explained.

'You have his license all ready?'

'No, I didn't,' Ed admitted. 'I started to make it out, but Mamie said if I did he'd know we'd been talking about him, and that would bother him, so I waited till they came.'

Will protested: 'Why didn't you say so? I had the permit all made out, but I can see Mamie was right, at that.'

'There weren't time,' Ed told him. 'The train had whistled in by then.' He added: 'Struck me this morning that maybe I wasn't supposed to sell a license to a man that'd been in jail, but I didn't check up. I guess nobody's going to bother him.'

'He don't look up this way at all,' Jem pointed out. 'Right now I wouldn't wonder if he thinks the whole world's down on him, holding their noses when they think of him. But she'll straighten him out.' He chuckled. 'The way she's made that place down there a regular park in the middle of the burnt land, it won't be no trick at all for her to make things right for him.'

Ed said: 'Damn it, I'm a mind to go slap him on the back, shake him by the hand.'

'Give him time,' Jem advised. 'You can't tell how he'd take it. He'll find out there's mostly friendly people in the world, 'fore he's through.'

The boat was loaded, the motor caught with a roar; and the three men watched in silence as it moved away. It went directly into the sun, so that it was presently a diminishing black dot silhouetted against a sea of radiant brightness. Ed said under his breath, with a lifted hand:

'Good luck, Mister Man.'

'He looks bad,' Will reflected. 'But the river and the woods'll fix him up.'

Jem said in a sober content: 'He's hoed a long, hard row, but she'll make it up to him.' They rose to return to their own affairs; but their good will followed Harland long after the motorboat was lost to view.

THE END